THE GIRL NOW LEAVING

Betty Burton is the author of *Jude, Jaen, Hard Loves, Easy Riches, The Consequences of War, Goodbye Piccadilly, Long, Hot Summer, Falling in Love Again* and *Not Just a Soldier's War,* as well as the collection of short stories, *Women Are Bloody Marvellous!* She has written for both television and radio and won the Chichester Festival Theatre Award. Born in Romsey, Hampshire, she now lives in Southsea with her husband, Russ.

D0833300

BETTY BURTON

The Girl Now Leaving

HarperCollins*Publishers*

HarperCollins*Publishers*
77–85 Fulham Palace Road,
Hammersmith, London W6 8JB

This production 2011
1

First published in Great Britain by
HarperCollins*Publishers* 1995

ISBN 978 0 00 790583 6

Set in Bembo at
The Spartan Press Ltd,
Lymington, Hants

Printed in Great Britain by
Clays Ltd, St Ives plc

The Girl Now Leaving is for the generations of workers in the staymaking industry whose important contribution to the economy and development of Portsmouth has been given neither the credit nor the place in history it deserves.

THANKS

Although this book is a complete fiction, I acknowledge and give thanks to the many women who so generously contributed their time and experience of the industry – some from more than sixty years ago – so that I might get it right. They include:

Iris Idellier – Portsmouth; Mrs K. Godden – Bristol, Chilcott & Williams; Miss Florrie Allnutt – Portsmouth, Leethams Twilfit factory; Mrs B. Appleby – Tyne and Wear, Marina Corset factory; Mrs Mary Griffin – Milton, Twilfit; Mrs N. Wandby – Copnor, Sultan Road factory; Mrs B. Emmett – Copnor; Mrs S. Bailey – Farlington, All Saints Road factory; Mrs V. M. Head (Alder) – Bideford (father owned Alder's Corset factory); Mrs Nellie McCann, her father, mother and great aunt – Gosport, Allens factory; Mrs D. Ramage – Southbourne, Emsworth, Weingartens Ltd; Mrs Doris Smith (Stapleton) – Gosport, Leethams factory; Mrs Jackie Wilson – Havant, Twilfit; Mrs I. P. Mapletoft – Nottingham, Twilfit; Mrs P. Loader – Portchester; Margaret Stevens' mother; Mrs Hoad (Connie Stoner) – Havant, ACTA factory; Marjorie Jermy (Townley) – Portsmouth, Regent Street & Mile End factory; Mrs Elsie Marland – worked in administration; Barbara Avis – Bedhampton, fifty years in the industry; Mrs Marjorie Jeram – Fareham, Twilfit; Mrs Dolly Cox and Mrs Audrey Arnold (mother and daughter) – Havant, Twilfit, Corners; Joan Sadden – Gosport; Joan Archer – Barrow-in-Furness, Twilfit, Berlei, Alders, Fletchers; Mrs Iris Hayward – Isle of Wight; Mrs S. A. Newton – Fareham, Landport factory; Mrs Horder, her grandmother and six others of the family – Portsmouth, Twilfit; Mrs J. Gray – Waterlooville, Charles Bayer; Mrs D. Dyer – Waterlooville, George Curtis' factory; Mary Stokes – Havant, Izods Corset factory; Mrs Olive Samphier (Cowdrey) – Portsmouth, Chilcott & Williams; Margaret Windsor and her sister – Portsmouth, Goldsmith Avenue factory; Mrs Stallard – Eastney; and Mrs Doris Young – Liss, Ward Road, garment factory. As Doris Watt, whilst still in her teens, she formed a branch of the Garment Workers' Union, received a medal and citation from Sir Walter Citrine, and was interviewed for local and national newspapers of the time.

Also to those many others whose names I am not able to record here because it was only in passing that they made their contributions – in the street, the swimming pool, the supermarket, at Weightwatchers, Guilds, women's groups, meetings, Institutes and writers' circles.

Leaving For The Country

Louise Vera Wilmott was born in Portsmouth on the south coast of Hampshire on Midsummer Day, 1917. This account opens in the spring of 1929, the year in which she becomes twelve, and is gathering strength for her headlong flight into the unknown territory of womanhood.

Clear morning light is everywhere here. The spring sun is up. In Hampshire, in country churchyards throughout the county, it picks out pale moon-yellow delicate blooms of wild daffodils flowering by the scattered thousand. It slides over garden walls of parsonages where grosser, fleshy daffodils stand in brassy, regimented rows. Early morning in an early spring, and God's most favoured county appears encased in a dome of fragile aquamarine glass. Here, it is easy to believe that in some ancient time the Holy Lamb of God was in its pleasant pastures seen.

The unclouded landscape undulates softly and, where it is threaded and crossed by the courses of small rivers, by laid hedges and ancient hedgerows, a panorama of patchwork in green plush and sepia corduroy is created, and upon it the Countenance Divine does indeed shine forth, highlighting barrows that still clasp ancient knowledge, and sending needle rays of brightness into dark pagan circles of yews. The sun is unseasonably warm, and having got morning started in Kent and Sussex, it now illuminates the surfaces of trout streams and brooks, it glosses the facets of napped flint, and dries the earth's chalk bones where they poke through the fertile crust of Hampshire.

The Earth continues its steady cycle, so that before long morning dawns over Cranbourne Chase and the Blackmore

Vale and paints out the warm spring night, still on and on, westwards until it catches the crashing rollers off Cornwall, sparkles Devonshire's coastal waters and bleaches its shores.

But young Lu Wilmott, although she was born in God's own county, is not out there in the pleasant pastures, not under the aquamarine dome of sky. Lu lives in Portsmouth, the great naval and military city, in that area where jerry-built terraces have been crumbling into slums since the time they were slung up by the inadequate hundred. A bad area in which to be born. The odds of getting beyond childhood in the Lampeter area are no higher than they are in the Satanic mill-towns of the northern counties.

Lu is peering out from a narrow-fronted terraced house whose paint has peeled long since. It consists of a living room, scullery, lavatory and coal-house outside, and one and a half bedrooms. This is her home, 110 Lampeter Street, Lampeter, Portsmouth. Here she lives with her mother Vera, and her two brothers, Ralph who is twenty and Kenneth who is fifteen. Theirs is the smallest family by far in Lampeter Street. Lu Wilmott has a father, but she has not seen him for a long time. Arthur Wilmott is a sailor, with the Royal Navy, a real Jolly Jack Tar sailing the southern seas.

Vera Wilmott is a beached woman, one of a great sisterhood who at some point in their own young lives became entangled in the lives of sailors and soldiers 'gone foreign'. For twenty years, Vera has lived on whatever she can earn piecework. Because she has never had the essential document of proof that she is married to Arthur Wilmott, she does not receive even that tiny allowance allocated by the Navy to one of its wives. Beached women usually have a child for every year the ship comes in. Some of them have more because this is a town where there is never any shortage of randy sailors ready to get any woman lit up with three penn'orth of gin. Vera's three children are all Arthur's. Only three because the vessel on which he serves does long tours of duty in waters thousands of miles away, and because she considers herself to be a respectable woman.

Women like Vera Wilmott are beloved of employers as a vast reservoir of cheap and docile labour. Particularly so the owners of the numerous staymaking factories with which Portsmouth abounds. Since the first refugee with a pair of scissors and pattern for stays set up shop generations ago, the great staymakers have prospered on the back of their efforts, because soldiers and sailors go away and leave women like Vera high and dry and with a family to bring up. Although in the sight of the Royal Navy she is not the legal wife of Able-bodied Seaman Wilmott, Vera has done well by their three children, and kept their mean home going unaided by gin and randy sailors.

The visible plane of sky young Lu can see through the window of 110 Lampeter Street is neither a fragile-looking aquamarine nor clear. Although it is still early, the streets of Lampeter are already stale for, even though the sea is quite close by, the air has not moved all night and has held on to the unseasonal heat which all day yesterday was absorbed by mile upon mile of squalid red brick, dull grey slate and drab tarmac.

Lu Wilmott is within sight of her twelfth birthday, but her face, as it peers out apprehensively through the street-grimed window-pane, might be that of a dispirited old lady or a pale and loitering ghost.

Lu has been sick. Very sick indeed. Her large, brown eyes are sunken in deep sockets, her skin is rough and sallow, her cheeks hollow and her thick, bronze hair appears too heavy for her thin neck.

Lu has had 'The Dip', which clogged her throat until she could hardly swallow or breathe.

This last winter, there have been schools all over the county which were lashed by this dreaded disease. In Lu's school alone diphtheria caused the death of three young children, Lu was one of the lucky ones: 'The Dip' roared through her body, thickening her air passages, boiling her blood to fever and her brain to delirium until, after a long night of struggle, her lucid spirit returned to her emaciated little body. That day, quite recent, she opened her eyes to see Ralph wringing out a towel in a bowl of water and smiling down at her, and to an awareness that her mother was slumped in a chair asleep over her sewing. Although her brother was smiling as he whispered, 'Well then, our Lu, you come back to us then?' tears were rolling down his cheeks. Lu had never seen Ralph cry – he was a man – yet he never made any attempt to hide it.

That was a week or two ago. Now she is on her feet again, waiting anxiously for Uncle Hector Wilmott's beer lorry to arrive in Lampeter Street. Her stomach churns with worry as she thinks of all the things that might go wrong. On her own territory she is as fierce and brave as any Lampeter Street child has to be, but where she is going today, she could get lost. They could forget the address where she had gone, perhaps forget on purpose because Mum was always saying she didn't know how they were going to manage. She wishes Ralph could have been on late shift, then he could have seen to it that Uncle Hec made sure she got there all right. They all know that Uncle Hec drinks his beer allowance as well as a pint at every pub he delivers to. Her ungratefulness made her feel guilty; everyone has said how lucky she is to have an uncle who lives in the country, and another one to give her a lift right to their door.

Ever since the letter from Aunty May arrived they have all been on about recuperating in the country, which makes Lu feel like one of the mouldy hens Dotty next door keeps behind their shed.

* * *

Ralph, who works for Southern Railway, is on early turn at the station. Before it was even light he had come into the front bedroom and shaken her shoulder. 'I brought you some tea, two big spoonfuls of condensed milk, nice and sweet. Big day, Lu.' She had shot up and put her feet out of bed in one motion, causing her mum to drag the cover over her eyes and say, 'Oh, Lu, for God's sake!' at which Ralph had picked up the tea again and indicated with his thumb that she should drink it downstairs. The glass panel in the front door had showed that daylight was beginning to make the yellow light of the gas streetlamps fade. The house was warm and the crumbly lino sticky to walk on.

In the kitchen, Ralph had had his shoes polished and ready; sometimes of an evening he would sit for ages listening to the wireless, rubbing round and round, spitting occasionally on the toes until they had a glossy finish. His hair too was glossy, parted at the side, Brylcreemed and combed sleekly. Several times since she had got over 'The Dip', unable to sleep, she had gone down early to sit in the scullery, and watched as Ralph, still clad only in trousers and vest, went through his morning ritual of washing, shaving, scooping out a finger of Brylcreem, then massaging it into his hair, combing and brushing until every crinkle was under control and greased down.

Today, as she had watched, a lump had risen in her throat until she choked over the sweet tea. Ralph hadn't said anything about her crying; he had just taken the mug from her and, enveloping her in a cloud of the smell of shaving-stick and hair-cream, had given her a long hug. 'Now, Lu, listen to me, I'm going to talk to you like a Dutch uncle. I know it's a big thing and all, but I promise you, you won't have been there more than a day and you'll wonder you was such a daft ha'porth for not wanting to go. I know you'll like Aunty May and Uncle Ted, they aren't like any of the other Wilmotts, they're nice Wilmotts,' he winked, 'like us. Mark my words, you'll come back your old self. You been really ill, Lu, but you're over it now and all you need now is feeding up and a bit of country air.'

She knew that. She had heard how she had been dragged back from Death's door.

'It's a long way from home, Ray.'

'No . . . it's not really. It probably seems it's a long way because you haven't never been anywhere before. It can't be that far because Uncle Hec drives his lorry over there every week. He bees there, off-loads at Suthick and is in Wickham by nine o'clock. And I promised I'd cycle over, didn't I? And you know me, I shouldn't undertake doing a bike ride that was *that* far.'

'I know, Ray, you told me all that, but it's just – '

'The first time. I know, but there's going to be a lot more first times. You've done plenty already, you was only five the first time you went to school and you done that good enough.'

'That's not the same, I knew people, and it was *here*. Supposing they don't tell me where the lav is, or what time I got to get up, and where I got to put my shoes and that?'

He had stood up and ruffled her hair. 'You got a tongue in your head, Lu. The world's full of things none of us knows, and if nobody don't tell you then you got to speak up and ask. You soon found out where the school lav was, didn't you?' He had gone back to the mirror again, his reflection looking at herself, grinning as he had fastened his collar on to the back-stud of his shirt then, letting it snap round his neck, stretching his chin upwards whilst he inserted the front stud and tied his dark blue tie in a tight knot.

'Wouldn't it be nice if sisters could marry brothers, Ray? Then we could get married and I could watch you do your hair and put on your collar every morning. Why can't they?'

'It's just a rule. Go on, drink up that tea now. I made it for you.'

She had done as she was told, drinking the dark tea, sweetly sweet as only condensed milk could make it. This was her favourite drink; she drank it to the dregs. He had handed her his little clothes-brush and, as on other mornings when she had watched him get ready for his early turn, inspected the navy-blue nap of his shoulders for hair or specks. He had buttoned his jacket, tugged it and saluted. 'When you're ready for marrying, our Lu, you won't give a second glance at a short-ass like Ralphy Wilmott.'

'You aren't short, Ray, you're a head taller than me, look.' She had demonstrated by standing beside him at the spotty mirror that hung over the scullery sink.

'Look how tall you are already. By the time you're thinking about marrying, you're going to be looking for a chap who's taller than five foot six and a half – ' his kind smile broadened into a grin – 'else he's going to want an orange crate to kiss you goodnight. You got the makings of a Presley for height. The Wilmotts all suffers from their bums being close to the deck.'

Lu had elbowed him and he had made a play of being knocked for six by her. 'I'm sorry, love, but I'll have to get going or I shall be up before the beak.' He reached deeply into his trouser pocket and drew out two sixpences. 'Now, when you got yourself washed and dressed, run along to the paper shop and get *Dandy* and *Beano* and some of the raspberry drops you like – they got a lot of sucking power; but careful because they say it's sugar rots your teeth. Keep the rest for pocket-money. You needn't tell our Mum voluntary, and don't tell Ken, he's always on the ear'ole for me to buy him a comic. Just put them in your bag, and don't start eating the sweets before you get to Aunty May's. Iron rations just in case you feel in need of a bit of a boost the first evening there . . . well, maybe one or two

7

to suck on the way (but remember to offer one to Uncle Hec – he won't take it, raspberry flavour don't go that well with bunker-beer). And offer the bag to Aunty May.'

He had talked to her as though she was still seven, but she liked it.

He had opened the back door, given her a quick bit of a hug and a kiss on her cheek, and another breath of sweet, warm hair-cream and shaving-soap. 'I'll borrow his bike at the paper shop, probably on a Sunday, and I'll ride over to see you.'

'Promise?'

'No, you don't need a promise. I said I would and that's good enough.'

She had followed him down the back-garden path, and watched as he unlatched the lane gate. He turned and winked. 'You'll love it, Lu. Guaranteed. Just remember, it was Aunty May and Uncle Ted invited you, it wasn't us that asked them to have you, so you'll be welcome. I'll bet they'll spoil you to death.'

Ralph was at the centre of Lu's life. She knew that he would hate it going off to work and seeing her sad, so she gave him a grin and said, 'They'll fatten me up like one of their pigs, I expect.'

'Then Uncle Hec won't have to come and fetch you, you'll be able to roll down from the top of Portsdown Hills and I'll wait at the bottom with a handcart.' He winked and was gone.

Very few letters indeed were ever addressed to 110 Lampeter Street, so it had been an occasion when a week or so ago the postman had rapped and pushed the small envelope through the letter-box. 'Just listen to this,' Mum had said. 'It's from your Aunty May out at Wickham that married your Dad's brother Ted (Ralph and Kenny would remember them, they came down to Portsmouth; but that's a good many years ago: you were just a babe). It says, "Dear Vera, As you know Ted's brother Hector drops in here sometimes when he is this way, and when he came last time he said that your youngest had had the diptherier and had been very poorly which had left her peaky and off of her food so me and Ted thought it might do the girl a bit of good to get out of Pompey and come over here and get out in the fields a bit. We got plenty of room to spare, as you know there is only Ted and me, and my dad rattling around in this big house, and having a bit of land of our own, there's always a decent bit of food about. We got ourselves a nice little Jersey heifer a year or two back, and she is now milking very well, and I make our own cream and butter, and I'm going to have a go at some cheese. I have always been a great believer in plenty of milk to build a person up after a bad time. It is my belief that Jersey milk, which is full of fat, is far the best of any. We would be very glad to have her, no need to write, just tell Hector the day she will come. Blessings and good wishes to all, your sister-in-law May Wilmott."'

Lu's mother's eyes had gleamed with pleasure. 'Well, would you believe it? Isn't that a nice offer? On your way to work, Ken, you can call in at Hector's and ask Aunty Elsie if she'd get him to call round here next time he's going that way. What a nice thing of her to do. I always liked Ted and May, he's the best of the Wilmotts.'

It had all been settled without reference to Lu. Uncle Hec was a drayman at the brewery and had said he would take her over on the dray, but she would have to keep her head down till they were clear of the city, because a drayman isn't supposed to take passengers except his mate. Uncle Hec preferred to call himself 'a drayman' rather than a common lorry-driver. 'Room for a little'n, eh Luey? Not that you're going to be a little'n for much longer. She got your height, Vere. Not a lot of Wilmott about her.'

They all said that. The reflection of hers and Ralph's heads looking out of the mirror showed how different they looked – him with black hair, blue eyes, a snub nose and round head; herself a 'Copperknob' with brown eyes and a straight nose. Something like her mother, except that Mum's hair was more reddish: she did it with a tu'penny 'Tonette Coppertone Wrinse'.

Lu supposes that she must take after the Presleys.

Ken puts his head round the living-room door. 'All right then, our Lu. Don't get lost, and don't get near the goats, they eat people's clothes off them. See you when you get back,' and he was gone. Not for the first time she wonders what it must be like to go to work each morning and spend your day among coffins and dead bodies. He says that some corpses will sit up and groan and make you jump out of your skin. She doesn't know whether to believe him or not. He works at the Co-op Funeral Department. He says dead bodies don't bother him, doesn't even notice them, but Lu doesn't know whether to believe that either. You surely can't work at the undertaker's and not notice dead bodies.

As she walks to the newspaper shop to get her sweets and comics, she sees Eileen Grigg and her little brother. She's never called Eileen except for the Register. Lena. Lena Grigg is mean and nasty to everybody but especially to Lu. She is envious of Lu who gets things, whose Mum isn't always whacking her, and who has two older brothers who are nice to her whilst Eileen is the drudge of hers.

The reason why Lu is her enemy is that somebody had to be. How else can Lena give vent to all that rage and bitterness she's got to bottle up at home. It must be Lu Wilmott because she is the girl Lena Grigg would most like to be. The Wilmotts have got a tin bath, Lu gets hair-washes in the scullery, they haven't got no babies or kids, and she don't have to sleep with nobody except her mum. Who else is there more deserving to be Lena's object of hate?

From the first day at school, when Lu wouldn't hand over her hair-ribbon, they had scrapped in the playground.

Eileen had supposed that because Lu had been a little goody-goody in class, she would do as she was told by Eileen. 'Give us that ribbon!'

'I'm not!'

'Give us it or you'll get my fist in your mush.'

But the little goody-goody hadn't waited for the punch; she got one in first, made Eileen's nose bleed, and finished up rolling in the playground dirt until a big girl told them to stop or she was going to fetch Miss Lake.

This morning, when she sees Eileen trying to hurry up her brother by slapping his legs, Lu's aggressive spirit makes her need to go over and slap Lena's legs so that she will know what it feels like. The thought of it makes her clench her teeth. Lena Grigg smells and gets scabies and nits, Lu has always had to fight her. Lu knows which of her scars have been given her by Eileen; the worst is the one which runs like a glove-seam around her left thumb; she had bled like a stuck pig and everybody at school said that Lu would get lockjaw and they would tell the police on Lena Grigg. Not that Lena doesn't carry scars given by Lu, but these don't really compare with the others, the ones she has collected at home. At the same time as she feels hostility, there are moments when Lu feels almost sorry for her, even though Lu can never have something nice unless some of the pleasure is taken away by Lena Grigg. Lena's brothers don't give her money for sweets, and she is always being sent on errands or minding her little brothers and sisters, or dragging home stuff from the market or wheeling coal in an old pram. It would be the worst thing in the world to be Eileen Grigg, and although she's never been afraid of Lena herself, Lu has a horror of becoming her, which would be only too easy in Lampeter Street.

Of course, she is too young to understand that yet, but it is that fear which daily fuels her hostility to this model of an abused slum child of a beached woman.

This is the first time Lu has seen her enemy since she went down with 'The Dip'. During Lu's period of delirium, Eileen has hung about hoping to catch a glimpse of something, but somebody always told her to clear off down her own end. Lu of course doesn't know that. She hopes Eileen won't start anything now, because she is still too wobbly to fight. The only thing she can do is not to give her a chance of sticking her face into Lu's and saying, 'What you looking at, beanstick?' Eileen flips her little brother in the face and makes him stand still while she crosses the road. Lu still keeps going, but Eileen blocks her way and says accusingly, 'You're going off away, ain't you, Beanie?'

Lu stands her ground. 'I wouldn't tell you if I was, Lena Grigg.'

'I suppose you think you're the Princess of Lampeter Street just because you're going off in that old beer lorry.'

'What's it got to do with you?'

'It don't matter, everybody knows you are. Anyway, who cares if you got a new skirt? Who'd want a skirt that looks like it was made from her granny's old drawers?'

'Mind out the way, Lena Grigg, I've got to go to the paper shop.'

'What you got in your hand?'

'Something that's mine and nobody else's.' It is only Lu's determination not to let Eileen Grigg get the upper hand that keeps Lu on her feet. She feels sweat spring out on her forehead.

When people said Lu Wilmott was going to die, Eileen felt that it served her right for showing off for having curly hair and thinking she was better than everybody. She can see Lu's sweat; everybody says she hasn't got hardly an ounce of blood left in her veins. She's as skinny as a herring and can't have the strength of a louse, but she doesn't give in. Something tells Lena that, even if she thumped her enemy and got her down in the gutter, Lu Wilmott would still be the winner.

The angry girl has no conception of a strength that is superior to fists and boots. Eileen has never been afraid of Lu before, but she is now. She shouts across at her brother, who is swinging on a rickety gate, 'Stop that, or I'll give you the biggest walloping you ever had', then pushes her face close to Lu's; it is screwed up with malice, her eyes look as though she's about to cry and her lips are wet with spit. 'Everybody said you was goin' to die, Lu Wilmott. I jiss wish you 'ad!'

Until that moment, Lu has never thought there was anything more to their mutual antagonism than that they were naturally against each other. She doesn't move, doesn't even blink. Eileen Grigg runs back across the road, wrenches her brother from the gate and runs down the road with him, his feet scarcely touching the ground.

The pleasure of choosing things at the paper shop is diminished.

Vera Wilmott comes back from the corner shop carrying a bloomer loaf under her arm and a skit with potatoes in it.

Monday: that means a fry-up of bubble-and-squeak done with a penn'orth of butcher's beef-dripping with jelly. By the time it is ready to eat, Lu won't be here. Going to Aunty May's is supposed to make her better, put her on her feet again, and all that has happened so far is that she feels anxious and lonely and worried – and she hasn't even left yet.

'You ready, Lu? I just seen Hector's dray turning the corner. Get your bag, and do up your cardi.' Lu's mother puts down the rush skit, tugs Lu's skirt and smooths her cardi. 'Remember everything I said. Look here . . . this postcard's got a stamp ready on it. In a day or two when you're settled in, write a line home. Oh, and here – ' Vera Wilmott folds Lu's fingers over a paper bag, as though the contents were secret or embarrassing – 'I got you your own toothbrush. If May don't have any "Gibbs's" or anything, just do it with plain water.' Amazed, Lu clutches the wooden handle. Nobody in their house has ever had separate things, like face-cloths or a tin of toothpaste, until they went out to work and earned enough to buy their own. As far as she knew, she was the only one in her class who was made to clean her teeth. She has never told her friends: they'd think it was daft. 'Can I keep it for myself when I come home?' Vera has never explained that, before he died, her father had been partner in a dental practice. Vera Presley's origins are past history.

Her Mum smiles. 'Of course you can, I said I got it for your own. I've been going to get you a little something . . . when you had "The Dip". I hardly lost any piecework in that fortnight, what with Ralph helping out and you being such a good little patient . . . ' Being paid by the piece for her work – which was hand-sewn finishing and trimming of garments – ruled virtually every move Vera Wilmott made in the working day. Normally Lu helped with the less than fine sewing, making up the weekly numbers that had to be turned in to the factory.

'Here's Hec's lorry. Be polite and helpful and speak nice. I always been proud of you, y'know, our Lu.' Taken aback at this revelation, Lu can only nod. Uncle Hector stops his lorry but leaves its motor running. She stuffs the new toothbrush down into the bag, along with the treats from Ralph. It gives Lu a peculiar feeling, part pleasure, part apprehension spiced with a bit of smugness, to have a bag in which everything belongs to herself.

Vera gives Lu's shoulders a smooth.

Hector Wilmott lifts her up by the waist into the cab and gets back behind the wheel. 'Don't you worry, Vere. In twenty years as a drayman, I haven't so much as dented a bumper.'

Charlie Barrit, drayman's mate, takes her bag, makes room for her, and fusses a bit of blanket to cover her knees, 'Can be a bit draughty when we gets on top of the hill,' he says, tucking her in.

Vera Wilmott stretches her neck to see her little girl settled between the two men. She looks as though she could be snapped like matchwood. *I'm going to miss you.* Vera doesn't say it, because people don't, and it would only upset Lu even more. But she will miss her. She hadn't wanted her, hadn't wanted any baby – not then, just as Kenny was off to school. She had taken doses of Woman's Comfort, but all that famous elixir did was to purge her and make her bleed. After a week of this, Vera concluded that this baby was determined to come. Half a crown would have certainly got an abortion. Dotty next door said at the time that babies you can't dislodge except with the knitting needle should have their chance, and although Vera knew that this was just one more of Dotty's platitudes offered because she liked people to cheer up and make the best of things, she decided to leave things alone and only hope that all the bleeding hadn't damaged the child. The following June, when Arthur was off again on the other side of the world, Lu had come, and had looked so wholesome and pretty and unaffected by all the Woman's Comfort that Vera decided that, come what may, she would never give in to Arthur again. She had never stopped feeling guilty about her pre-natal treatment of her pretty little girl. She had a lot to make up for to Lu.

The lorry rolls slowly forward and laboriously picks up speed, watched by half the mothers from the shop end of Lampeter Street who stand in their doorways waving.

And they are away.

To Wickham, twelve miles away.

Her punishment for trying to interfere with Lu started from the time she got on her feet again after the birth. Everything dropped down. A common enough condition. Doctor Steiner, who was the Penny Club doctor, had said that it could probably be put right. But to have a man's hands inside, stitching everything back in place? Too frightening a prospect for most women and, in any case, in those days Vera hadn't been able to afford a Hospital Club as well. So, all these years later, Vera is still an outworker, collecting piles of pieces from the factory to be hand finished, paying for her own needles and cotton, working like a slave for a few shillings.

Times are not quite as hard as then. Kenny isn't earning yet, but his apprenticeship isn't taking money out, and Ralph is a white-collar railwayman. There are very few railwaymen around Lampeter Street, even fewer clerks. A railwayman's wage too. It wasn't so much the wage as the security of it. Vera was never more thankful than on the day when she saw both her boys out of the danger of having to go to the dock gates and fight their way to be picked out of the crowd for a few days' or a few hours' work. She had always promised herself that she would not make plans for Lu, except that she would use her own knowledge of teaching to give Lu some sort of homework or tuition. But Vera had not counted on her own health giving out on her. She had grown steadily more tired, then fatigued. Dr Steiner gave her big bottles of iron tonic that stained the teeth but didn't halt the anaemia. By the time Lu was school age, it was as much as Vera could do to get her outwork done, so Lu was left with the same standard of education as the rest.

Ralph was good, though: he bought a paper every day, and in the evening he read it aloud. Vera loved to listen to him; she didn't mind if it was the *Evening News* or Lu's *Rupert Bear* book. The man of the house reading aloud. Something good from her respectable middle-class past, from before the time when she had allowed her future to become entangled with the tribal Wilmotts. Most of the Wilmotts despised her for her class, and for flaunting it before them with her grammar and posh voice. But that was no longer relevant, these days they could despise her for being an outworker. Lowest of the low. All Arthur's sisters and nieces were staymaking machinists.

All of that because she had experienced the kind of lust for a rough, Pompey matelot that girls of her sort were supposed to consider beneath them.

In the throes of that intense passion, her intelligent, teacher-trained self couldn't see further ahead than the next time she would recklessly arouse him. Her thoughts dissipated, except for those to do with her unashamed fantasies of desire and passion. Her moist body in a state of aching readiness, to be satiated, aroused, then gratified again, endlessly. Her senses heightened – hearing coarse words and saying them herself; smelling work sweat, foreign spiced hair-oil, twenty-year-old maleness; feeling fingers sliding, mouths slavering, tongues thrusting, hands kneading, nails clutching, clawing; watching the moment when he lost control because she let him. How powerful it was to be a woman, to know that she could bring a self-assured man like this tough sailor to a state of pleading – pleading for what she wanted anyway. There had been, too, such shameless pride in discovering that she was desirable – he'd told her his mates were green with envy; he'd boasted that he was having it all with the hottest piece of goods this side of the Line, a real bit of class. And she had loved it all. For the period of that one erotic fling she had been like a foie-gras goose, overstuffed to destruction.

All of that, everything, because when she was young, and a virgin, a good-looking sailor had touched her in such a way that mating hormones had surged through her, had filled her with such intensity that for a time she was no more responsible for her actions than had been her primitive female ancestors who had mating seasons and went on heat. As Arthur had discovered, it hadn't taken long for her to cool. Not much chance that he would want her as she was now, thank God.

Ralph, a clerk with the Southern Railway, hard at work poring over the spring timetable newly sent down from the statistics office, looked up and saw that the time was five to seven, the time when Uncle Hec said he would pick Lu up, and again hoped that he was right about Lu being sure to enjoy herself. He'd never forgive himself if this holiday didn't live up to the promises he'd made her.

At work his contact with other people went in bursts, such as when a train was in and the guard supervising the loading of the goods van exchanged a burst of chat with him, usually about PFC and football generally, or a bit of gossip that was of interest only to Pompey men. This morning there was no one around, though, and he kept finding his mind going back to Lu and then to his mum.

Naturally she and Ray never spoke about it, but he knew well enough about his mother's woman's problem. It was the reason why she had been forced to take out-work, because she couldn't sit on the machinists' backless stools. You could see her problem in her face, weary, dragged down and fit to drop, even though she did her work seated in a low, easy chair. Sometimes he would come in and find her with her hands cupped beneath her 'high' stomach. How he hated to see it. But she'd always make herself perk up and say, 'Oh dear, Ray, look at me, I was miles away.'

He wished he earned enough so that she didn't have to do it. He had been stupidly blind at first, but now he realized there could be only one reason why she didn't draw a Navy allowance. Once, and once only, he had been thoughtless enough to bring it up. She had flushed bright red, and plucked at her lower lip, and looked as though he had caught her out in some shameful act. The pause when she couldn't answer had seemed so long. Even if she had at last come up with an answer that could have salvaged her respectability, he hadn't, by then, wanted to hear it. It was a moment when he had loved her so much that he wished he had known how to tell her, instead of which he had said, 'If I don't mend that fire now, it's going to go out', and had gone to the shed and sawn off a length of old railway-sleeper hard as iron.

That weekend she had got him a new tie from the tallyman. 'Go on, you have it,' she had said when he'd insisted he didn't need another one. 'You're good to me, Ray, and I never like to see a man go out in the evenings wearing his working tie.'

The best he could do was to see to it that she never had to do anything heavy. Ken brought in the coals for the range, Ralph filled and emptied the copper-boiler on wash-days, and ever since she'd been able to reach, putting washing through the mangle and out on the line in her school dinner-time had been Lu's job; she also ran errands to the Co-op for potatoes and other heavy shopping.

'What you think of that then?' Mr Barrit points to the harbour far below. 'Looks like a toy town, don't it?'

Hector Wilmott's lorry, rattling its crates of bottled beer, has laboured up the narrow winding road that leads out of Portsmouth, and has halted on the crest before taking the smooth run down over the Portsdown Hills. The sun pours down, sparkling the distant sea. In the hedgerows, last year's brown grass is already being overgrown by new green, and buds are showing on everything except the brambles, but even their purple stems are engorged and saturated with their life-force.

Lu nods, solemn and wide-eyed, slowly dissolving a sweet in the hollow of the roof of her mouth with her tongue; sees her home town spread out far below. It is a strange feeling, from here Portsmouth looks like a map with models on it. A working model. Trails of smoke where trains are being shunted in the goods yard. Ships slide out of harbour and past the Isle of Wight. Dockyard cranes dip and swing. She wants to be pleased because of Mr Barrit and Uncle Hec, but apprehension makes her stomach knot and her skin cold. She doesn't want them to know that she's not excited, but she doesn't want to tell them lies; they've been so nice to her, telling her old riddles and asking if they still learn the same poems at school. They think this must be the greatest treat in the world for her.

Without her mother to correct her, she automatically slips into Lampeter Street cockney, which is how Mr Barrit and Uncle Hec talk. 'We was going to come up here with the Sunday school outing, but last time boys kept running down the steep part, so the teachers said they wouldn't come no more, so we had a picnic and games on the common and a paddle in the sea, and we never come up here. It was nice though.'

Mr Barrit says, 'Is that a fac'? In my day we never had picnics.'

The lorry rolls on down the road on the other side, allowing Hector, the driver, to return his attention to the conversation. 'You learnt to swim yet, Luey?'

'No. Ray said he wouldn't mind teaching me, but he's got to learn himself first, and he haven't got bathers yet.'

'All Pompeyites is the same. Live by all that sea, yet how many of us does more than have a bit of a splash around? I don't reckon there's a Pompey matelot ever taught himself to swim.'

When Uncle Hec said he would tuck her away somewhere in the cab, she never expected a journey where she would ride so high up, with windows both sides and in front. It is better for seeing than even upstairs on a bus, but, now that they have left the streets and houses, she is not so sure that she wants to see. Now they are over the crest, Portsmouth is lost behind them and there is only a vast, empty green land to be seen.

'There you are then, Lu, what do you think of that? There's your proper country for you.' He switches the engine off and indicates the emptiness to his right, and as Lu bends forward she is exposed to rural Hampshire for the first time in her life.

She does not see those pleasant pastures, nor any un-clouded hills, and the great aquamarine dome covers emptiness. Whichever way she looks, there is nothing but open land. She has grown up with the sea within walking distance, so she is not unfamiliar with a distant horizon, but back home there are always the hills of the Isle of Wight not far away. There the sea is never still and quiet.

This vast, uninhabited, empty land is still and quiet and very, very alarming.

Yet this empty space is The Country where she is being sent, where she is supposed to enjoy herself and get well.

Her stomach clenches with anxiety. She had never im-agined it would be empty or so endless. In the clear air, for as far as she can see to her right, there are just fields and fields and fields and fields. No guiding landmarks, no roads, no houses or people, just a few little trees. How can anybody find their way in a place with no houses or shops or churches? The map on the classroom wall shows England as such a small country. Miss said that millions of people live in England, so Lu had supposed that every-where was like home. Miss had shown them a picture of the Russian steppes where people didn't live, and the Sahara which was empty and where there were mirages and no water. But she never said anything about empty England. Yet its emptiness was only just the other side of the hill from home.

'There aren't any people, Uncle Hec, Where are they?'

'What people, my lover?'

'People who lives in the country. There isn't no houses.'

The Dutch courage that Ray had given her is draining away. He said she would like it. How did he know? Pictures of the country in storybooks always had cows and sheds, and pretty cottages surrounded with trees, and mothers standing at the doors watching children and sheep. But it was all empty, like the red dreams in her

21

Dip fever, where any people who did come shrank down to dots till they disappeared.

And here, just like the Dip dreams, you could run and run and never get anywhere.

What would happen if you got lost or hurt? Who would hear you?

Where did people get their food if there wasn't a Co-op or a greengrocer's?

Her stomach rumbles and she feels chilly from Uncle Hec's open window.

'Oh, there's villages up over yonder. There's Soake and Denmead; there's even World's End. Don't you worry, there's plenty of people about. A lot of them'll be out there somewhere, ploughing and planting and that. Your Uncle Ted will be out on his land drilling or something.'

Charlie Barrit sings, 'Oh to plough and to sow and to reap and to mow.' Hector joins in. He has a deep, tuneful voice. 'And to be a farmer's boy-oy-oy-oy, And to be a farmer's boy. You know that, lover?'

Lu nods.

'Well, come on then, let's hear you.'

She drags her dismay away from the wilderness on her right and, as Uncle Hec gets the lorry going again, fixes her gaze on the road ahead where her attention is at once caught. 'Look! There's Buckingham Palace.' And so it looks to Lu who is quite untutored in palaces. Ahead and to their right stands many-windowed Southwick House. Its façade with the sun on it appears finished in cake icing; a flag fluttering from its mast, it rises out of mature woodlands of full-grown oak and elm.

'Nah, Buckingham Palace is half a hundred miles away,' Uncle Hec says. 'That's Suthick House. We're going there.'

'Ah,' says Charlie, in his playful tone, 'but only to Suthick village. We forgot to bring our invitations to the palace. Dang me, what a stupid I be.'

'Have you been there?'

Uncle Hec shakes his head and takes his eyes away from the road to look at Lu and Charlie. 'Not really our type, are they, Charlie?'

'A bit on the rough side.'

And now she knows that they are pulling her leg. And now they are clear of the scary, empty land. And now there are big trees and a long stretch of high wall. The sight of such a long stretch of red brick settles her stomach and encourages her blood to circulate. She says, 'It's a long road, what's it called?'

Mr Barrit says, 'This is the Suthick Road, goes on far as Wickham.'

Hector corrects, 'Goes on as far as Winchester, Charlie.'

'That's true. And if you follows it to Winchester, there you got a choice: you can carry on north and go to Newbury, or turn east and go to Devizes.'

'No, Charlie. If you're going to give the gel a geography lesson, make sure you haven't got it ass about face – it's *west* to Devizes.'

Charlie Barrit pulls a face and puts his hand over his mouth like he was a dunce. 'Your Uncle Hec's right, I never can remember which is my left hand and which is my right.'

Lu says, 'Ralph says that's a sign of being intelligent.'

'There you are then,' says Charlie. 'I always said there was a professor's brain hid away somewhere in here. I think I'll ask for a raise.'

Hector says, 'Now asking for a raise don't strike me as a very intelligent thing to do, Professor Barrit.'

The two draymen laugh, disposing of some of the apprehension about what it is going to be like when she is dropped off at Aunty May's, and making Lu begin to imagine that she has sat between them and done this journey a dozen times. She knows very well that this chit-chat and joking is for her benefit, but that doesn't lessen her enjoyment. The lorry is a small, enclosed place and she feels, hears and smells the big men who rock from side to side, their hard, strong, safe arms that can lift a beer-crate crushing gently against her own arms. She likes the feel of the lorry, thrumming and swaying; the smell of the men's blue overalls, oily, dusty, beery; the soap-smell of their shirts fresh on that morning because it is Monday; she likes the thought of the contents of her bag, her comics, her toothbrush and the skirt and top made specially to go to Aunty May's from a couple of Bon Marché remnants.

She shouldn't have had those doubts about Ralph. She was going to stay with her aunty and uncle, they were relations, Wilmotts like herself.

'Are you sure you wouldn't like a raspberry drop, Uncle Hec?'

'Well, now you mention it, I could just do with something to take the taste of this dust out of my mouth till we gets to Suthick.'

The three of them sit sucking with noisy enjoyment until they come to a signpost finger pointing to Southwick. Hector puts his arm out of the window and signals with a stiff hand that he is turning right, and they all scrunch quickly.

The narrow winding village street and the huddled little houses might be seen – by a stranger who knows nothing of their unhealthy interiors – as most picturesque and romantic. The Bells is the pub where they are to make the first delivery. It is a white, thatched building, set at the edge of a birch and hazel spinney. It looks secure and comforting.

'Now, if you wants to go to the you-know, just go round the back and you'll see the "Ladies" sign on a shed. Come back and sit on that bench outside the tap room over there. We shan't be long about.'

Lu doesn't want the you-know, which is as well for it is a privy with a wooden seat over a pit. But because she is curious about the back of the pub, she goes where Uncle

Hec had indicated. Lu has never seen the likes of a pub like this; pubs at home are bigger and many are done over in shiny tiles with letters that read 'Home Brew – Stout – Porter – Best Wines and Spirits'. They were some of the first words Ralph had taught her; then he had bought a *Rupert Bear* annual for her fourth birthday and begun to teach her to read properly. She wishes there was some way to get a message back to Ralph to tell him that he was right, it is lovely to ride in a lorry.

The Bells has been an inn for centuries, and over that time it has expanded, taking over a couple of adjoining cottages, its uneven exterior and undulating roof-line showing the expansion. Its only cohesion is in its overall lime and rubble finish, and the shaggy thatch used by birds and mice at nesting time as a kind of builders' supply depot. Small windows are overhung by the roof, and at the front is a narrow door shielded by a stone-built weather-porch. It is old. In the seventeen hundreds, no drays called to roll wooden casks of ale into the cool, windowless outhouse; in those days the ales, beers and ciders were brewed on the premises, often by the innkeeper's wife who made do with vessels filched from her kitchen, vessels with names that had by the twentieth century become almost obsolete or at least curious or romantic, the pipkins, the pins, the gugglets and the jeroboams. In many ways the original inn, minus its extensions, is so little changed that its original occupants would feel at home. Only recently a white ceramic hand-basin, bath and indoor flush lavatory have been installed, but these still drain into an ancient cesspool.

The Bells at Southwick experiences in winter a climate which can be much foggier and degrees colder than on the seaward side of the Portsdown Hills where the air is warmed by the Solent and Spithead waters. Even so, The Bells is still in the cosseted south, where spring and summer gardens can bloom five or six weeks earlier and last longer than those in the north. It is not yet April; even so the spring season is especially advanced when Lu Wilmott is drawn into the garden of The Bells.

Seen through her eyes, here is a birthday cottage she believes in. Familiar flowers, some of whose names she knows like the cherry-blossom, tulips and daffodils that grow in Portsmouth parks. She hears a church bell distantly and counts as it strikes the hour. Seven . . . eight . . . She can hardly believe that it is only eight o'clock and here she is in another world.

She sits in the sun, her knees tight together, her hands clasped to stop herself worrying again. A lady, nothing like the rosy, picture-book mothers, comes out through the porch-door carrying a tray of drinks which she puts down on the table where Lu is seated. Her hair is long and fair, done in deep waves clipped back on one side in a long hair-slide, a star of sparkling diamonds with a tail of diamonds shooting out of it. In her ears she wears little white birds. Her silky, rose-printed dress has two rows of frills instead of sleeves. She is lovely, made up like a film star and smelling of scent.

'Hello, sweetheart. You must be old Hec's little niece.'

Lu jumps up, her face flushed with shyness. 'Yes, miss, I'm Lu.'

The lady smiles, 'Hello, Lu, I'm Peggy – Vera really, but nobody ever calls me that.'

'My mum's called Vera, Uncle Hec calls her Vere, and it's my second name.'

'Just fancy that. Uncle Hec your mum's brother?'

'My dad's, he's in the Navy.'

'One of the boys in blue. You wasn't surely christened Lu?'

'No, Louise.'

'That's a beautiful name. Why do you let people call you Lu?'

Lu thinks for a moment. 'Because I never thought of it.'

'Well, if it was me, I'd start thinking about it. Louise has got a real touch of class . . . style. Louise Wilmott, that sounds nice.'

It did!

Peggy smiles at her again. She is so beautiful, all made up with red lipstick, eyelashes black, and blush on her cheeks: Lu longs to be her. On special occasions Lu's mum does herself up like this and is changed like magic; Lu loves it when her mum makes her face up. 'Sit back down, sweetheart. Here, I brought you some cherryade and crisps, help pass the time till Hec and Charlie are finished down the cellar.'

Peggy pushes the red drink and packet of Smith's potato crisps to Lu's side of the table. Lu sits down and Peggy joins her, holding her own clear bubbly drink in one hand, and a cork-tipped cigarette in the other. 'I hear you are off on holiday then.' Lu is about to say that she has had the Dip and is going to her aunty's to recuperate when she realizes it sounds better to say that it's a holiday. Sounds more like Peggy's dress than next-door's moulty chickens.

'Yes, miss, I'm going on holiday to my aunty and uncle's who's got a place at Wickham. Have you heard of Wickham?'

'Oh yes, everybody round here knows Wickham. It isn't far along the road here. Nice little place, big square with little shops all round, a bit sleepy for me . . . Still, a bit livelier than Suthick, though. Come on, eat up, if I was slim as you I'd have a packet too. Or would you rather have biscuits?'

'No, thank you, I love crisps.'

Suddenly Lu is no longer lanky, thin or skinny. She is slim. Adverts always say things like that: 'Slim-waisted style', 'Slim fitting', 'Be slim!', but never, 'Be a skinny beanpole!' She smiles at Peggy, takes a swallow of cherryade, breaks open the crisps and finds the blue knot with the salt, offers the bag to Peggy who shakes her head and

27

raises her cigarette, then crunches the brown, oily treats. At tuppence a bag, it is only once in a blue moon that Lampeter Street kids get such treats. 'I'm supposed to be going away to get some flesh on my bones.'

Peggy smiles and blows smoke at the same time. 'Well, that'd be a treat for some of us. Mind you – ' she leaned in Lu's direction and held up her glass – 'this don't help.'

'What is it?'

'Gin and tonic. Mother's Ruin. It's no good for anybody, you know. Don't let anybody start you on it.'

'Isn't it nice then?' Lu found it so easy to talk to her.

She laughed again. 'Oh yes, it's lovely, that's the trouble, once you had one you soon want another one. I suppose it's not much good living in a pub if you got a taste of it.'

'Do you live here?'

'Sort of, I'm the barmaid. The landlord's a widower, so I'm a sort of substitute landlady. Right out here, you got no choice but to live in.'

'It's a pretty house.'

'Yes, it's all right. I never thought I'd make a country girl, but I reckon I could take to it, given the right sort of persuasion. Needs a car though. Hello, here's the happy wanderers.'

Uncle Hec and Mr Barrit come out, each carrying a half-empty tankard of beer, Mr Barrit wheeling the handcart which he returns to its place under the bed of the lorry. Lu is almost sorry to see them; she has never met anybody like Peggy, who speaks to Lu as though she were a real person.

'Now then, Peg, what you been putting our little gel up to?'

'I wouldn't put her up to anything, Hec. She's a really pretty girl, and she speaks lovely.'

'That's her mum, a reg'lar crack-jaw she can be when she wants.'

She turns to Lu and smiles, 'You're lucky then, Louise. A pity a few more children didn't have mothers that taught them how to speak decent. Now, you make sure these two brings you in when you've had your holiday.' She turns to Uncle Hec. 'I want to see what she's like when she's back on her feet.'

Uncle Hec drinks the last of his beer and wipes the froth from his mouth with the back of his hand. 'Thanks, Peg, but this won't get the baby a pair of trousers!'

Lu drinks the last drop of cherryade and puts what is left of the crisps in her cardigan pocket. Suddenly she wants to pee. Uncle Hec is tying down the tarpaulin, so she would have time, but she doesn't like to ask in front of everybody. Peggy says quietly in Lu's ear, 'Might be a good idea to go while you got a chance.' Lu nods vigorously, grateful for Peggy's kindness. 'Come on, don't go round to that old bog-hut, there's one indoors.'

When Lu comes out, Peggy is holding a full bottle of cherryade and several packets of crisps and biscuits. 'I'll just pop these in a bag and give them to Hec to put in the cab for you. It's not much, but I know it's nice to have a little treat when you're on holiday.'

Lu blushes at not having the words to thank her enough. 'Thank you *ever* so much. Do you know, I got some new comics, my brother bought them for me, and some sweets, and a new toothbrush.' She grins at Peggy. 'I've got ever so many new things.'

Peggy stands for a few seconds looking at Lu, then, taking Lu's hair in a bunch, she unclips the sparkling hair-slide from her own hair, and with it clips back Lu's. 'How's that, then? Shows off those lovely eyes and this beautiful hair. You'll find it cooler off your face.'

'Can I wear it?'

'It's yours. You'll be a star yourself one day, just you see. Come back and see me when you are.'

Lu doesn't know what to say. A star of diamonds must have cost a packet.

'Now get on your way, or your Uncle Hec will blame me if he don't have time for another pint when he gets to The King's.'

Lu longs for words that sound equal to her feelings, but can only think of the tallyman who always says, 'Obliged to you, Mrs Wilmott, much obliged.'

'Thank you, ever so much . . . really. I won't lose it.'

Back inside The Bells, Peggy poured herself another small gin as Dick came up from the cellar. 'Did you see that little girl Hec Wilmott had with him, Dick?'

Dick Briardale, the landlord of The Bells, shook his head absently. Dick Briardale, widower, nicely off, handsome and with healthy appetites, had had his thoughts engaged elsewhere for the past half-hour.

'You should have seen her. Breaks your heart to see a kid looking like that. She's being sent to some place in Wickham hoping to get her better.' She shook her head sadly, sipped and held the spirit in her mouth before swallowing. 'Breaks your heart . . . Kids like that haven't got a chance; they don't have anything in reserve.'

Untying his leather cellar apron, he came close, pressed his belly against hers and cupped her shapely, generous left breast. 'You got a soft heart, Peg.' His other large hand parted her legs and moved upwards without any of the preamble or finesse in 'courting' that, in her younger days, before she became wise to them, Peggy had always believed a decent man would show. In other ways, Dick Briardale was a decent man, and according to Dick himself, a good ladies' man. A big ladies' man, and don't they love it? Handsome and knew it. 'Soft and warm,' he said, playing around with her in a way he knew softened women up a bit.

'Oh, Dick,' Peggy said, 'you get worse. It isn't hardly half-past eight.'

'Just a refresher, Peg, it don't take five minutes. Go on, undo me, you know you're dying to . . . Go on, I haven't got three hands.'

He wasn't asking. She was under his roof, in clothes he had paid for, his gin inside her. A year ago he had become a single man again, with a nice ale-house and a decent trade. There were plenty of other women who'd like the chance to know what it was like to sleep in Dick Briardale's bed at nights, and stand up for Dick Briardale when he was full of eggs and bacon and perky from a wash and shave. And there had been several women, since his wife had died, who did already know. But he liked Peg, she wasn't any sort of a prude. No, sir! Not one bit. So he wouldn't mind if she stayed, which was why he let her twist him round her little finger.

Peggy lifted the silky skirt. The little girl had surreptitiously fingered it, probably hadn't felt silk in her life. She leaned back with her elbows on the bar so that her boss could take his morning exercise . . . his physical jerks, his daily dozen. His joke. Peggy, looking over his shoulder as he concentrated on her soft, easy body, knew that he was oblivious to everything except his gratification. Next time Old Hec called, she would ask him how the girl had settled in. Breathily she whispered, 'She looks to me as though she won't make old bones, Dick. Seems such a waste. Just a dried-up little angel with her big eyes.'

Dick groaned.

He hadn't heard a word. She hadn't wanted him to hear. She could say anything to him whilst he was grunting away, giving her what he knew a woman of twenty-five bloody well wanted. 'There!' he said. In the mornings he said, 'There!', and at night he said, 'You liked that, didn't you?' Sunday afternoons, he said, 'You shouldn't have let me eat so much, Peg.' Predictability was good in a man. Some men would kiss you one moment, slap you around the next. Dick wouldn't ever hit a woman, you could rely on that. Dick was all right: she liked his predictability. Surprises are never what you expect – Peg's joke.

He pulled away and she went into the toilet. Standing her gin on the little shelf under the mirror, a newly lighted cigarette beside it, she looked into her own eyes as she pulled down a long length off the roll and asked herself the same question as she'd asked before, 'What would he say if I stopped wearing my little cap?' He wouldn't know . . . accidents happen . . . they didn't guarantee caps to be a hundred per cent. He said it never bothered him that his first wife couldn't have babies, but when it came down to it, there wasn't a man born who didn't want living proof that he could deliver, that he wasn't all talk and trousers. Southwick itself wasn't much of a place, but The Bells was all right. She was doing better here than she'd done for ages. Pity to risk it just because she got broody. So what if he did give her the heave-ho? He wouldn't be the first man to do that. She could still pull a man. She peered closer, inspecting the fine lines. What about in five years? Ten? She'd be thirty-five. She bit on her lips which she had repaired with bright red lipstick. Then again, she might be pushing up the daisies. Pity to pop off and not know what it was like to do what women are supposed to do. Anyway, Dick might get the idea himself; he'd been soft enough over the puppies his pedigree bitch had gone and got without letting him know she was even interested.

Two of the few things that were her own she had given away that morning. What she had given Dick he didn't see as being a gift, but the hair-slide that she had given to that little Louise, the girl'd treated as though it was the crown jewels. Her mum was called Vera; what must it be like to have a little kid, bring her up, and then have to look on, helpless, as she wasted away. Peggy felt like weeping. 'This is all your bloody fault!' she said to the gin as she tossed it off.

* * *

The rest of the journey seems to go in a flash, with Mr Barrit keeping saying, 'Not long now', 'Only a mile or so', 'Nearly there'. They turn off the main road and go down a long narrow lane with fields on both sides, but these ones aren't endless and empty, there are rises and hedges and trees. And suddenly they are there. A proper painted notice on a post says, *Roman's Fields. Proprs. Strawbridge & Wilmott. Strawberries and veg. in season. Wholesale and retail. Eggs. Chickens. Honey. Call at side door or in fields. Ring bell for service.*

'Look, Uncle Hec. Wilmott.' Her own name in curly letters on a proper notice like outside the church or over a shop. She had never known that the May and Ted Wilmotts were posh. Ralph said that, except for the Lampeter Street Wilmotts, the Wickham ones were better than all the rest. Uncle Hec had been really nice today, so perhaps Uncle Ted would be too.

Absently, because he is manoeuvring the lorry, Uncle Hec says, 'Yes, my pretty, that's our Ted.'

Uncle Hec slows down, Mr Barrit jumps out and swings open a wide gate, and Lu watches as the lorry is manoeuvred into a kind of yard surrounded by sheds and outhouses. Mr Barrit holds out his arms and helps her down. Her legs feel shaky and her stomach is turning over with alarm. As she is looking at the outhouses a voice behind her says, 'You got here all right then?' and Uncle Hec says, 'Course we did, May, here's the little maid safe and sound.' Lu swallows on a dry mouth. There is no turning back now; she turns and sees this unknown aunty in whose house she will have to stay.

Aunty May is nothing at all like her other aunties. She is pretty, a lot younger than Mum, about the same age as Peggy, and she has the same low, slow way of talking as her too. Aunty May is wearing leather sandals with buckles, and a wrap-around apron with no sleeves. She is so different from anything Lu had imagined. 'Hello, Lu,' she smiles. 'I'm so glad you could come and visit us. We've been looking forward to it that much.' She takes Lu's hand and holds it between her own two. 'Are you cold, pet? I hope Hector didn't keep the window down.'

Lu can only shake her head. She tries to smile but feels that it is coming out all wrong, and her hand really does feel cold, enclosed as it is between the two very warm ones. Because of Aunty Else and the other aunties – Glad, Ethel, Rose and Vi – Lu had created Aunty May from a composite of them.

No wonder May Wilmott was such a surprise: the other aunties were hard-voiced and bony-faced and in their forties, mothers of several children. The other aunties always appeared to frown and have their arms folded close across their bodies. Such faces and arms are familiar to Lu, because she has grown up among women who have spent their lives living on a diet that lasted a long time in the stomach: combinations of potatoes, bread, belly-pork, lard and suet. Protein was usually fish in batter or sausages. Few fresh vegetables or fruits, and a great many daylight hours spent in ill-lit factories bent over sewing machines, score deep creases in their grey faces.

Lu, of course, does not realize that her grim Pompey aunties have good cause to look grim. All she sees – to her great pleasure – is that this aunty is very pretty, with a kind face and a gentle voice.

She stands with her hand held as Aunty May asks Mr Barrit if he would mind bringing Lu's bag into the house.

Aunty May's hair is as light as Peggy's, but not the same goldy colour; nor is it shiny and neat, but spills out in little twirls from the sides of a blue handkerchief which is knotted at the back. It is not reasonable to expect Lu to take in much else, for she is held by Aunty May's beautiful eyes. Lu has heard of 'smiling eyes', but until Aunty May, she has never seen eyes that do this. As Aunty May turns to Lu, the smile spreads to her lips as well.

A minute ago, when May Wilmott saw her waif-like little niece in her cheap plimsolls and ill-fitting cardigan, she needed to put her hands together in order to stop herself clasping the girl herself. Instead she took Lu's hand; a bone-cold, bone-thin, sinewy hand which, except for the soft skin, was like that of a very old lady. What a pathetic, sick-looking child. How overwhelmed she must be. All those weeks of illness, and now being uprooted and put down in a place that must feel very strange to her. May has promised herself that it must not feel strange for long. She says again, 'We've been so looking forward to it, we don't get many visitors, so it's a real treat.'

Lu's blush is noticeable on her pale face. Vera has most likely given her a talking-to about good manners. Vera brought them all up like that. May hears the Pompey cockney of back-street Portsmouth as Lu hands over a neat packet. 'Thank you for asking me. These is from Ralph, he saved all last week's *Evening News* for you. He said Uncle Ted would probably like to know what's been going on in Town.'

May was touched by the simple present. 'Well now, isn't that good of Ralph to send something interesting. It's not often we get to see the Portsmouth papers, that's true. I've always remembered Ralph as such a nice boy.' The winsome girl, whose face seems to be overburdened by her large eyes, and her head by such heavy, lank hair says eagerly, 'He is, Aunty May . . . and he's going to get a "priv" and come over and see me when he's on the right shift, or he's going to borrow the paper-shop bike.'

May suspects that this statement is to get the proposed visit established right at the outset. 'Well, pet, you'll have to tell me what he likes, because we'll have to make him a special dinner. Now come on in, your Uncle Hector and Mr Barrit will want a ham sandwich before they get off down to Wickham.'

* * *

The first night at Roman's Fields. Lu, having embarrassingly fallen asleep over her supper, now finds herself wide awake, her mind in turmoil with the events of the day. Peggy swims in and out of her mind; her bird earrings and the roses and frills of her dress; the way she talked as though Lu wasn't just a girl, but a person. Then Aunty May's kind, pretty face smiles out of all the new faces. She raises her eyebrows when she smiles, as though she's being given a surprise present.

About this characteristic, Lu is quite perceptive. May is a woman given to acknowledging enchantment whenever it presents itself, and if it should slip by unnoticed, she's likely to say later, 'That was really nice. I don't know why I didn't notice at the time.'

Ever since Hector had mentioned how worried Vera had been over the girl, and how when it had come to the crisis it had been touch and go, May had planned to ask Vera to let the child come to stay. May's visits to Portsmouth always appalled her. Whenever she had visited the city, on her return to Roman's Fields, she and Ted had virtually the same conversation. 'Oh, I like the city itself well enough, it's a change to be in a place where they're so rich the town hall looks like it come from ancient Greece. And I always like a chance to go to a play or a show. And I have to admit, Joycey's in the village isn't quite the same as that big new Co-op, that's all nice when you come from the country.'

Ted would say his line, 'There's not many Pompeyites lives in the guildhall.'

And, as though Ted had never seen his own birthplace, May would bring out the piece of stone that weighed heavier than any of the purchases she had brought home with her. 'It's only when I see it all again that I remember how bad it all is. There's poverty enough around here, Lord above we all know that, but all that part of Pompey where your people live . . . it's all so mean, squalid, and the air tastes like sulphur. And they have to go on breathing it every day. All those families packed together in those dreadful narrow streets. I don't reckon there's hardly a house can open a window or door properly the frames are that warped.'

'It was throwed up overnight, cheap bricks held together with hardly anything 'xcept sand and water.'

'And how the place did smell. I tell you, Ted, all those streets round where the market is . . . well, our goat shed was a sight more sweet than they were.' Finding Ted's only response was to shake his head, May would ask the same question she had asked before. 'Why do people stand it?'

'You know why they do, May – because we're born to it. You know what it's like if a rabbit's born in a old orange-box that's full of droppin's and old cabbage leaves . . . He don't know nature intended him to have a decent nest down a warm burrow. Well, people born in slums don't know nothing else.'

'Ah . . . but if you showed your rabbit a green field and opened his box, he'd be gone before you could blink. I mean, human beings actually know it isn't nature to live so cramped up with hardly a green leaf in sight. Why don't they all just get out, live in a tent? Eli bringing up his family in our old barn is better housed than your people, Ted.'

'Eli Barney's born a gypsy – he knows how to turn a penny and live off the land . . . There isn't a Wilmott in generations who'd know about livin' off of the land.'

'You do, Ted.'

And Ted would smile, shaking his head ruefully. 'And a pretty fist I made of it at first. If it hadn't a been for your dad, I'd a gone back and lived in my old orange-box, droppin's, cabbage leaves and all.'

Of course, May Wilmott knew only too well how and why slums existed and how and why it was virtually impossible for people trapped in them to escape. But, although May no longer thought of herself as a Quaker as

37

her parents had been, she still saw the world and its people with a particular view of what was right. Her mother had died a long time ago, but Gabriel Strawbridge, her father, now arthritic and losing his sight, still lived on in Roman's Fields. He had inherited the few acres and a house from his father, whose forefathers had squatted on the bit of land which had been overlooked by the big estate at the time of the enclosures. Each generation of Strawbridges contributed something to the betterment and fertility of the smallholding; now, when May and Ted are working it, it is about as productive as a bit of land can be.

The sad thing for Gabriel Strawbridge, and for May and Ted themselves, is that there are no children to carry on Roman's Fields. Gabriel would have liked to know that it would be kept up by somebody who loved the place. May, although she would like to have had a child, had never dwelt on it, instead enjoying the presence of other people's children – Eli Barney and Ann Carter's children came and went at Roman's Fields almost as an extension of their own encampment. So, when Hector said how sick Vera's girl had been, the opportunity to do something worthwhile arose, and she had sent the letter that had caused such a stir in Lampeter Street. Vera's message in reply had caused an equal stir at Roman's Fields. Every evening for a week she spent preparing one of the rooms for her niece, sometimes with the help of young Bar Barney, Eli and Ann's girl.

In a way, it was history repeating itself. Ted had come to the farm as an ailing youth, with a damaged arm. The arm had never grown as the youth had grown, healed as the rest of him had healed. Withered and useless on its own, Ted's left arm hung around waiting for his right hand to move it. Once in position, his left hand functioned reasonably well and was able to grasp a hoe, carry a bundle, push a cart and even grip the steering wheel of a van. And now, late in the evening of the first day of Lu's visit, May was out in the garden with Ted, lamenting quietly at how ill the child looked.

'Have you ever seen such stick arms, Ted? I never have, she looks as if you could snap her in two or a breeze would blow her away like thistledown. It breaks my heart to see her, Ted, and that's a fact.'

Ted hmmed agreement. 'You'll soon put her on her feet, m'dear. You're the best cook I know. But if you'll take notice of me, you'll have to take it steady, little bits of this and little bits of that. You'll have to treat her like she was a runty piglet or an orphan lamb.'

Seeing a snail in the beam of her torch, she picked it up and deposited it in a pail of salt water where it expired along with others of assorted sizes and colours. 'Thank you, Ted, but I do know what I'm doing. Little and often, sweet and savoury, pretty to the eye and tasty in the mouth.'

'Ah well, yes, May, I was only sayin', I wouldn't attempt to interfere, it's just that I'm as keen as you to see the girl grow back to health and spirit.'

'I doubt her spirit's ailing.'

'Nor her intelligence, she's bright enough . . . There, look, May, by the forcing bell, one of them great yellow ones.'

'You know I can't abide to touch a slug,' and she trowelled it to its saline doom. 'Did you hear what she said about the barmaid at The Bells?'

'I thought I'd smile.'

'Never mind smile: what she said was observant for a girl of her age. She was the kind of lady that people down our street would say things about behind her back, without even knowing she was nice, she said.'

'I know, I heard her.'

'She said, "People don't think somebody like her would care about children, but she did, she was kind to me." She's only young, after all, Ted.'

Ted, sounding as though he was smiling: 'And I can hear you telling it her back when you're old and grey.'

'Well, I thought it showed a perception. It's the sort of thing sticks in your memory.'

'I an't arguing about it. She's a nice little thing. A Wilmott in name only, though.'

May did not respond at once, until she had despatched another half-dozen snails. 'I reserve judgement on that; she hasn't been here a day and a night yet.'

Having gone the length of the garden, they stood up, Ted rubbing the small of his back as he always did when he straightened his spine; not because it ached, for he spent many hours of his adult life stooped over one or another of the Roman's Fields crops. Leaving the night's catch beside the compost pit into which it would be consigned tomorrow, they ambled amiably back towards the house, Ted to write up his daybook, and May to get Gabriel his supper and turn down his bed.

Although Lu could hardly remember her father, the photo on the mantelpiece at Lampeter Street taken before she was born (Mum holding baby Kenny, Ralph standing by Dad in his Navy uniform against a picture of the sea and a sailing ship) shows that Dad and Uncle Ted look quite alike, except that Dad is younger and his hair is cropped right off, the horrible baldy, short at the back and sides that Navy men have to have done.

Gran said she always liked Arthur best. Arthur was always a bit of a lad. He likes his grog. Always one for the girls. He throws his money around like a sailor. Children whose fathers are on the railway always have better things, and it isn't so essential for their mothers to have to work in the clothes factories. Lu has often wished that she had a railway dad like Kate Roles did. Aunty Vi said Kate Roles was spoilt, but Lu didn't think so; Kate was pretty and happy and came to school with a red bow in her yellow hair. Lu wonders whether she will be allowed to wear her diamond star. It is an exciting prospect. Lena Grigg would be jealous as anything.

She hears a murmur of voices coming from below her window, and creeps out of bed to look. Aunty and Uncle are going round the garden with a torch picking something. She can't imagine what must be picked at night; she can only think it might be mushrooms which Ray sometimes went out to pick at night, but she really doesn't know about mushrooms. Now that she is out of bed she leans on the windowsill and looks out at the night. There is a line of orange on the horizon and it occurs to her that it might not be night, but Aunty and Uncle are 'up and about early', as they said they would be. This reminds her that Ralph is on early turn, and she watches him again rubbing Brylcreem into his hair to make it stop down. She wonders why he doesn't just let it be its own crinkly self. But then it might grow like Uncle Ted's, which is a frizzy bush.

Lu is struck by the slow, easy way they walk, quietly talking. She has never seen people behave like this. The whole scene has the same contented but a bit anxious feeling she gets from reading her only book, the *Rupert Bear* annual. Their voices are too low to reach her. Ted is saying, 'Is that a face up in Pa's old room?'

'Oh, poor child, she must feel strange not having any houses round her. I'll take her a drink of milk.'

'You had your turn at fussing her, let me go up.'

Lu is now back in bed. The bedroom door is not closed; she hears a quiet humming in time to the slow, light tread on the stairs. Uncle Ted seems to hum and whistle a lot of the time, so she knows that it is him when she hears a quiet knock on the door.

'All right if I come in, Lu?'

'Yes, Uncle.'

She is leaning on one elbow looking anxiously towards the door. Uncle Ted is carrying a mug in his ordinary hand

and a book under his arm, the arm that doesn't work properly hangs down swinging slightly. At supper she had found the arm fascinating. It was thin and looked as though it belonged to a different sort of person from Uncle Ted, who was strong and brown. She thought it looked as if, although his hand could remember what to do, his arm couldn't. If he wanted to pick up his fork or cup, his right hand would have to put his left hand in place before it could do so; then it was all right.

He stands uncertainly just inside the room. 'Can't sleep then?'

'I was asleep, then I woke up and I didn't know if it was morning.'

'I dare say it seems a bit dark without any streetlights.'

'It was quite nice. You get ever such a lot more stars here than we do.'

'Your Aunt May thought you might like a bit of a drink of warm milk, but I thought a story.' He approaches, puts down the mug of milk on the night-table, then perches on the bedside chair. 'Could you manage both?'

Lu gives a little smile and nods. 'Ralph used to read to me at night when I was getting over the Dip.'

'What did he read then? Go on, drink it whilst it's nice and warm.'

She tastes, then drinks. '*Rupert Bear*. It's the only one I got, but it's my favourite. Ralph bought it for a present when I was four.'

'I'm afraid we haven't got *Rupert the Bear*. Only one I could find was this. I don't know whether . . .?' He turns the spine to face her, and she reads, aloud, '*The Children's Golden Treasure Book* – Brimful of Joyous Entertainment. That's a thick book. What is in this milk?'

'Nothing except milk. Don't you care for it?'

'Yes, but it's sort of sweet and thick.'

'Ah, that'll be because it came from a cowslip.'

Lu gives a little smile, showing that she knows that this is a joke.

'Cowslip's the name of May's little Jersey cow. When you're feeling up to it, I dare say she'll take you down at milking time. May was going to put in some honey, but decided best not in case you don't like it.'

'I never had none of that. Isn't it what bees have?'

She'd never had no honey? Best not tell May that or she'd be on about 'poor little mite' again, and that wouldn't do the girl much good; she really don't realize there's much amiss with her.

'True, it is what bees have, but we has a share with them . . . Well, no, they share it with us, but in return we give them a bit of sugar in the winter. But it rightly belongs to them, the honey. I reckon it's the best sweet taste in the world.'

Ted remembered the lump of raspberry drops she had offered round, looking pleased when he and May took one and May popped one in her father's mouth. 'Well, maybe you'll think your sweets are better, but I promise you the honey has more goodness. Country people put it on wounds, and sores. It's a gift from the bees us humans don't always deserve. I'll tell May to give you some on toast in the morning, see if you like it.'

'Is there bees' seeds?'

Ted frowns. 'Bees' seeds? Not that I ever heard.'

'Oh.'

'What are they supposed to be?'

'I don't know, only people say "mind your own bees' seeds".'

His eyes smile as he recalls his Pompey boyhood. 'You mean like kids say to each other when they'm being a bit assy with each other? Like "Clear off you, mind your own bees' seeds"?'

Lu nods vigorously. 'Yes.'

'I always took it to mean "mind your own business".'

43

'Yes, but why bees' seeds?'

'You got me there, Lu. I'll have to sleep on that one. Now, where was we? What shall it be then, a lucky dip? Go on, you just open the page, any page, and we'll see what comes up.'

'Start at the beginning.'

'So we shall. I come by this in a box of books I bought at a house sale. I never thought to read it, so it will be a mystery tour for me and all.'

When he opens the book and turns the pages, Lu is at once reminded of Ralph, who turns pages one by one, gently flattening them along the stitching with the tip of one finger.

'Right then, if you can't drink no more, you could put the rest of your milk on the night-table if you like, in case you get thirsty during the night; lay back comfortable on your pillow.

'Here we go . . . "Candida's First School" by Katharine L. Oldmeadow. "Chapter One – Enter Candida. The Dresden china clock on the mantelshelf struck three little silvery strokes, and Miss Elizabeth Wymer put down her pen with a sigh of relief, for at three o'clock she had promised herself a cosy rest near the fire before tea, with a new number of *Punch* as companion.

'"The room in which she sat was oddly unlike the usual sanctum of a busy schoolmistress . . . "' He reads on to the bottom of the page, looking up as he turns over and sees her large, overbright eyes absorbed in this Miss Wymer getting herself comfortable in her chintzy room before a glowing fire on a dreary January afternoon. The doorbell rings in an ill-bred way and the Candida of the title arrives on the scene. '". . . tall for her age, and was extremely thin. Her little oval face was very pale, her eyes were so darkly blue they seemed almost black, and deep shadows of weariness lay beneath them. Masses of thick black silky hair, unconfined by ribbon or plait, hung to her waist in a dark cloud . . ."' Again he glances up and receives a wide smile that shows in her eyes. Ted gives her a little friendly wink.

'Uncle Ted? Would it be rude if I went to sleep now?'

'No, my dear, it would make me and May very happy if you did.'

Lu let out a deep sigh and wriggled her head into the pillows and was almost asleep before Ted had put a marker in the page and placed the book beside the mug of milk. She had gone to bed in knickers and a sleeveless vest; he felt he should cover her stick-like arm that lay on the plump eiderdown, but was afraid she would be disturbed.

He stood looking down at that arm which reminded him of his own first night under this roof. A damp, foggy night, like many he had experienced here since that one. It was the first time in his life that he had slept on two pillows, and each with a clean pillow-cover. As he listened to Lu's heavy breathing, he reached over and cradled his own damaged arm. He had learned to forgive the man who'd done this to him, Gabriel had taught him that. But he would never be able to forget the injustice and indifference that came after – his dreams still reminded him. But then neither could he forget the altruism of Clara and Gabriel Strawbridge. Now, here was the second of the Wilmott tribe to feel the balm of a family whose motto (if they had ever been so vain as to think of such pretentiousness) would be 'I am my brother's keeper', and who lived by it.

Downstairs, he said to May who was standing ironing sheets on the table, 'She got a lot better manners than I had at her age.'

May said, 'She seems to have a nice nature altogether . . . Ah, but so pathetic, those great dark eyes sunk in like that: she makes my heart bleed. I'll say this, even though Arthur's your brother, Vera and young

Ralph have made a better job of making his baby into such a nice little thing than he'd have made himself . . . '

'Young Ralph was always a nice sort of lad . . . and a course so was Vera nice. Nobody thought she'd stick to our Arthur – he was the roughest of all of us brothers.'

May, changing flat-irons at the range, pecked him on the cheek. 'And who was the best?'

Ted shook his head. 'Not Ted Wilmott in his younger days, that's for sure. It took a man like Gabr'l to smooth down the rough side of me.' After a few minutes gazing inwardly, he said, 'You know Vera don't get an allowance from the Navy, don't you?'

'Don't get an allowance? Why shouldn't she? Your Arthur's signed on for twenty-five years.'

'He isn't married to Vera.'

May put down the flat-iron and stood smoothing the warm sheet. 'Not married?'

'No.'

'Lord's sake, Ted, then it's high time he was.'

'That'd make him a bigamist. He got a wife somewhere up the north of Scotland. Got married at Gretna Green when Arthur was under-age.'

'I can't hardly believe what I'm hearing.'

'It's true.'

'Why haven't I heard about it then?'

'I don't know . . . I suppose when it happened, you and me hadn't got together . . . He said he'd made this terrible mistake and he couldn't talk to anybody else in the family.'

'What about her then, his proper wife?'

'Arthur reckoned she got fed up as quick as he did, but she was from one of them strick churches they have in Scotland. Her father was something like equal to a vicar, so there it was.'

'Is she still alive then?'

'Don't ask me. No reason why she shouldn't be; she was only about ten years older, so she'd only be about my age.'

46

'So what about Vera?'

'I tackled him about it – he says she knew.'

'But they had a wedding and everything?'

'No, they never. When they was supposed to have gone off and had a run-away wedding down in Devonport, they never. They had a photo done, with Vera in a white frock and flowers, and one of Arthur's shipmates, but that's all the wedding amounted to. It was all done because Vera was expecting Ralph, and she didn't come from that side of the tracks where a girl can go home and tell her mother she's got herself in trouble. She thought it was better for everybody if they thought she was married.'

May spat on a reheated iron, then waited for it to cool down. Ted sat fondling May's fat black half-bred Persian cat, which rumbled with pleasure. 'Why haven't you ever said anything?'

'Because I said I wouldn't. They didn't want none of the families to know . . . can you imagine how the Wilmotts would have treated Vera – at least Arthur had sense enough to understand that. Vera didn't want her family to know; it was bad enough for the Presleys having a daughter who they expected would marry a middle-class chap running off with a Pompey matelot. You can imagine what it would a done to them if they knew they wasn't even married.'

She was hurt. 'I suppose saying you wouldn't tell anybody, included me?'

'You're the one who's got the scruples here, May.' As soon as he said it, he wished he hadn't. 'Well, now I've told you.'

May laid out a flannelette sheet, and ran back and forth over the same piece. 'So you have, but you waited a long time.'

'What would have been the point?'

'We might have helped Vera, is the point.'

'It's all very well to say that, but Vera's just as proud and independent as you are, May. Put yourself in her shoes. Would you have wanted to live amongst the Wilmotts having them look down on you? They never liked her much as it is, her talking proper and being to college . . . wouldn't they a just loved taking that out of her. I knows my own, May.'

'Then why have you chose tonight to decide to come out with it?'

'I should a thought that didn't want much fathoming. The plain fact of Arthur's irresponsibility is upstairs asleep. It wasn't until I stood looking at her, lying there like some little waif, that I saw in the flesh the depth of his wickedness. You can't blame Vera.'

'What for?'

'Well . . . I suppose for having two more children even after Ralph.'

'Blame Vera? Your Arthur could twist her around his little finger. She gave up everything for him. What do you reckon he gave up?'

Having finished the sheets and pillow-slips, May put them on the airer, then pulled it up to the ceiling above the range. Ted sat silently petting the fluffy, fat cat under its chin, making it squirm with pleasure until May took it from him and dropped it unceremoniously on the floor, and sat on the kitchen footstool close to Ted. 'There's bound to be things husbands and wives don't tell each other about, and I suppose it don't matter whilst they remain in ignorance; but when it gets out it hurts . . . No, no, let me finish. You were right, you said you'd keep it to yourself, and it wasn't anything that affected me. And as for Vera, she fell for a Wilmott same as I did, and I don't suppose I'd have acted much different in the same circumstances.'

'The thing is, May, I hope you wouldn't have had to. I thought more of you than to deceive you the way Arthur deceived Vera.'

May squeezed his good hand, without looking at him. 'I know that.' The cat insinuated itself on to May's lap. 'Poor old thing, I haven't fed you yet.' She draped the cat on her shoulder and picked up its bowl. 'What about the other one? Do you know if she had any children?'

'I don't know. I never thought about it.'

'Well, at least she's entitled to the Navy allowance.'

'I never even really thought about her as being real.'

'Best leave it like that. Don't do any good to turn over too many stones.'

Ted, thankful that May was closing the door on the incident, helped to change the mood. 'I'll just go along and see if Gabr'l wants a bit of supper then.'

'No, leave him. I took him something whilst you were upstairs. He'll probably be asleep by now.'

In another downstairs room, because sometimes, in cold weather, climbing stairs gave him chest pains, May's father, Gabriel Strawbridge, could not sleep for several reasons.

Firstly, it had been another unseasonably warm day, and his room was stuffy. May would insist on shutting his windows at night, a thing he had never been used to in his life until this last year or two. He had had a bad bout of bronchitis and had gone along with May about keeping out the night air, but he was well now, and they were being blessed with an early spring. When he heard them go up to bed, he would get out and let in some fresh air.

Secondly, there was a lot of talk going on tonight: first Ted's voice coming through from up above, then the both of them out in the kitchen talking for ages; they probably didn't even notice that they had the wireless on. May had done a lot of creeping around late at night lately. One night she even distempered the walls after midnight. 'I hope I didn't disturb you, Father, but I've been doing out your old room. Pale peach, it's for Ted's little niece; she's had diphtheria, so I thought we could get her here for a week or two to recover her health.'

Thirdly, and this was what kept him wakeful, he could not put out of his mind the feel of the child's young hand when he held it for a moment after she had been prompted by May to shake hands with him. The hand was not just small, it was wasted: cold, dry bones in a thin covering. He had held it briefly, moved by what it told him. Had it not been for the strong life-force he felt within it, he could easily have believed it was the pathetic hand that Ted had reluctantly pulled from his pocket twenty-five or more years ago. Perhaps when she knew him better, the child would allow him to look at her through his large, old-fashioned magnifying glass. His left eye had the beginnings of a cataract, and the vision in the other was now dimming, so that he had not been able to see her face clearly. She appeared tall for her age; May had described her eyes as 'brown as new chestnuts' and her hair 'like copper in need of a bit of a polish'. But such a bag of bones. So many were . . . so many are . . . so many had been over the many years and in the many places his wanderings had taken him. And himself an old man who did not need the nourishment, given meat and bread at every meal, and milk and eggs in plenty.

As he lay back against his pillows, Gabriel Strawbridge welcomed his guilt, his conscience, his impotent rage; he had little else these days. He needed to have his complacency halted. He had allowed old age and ailments to excuse him from responsibility. All over the world there were men and women who were suffering from the infirmities of old age by the time they were thirty, and children suffering mortal ailments, not mere stiff bones and dim eyesight.

As soon as he felt that hand, emaciated as it was from the battle with disease and malnutrition, he had begun to feel a kind of vitality flow into his own diminishing spirit.

All evening he had been sitting, thinking, wondering why it was that he had allowed himself to listen to his doctor who said that he must rest, must be calm, must stop becoming involved in matters best left to younger men. He had been weak enough to collude with his doctor's advice, and so had May in her eagerness to preserve him for a few more years; the advice amounted to leading an uneventful, dull life. Between the three of them, Gabriel Strawbridge had become an old man; not merely old, he had become useless. He took from society and returned nothing: the very thing he had always been against. Who had the right to a free ticket to ride the planet? No one unless they were incapable, and for them, the rest must put in a bit more.

He had always firmly believed in that. It was supposed to be the basis of the Christian religions, but did any of them practise it?

It had not been old age, shortness of breath or dim vision that had persuaded him to stop putting in; it had been surrendering to the belief of younger people that a gerontic mind is the same as a senile mind. No good blaming May, she mollycoddled him because he was her father and she loved him. He knew perfectly well that he was not senile. Ted recognized that. In an argument, Ted never gave any quarter out of concern for Gabriel's age.

Well, here was the very opportunity to do something. At this time of year, May and Ted worked from dawn to dusk. May wouldn't hear any argument that it was too much for her to work in the fields the same as usual as well as caring for a sick child. She'd do both: May was like that. She'd inherited the Strawbridges' liking for a hair-shirt. It was a good thing that the sick girl and young Bar were of an age: young Bar knew the house inside and out; she'd be a great help. Would two girls with such different back-grounds and upbringing get on; would they understand one another? A child of Portsmouth's narrow slums, and a half-wild girl whose parents were outcasts and lived life very close to nature. He looked forward to seeing them together.

The narrow slums . . . He had known them from boyhood, from the years when he rode on horseback with his father to attend meetings of the people who were then brethren, taking what paltry few goods for the poor they could manage. Ted had come from there, not as emaciated as this child, but underfed, and with a constant run of mucus, and bow legs, a sure sign of the poorly nourished. As a young man, Gabriel had known that his journeys into the slums, with what surplus from the smallholding as could be managed, were partly to scratch under the hairshirt at his own feelings of guilt because he'd been born into better circumstances.

He had never believed otherwise than that the baskets of fruit, crates of eggs and jars of honey were but a drop in the ocean of needs of the poor in that city, and there were backstreet slum children in every city in every country in the world.

In those days there was only one way for a boy to get out of the slums, and that was by signing up and becoming a cog in the war machine. Portsmouth being a seaport gave its poor boys the opportunity of being taken into the Navy. There they at least got fed and clothed, or they did until they had the misfortune of coming a cropper – as young Ted had done. For a minor misdemeanour, he had been lashed. He had only been a boy sailor, not yet grown enough to take sea-dog punishment. The beating had been so violent that his left arm had been rendered useless, which naturally rendered him useless to the Navy.

Even now, after all these years, he still felt the defeat of not being able to win the fight against Whitehall on the lad's behalf. Well, at least they'd done something with Ted: he and Clara had made a man of him. And here was history almost repeating itself. He still missed Clara every day – how could he not when May was the living image of her?

Waiting for the house to go quiet, he lay back and planned what would be best. He would get May to go down into the village and get some Scott's Emulsion, some Marmite, and a tin of malt. Clara had believed these three taken once a day were a cure-all. May knew it worked; more than once she had brought on a kid on it. Gabriel himself favoured the addition of citrus fruits to a convalescent diet.

Damnit, no! He would go down to the village himself. If he didn't know the way there by now, then he never would. He made his way to the casement window; when he opened it his reward was the perfume of mahonia and winter-sweet.

Next morning, when Lu awakes, she is surprised to find the sun streaming in through the curtains that are billowing into the room on a warm breeze. There is no momentary puzzlement as to where she is, for, having never experienced such bright morning sun, she knows at once. She slides out of bed and looks out on the garden below which, like that at The Bells, is a hotch-potch of flowering bulbs and green plants bathed in sunlight; then she patters across the floor to a small cupboard which contains a daisy-speckled pail with a lid which, along with a striped face-flannel and towel is, as Aunty May had told her yesterday when they had come up and put her things in a drawer and on the night-table, hers to use whilst she is staying at Roman's Fields. She then patters to the daisy-speckled water-jug and bowl, beside which, to her great pleasure, is a daisy-speckled beaker that hadn't been there yesterday, in which is her own toothbrush and . . . a new tin of toothpaste. With this discovery, she confirms what she has suspected, what with this being a house with so many rooms: that Uncle Ted must be rich.

Hearing footsteps coming upstairs, she quickly puts her cardi on over her vest and knickers, her cardi being a woman's size that has shrunk, but it still comes well down over her knickers. She waits expectantly in the middle of the room for Aunty May to come in and tell her what to do. But it isn't Aunty May.

The door swings open and a girl, about her own age, stands there. She is short, brown. Her black hair is like a fuzz-bush, longer even than Lu's own; it is tied back with a bit of creased red ribbon. She doesn't move but stands there looking. Staring quite rudely, is what Lu thinks.

'What you looking at? A'nt you never seen bare legs before?'

The girl bites her lips and hangs her head. 'Sorry, I waddn't meaning to stare, you caught me out because I never expected to see nobody up. I thought you was still asleep. Mis Wilmott said I got to be quiet and not wake you but to look round the door to see if you was.'

'Well, I'm not.' Embarrassed at having made the girl embarrassed, and knowing she is in the wrong, Lu pulls her cardigan around her even more tightly. Lu stands and the girl stands, and they say nothing until the other girl speaks, not actually looking at Lu. 'Mis Wilmott left me to see you got a good breakfast.'

Lu panics a bit. 'Where is she then, where's she gone?'

'She's only gone to work.' She has a slow, broad way of speaking, pronouncing it, 'gorn a werk'.

'To work?' Lu feels herself abandoned, tricked. Nobody said Aunty May went out to work. She hadn't been to work yesterday.

'She'm only gone down the strawb'ry beds. Look – ' she points through the window and to the left – 'you can see her 'at. She said I was to see you got your breakfast and then go down there and tell her you was awake.'

Lu looks to where the girl is pointing and, yes, she can easily see a large, yellowish hat moving.

'See her?' The girl's voice is pleading with Lu to be pleased that her aunty hasn't gone far away.

'Shall we wave?' She hooks both her little fingers on to her bottom teeth and lets out a shrill whistle. 'There, she's seen us. Wave. Go on. There see, she isn't very far off.'

Lu nods, ashamed at her babyish behaviour. 'I thought you meant she had gone away to work down a factory or somewhere.'

The girl looked very serious and shook her head. 'Naah . . . we a'nt got none of they out here. We only got farms and small'oldins.'

Lu knew the latter term, but didn't quite know the meaning; she wasn't going to ask and show herself up further in front of a girl who, from the look of her, might be younger than herself.

'Well, do you want some?'

'What?'

'Do you want yer breakfast?'

'All right,' Lu says cagily. 'What is it?'

'Mis Wilmott said, toast and honey and a glass of milk and if you was still hungry a Shredded Wheat or a Sunny Jim's. They got all kinds here.'

The girl seems so knowledgeable and off-hand, but milk and toast are the only items on the menu with which Lu is familiar. 'Do you like honey?' she asks the girl.

'Everybody likes honey.'

That sounds safe enough, and Uncle Ted had said it was heavenly sweetness itself. 'Which do you like out of the other things?'

The girl flicked her a look. 'I don't know, we don't never get much stuff out of shops, we haves fermity or bread.'

'Perhaps I'd best come down and choose.'

'You don't have to, Mis Wilmott said you could have it up here on a tray. Why don't you? I would if I had half a chance. Go on, you stop there and let me bring it up, and I'll sit here with you. A'nt it a lovely room, I bet you liked it sleepin' here?'

Suddenly the girl seems to change from the cocksure little intruder who had barged into the room into a short, dark, nice friendly girl who wants to please Lu. 'What's your name then?'

'Bar Barney . . . well, it's Barbara by rights, but nobody don't never call me nothing except Bar. I know yours, it's Louise.'

'My aunty told you.'

Bar nods. 'And she told me I got to try to see you got something inside you. Go on,' she wheedles, 'let me bring you up some on a tray, your aunty left it all laid up for you. It a be good fun.'

Oh, how nice everything seems to have become all of a sudden. 'All right then,' Lu clambers back on to the bed, 'but not much, I don't get that hungry and I don't want to upset Aunty by not eating it up.'

'Don't mind about that, I'll finish up what you don't want.'

'Will you? OK, let's have the toast and I'll try the honey, and a bit of both of those others if you like, then we can see which is best.'

Bar whizzes out of the room and thumps down the stairs two at a time. She is gone about ten minutes, during which time Lu puts on the frock Aunty Elsie has made for her out of a skirt of her own she never really liked. It isn't new, but it is new to Lu. The frock has short sleeves which makes her feel conscious of her arms, so she puts her cardi on again and is just brushing her hair with the green celluloid-backed brush that Aunty May said she could use, when she hears Bar rattling back upstairs. She doesn't plait her hair as she usually does, but ties it back with the string that had held her bag together. The diamond star, she has decided, is only for Christmas and birthdays and perhaps Empire

56

Day when they only have to go to school for prayers and then it's a holiday.

Grinning, Barbara stands in the bedroom doorway, carrying a wide wooden tray with handles that appears to be loaded. 'There, see, didn't take long, I only had to do the toast and put out the boxes. The Sunny Jim's looks like cornflakes; we had cornflakes last year when we went to tea at my Gran's, only these Jim's is brownier and crispier. I tried a couple, I think they got a nicer taste. Your hair looks nice. I wish mine would ringlet like that instead of this ole fuzz-bush.' She puts the tray down on the bed whilst she clears the night-table on which she then lays up an enticing breakfast and pours a glass of milk from a large jug. 'There, what you going to have first?'

This is the kind of decision which before today has never troubled Lu.

Bar advises, 'Why don't you eat the toast first, then it won't go cold. Honey's best on hot toast, Mis Wilmott gives me a slice sometimes when I been helping out. I'll do it for you. Look, if you sits up in bed, I could sort of hand it to you if you like.'

'I don't want to get nothing on the covers.'

'All right then, sit sideways with your legs out and I'll put the towel over your lap. Then you'll be sort of resting and up at the same time.'

Lu allows herself to be suggested to and be gently bossed about by the small, brown-haired girl. Lu wouldn't have known how to go about getting a tray ready or how to eat breakfast in bed, except that when she was getting over The Dip she was given things to eat sitting up, but it was usually bone broth with pearl barley which she spooned out of a mug. She can't decide whether she likes honey or not, it doesn't taste like anything else, but it is sweet and Lu has a sweet tooth and manages half of the slice of the toast Bar prepared for her.

'You going to try these?' She pours milk from the large jug, and sprinkles Sunny Jim's liberally with Barbados sugar.

'What's that stuff?'

'Brown sugar,' says Bar enthusiastically. 'An't you never had it? Here, taste,' and she picks out a dark brown knob from the bowl, and Lu, not wanting to appear even more foolish in her lack of knowledge, lets her put it into her mouth. Lu is surprised. 'That's lovely, it's got a taste as well as only being sweet.'

'I know, we don't have it at home, it's dear and my mum don't like shop stuff. But it's good for you.'

Lu eats a little of the cereal and feels full. 'I don't want any more, do you want it?'

'You sure?' Bar clears the bowl in seconds. 'I wish I could have one of them every day. You'd better just try the Sunny Jim's, then you'll know which ones you like best,' and without hesitation pours out a liberal portion from the packet and covers it with sugar and milk. Lu takes back the spoon from Bar and tastes. 'I think I like these best, they got a nice crunchy feel. Only I can't eat any just now.' Again Bar clears the bowl then heaves a sigh of satisfaction. 'Lovely. Waste not, want not. If you don't want that other slice of toast, shall I clear it up for you?' Lu nods and watches in wonder as the girl, who is much smaller, wolfs down the fingers of toast one after another, and then hands Lu the glass of milk she had already poured. 'You got to get this down you. Mis Wilmott said you was to try to drink a whole glass of milk. You don't have to drink it all at once. Oh look! There's your aunty, she's looking this way again.' She goes to the window and waves heartily. Lu jumps down and joins in the exchange of waves. Apparently satisfied that all is well, Lu's aunt returns her attention to the strawberry bed.

'Your aunty is nice, I like working for her. I does a bit of work for old Cat, who lives near the village. I hate her.

58

She's the same to everybody that works for her, nobody can't never do a thing right.'

'How come you go to work?'

'Only when I'm not at school, weekends and after school and school holidays. Our school's shut for a while, because of the foundations. Mis Wilmott said I could come and help out every day whilst you're here. I was e' so glad, because that means that old Cat will have to find somebody else to pick holes in. Mis Wilmott don't never do that. If you does it wrong she says, "Look here, Bar, if I was you I'd try it like this, and you a find it's a bit easier", or something like that, she don't make you feel you're daft. You finished?' Bar starts to collect the dishes together. 'You get your plimmies on while I washes these up and then we can go down and see your aunty. Only if you want to go, Mis Wilmott said if you wanted to stop in bed then you was welcome, there's nothing to get up for.'

But there was.

For one thing it was necessary to see the downstairs again. Yesterday it had seemed to be such a maze of passages and rooms and larders and cupboards, that she needs to refresh her memory of their lay-out.

Bar picks up the huge tray with apparent ease. 'If you can't manage your pail, I can come up and get it.'

'No!' It was all right Mum carrying the slops when she couldn't move because of The Dip, but she wasn't going to have a girl carrying her pee-pail downstairs. 'I can do it myself all right.'

It takes her only a minute to wash her sticky face and hands, empty her washing water into the slop-pail, put on her plimsolls and hat. The vicar's wife had brought the hat, just as the vicar's wife had brought in some vests and knickers. The vicar's children went to a posh private school where they had to wear velour hats in winter and Panamas in summer. The vicar's wife had removed the blue silk band and school badge before giving it away; Lu wouldn't have been seen dead in a hat with a badge anyway. Private girls were the enemy – not that the two camps ever saw much of one another; but when they did, the common kids stuck out their tongues and pushed their noses up into snouts. Aunty May had said it was a very decent quality hat and was just what Lu would need when she was out in the open.

Bar is standing on a duckboard, reaching into the deep kitchen sink and scrubbing away with scouring powder. 'I finished.'

The big whitewashed outhouse houses a whole roomful of tools and other stuff and three sizes of tin baths, a queer wooden bench with a hole for a lav, but Aunty May said she shouldn't empty her pail there, but in a pit round the back which contains all sorts of vegetable waste. Lu does so, then scoops water from a long stone trough, rinses the daisy pail and hangs it on its hook in the outhouse. Aunty May had explained how the rubbish pit works. If you piled cabbage leaves, peelings, carrot tops and weeds into a pit and put in hay and wood-ash from the fires, and earth and poured slops on it, the rubbish turned back into a good sort of dirt that made vegetables grow like nobody's business. So Lu, supposing it must work if Aunty said so, after adding her contribution to the unlikely process, goes back into the house where Bar is putting the big tray back into a cupboard.

'There! I'll just get the bag. You ready, Louise?' She puts one arm through the long handles and carries it on the same shoulder, in the way that sailors carry their knapsack.

Lu nods, hoping Bar will take the lead about which way to go: it would be easy to go off in the wrong direction and find yourself out there in all that space and never finding the right way back. On her way here in Uncle Hec's lorry, they hadn't passed any houses for miles and miles, and when Lu had looked out of the window this morning, there were just fields and fields that went on for ever. 'You want to go round the stile way?'

'I don't mind.'

'All right, we can go up through your aunty's garden then. You been right to the top?' Lu admits that she hasn't. 'It's e' so nice, you just got to keep out of the bee-paths, but I'll show you where they are.' It is obvious that Bar is getting a great deal of pleasure from being the one who knows what is what. 'It's only cuz you're new. I'm bound to know the place, I been coming up here since I was really little, I just used to run errands for them then, but now your aunty lets me do proper work. She let me do straw-ing last year and paid me proper money and give me my dinner and tea. Perhaps she won't want me this year if you're here. Not unless you an't feeling well enough.' She halts, bites her lip and stops her chatter with a brown, cupped hand.

'What's wrong?' Lu asks.

'I'm sorry, I'm wasn't supposed to go on about your not being well or anything.'

'Why's that?'

'Mrs Wilmott said she wants you to forget you ever been bad, and people gets over illnesses if they don't dwell on them.'

'Oh.' Lu leaves that to think about later.

'This way.' Bar leads the way out of the part of the garden that was like the one at The Bells and into a big open, grassy part, bounded on one side with a tall, mixed hedgerow, interspersed here and there with tall trees which Lu will eventually get to recognize as spruce. The only hedges in Lu's part of the world are some old privets that divide some of the Lampeter Road gardens, leggy because they were seldom trimmed, and seldom trimmed because nobody owned shears; occasionally they were chopped at out of sheer exasperation because children made dens there. After a good chopping, fresh new growth would spring up and fill in some of the gaps. In time somebody will tell her what these flowery sort of hedges are made of.

Barbara chatters, leading the way like a tracker leading an expedition, pointing out buried stones, fallen branches and holes that could break your ankle. Lu walks behind, admiring her knowledge and assurance, and takes in what she had not before.

Bar's black hair is almost frizzy, not like the crinkly Wilmott hair, more a tangle of small C's. Her dress is dark green, little more than a small tent through which her head and bare brown arms emerge. She is wearing dark blue knickers, one leg of which is clearly visible because it has lost its elastic and hangs down level with the hem of her dress. There is no sign of a bodice or vest or petticoat, which the original wearers of Lu's Panama hat would have expected. In the world of Bar, Lu and the girls of Lampeter Street, knickers are often the only underclothes worn. Barbara's feet are encased in heavy black shoes with a strap and button, except that the button of one is missing and a string has been poked through the place where it had been, then through the button-hole where it is tied in a knot. The shoes slock a bit but Bar doesn't seem to notice and it is only because Lu is sizing up this new person who has suddenly come into her life that Lu notices at all. It is only natural, them being of an age, that she compares.

Hand-me-downs, Charlotte Street market bargains and charity clothes are normal in the Lampeter Street neighbourhood and, as in other similar neighbourhoods all over the poor parts of town, every item of clothing is circulated, swapped and handed around until nothing can be done with it except to make it into pegged mats, washing-up or floor-cloths. Occasionally new clothes are introduced into the cycle. This is when piecework factory hands earn enough to pay a tallyman or clothing club, usually not until they are sixteen. In the case of dockyard apprentices, often not until they have finished their time, and have apprenticeship papers. Not too many Lampeter Street boys own the papers which are the means of a leg-up. Lampeter Street is in a 'Slum Clearance Area', not that children of Lu's age know what that is; Lampeter Street is just the place where they live.

Barbara suddenly stops, spreads her arms wide. 'You have to watch out here. This is one of Mr Wilmott's bee-paths. The warm weather's brought them out after the blackthorn, I expect.' Lu searches the ground ahead but can see nothing but short grass, then Bar points to the right. 'There's one lot of skeps over there, see?' Lu looks and sees three little white houses with no windows but a small door.

'What's a skep?'

'A beehive, it's where the bees live, where they go to tell each other where there's a new lot of flowers opened. Inside they makes their honey and wax, and the queen lays her eggs in the combs, and they all sleep at night – except for the ones that guards the opening. Get your aunty to give you a look in next time she takes the honey. You don't have to go near them 'less they know you. They know you were coming, your aunty told them.'

Lu does not know whether Bar is having her on, but she doesn't seem to be, except the bees telling each other, and having guards, don't sound like normal insects, so she gives a non-committal, 'Oh. Where's the path you said?'

'There, look.' She indicates a yard or so ahead at eye-level, where Lu sees a few bees flying purposefully in two directions.

'Yes, I see, I see now, I thought you meant a path on the ground.'

Bar gives her a sweet, understanding smile. 'Well if you haven't never seen a skep, then you wouldn't know where the bee-paths are. It's we who has to get down on the grass, unless you want to go right round the back of the skeps.' Not getting instructions, Bar gets down on her hands and knees and crawls forward. 'Come on, they won't bother you if you don't walk through them.' Bar having got past unscathed, Lu follows, crawling well beyond the bee-path before turning to see that she is well clear.

'We could go on up past the goat if you like, or get over the stile here.'

Lu, having got clear of the bee-path, is not yet ready for another new experience, so says, 'Over the stile.'

What lies on the other side when they climb the divide seems in marked contrast to the part they have just left with its lush spring grass and plants, hedged around by a variety of shrubs and trees; here it is open, flat, milky-coffee-coloured fields, dappled white and striped green with ground-hugging plants, each row of which follows the small undulations of the land.

'There's Mrs Wilmott over by the straw bales.'

Without having to ask a foolish question, she is given the answer as to how strawberries grow – Aunty is in the strawberry beds, and Aunty is cutting open a bundle of straw. She waves and makes a sign that she is mopping her brow. 'Am I glad to see you, I was just dying for a drink of tea.' And here is the answer to what Bar has been carrying in a long bag woven from leaves, like the leaves of Palm Sunday crosses.

Aunty May pats the ground in the shade of the stack of straw bundles. 'Come and sit by me. Now, pet, did you have your breakfast all right? I'm sure you did, Bar's really clever in that direction.'

'Yes, Aunty.'

'And she drunk up the whole glass of milk like you said, Mis Wilmott.'

'Well, that is good.'

'Do you want me to lay some straw?'

May Wilmott considered. 'If you like, just whilst I have my breakfast, go on along that row where I left off.'

Bar picks up a bundle of straw under each arm and, on

reaching where she has been told, kneels down and, taking handfuls of loose straw, tucks the material around the plants.

May delves into the rush bag (one of Bar's mother's making) and takes out a green-glass bottle containing cold tea, and bread and something wrapped in a cloth, this having been the traditional meal of agricultural workers for generations. She takes a long, satisfying drink from the bottle, then a bite from two very thick slices of bread toasted on one side, smeared lightly with a little honey and sandwiched together. Lu sits quietly beside her and watches Bar moving quickly along the row. May chews well but eats quickly; there is no master to come and chide her for taking time out, nor has there been on Roman's Fields for generations, but old habits die hard. When she has eaten, she re-corks the bottle, takes it back to hide in the shade of a hawthorn bush that grows by the stile, and sits back down beside Lu. 'Were you all right with me leaving Bar to see to everything?'

'Yes. She showed me out of the window where to look for you.'

'Well, the thing is, these mornings it starts getting light early, and what with this sudden warm spring, the flowers are coming on fast, I thought I'd better get on out first thing. We've got one or two casual workers coming in, but they don't leave off at their other place till tomorrow. I looked in on you and you were sound asleep, so I got Ted to go and tell Bar to come over early. I hope you like her, she's a good little thing; always gets on with whatever she's told, don't need telling twice. She'll make somebody a good worker some day.'

Lu had expected her to say 'good little wife' which was the usual compliment to a girl who doesn't mind hard work.

'She likes to get up here, I could hardly keep her away when I was getting the room ready for you.'

Lu has a sudden picture of Aunty May and Bar. busy together preparing the room, before she even knew what either of them looked like, then felt a flush of shame as she recalled the way she had greeted the girl who was only doing what she had been told. *What you looking at?* 'She was ever so helpful, and it wasn't her fault that I couldn't eat much after the toast.'

Aunty May smiles and nods. 'I never expected you to. You drank the milk, though.'

'Yes, I did, but it fills you up. Uncle Ted said there wasn't anything put in it, but it tasted thick. We don't have that much drinking milk, except at school.' May guesses rightly that Vera, like a good many mothers trying to make ends meet, buys tins of skimmed sweetened condensed milk which is hardly milk at all, but a concoction of skim and sugar which quickly establishes a taste for it in young children and rots their teeth. There is an Unfit for Babies warning on the label, but May knows that many babies are weaned from the breast with a mush of condensed and stale bread. As well as establishing the idea early on in children's experience that 'condensed' is milk, it solves a problem for the mother in that, once the baby can eat mush, the child can be left in the care of a granny, while its mother is able to return to earning to pay the rent and something off the bill at the corner shop. 'Did he tell you it was "Cowslip milk"?'

Lu nods.

'It's his little joke, he don't seem to tire of telling it. But the thing is, the milk Cowslip gives is creamier than anything.' One thing to do with food production about which Lu wasn't ignorant was milk. The Co-op had let the over-tens go round the dairy and see the milk right from when it was brought in huge churns, through the pasteurizing, the cooling and into the bottles. The man had said Co-op milk was one hundred per cent pure, and soon after that they got free school milk. Not many of them liked it because it wasn't sweet, but teachers kept watch to see it was all drunk up.

'I did drink it all, honest.'

'I'm sure you did. It will do you the world of good.' The first time Bar Barney was offered it, she made a 'eyuk' sound. In the Barney family, once the children were off Ann Carter's breast, they drank water. But gradually, over a year or two, Bar had come to take milk until she had come to not mind too much if there was no water to be had. 'Look, pet, if you don't mind, I'm going to keep going with this field whilst the weather holds. You understand? If we don't get on, and this weather keeps up, the buds will be out before we know where we are.'

'No, I don't mind.'

'What would you like to do? Go back to the house with Bar? She knows where everything is when it's dinnertime. Do you like cold ham?' Lu nods uncertainly. 'If you don't there's some of yesterday's soup left – you liked that, didn't you.'

'Oh, yes.'

'You just have what your fancy takes you. Better to eat plenty of what you like than to leave a plateful of what you don't like.' She laughs. 'Nothing gets wasted where Bar is.' Lu grins, but says nothing. 'I asked Ted to fix up a swinging-rope in one of the trees where the goat has cropped the grass, and there's a couple of balls on the shelf next to the big bath in the outhouse. I think we got a couple of tennis bats somewhere, I'll look them out for you.' Lu had noticed the balls yesterday when she was sitting in the outhouse on the strange, wooden seat, feeling so apprehensive that she couldn't make herself pee for ages. 'Anyway, you sit there for now, and I'll go on back to work. I'll let Bar finish the row before she comes back; she tries to see if she can earn more in a week than her brother. Any time you want me, you know where I am. You be all right then?'

'Yes, Aunty.' Already she feels confident enough to say so, even though here she is out in the country, with not a single house in sight, not even Aunty May's and Uncle Ted's, and the only people visible are Aunty May and Bar. The presence of these two happy, friendly people is reassuring. She leans into the pile of straw which smells nice and which, although a bit prickly, is warm and comfortable. Bar waves, and Lu waves back and watches the two figures as they get smaller and smaller.

Back at the house, Bar's brother had seen the signal (a blue rag tied to the gate) that meant they wanted him to call at Roman's Fields. There were several houses where similar signals were put out, all offering him an hour or so's employ. He answered to the name of Duke, which wasn't the one his father had given him, but the only one he would answer to.

Duke Barney was older than Bar, a bit taller, a shade browner, and his mop of curly hair shorter. He wore a pair of dungarees that had seen better days, and apparently little else except a long-sleeved workman's vest. His feet were bare. He didn't look very clean, but that was misleading, because even after a wash with soap the downy black hair on his arms and around his mouth kept him looking much the same as before. His feet actually were dirty, which wasn't surprising: he had already gone errands in the village, cutting across the fields rather than going round the lanes. He rattled the door-latch at the Roman's Fields house and gave a short, piercing whistle. 'Anybody 'ome?'

Gabriel Strawbridge called out from his room, 'Is that you, young Duke?'

'Yes, Master Strawbridge. Shall I come in?'

'How's your feet?'

'Dusty, but no dung.'

'Come on through then.'

Duke knew his way through the passageways to the room Mr Strawbridge slept in. The door was open and the old granfer was up and dressed in his everyday out clothes, even to his boots.

'Ah, good, Duke, I hoped you wasn't going to be too long. Have you got Pixie?'

'She's tied up by the hedge.'

'Good, then get out the little governess cart.'

Duke looked delighted. 'The cart! You and me going out then?'

'What did you think we're going to do, with Pixie harnessed to the governess cart then, m'lad?'

The youth grinned, 'I'd say we was going out, Master.'

'Down to the village. Now get along and don't be long.'

By the time Gabriel had taken money from his cash-box, and made his way to the yard, Duke was waiting with Pixie and the governess cart. Gabriel Strawbridge's governess cart was something out of the ark and, had it not been for the fact that he was old and respected, the tableau would have drawn smiles as he, his knees bent double, his large body seeming to overflow the driving seat, held the useless reins whilst Duke, riding Pixie bareback, guided them along.

It was a bright, fresh, beautiful morning. Even before dawn, birds had been singing and twittering, building, mating. The trit-trot of Pixie's dainty hooves was by far the better accompaniment to their voices than the green single-decker that came hourly along the main road to the village. But Duke and his passenger went along narrower roads: Frith Lane with its hedges and oak trees, into Mill Lane with its gravel surface and the rushing River Meon, into Bridge Street, ancient and narrow, then turning into the broad village square where Duke jumped down outside the chemist's shop and took the reins from the old man. At the time when the cart was new, there had been plenty of hitching posts and mounting stones, but with modernization had come tarmac and buses, then every assistance to the traveller with live horse-power removed.

No sooner had the doorbell clanged than Mr Farnsworth junior came forward and said, 'Mr Strawbridge, what brings you out today? I heard that you were house-bound.'

'Well, young sir, if you believe only half what you see and nothing of what you hear, then you might get somewhere near the truth of it. I am very well, as you can see. I'm expecting soon to go and see a man who does good work on cataracts.'

'I'm glad to hear it, Mr Strawbridge, but you know what this village is like for gossip.'

'If I don't after eighty-odd years, then I don't know who does.'

'You're right there. Now what is it I can do for you, Mr Strawbridge?'

'Scott's Emulsion – large. Marmite – large. Horlicks Powder – large. Cod-liver oil and malt – the one in the red tin. Slippery Elm. Arrowroot.'

'Ted's niece arrived then?' He knew of course that she had arrived almost as soon as Hector Wilmott and Charlie Barrit had rolled the first barrel down the chute at The Star. The family up at Roman's Fields had always been of interest to the village proper – not that the Strawbridges were ever anything but villagers, but, being that bit further out, away from the huddle of dwellings and shops that made up the ancient village, their goings on were not always capable of interpretation and discussion. Also, Gabriel the elder had been a religious but unorthodox preacher, and the present Gabriel was a known Liberal (even a radical, some said) in his time; young May Strawbridge had married the help with a withered arm who had suddenly appeared one day and was a good few years older. And as well as all that they didn't mind gyppos camping on their land.

The Strawbridges had always kept themselves to themselves; not hoity-toity, but just wasn't interested in fermenting village life with a bit of gossip now and then. The Strawbridges taking in a convalescent child was interesting; one snatched from the jaws of death was better. The fact that May and Ted had neither chick nor child was of speculative interest to those who said that a child in the house could beget other children. May's waistline would be observed for the next year. Old wives' tales they might be, but they had been proved to be true time and again.

Gabriel Strawbridge knew that his purchases here this morning would be of interest, the fact that he had come down for them himself worth five minutes' mulling over. 'I can't say that any of the rest of us is in need of oil and malt or Horlicks drinks.'

'Only too right, Mr Strawbridge: you all always look pictures of health.'

Farnsworth junior collected the purchases, wrapped them in white glossy paper, each packet separately tied with fine string, then placed them in a large brown bag. 'Want me to send this up for you, Mr Strawbridge?'

'No, I got the governess cart outside.'

Farnsworth junior peered through the several notices on his shop door and saw Duke Barney holding the head of one of the Barneys' little horses.

'I hope the little child is soon back to health and fitness. I think you might find that a siphon of soda-water and a fresh orange squeezed with a good spoon of glucose is very good when there's been sickness in a child.'

'Is that so, Mr Farnsworth? I'll take note of that and see if I can't find a bag of oranges.'

Farnsworth junior opened the clanging door. 'There's a little step up, Mr Strawbridge.'

'I remember,' and raising his hat said, 'I see my carriage awaits. My regards to your father and mother. I shall remember the oranges and soda.'

Farnsworth the chemist deposited the bag of purchases in the little box at the rear of the cart and watched as the elderly gentleman stepped with the assurance of a fully-sighted man on to the running board and the seat. 'Just walk on, Duke. The sweetshop and then the grocer's.'

Hopefully, Duke made their first stop at the sweetshop.

'Go inside and ask Mrs Southey if she would oblige me by coming out,' confiding, 'it's years since I was in there, and I can't remember whether it is one steep step and then a low one, or the other way.' Securing Pixie's reins around a streetlamp he disappeared inside, quickly returning with Mrs Southey senior.

'Lord above, Gabriel Strawbridge, it seems half a life-time since I last saw you.'

Gabriel Strawbridge raised his hat. 'I might say just the same thing, Beth Southey, but don't tell me you thought I was house-bound or I shall feel that we are both past it.'

'Well, 'tis not all that long. Wasn't it at the last Harvest Supper we sat close by together?'

'Harvest of '27. May came on her own last year; Ted was laid up with a gash in his foot and we said she should go and I would see to Ted.'

'Oh, you missed a good supper last year, Gabriel. You just see to it you all comes down this year. I really think that's the highlight of my year – unless it's Fair Day. I always liked Fair Day.'

'And it always sees you trotting to the bank next day, Beth, I'll be bound.'

'Can't say we does badly, Gabriel. Now, what is it I can do for you? I'm not in the shop so often now, Dick's wife runs it mostly now, but she's lying-in. Did you hear she and Dick had a son?'

'I did, Beth, and congratulations.'

'Dick's pleased as a dog with two tails. Mary and me didn't mind what it was, just as long as it had everything it's supposed to have. And my word this one has – nine pound twelve, and a tooth at birth. Keith. They don't go for the good old names these days.'

'True, I can't see any woman agreeing to give her pride and joy a name like Gabriel.'

'Ah, you can't never tell. When the time comes, your May might want to see a fine name carried on. I hope and pray it comes to you.'

'Thank you, Beth. But if it doesn't it will be the way of things, and it is no good fretting for what you can't have.' Long ago, long, long ago now, Gabriel and Beth had had a summer romance that had faded, but had left them with an affection and respect for one another, and a friendship that was too long-standing for either of them to say anything that was not meant. 'I'll tell you what I came for. You no doubt heard that Ted's niece has come to stay with us – we hope for the rest of the summer, but we shall have to see. She has had diphtheria and she's like a little walking skeleton, but it isn't that, May's got the feeding-up department all sewn up . . . but I thought I'd come down and get a few extras – some Scott's and such from Farnsworth's. But I wondered what sort of a little treat a girl of that age might just like.'

'In the sweet line, do you mean?'

'That would be nice, but if there's anything else. You know all Ted's brothers and their families have a hard time of it, I don't suppose the child's had a treat in her life. Her mother bought her a toothbrush of her own because she was coming to us – I tell you, Beth, I could have wept for her and all children like her.'

'Oh, Gabriel, you don't change, do you? You been weeping over people since the time when you should have been out enjoying yourself without a care in the world.'

'I've been a very fortunate man, Beth, and I don't ever forget it.'

'What about slippers?'

'For the girl? What a good idea. How would I know her size?'

'I reckon if you tell Joycey how old and how tall, Joycey won't be far out, and she will always change them.'

'I'd rather get it right.'

'Then get a larger size and some of them fleecy insoles in case they are loose. Do you want me to come with you?'

'Would you, Beth? Just put a few licorice straps in a bag for Duke, I know he likes them. And something special for Louise, that's her name. And young Bar Barney as well. May's appointed her nurse at the moment.'

'I wouldn't have any of the Barney family running loose in my house.'

'Ah, well, Beth, you'd be missing a lot. They are decent people. Ann's no different now than when she was a girl living in the village, and Eli knows more about the country than you and I put together. They're as good neighbours as you could wish for. The fact that they've chosen to suit themselves instead of the village is nobody's affair except theirs, now is it?'

'Ann Carter might as well have run off with a black-skinned Moor as to take up with a didecoi.'

'Beth Southey, that's not you talking, that's the gossips that stand around in your shop. You know very well that Eli isn't a didecoi. The gypsies are purer-bred than the likes of us. I make no apologies for having them stop on my land. And I do like having young Bar and Duke around; they've got some fine old-fashioned manners, and they aren't afraid of hard work. Not many can say that of youngsters these days.'

'You think you can make silk purses out of pigs' ears?'

'I'd rather leave the pigs to make what they will out of their own ears.'

'And Gabriel Strawbridge would have no use for a silk purse anyhow, would he? You haven't changed over these umpteen years.'

'And you, Beth Southey, are still as bright as you were when your name was Possett.'

With 'Southey's Village Sweetshop' latched, a 'Back in ten minutes' sign on the door, and Duke contentedly leaning and sucking black-strap, as he went to the greengrocer's for some 'best juicy Jaffa oranges for Mr Strawbridge', Gabriel, with Beth unobtrusively guiding, walked slowly along the pavement to the shop that held a prime corner site. 'Clothiers, Haberdashery, Shoes, Linen, Fabrics' in letters of gold eighteen inches high stretched the full length of the shop-front.

Beth told Joycey what was wanted, and soon six pairs of slippers were set out for Gabriel's consideration. With his large magnifying glass he inspected closely. 'What do you think, Beth. What would you have chose when you were a young girl?'

'Why the pink of course, girls always like pink.'

'What about a kind of peachy colour – May has done the room out that colour.'

Joycey said there was no call for peach.

Beth Southey said, 'Well, hasn't she been busy then? Making quite a fuss over the girl.'

Not expanding on May's improvements, he said, 'You reckon pink? All right then. And the insoles.'

Joycey asked, 'Felt or fleece?'

'Fleece, I reckon,' Gabriel said.

'More than twice the price,' Joycey warned.

'It isn't every day I buy pink slippers,' he said, causing Joycey and Beth to flash one another a look of satisfaction. They had all thought they had seen the last of him calling in at the village shops.

Back in the governess cart, Gabriel Strawbridge told Duke, 'Go down Bridge Street, and home along the Alton Road.'

'It's a main long way, Maaster.'

The use by Duke of the word 'Master', pronounced in

all its rural breadth, did not indicate any subservience, but arose from the fact that Duke's education had been imposed by tradition rather than by the state. He had been around horses since the time he could sit up, and when selling he had learned from his father the tricks of breeding and trading in horses. One being to flatter the buyer into believing that it is he who is making the running. By the simple use of 'master' as a form of address, the horse-trader puts himself in an apparently subservient position. If the master is not fly enough to see the true situation (which is that the trader has had a lot more time in which to know his horse), and lays out good money because he believes himself the expert, well, is the trader to blame? Hence Duke's instinctive use of the word, even though Duke was as independent as his forefathers and worked for the Strawbridges on his own terms.

Gabriel Strawbridge and Eli Barney each accepted and admired the independence of the other. They had a working relationship that acknowledged the freedom of both. The Barneys occupied a corner of Roman's Fields, for which they paid a peppercorn rent of a silver threepenny-bit a year. If Eli chose to disappear overnight, there were no ties. The Barneys were the 'gyppos' whom the villagers disapproved of and distrusted, but against whom they would lay no complaint other than that they did not 'fit in'.

Gabriel, who had always believed that without tribal-ism, nationalism and religious differences, the human condition would be vastly improved, had become involved with Eli Barney years ago. The same emotion that had brought Ted Wilmott to his notice had also brought Eli Barney, for Eli Barney had taken up with Ann Carter. That had put her beyond the pale, but Eli and Ann were strong enough to withstand the pressures put upon them. Gabriel had offered them a small corner of Roman's Fields on which there was a bit of stabling left unused since the days when horticulture superseded farming. Eli and Ann repaired the buildings, part of which they lived in, part of which they used when a mare was foaling. The breed, being as hardy as wild horses, lived out as wild horses do; to a great extent Eli, Ann and their four children lived likewise.

'A main long way or not, Duke, if you aren't wanted by your father, then I should like to make the most of it.'

'He knows I'm with you. 'Twas he who told me the flag was up and said to take Pixie. He's going to take her down to Wickham Fair, and he wants her main used to highways by then.'

For the Barneys, Wickham Fair was always a testing ground, for this was the annual local fair when both their families would be on common ground. For Eli to take his horses there was to run the gauntlet, at least of fierce resentment and ostracization, at worst violence. But every year Eli stood his ground. He had the same rights to run his horses there as anyone.

As they went under the railway at the end of Bridge Street, a train rumbled over, but Pixie continued to pick up her dainty hooves and trot on up the incline without concern. 'Not a twitch, eh, Duke?'

'She's a good little mare. I reckon we should keep her to breed out of, but Father says we need to sell her. He knows I'm right, but he's just pig-headed. I reckon I might talk him round. Else I shall have to make him an offer and buy her meself.'

They were now clear of the village, and Gabriel could smell the spring in the hawthorn and fresh grass. Although his eyesight was not good, he still had the experience of scores of earlier springs to draw on. Morning light filtering greenly through translucent leaves, and tufts of new larch, catching the many yellow flowers growing in the new grass; primroses springing from rosettes of beautifully-veined leaves; coltsfoot flowers golden and tuft-headed on stems like green ropes; on the sallow-willow male flowers heavily yellow with pollen-grains, and in the ditches king-cups. It is the evocative smell of the warming earth that brings to mind those sights he had so delighted in, especially when he had Clara to enjoy them with.

'Tell me what you can see about you, Duke. I hear a hedgeful of nestlings and I reckon I can smell the hawthorn main strong.' Duke turns and sees that the old man is smiling.

'You don't catch me. 'Tis the *blackthorn* is full out, and there's thrushes and blackbirds with young hatchlings. There was a couple of brimstones about up this morning, you know that old buckthorn? It was by there.'

'It's where the brimstone caterpillars always feed.'

'I know, well enough. All I was saying is that it's early. The season's too far on: we shall suffer for it later.'

Gabriel was inclined to agree with him. 'Come on, my eyes, what's about in the hedge-bottom?'

Pixie trit-trotted, and the wheels of the cart crunched on accumulated road-grit at the verge of the main road. 'Celandines . . . garlic . . . '

'Which?'

'Garlic mustard.'

'No primroses?'

'A course there's primmies, what d'you think – there's always primmies this time a year, the bank's as covered as it ever was, you don't catch me like that neither, Master. I know you can smell them primmies . . . creeping ivy . . . cuckoo-flowers.'

'I thought I heard one this morning.'

'Nah, they won't have hardly arrived yet.'

'Well, I wouldn't back money on it. You said yourself, Duke, the season's far on.'

'It probably wasn't no cuckoo-call. Anybody can be fooled by a young pigeon this time of year.' Duke liked to be the first to hear the cuckoo-call, but he knew the old man with his acute hearing was a strong competitor to be first. 'I'll tell you first time I hears him.'

They journeyed on like this for a couple of miles, taking the long way home, then Pixie, of her own accord, turned into the Roman's Fields yard. 'I'll take the packages, and you see to the cart, Duke. A florin see you all right?'

Duke made to take the coin, but drew back. 'Father said I wasn't to ask anything, he owes you for the straw bales; anyway, you give me the black-strap at Southey's.'

'Tell your father, you didn't ask, I offered. It isn't long to Wickham Fair, you'll be able to shy at coconuts all morning with a florin. I haven't enjoyed myself like this for many a day. I'm obliged to you, Duke.'

Spitting on the coin for luck, Duke said, 'And I'm main obliged to you, Master Strawbridge.'

Cheeky young devil. The grin on his face was audible in his voice. He was a decent lad, more Eli than Ann in him, missing out on so much schooling that the beadle had trodden a path to the Barneys' camp. But it hadn't seemed to have done much harm to Duke's ability to turn sixpence into a shilling.

Back in Portsmouth, when Ralph came off his shift, the air was as heavy and warm as summer. He wondered whether there would be a card from Lu by second post, but realized that, as she had only been away for a day, that was unlikely. It seemed longer than that.

Chick Manners caught him up. 'Where you going at a rate of knots? You look as though you got a right 'ump on you.'

'Not really. I was thinking of Mum, she didn't look too good when I went off this morning.'

'What's up then?'

'Women's trouble.'

'How about coming down on The Common this evening. We got a scratch game of footy, and we thought we might try a dip afterwards . . . water's still cold as a witch's tit but first dip of the year always is.'

'I'll see. If Mum's OK I'll see you down there.'

'Good, kiddo, we'll have a couple of halves in The Wheelbarrow and home to bed like good boys.'

'That'll be the day when you go home like a good boy.'

Chick was the gay Lothario of a fivesome of young men who had stuck to one another since their days at Lampeter Road Boys' School. They felt themselves to be special because, in the face of growing unemployment, they had all got taken on either in the docks or on the railway. Chick and Ray were the two who wore collars and ties to work, and were inclined to stick together because of that. Ray had a good many 'oppos' but Chick was the only one to whom he would have said anything about his mother's ailments.

At the crossroads they parted company as usual, Ralph pressing on into the Lampeter area, notorious for its poverty – famed for nothing else to some – home to scores of families, most of whose lives were spent keeping their heads above water. Some failed and sank, children being taken into care and parents going God-knew-where, leaving a bit of space for some other family to fill. That morning, Ray heard that his father's ship was to return to home port this year. That thought, and his mother's condition filled his mind.

He scarcely knew his father. Once or twice a year they would hear from him, usually by postcard depicting a scene from the place where he went ashore. These had been fixed around the frame of the only picture hanging in Number 110. A framed picture in Lampeter Street indicated that Vera Wilmott still held on to the remnants of her pride.

As he neared home, he was forced to think about the homecoming in relation to his mother. What Chick Manners had thought was Ray having the hump about something was in fact intense anxiety. What he had seen that morning had scared him to death. When he was almost ready for work, he did as he usually did on early shift, taken her a drink of tea and a bit of toast. He gave himself ten minutes extra because he knew that she would be fretting about Lu and he had planned to sit with her and have a chat.

When he had tapped gently on the bedroom door and put his head round, they had both jumped out of their skins. His mother had obviously not heard him come upstairs; Ralph had jumped because of the state she was obviously in. He had slopped the tea and turned his head away, whilst she had dragged the top coverlet around her. He'd almost been too embarrassed to move. She'd sat down on the edge of the bed clutching the cover, as embarrassed as he, and for a moment or two each had been at a loss to know what to say.

But it was no use pretending, he had seen the state she was in, and she knew that he had. The old-fashioned petticoat she used to sleep in was soaked with blood; there was a pool on the floor and her feet and legs were smeared, as was the coverlet with which she had been trying to mop herself.

'Oh dear, Ray, I'm so sorry. It looks worse than it is. I didn't hear you come up.' She was near to tears and afraid, and no wonder.

Scared as he was, he hadn't been able to bear her polite stoicism, and it had been that which gave him the impetus to go into the room. He put the tea down on the stool that served as a bedside chest and stood hovering. He hadn't dared touch her. 'What is it, Mum? What's wrong?'

'Don't worry, Ralph, I'll be all right. When you hear Dotty putting her ashes in the dustbin, just ask her to pop in.'

'Pop in be blowed, Mum. Put your legs on the bed and don't you move. I'll go and fetch Dr Steiner. Here, have a drink of tea, it's sweet, that's good for shock.' He hadn't listened to her protest, but had wrapped her around with the coverlet, shaken Kenny roughly awake, told him that Mum was in bed and to get his trousers on and watch she didn't faint.

'What's wrong then?' He looked stupid with sleep.

Ralph, who was not one to panic, hauled Ken out of bed and flung his trousers at him and said fiercely, 'For Christ's sake, put a move on, she'll bleed to fucking death if I don't run for Dr Steiner quick.' The use of this obscenity, which was rarely heard in any family home, spurred Ken to leap into action.

Dr Steiner was not only the GP in this most unfavoured part of town, he was, with the splendid Mrs Steiner, a confidant, educator, occasionally a dispenser of potions for women in trouble, or of the strong green stuff for patients who had reached the extreme of endurance with pain and wanted no more. Abortion and euthanasia? Perhaps. Dr and Mrs Steiner never made a move that wasn't compassionate. He was in Number 110, his trousers and jumper pulled over his pyjamas, within a few minutes of Ray's ringing of the emergency bell. Shortly after that Vera Wilmott was in the ambulance and on her way to St Mary's.

Now, before Ray reached Lampeter Street, he turned in the direction of the hospital. He had left Ken to tell the other Wilmotts. Important, because there would be family ructions if they heard the news second-hand. The Wilmotts were easily slighted and quick to take offence. Ray wanted no irate aunties on his back, nor did he want anybody letting Lu know about it; he impressed on Ken that he must make that clear to Uncle Hector.

Inside the hospital he was close-questioned about his relationship with Vera Wilmott and, having established that, in the absence of Arthur Wilmott, who was somewhere in the South Atlantic, he was her nearest relative, he was escorted along the glossy, carbolic-fumed corridors, upstairs and along even more dangerously glossy corridors and told to wait in the corridor. Eventually he was told, Doctor will see you.

The doctor was not one of St Mary's regular specialists in gynaecology, but a visiting surgeon – a mister, in fact. Surprisingly young for a specialist. He fiddled with some notes without looking up and waved Ralph to a chair. 'Be with you in seconds.' Ralph forced himself to sit with his back against the chair. His white knuckles and working jaw muscles indicated his state of mind. He cleared his throat nervously as the surgeon looked up. 'Your mother, right? Mrs Vera Wilmott, 110 Lampeter Street. Mr Wilmott is a rating serving in the Navy, at present aboard his ship?' He spoke slowly, as though Ray might not understand, or that these were important facts to consider.

'Yes, I told the nurse that.'

'Well, Mr Wilmott, I am Mr Bathouse, a gynaecological surgeon.' He said the latter as though to query whether Ray knew what that might be. Ray nodded. 'I have to tell you that in the absence of Mrs Wilmott's next-of-kin, I was forced to take a decision to remove the womb.'

Ray clutched the edge of the chair. In spite of the mixed emotions he was experiencing, he held on to his dignity.

'Normally one would consult the husband, but in view of the haemorrhaging, there was no option but to go ahead with the procedure to perform a hysterectomy. In any case, Mrs Wilmott was able to agree to the surgery her-self.'

'How is my mother?'

'She is recovering quite well from the anaesthetic.'

'I should like to see her.'

'Too soon, I'm afraid. She is barely back from theatre. Anaesthetics take some time to wear off, and then she will be sedated and given a strong analgesic . . . pain-killer.'

'I realize that. I just want to see her. I don't care if she hasn't come to, I just want to see that she's alive.'

'My dear young man, of course your mother is alive, very much so. Indeed, now that she is rid of her enormous fibroid, she is likely to feel better than she has for years.'

'I shan't be any bother . . . I just want to see her.'

'You will be allowed in at visiting time tomorrow.'

'I must see her today.'

The important man spun his fountain pen impatiently.

'Listen, sir, if you had taken your mother a cup of tea up and found her standing in a pool of blood looking as if she'd been attacked by a mad axeman, and then seen her rushed off in an ambulance and been told you couldn't go with her; and then if you'd had to go to work and keep your mind on it as if nothing had happened; and then been told that she'd been cut open and bits of her taken out, wouldn't you want to just have a look at her . . . sir?' Ralph was pale and stiff with the stress of speaking his mind to such a powerful and important man.

Mr Bathouse tapped his teeth with his pen, opened a packet of cigarettes and said, 'Have a smoke, Mr Wilmott.'

Ralph drew a deep breath and then expired deeply. 'Thanks, but I don't.' There was a pause whilst the doctor lit up. 'I'm sorry, sir, if it sounded as if I was blowing my top, but I've been that worried at work. I shouldn't have been so personal.'

'I wish that I could say that I understand, Mr Wilmott, but I'm afraid that is beyond me. I haven't had a mother since I was four.'

Ralph would have liked to cry. He didn't really want to hear somebody else's troubles, but he didn't want to get on the wrong side of this man either.

'But you are right, Mr Wilmott, in my profession it is not always easy to remember that there is a person under the sterile sheets. Rather it is an interesting case . . . a human being, of course, but detached; a person in a vacuum, perhaps. Mine can often be a dramatic profession, as it was with your mother's emergency: the operating room is not called a theatre for nothing.'

'Perhaps I could come at visiting time this evening then?' Ray said hopefully.

84

The surgeon rose, stubbed out his cigarette, went to the door and called, 'Nurse!' The response was immediate. 'Take Mr Wilmott to the recovery ward.' The nurse raised her eyebrows. 'If Sister queries it, then refer her to me. Now, Mr Wilmott, no conversation with my patient.' Ray nodded agreement and Mr Bathouse smiled, 'I'll be on the carpet before Sister if you do.'

'Promise, sir. And thank you for . . . you know, what you did for her this morning. I can tell you, when I went in that room it put the wind up me.'

He saw her, a glimpse only, but it was enough. He was glad that she was still out, he couldn't bear to think of what was covered by the stiff sheets, or of how she would feel when she came round. She looked dreadful. The nurse reassured him that this was normal and that everything was fine, and that he should bring in these things. She gave him a list of necessities. He left the coolness of the hospital and went out into the warm air and sat on a wall and read the list. It seemed very long.

He contemplated asking Dotty or the aunties to go and get the things, but just now he couldn't face them, so he went down to the Co-op himself and drew a Clothing Club cheque for five pounds to be paid back over twelve months. When he had paid off the last Clothing Club, he had said that in future they would try to steer clear of buying anything on tick, and his mother had agreed. It hadn't been easy all that time when Lu was sick, the Doctor's Club had lapsed and they already owed Dr Steiner for that, and now there would be other fees and bills. Had their mother kept up the hospital insurance? It was something like a pound a year, the first thing people in debt let go. Ah well, it's no use worrying about that now; time enough later.

The brave face he had put on when standing up to the surgeon held sufficiently for him to go to the ladies' clothing department and ask if he could speak to the manageress. She was charming and understanding and invited him to sit in the staff room and wait for her to send around to the various necessary departments. 'Slippers are not listed, she would want slippers, and toiletries, perhaps eau-de-cologne?' Having agreed that she should use her discretion, Ralph relaxed for the first time that day and waited. A shy assistant brought him a cup of tea. He was slightly embarrassed at having to approve the choices. Three night-gowns, blue, pink and green with a sprig pattern. Three hand-towels, two face-flannels, soap in a soap-dish, and various other items deemed essential. He also approved a tube of Innoxa hand-cream because the manageress assured him that the air in hospitals was very drying to the skin. Ralph was past caring and approved everything. In for a penny, in for a pound, he told himself. He'd ask for a bit of overtime. Overtime was often given to men who needed to earn an extra quid in an emergency. Freemasons were not the only men who saw one another right in bad times.

Not long after Ray had left, the sound of his voice had reached her consciousness and Vera Wilmott had lifted her eyelids a fraction. Bright sunlight filtered through the neat, pleated cotton screens. She closed them again and drifted off to where voices echoed, words that she could not quite understand. Footsteps. She drifted back to the sunlight and heard a distant clatter of plates and cutlery. Potato and apple. The smell made her feel nauseous, but before it could bother her she drifted off into warmth and restfulness.

Later she was drawn back, to become aware of a dull, aching, painful, sore hollow that seemed to stretch like a band across her belly. It hurt, the pain was raw, but in its way it felt cleaner and more bearable than the pain she had put up with for so long. Too tired to open her eyes again, she lay still, slowly becoming aware of her surroundings.

She had had the big operation that all women dread, taking it all away. This pain she could stand. This pain was welcome. This pain was almost cheerful because she had signed for the surgeon to take it all away. No more mouths to feed when Arthur went back to sea. She remembered Lu. Thank God she had gone over to Ted and May's. Now, Lu would always be her youngest. Perhaps when she was on her feet again she might be able to get back to the factory. On piecework, they might get out of debt.

The screens were rolled apart sufficient to allow a nurse to slide in. 'You're back with us then, Mrs Wilmott.' Speaking as though Vera might be simple and hard of hearing.

Vera hauled up her eyelids and the corners of her mouth, and agreed that she was.

Lu realizes that she must have dozed off. She looks up and discovers that Aunty May and Bar have moved on several rows and are now walking back. She jumps to her feet and falls back into the straw, her head spinning, and hears Aunty May say, 'Whoops', as she runs along the strawberry rows. 'Oh dear, pet, perhaps you been too long in the sun?'

'I fell asleep.'

Aunty May feels her brow. 'You are a touch warm, best be careful, though I dare say it's just that you jumped up too quick. You look fine to me. Why don't you and Bar go on back down to the house? Have a bit to eat, there's things in the big larder, but don't cut into the new pie, and put a bit of something on a plate for Mr Strawbridge, will you, Bar? I'll be upalong when I finished to the fence. I made some lemonade.'

Bar, having clocked up another hour in the fields, doesn't mind at all going back to the house. Mrs Wilmott has pies, something they only get at home if their ma buys one – and that's not often.

Aunty May says to go back along the lane way because it's shadier.

'Your aunty says you got a new skirt, that right?'

'One of my other aunties run it up in the stay fact'ry, and a top to go with it.'

'What's the stay fact'ry?'

'It's where women go to work and they do the corsets.'

'What d'you mean?'

'Well, you know corsets, don't you?'

'A course, it's they pink things they sell in the shop.'

'It's for making ladies' stomachs flat.'

'I shouldn't like that.'

'You have to when you grow up.'

'I won't. I'd sooner have a round belly like my ma's. Anyway, I shan't have no babies, then it will stop flat down.'

'Why won't you?'

'Because I'm going to live by myself, in a little, tiny house, with a nice chair and a bed and a fire inside the house.'

They dawdle idly. It is April. Bright dapples of midday sun come through the ancient trees on one side of the lane. Lu is surprised at how close they can go to some birds without them fluttering; even then they only fly a few yards away. It seems hard to believe that it was only yesterday that Uncle Hec's lorry came along here, brushing aside the twigs and buds as they hit the windscreen. Perhaps it is because she has fallen asleep three times and each time she awakens the place seems to be a bit more familiar. She points into the hedge bottom. 'We got flowers like that back home.'

Bar looks a bit mystified, for they are celandines, the most common and long-seasoned flower imaginable. 'Celandines.' She picks one. 'Louise . . .? What's your other name?'

'Wilmott, of course.'

88

'Oh, a course it is. Louise Wilmott, do you like butter – very much, much, a little, or not at all? Answer the truth, or you shall pay a forfeit.'

'Very much.'

Bar holds the flower close to Lu's chin. 'You tell the truth. Now test me. You have to say the whole thing, else you can't make me pay the forfeit.'

Lu does as she is told, standing in the middle of the lane, a thing that would be impossible to do in the streets back home. Bar answers, 'Very much', and Lu does the test that children have done for unknown generations. 'Not true, not true, it hardly shines at all. You have to pay a forfeit.'

Bar grins. 'I know, it don't never shine much on my skin, I expect it's too dark.'

Lu tucks the flower in Bar's hair. 'It looks lovely in your hair though.'

'What about my forfeit?'

Lu thinks. 'Why did you say you wanted a fire inside the house?'

'That's not a forfeit; you're supposed to make me climb a tree or jump a wide ditch, or carry you.'

'I know, I just wondered why you said it.'

'Because that's what I'd like. A cooking fire with a black oven, inside, like Mrs Wilmott.'

'I mean, what do you mean *inside*? Where else could you have a fire?'

'Outside, of course, like ours is.'

Lu is puzzled, but doesn't like to show her ignorance more than she has already. 'Your forfeit is that you must come again tomorrow.'

Bar laughs. 'That's an easy one. Mrs Wilmott wants me every day you are stopping here. I'll tell you what I'll do for a forfeit. I'll weave you a wreath to go all round your hat.'

Lu has never seen anyone wind and plait so swiftly; two lengths of thin willow, still with its new pussy-buds, a strip of new ivy growth, and into these she binds flowers of the

April hedgerow and some premature May finds: pink campion, brittle stitchwort, white cow parsley, yellow Alexanders and celandines. When she has finished, she bands Lu's charity hat. Lu takes it off to look at. 'That's lovely!' and tries the hat on Bar. It sinks down well over Bar's brow, making them giggle.

'I wish I could do that.'

'What?'

'Make a crown like that.'

'Why can't you?'

Lu shrugs her shoulders. 'We haven't got any of this stuff at home.'

'It's only hedge flowers.'

'We haven't got hardly any . . . well, only celandines and dandelions and ivy. We haven't got this other stuff, only those pussy-cats sometimes when our teacher brings them in. Not often.'

'Well, she couldn't, could she? They only comes out now, and next week about, they a be going over.'

They have reached the picket gate at the side of Roman's Fields house, leaving both girls with questions about the other.

If Bar's house doesn't have a fire inside, where do they cook things?

If Louise can't find bits of common stuff that grows in every hedgerow, what kind of place does she come from?

Lu Wilmott has never encountered a gypsy, other than those who come door-to-door trying to sell their pegs to people who can hardly afford clothes, let alone clothes-pegs. She had no idea of Bar's unusual ancestry.

The closest Bar Barney has come to street-life is that of Wickham, whose main road is peaceful and whose ancient lanes are narrow and hoggin-spread: muddy in winter and dusty in summer. Unlike Lu, who, since yesterday, has journeyed, Bar has never been outside the village.

As they reach the yard, Duke is geeing up Pixie with his

heels; he at once flicks her lightly with a switch and she stands. Duke looks down from his greater height. 'Where are you going, Bar Barney?' he demands. Lu backs away from the horse, which looks unsafe without harness and uncontrolled by shafts.

Bar answers, 'To get the old grandfer a bit to eat. What d'you want to know for?'

'Askin', that's all. Is she her that nearly died?' indicating Lu with his head.

Bar screws up her eyes and mouth and approaches him fiercely with her fists clenched. 'I shall tell Ma what you said and then you'll get it.'

Duke, knowing that he had done what he was so often accused of doing, which was 'opening his gate too wide' when he had been told to keep it shut, knees Pixie and rides out of the yard, proud as a Bedouin astride a finely bred steed.

'Who was that?' Lu asks.

'That's only Duke. You don't want to take no notice of him. He thinks he's a man, and he isn't that much older than me. He just likes to show off like boys do. Come on, or Mrs Wilmott will be back and I shan't have it ready.'

Lu is fascinated by the wifely way Bar behaves when she is in Aunty May's. She even washes her hands at the high sink before going to the larder and bringing out the food as Aunty May has instructed: bread, butter, milk, a jug of lemon-juice and a flat pie on a plate. 'You go and knock on the old granfer's door and tell him it's ready.'

Lu looks alarmed. Her encounter with the old man has so far been brief and made embarrassing because of his blindness. 'I don't know where it is.'

'It's only just along this passage, look.' She knocks on the door and puts her head round. 'I got you a bit to eat, Master Gabr'l. Do you want it here?'

'I'll come through. Is Louise there?'

'Yes.'

'Good. I got some stuff I've got to tell her about.'

Lu finds the dinner-time interesting and the old man not so strange as yesterday. Nobody stops long at the table, but they all sit round, even Uncle Ted and two men whose place in the household mystifies Lu, though she guesses they must have been working with Uncle Ted – it wouldn't have occurred to her that they could have been working *for* Uncle Ted. Aunty May passes out pieces of pie which are put on the bare wooden table, and everyone tears off as much or as little as they want from a big loaf. Although no one says anything except, 'That all right for you, Lu?', she feels that her progress through the pie, bread and milk is of interest and being watched. The old man has placed his packages in a row beside him on the long dresser.

'You been out then, Gabr'l?' Ted asks casually.

Looking pleased with himself, Gabriel says, 'I've been down to the village with young Duke.'

'And you been shopping too then, Dad?' May asks.

'I have, and very well I enjoyed it. I should go more often.'

'Well, I'm glad to hear that,' May says. 'I was thinking you might be trying to root yourself.'

'She's been sucking the lemons again, Ted.'

Ted laughs at his wife's expense, but it is all good-hearted.

'What are we supposed to do about these then, Dad, pretend we don't want to know what's in them?'

'Nothing you need, May, mostly it's stuff to put the roses back in the cheeks of our young Lu here. Open them, May.'

Aunty May does and speaks the names as she opens the chemist's packages. 'Scott's Emulsion, Marmite, that's a big jar, Dad, I didn't know they came this big, and some malt, and what's this? Horlicks. Well, if she has all this lot plus a bit of fresh air and sunshine, she'll be fit to run back to Pompey.'

The men leave, Aunty May asks can she have John to help

with the strawing when the bean-sticks are done, puts covers over the food and returns it to the larder. 'Am I supposed to give Lu some of this, Dad?'

Lu looks up sharply. She has had enough recently of medicines, and this is what it seems to be.

'Of course, of course,' he says, 'it's all goodness.'

Lu is too apprehensive to object when Aunty May spoons out the white emulsion. But it's all right, fishy, and she hadn't expected that, but it is thick and not bitter like the medicines Dr Steiner had sent round. The stuff in the tin is lovely, a bit like melted toffee; she licks the spoon clean. Aunty May says, 'Will you look at that?' as though Lu has done a trick. 'Every last drop.'

'Good, good,' says Gabriel. 'Now she can have one of these.'

'Lord, Father, the girl will burst.'

'Just one, and here's a packet for little old sweet-tooth, Bar . . . What size are your feet, Lu?' he asks.

Lu looks at the old man, puzzled. No one has ever asked her that. 'I don't know.'

'Try these for size, they can go back if they don't fit.'

Like Lu, Bar's breath is taken away at the sight of the pink slippers, an item so remote from each of their lives that they haven't even dreamed of owning such luxury; they know no one who does. Aunty May takes over, kneels on one knee and supervises the fitting. Lu stands up and walks, the backs slock. 'She could have done with a size smaller, Dad, but she'll grow into them.'

Gabriel Strawbridge knows how to give gifts and puts yet another bag on the table. 'Then try with these.'

With the thick, fleecy insoles, the wonderful slippers fit, and Lu walks up and down the kitchen watching her feet flash colour as she does. Bar stands at the sink drying knives, sucking a sweet, smiling, for Bar Barney is one of those rare and agreeable persons who are not covetous but are pleased for anyone to have a bit of good luck come their way.

Lu is very, very conscious of her feet. Her attention is usually drawn to them by a leaky welt, a blister, chaps and chilblains, a hole or the pinching of an ill-fitting shoe; but now, with each step, they sink into the soft fleece, and the tread is lightened by the spongy soles. She looks at the old man shyly, and then at Aunty May, then back again; she knows he cannot see things at all well, and he has one white eye like Grandma Wilmott. His bad eyesight makes him peer, which makes Lu even more shy of speaking to him, but she is overwhelmed by the slippers and his kindness. Except for the things they gave her to bring with her, her mum and brothers only exchange small presents on birthdays and Christmas Day, but she has only known Mr Strawbridge about a day. She wants to tell him all of this but only manages, 'Thank you, thank you ever so much. I never had no slippers.'

'No thanks needed, but I *should* be pleased if you had a go at taking that nourishment I fetched you, and a slice of bread and Marmite before you go to bed. Vitamin B there is in that. Very good for you, Vitamin B.'

'Oh lumme, I forgot the card. Mum gave me a card with a stamp on for me to write home and tell her if I was all right. Now I can tell her about the slippers.'

'And are you all right?' her aunty asks.

'Yes, I am. Honest. Ray said I would be, but I never believed him. Well, I didn't know what it would be like, and it's all right, it's nothing to be scared of even though there isn't any houses except this one.'

Aunty May looks satisfied and as she puts on her wide straw hat with a handkerchief hanging down the back, says, 'Well, that's good. There's a pencil in the jar there, if you sit down now and write it, the afternoon postman will be along the lane in about half an hour; you can wait out on the verge and give it to him.'

'Haven't you got any post-boxes?'

'We have, but the postman comes this way, so he collects our letters.'

When Aunty May has gone back to the fields and Uncle Gabriel to his room to rest, Lu and Bar sit at the long kitchen table and try to convey in the space given for messages Lu's relief that she does not feel lonely or afraid, her pleasure at having a bed and a room to herself, her pride at the pink slippers, and the many, many interesting things that she has encountered. 'Are you my friend now?' she asks Bar.

'Can I be?'

'You can if you like.'

'Oh yes, I haven't got a friend.'

'Not at school?'

Bar Barney shakes her head. 'Nah, they won't let me because I an't a Wickhamite.'

'What are you then?'

'Romany.' She meets Lu's enquiring look as though ready to challenge.

Lu smiles, pleased. 'I've got an Eyetalian friend – her mum makes ice-cream and her dad sells it on the front – but I haven't got a Romany, I never heard of a Romany.'

Bar leaves her question about what 'the front' is, in her flush of pleasure at having got a friend. A better friend than any of the Wickhamites, who often won't let her play unless it's in a team and it's something physical that she's good at: nobody at school has a friend that has come from Portsmouth in a lorry, and is given a room of her own, a new skirt and top, a toothbrush, and a card to post back home. And pink slippers. Lu has let her try them; they are miles too big but the feel is like warm moss.

They compose the message in tiny writing – 'Dear Mum, It is nice here. I got a pretty room and a friend. She is Bar. Everybody is nice. Ray will like it.'

'You are supposed to put your name.'

'She knows because I said Mum . . . she give me the card.'

Bar sees the logic of that. 'Then you got room to say about the slippers.'

'Lor!' Lu can't think why she needed reminding and adds, 'I got some pink slippers NEW.'

Sitting on the grass verge, waiting for the postman, they compare notes about schools and are amazed that these can be so different; each envies the other some bit of her school-life; they exchange wishes and hopes; they hold back on some things, understanding that there are things that have to be revealed gradually, as the friendship develops. Lu is pleased that she has a brother like Ray to tell about, and they have in common Duke and Kenny who can't get through a day without teasing and throwing their weight about. With the card safely in the postman's bag, they return to the house and sit on Lu's bed reading *Dandy* and *Beano* over and over. Eventually Lu falls asleep again, Bar covers her friend's legs with the counterpane and goes downstairs to scrub some potatoes for Mrs Wilmott to put on when she comes in from the strawberry fields.

The first week slides by in a series of new experiences. In Lu's debilitated state, she drifts in and out, occasionally not sure which bits are real and which dreamed. This is a strange world, where routine is lax and governed not by factory hooters but by the sun and the weather. When Saturday comes, Lu can scarcely believe that five days have gone, and yet, strangely, it seems as though she has been here much longer than that. The days have gone by in a procession of new experiences, deeply-slept nights and just being here. Also, five days show their passing in the drop in the level of the Scott's, the Marmite, the Horlicks and the malt.

In five bedtimes Uncle Ted has finished reading the story of Candida starting at Miss Wymer's school, which has given Lu a lot to think about. At Miss Wymer's school the girls do not go home at night. Candida had jewels hidden about her. A box arrives containing Candida's unsuitable, 'unhealthy' clothes of green velvet, bright blue alpaca, a red silk blouse with pearl buttons and a pink satin party dress trimmed with white swansdown. It has not mattered that Lu is not familiar with buckram, leg-o'-mutton sleeves or lavish military braid; she can visualize the opening of Candida's trunk. Candida speaks French, but she is really Russian, and has 'strange ways' such as airing her mattress over the bed-rail; she dances with 'wild, passionate sadness, her feet hardly touching the floor'; her mother is dead, her father is dead, and she has come to the school that her *maman* loved so much. It was a long, interesting and sometimes baffling story. A school where the girls sleep and each has a room to herself. Were they all rich orphans? Uncle Ted explained every detail and then went back to the beginning so that they could both enjoy it more now that they knew about the complications and misunderstandings and the strange ways of people who had plenty of money with which to look after their children, but instead sent them away for somebody else to look after.

During the day, she rarely saw Uncle Ted; after the first day he took his dinner out with him, but as the week passed she looked forward to bedtime as a treat. Nobody told her when it was bedtime, but when she felt tiredness overtake her, she went upstairs, washed her face, and lay beneath the covers in her vest and knickers, hoping that Uncle Ted would put his head round the door again and say, 'Are we going to find out a bit more about what all these gels are up to at their fancy school?' The story lasted for such a long time because once Uncle Ted's rumbly, husky voice had read a few pages, Lu drifted away into a deep sleep. She was usually vaguely aware of Aunty May pulling the covers over her and lighting a night-light, and then it being daylight again. In five bedtime readings with

Uncle Ted, Lu has learned that *'petite'* is French for small, *'dame anglaise'* is 'English lady' and (for Uncle Ted can only guess until he can get his hands on a proper dictionary) *'jeune fille'* might mean 'young girl'.

Candida appears to have no faults, she is transformed, becomes beautiful, thoughtful, happy with very little, friendly, understanding and very helpful. Lu knows that she could never be like Candida; if she had a box containing clothes of glorious red silk or green velvet, she would never give them up to be like everybody else and wear a black serge skirt and a woollen blouse. On the second reading, Uncle Ted and Lu agree that they probably wouldn't like her if they met her in real life. Lu secretly covets a name like Candida, but much prefers to have a giggling friend like Bar who would never turn out to be a princess.

Each morning, whilst they carry Aunty May's cold tea to the fields, Lu retells each episode to Bar. They try to think of things to say to her about *petites jeunes filles* and *dames anglaises*. Aunty May says she is very impressed and teaches them a song in French, about people being called to arms and becoming glorious soldiers. The girls are thrilled at hearing the strange language spilling from their mouths.

Vera Wilmott was still in hospital. It had been agreed that Ralph would catch the midday train on Saturday and see May. Vera said, 'Lu sounds as though she's all right on her card she sent. I don't expect May will mind if she stops on till I'm out of here. Don't tell Lu I'm in here, not yet. If you bring me in one or two cards, I can write them and she'll never know what happened. I've thought over and over again since I've been laying here what a blessing it was Hector took her when he did. I should have hated her to find me . . .'

Ralph, as embarrassed about crises as herself, squeezed her shoulder briefly. 'You want to forget that; don't think no more about it; you just get yourself better. Ken said he'd come later on, when you're up and about.' Kenny had sent in a bunch of violets and a bag of sweets – without needing any reminding.

Vera was past caring how they were going to pay the bill; for the first time in her adult life she was in bed, warm, fed, with a nice hot drink at night and people concerned for her health. Painful as moving was, she could still do with six months of this life. Auntie Elsie was going to be allowed to come visiting in Ralph's stead. It would be a relief to tell a woman what she had been through. Elsie would say that it will be a long job, hysterectomies are the most major surgery, weeks hardly putting a foot to the ground, and six months before getting back to work. Nothing of which she has been able to discuss with Ray; in any case he has enough to cope with in seeing to everything at home. He said he didn't mind taking her things back for Dotty to wash, but Vera minded, it wasn't a man's job to do that, not a *son's* job. He had always been a nice boy, the best son a woman could wish for. If it hadn't been for Ray, Vera doesn't know how she would have managed these last few years. He had carried the whole house on his shoulders, her own bit of earnings and Ken's together hardly paid the rent and gas, but they had never gone without a meal of some sort.

She would like to see him with a nice girl to look after him; he didn't meet the sort of girl Vera wanted for him. She had always encouraged him to attend meetings that took him out of town, expenses were paid so it was a chance for him to get away, you never knew who you would meet going further afield. Ralph said 'fat chance', delegates hardly got out of the conference hall. She didn't believe that, he always seemed to be a lot happier, more full of life after he had been away for the NUR, especially if he had a chance to speak. She just couldn't picture her Ray getting up in front of hundreds of delegates. She hardly understood what a delegate was anyway, only that people had respect for a good union representative, and a young one at that – it showed brains. It was having brains that helped you pick yourself up by your bootstraps and get on. More than anything she wanted her children to get on – not just the boys, Lu had a good head on her shoulders. Once or twice when Vera had been daydreaming over her endless hand-sewn lacing, she had visualized Lu going to a place like Northern Grammar, wearing a Panama hat and gym-slip. When she was up and about again, she would find out about scholarships. There was plenty of time.

Roman's Fields was settling down around Lu, and she was beginning to find the quiet less strange and the spaciousness less uneasy, although she didn't venture beyond the out-houses and yard unless Bar went too. But there was no problem about that, Bar was at Roman's Fields from early morning till after supper, and gradually Lu was assured that she would not be trampled by horses or chased by cows if she walked over the fields. So Lu began to venture into unsignposted lanes, footpaths through woods and short-cuts. She learned how to tuck straw beneath strawberry plants and saw how bees could be calmed with a smoker and the basic knowledge about the getting of honey and milk, taking everything in through her large eyes with heavy, fatigue-darkened lids and sockets. Bar took her to look at The Swallitt, which was a pond in a wood, and made plans to take a picnic there; another time they went to the stream and brought back tadpoles with little legs.

On the day of the picnic, carrying their food in grease-proof paper and their lemonade in bottles, the two girls dawdle along the lane that runs by Roman's Fields, taking back a bill-hook Uncle Ted had sharpened for Mrs Cater-mole's gardener.

Mrs Catermole – old Cat – owns a number of cottages in the village, and earns very good rent from them. This, she considers, entitles her to respect and deference and a right to interfere in the lives of anyone with an income less than hers. Her house stands within a brick-built boundary wall, about a mile away from Roman's Fields and the same distance from the village.

Lu, having already heard of old Cat's rudeness, would have preferred to wait in the lane whilst Bar went in, but that seemed mean seeing that they were running the errand for Uncle Ted, and in any case Lu was daily growing more curious about the many people who inhabited Bar's gossip.

She viewed the long drive with misgiving; there was no house in sight but the drive was banked with shrubs and spring flowers. 'Come on, she won't eat you. You just don't have to take no notice of her. She's just mean from living by her own. She don't really need me to run errands for her: she got a housekeeper could do that.'

'Why does she then?'

'I expect she wants to have people go and see her, but they don't because she's rude to them, and she likes bossing people around, and she's nosy . . . She asked me everything about you, but I couldn't tell her much. Nobody likes going to see her, if she was nice to people, they would. She gives me a ha'penny for going to see if she wants anything from the village, and a penny for getting it. Most days she do.'

'So you get . . . '

'Sevenpence, usually. It's a lot, but she can afford it. I have to go and get it on Friday after school, which means she gets a call for nothing.'

'It's all right though, having sevenpence.'

'I gets more from your aunty. But if I'd a' know before you come that we was going to be friends, I'd a' come over and helped get your room ready anyway.'

'I didn't even know Aunty May knew any girls . . . I didn't know anything at all about her really, only that she married my dad's brother.'

'What's your dad like? He look like Mr Wilmott?'

Lu shrugged, 'I don't know.'

'Not your *dad*?'

'He goes away to sea. He's been gone years. I think I must of been about seven or eight last time he came home.'

'It must be queer, not knowing what your dad looks like. Perhaps you won't like him.'

Lu has already had sneaking thoughts of that. 'I expect everybody likes their dad.' She knows a lot of kids who hate their dad.

Bar nods, not really having considered until now whether she liked her own dad.

The house suddenly looms into view. Lu is astonished, she had expected Bar's ogress to live in a gloomy stone house. But this is the prettiest house Lu has ever seen. Built of small red bricks, over the entrance there is an archway of red tiles laid edge-on. The same tiles appear above the diamond-paned windows and again as ledges. On one corner is a small tower with diamond windows all round. The tower is capped by a tall, slender cone of copper.

The name of the architect would not have meant anything to Lu, but, as Mrs Catermole is forced to make clear to everyone, it was Sir Edwin Lutyens. It will take time and experience before Lu understands why it is that she thinks this is such a wonderful house. If she never knows why, it does not matter; it is enough that it is a beautiful house in its right setting. If she does get to know, then she will know that Mrs Catermole is justified in her boast of owning a house designed on a human scale, marrying beauty and function.

'Fancy having a place like that all to yourself.'

'Do you like it then? I reckon it's creepy.'

'No, it's not, it's the kind of place magic happens.'

Bar giggles. 'Perhaps she magicked the people away and she's the witch that's took it for herself.'

A sharp, shrill voice calls from beyond a line of cordon

apple trees, 'Is that your silly giggling I can hear, Bar Barney? Come here. Come to the garden.'

Bar pulls a face, 'She's got ears like a cony, only she don't run away like they. Come on, you'd better come and see the witch,' stifling another giggle.

The garden is as beautiful as the house, reinforcing in Lu's mind the notion that people who live in the country have gardens chock-full of flowers and trees. Things planted here don't give up the ghost as they do in Lampeter Street; here they don't grow up spindly and thin, or have leaves that look dull and dirty, and bark that oozes gum from damage. Here in the witch's garden, flowers and trees are not only dense and colourful, they are as clean and bright as a box of scallops. The lawn on which basket chairs and a table are set out looks as green and short as the bowling greens on Southsea front.

'Oh,' Bar whispers crossly, 'the blimmen old vicar's here – he's her brother,' and walks boldly barefoot towards him and the old lady, followed slowly and at a distance by Lu. Mrs Catermole is indeed Lu's idea of a bad witch; everything about her is pointed and sharp and dark, only her glasses are not, these are small, round and silver-rimmed. Waving away the proffered bill-hook to an undefined place out of her sight, she points at Lu, like a school inspector choosing a victim to test for arithmetic. 'You, child. Are you the Portsmouth girl come to Roman's Fields?'

'Yes, miss.'

'Speak up, speak up, lift your head so that I can hear you.'

'Yes, miss.'

'Oh, the Portsmouth cockney whine,' the cross-looking old lady says as she turns to the vicar. 'Diphtheria. She has been at Death's door. Half the places in that town are slums – naval towns are all alike. Disease goes through huddled backstreets like wildfire.' To Lu, 'Stand close, child'; to the vicar, 'She's perfectly safe, the contagion has long gone.'

Lu takes a few steps closer.

'Does your father work?'

'He's in the Navy, miss.'

'Show me your arms.' Lu, bewildered and embarrassed, does as she is told. Mrs Catermole pulls up the sleeves of her cardi. 'Look at that, Compton, sticks. May Strawbridge has her work cut out to put flesh back on those.' To Lu, 'Tell your aunt, Mrs Catermole said she should give you eggs every day.'

Lu feels incensed at being inspected like this and being told what Aunty May should do. At school everybody must submit to all kinds of inspections, especially skin, hair and fingernails, but she cannot see what right this lady and the vicar have to look at her arms and talk about her as though she isn't there.

The vicar, who seems to be soft and round in all the same places that Mrs Catermole is sharp and pointed, says, 'Have you thanked Jesus for making you well again?'

Lu is astonished. Jesus has his place and time within school – morning and evening prayer, RI, 'There is a Green Hill Far Away' at Easter, carols at Christmas, and a test on religious knowledge once a year after you leave the Mixed Infants – but not in gardens. She could answer that she has not spoken to Jesus at all, but guesses that Mrs Catermole would pounce upon her with that cross voice. Tell a lie and say that she had. It's not easy to tell a lie to a vicar.

Suddenly Bar leaps into action, grabs Lu by the hand and drags her stumbling awkwardly away. 'You got a bloody cheek, asking her questions, and feeling her arms like you feels Duke's pheasants!' Her cheeks are red as she shouts angrily over her shoulder, 'How would you like anybody prodding you?' She sounds furious. She looks furious. She *is* furious.

They have reached the edge of the lawn and they could have easily escaped, but Lu stops, turns and takes a few steps back towards the indignant couple. Her own indignation brings out her best Lampeter Street challenging tone. 'I haven't got Jesus to thank for nothing. He didn't do nothing, it's our Ray that did it.'

The vicar stands up, hands on hips, his head stretched forward menacingly.

'And my aunty already gives me eggs, and honey and milk, every day I been here, so she don't need nobody to tell her.' Lu, who has learned to stand up for herself in an area where people can be threatening to the point of carrying out their threats with fists and bottles, is only wary now because she doesn't know the rules out here in the country. The vicar doesn't scare her. Lena Grigg can scare more than that. Lu stares him down until he turns and joins his outrage to that of his sister.

Lu and Bar run down the drive, and when they have reached the lane again, Lu is breathless, her knees are weak and her hands are trembling, but she keeps running until they reach the wicket gate at the top of the Roman's Fields garden, when they slow down and sink into the long grass.

Uncle Ted's voice, coming from the other side of the hedge, surprises them both. 'Hello, what you two minxes been up to then? I thought you was going picnicking.' Smiling, he comes round a bend in the path carrying some long-handled tools over his shoulder. 'Lu, you shouldn't run like that, look at you, beads of sweat on your forehead . . . '

Bar speaks up. 'We ran away from Mrs Catermole and the vicar.'

Uncle Ted raises his eyebrows. 'Oh yes, what you been up to then?'

'Go on, Lu, tell him, or shall I?'

Lu hunches her shoulders, not wanting to tell; she has seen too many rows and fights between neighbours over children. 'She made me hold out my arms so the vicar could see, and she said Aunty May must give me eggs.'

Bar, whose nature is more placid than otherwise, is still angry that Lu should be spoken to so rudely, and she's angry at herself for taking Lu there, she should have known, but she had thought that a visitor at Roman's wouldn't get spoken to the way the village children are. 'She said about the slums . . . and it was safe to get near her – anybody'd think Lu had horse-scabs! And the vicar said did Lu thank Jesus? They got my blood up for being so rude.' She exchanges looks with Lu.

Ted knows about getting the Barney blood up. Eli, always conscious of prejudice against his family, has taught his children to be proud of themselves and to stand for none of it.

'Bar didn't mean to be rude to them, but she knows I don't like people looking at my arms now they've gone skinny.' Now Lu feels cross.

'I *did* mean it! I told her off another time – she asked me if I ever washed my feet. Cheek!'

Uncle Ted settles down on the grass with them. 'Your arms are all right. There's nothing shameful in losing a bit of weight because of a fever, it's a natural thing, but I don't think it is up to Mrs Catermole or anybody to assume that they have any right to make comments. Being old doesn't give nobody the right to ask personal questions.'

Bar couldn't leave it, her adrenalin was still running. 'She said Lu's been at Death's door.'

Neither could Lu. 'And did I thank Jesus for saving me? It was our Ray who saved me, not Jesus, so I told him, that vicar.'

Ted Wilmott cannot prevent the flush that reddens his face, but he does keep emotion out of his voice. 'Is that a fac'? Death's door . . . what a daft thing to say.'

The two girls nod vigorously, and Bar says with as much humility as she can muster, 'And I cursed at him.'

Later, when he relates this to May and Gabriel, he will let out the smile that threatens now, but it is not really quite the thing to smile at the thought of that Holy Joe being cussed at by Bar Barney. She is 'the gyppo's child', whose father doesn't have a great deal of time for vicars. Eli knows to an inch how far Christian charity stretches; not far enough to reach a man who wears a gold ring in his ear and deals in horses.

'Now you two go on your way and enjoy your picnic.'

The only people who know exactly what transpired at the Edwin Lutyens house are Mrs Catermole, her Holy Joe brother and Ted Wilmott. When Ted returns to Roman's Fields twenty minutes later, he breathes a heavy, satisfactory sigh and says to May and Gabriel over their midday bread and cheese, 'I never was a man for having my say unnecessary, but there's some things – specially when you've needed to have 'em out for a long time – feels very satisfying when the chance comes and you can tell people to their face exactly what you thinks of them.'

Old Cat does not spoil their picnic. Later, beside the brook in the woods, where it trickles over into a dip creating the Swallitt Hole, watching Bar expertly weave rushes, Lu falls into a light sleep. Her initial apprehension about being where there were so few people is fading. She is becoming used to sleeping where sounds were not human or familiar ones; the owl is still mysterious and eerie, but after dark a night-light glows comfortingly in her peach-coloured room.

When she opens her eyes again, it is to see Bar has taken off her frock and knickers and is naked except for lengths of ivy draped around her, and her hair stuck all over with flower-heads and silver pussy-willow. She is engaged in some strange dancing game like nothing that Lu – who is an expert of playground rites and games – has ever seen before. Bar is twirling round and round and round on the spot. She looks so different from the Bar who looks short and shapeless in her old dress and droopy knickers. Without her clothes, she isn't even a girl. Lu is fascinated. She has such a tiny waist, and her chest is swollen into real little breasts, with bigger and blacker circles than Lu has ever seen put into the mouth of any of the babies suckled by their mothers on the doorsteps in Lampeter Street. There is a line of black hair in her armpit, and she has a black triangle of curls that is decorated with more pussy-willow flowers.

With her arms outstretched and her eyes closed, she tilts her face upwards. She is obviously enjoying whatever she can see behind her eyelids, because her lips are turned upwards into a faint smile.

Twirling on the spot is a playground activity that comes and goes in its season. The competition is to see who can do it the longest without falling down giddy. But what Bar is doing is nothing so silly and knock-about, but a kind of undulating, spinning dance with her toes not moving from the same spot of grass. She looks lovely, but alarming too. Round and round she spins on, her flowery hair flying round behind her, never catching up with her face. Faster and faster. As her speed increases, she gradually raises her arms. When they are above her head, she crosses her thumbs, puts her palms together, fingertips pointing to the sky, and stretches up to her fullest extent. Then she stops, not breathless, but standing erect. She does not stumble or fall about drunkenly as happens in the playground game, but stands unmoving, and then slowly lowers her arms until her hands, pointing heavenward, are level with her face. Her eyes remain gently closed and her mouth holds its smile. Only her mass of hair is not stilled; it seems to have doubled its bulk and is moved restlessly about by every small current of air.

Lu sits spellbound, wondering what might happen next. It is as though, for those few minutes, Bar has been changed from her brown, practical self and has become an enchanted figure who might have just been magicked out of the woods.

Bar opens her eyes. 'Oh good, you've woke up.' The spell is broken. In a moment she has put on her frock and pulled up her thick knickers over the heads of pussy-willow. 'Look, I found my old pickle-jar I left here before. I was going to get some taddies to take back. Your aunty wants some more for her old frog-tank she got sunk in the ground for – '

The rest of Bar's explanation was lost on Lu, who interrupts, 'Oh, shut up about frogs, what was that you were doing? That dance?'

Bar shrugs. 'I was just getting rid of Old Cat,' she says off-handedly, poking a stick into the pickle-jar to fetch out a rotted leaf, then she looks up and giggles. 'Oh, Lu, you do look queer, are you grumpy or what? I was trying to get it out of you too.'

'A' course I'm not grumpy. What about Old Cat? What were you doing to her?'

'Not to *her*, just the bad feelings she give us. We din't want them rotting away inside us, did we? So I got rid of them.'

What with the ivy fronds, the flowers all over her hair and her flushed cheeks, she looks pretty in a way Lu has never seen anyone else look. It is as though the old frock and knickers are a disguise. 'Don't be such a blimmen tease, Bar Barney. Nobody does things like that without their clothes on. You're just pretending it wasn't no-thing.'

'I'm not. It's special, and I wanted you to see, only I din't know if you'd think it was daft.' She comes and settles herself down beside Lu again, ferrets around in the picnic bag, and brings out a couple of sandwiches, one of which she gives to Lu, who eats hungrily. 'It's just . . . well, don't go thinking it's magic or anything like that, anybody can do it . . . Still, you'd best not try till you got all your blood strong again. That stuff Mr Gabr'l give you will do that in no time.'

'What *is* it? A spell?'

'I told you it wasn't nothing like that. It's just dervishing. You starts turning round slow with your arms out till you got your balance, then you closes your eyes, and when you got the proper way of whirling, you just keep going until you've got as fast as you can.' She takes a swig from her water-bottle. 'Was I going fast?'

'Ever so fast, couldn't you tell?'

Bar shakes her head. 'It's like there's a thread or something hooked on to the sky, it goes down through the top of your head and out between your legs, and it's like you been set off like a spinning top, and you just keep going as long as you like, then when you're ready to stop you catch hold of the thread between your hands and the dervishing stops.'

'Do it feel nice?'

'A' course it does. It feels lovely . . . like nothing bad is left inside you.' She gives a Bar-like giggle. 'Sometimes you get a feeling like when you pinched a mug of new scrumpy, only you don't get the runs or a headache after.'

'Will you teach me?'

'Easy, yes. We'll do it together when you're be . . . when you feel you're up to it, only I don't want to get into trouble with your aunty, so we'd best wait. When it's summer.'

'I might be gone then.'

'You won't! You don't want to go back yet. It's a lot better in the summer. We could come here and go swimming, if you like, and you could help your aunty at picking time. I always help with the picking.'

Lu is still thinking about hanging by a thread from the sky and being out in the open without your clothes on. 'Do you *have* to take your clothes off?'

'You don't have to, but it's better when you do, you can feel all the hairs on your body standing up like a fritt cat . . . listen.' She leans her head against Lu's and her hair crackles.

'You have to find a place where nobody don't come, else the daft old villagers would tell on you for being a witch.'

'Don't the kids from your school come here to swim?'

'No, they get the bus down town to that swimming pool they built. They said it's blue water in a hole as big as a house, and it's clean because it's full of stuff that smells like Conde's Fluid. They think it's awful swimming with frogs and fishes, but that's the proper place to swim . . . and they say this wood's been witched. Only me and Duke come here.'

'It's not witched is it?'

'Only Duke's sort of witching. He goes out looking for fox-skulls or stoats', and he hangs them up in a tree. They're all daft down there in the village – old fox-bones can't witch anybody. If you gets scared of a place, it's only what you do to yourself. Me and Duke don't mind if they think that . . . they don't come making any bother on us.'

This may have been Lu's initiation into life on the other side of the hills, for it was from here on that she began to feel that she was no longer a visitor or a stranger.

So another week passed magically, Lu getting healthier by the day, regaining her appetite, sleeping deeply at night. It is Saturday again, the Saturday after the old 'Cat' incident and the picnic by the stream. Aunty May, who is still in the house when Lu comes downstairs at half-past seven, says, 'Half day today, the soil's so dry the slugs will have a hard time of it. I'm going to have a good clean through, so you and Bar had best make yourselves scarce. I think my father has something up his sleeve. I'll be all done by dinner-time, then I'm just going to do a couple of hours' weeding in the house garden.'

Lu likes the way that Aunty May, although she works long hours, still seems to be there to talk to and see to things in the house and when she is in the fields she lifts her head and waves, or walks over and sits for a while, asking if everything's all right. She never rushes about and, when she is asked a question, always stops and looks as though she's thinking about it before she answers.

What Lu perceives without understanding is May Wilmott's tranquil nature, which pervades the entire household. She is a woman blessed with good health, boundless energy and contentment with her lot, most of which she inherited from Gabriel.

Father and daughter have in common, too, a tendency to anarchy. Perhaps that is too defined a tendency – rather, they have a philosophy which allows that there is no 'right way' in which anything must be done. This is why they have never had anything to do with orthodox religion or party politics, both of which thrive by constantly trying to impose *their* 'right way' on the rest. This belief, which pervades the Roman's Fields household, possibly stems from Gabriel's experience in his youth, when he worked his passage to South Africa to try to discover for himself the truth about the power struggle going on there, about British rumour and Boer counter-rumour. He had returned wretched with shame. Not only had he seen monstrous acts of cruelty committed by the British against the Boer women and children, but the Boer, too, when it came to wanting power over the native bushmen and their lands, behaved with equal barbarity.

After that experience, he came to believe that tolerance grew out of knowledge. And here is Lu Wilmott who, as he very soon realized, was a child with her intelligence unprospected, her experience limited to a poverty-stricken way of life, her schooling mean and niggardly. And here too is Bar, with a fuller, more wholesome childhood. He applied his mind to how he might offer them some new experience, perhaps something that might light a flame which might perhaps illuminate some part of their minds. If not, then no experience is ever wasted.

The warm weather persisted, and from observations of

rooks, haws, clouds and bones, plus some hope and guess-work, local soothsayers foretold a good summer, but in case it should happen that they were wrong, Gabriel decided to get out whilst the going was good. Yesterday, he had arranged with Duke to bring Pixie, and arranged with May that he will take the children away from the house for the morning.

Lu has never ridden in any kind of horse-vehicle, and is both excited and apprehensive. Unused to the motion, she grips the side and tailboards. Bar, who is wearing a black flared skirt and top which makes her look older, perches easily, without needing to hold on. Duke stands up like a Roman charioteer, his long, curling black hair blowing heroically. Lu wishes she did not feel so apprehensive; by the looks of Bar and Duke, there is a lot of pleasure to be had from a ride in an open cart. 'Don't you want to know where we are going?' Gabriel asks.

Bar says, 'Duke said he was going after conies.'

'Well, Duke is a businessman, he's got a living to make, but we shan't be cony-trapping.'

'I don't care where we are going, I just like being in a cart. And I expect Louise don't like to ask, do you?'

Lu suggests, 'To the village?'

'No,' Gabriel says, pleased at being out in the warm air with nothing but the prospect of a small pleasure in mind, 'further than the village, but not very.'

Lu is still a little shy of the old man, but Bar, who has known him since she was able to know anyone, since before his cataract, is not in the least shy. 'Where then?'

Duke says, 'Three miles t'other side of the village. Howton's Ford Farm.'

His sister is scornful. 'Well, of course *you* know, you been told.'

'Ah, but my driver doesn't know why we are going, Bar. You'd never guess in a month of Sundays.'

And neither would they. 'It is what is called a field-walk,' he says. 'A bit like a treasure-hunt. You might not think so at first, but just give it a try, and I'll be jiggered if you don't want to do it again.'

Duke's interest is captured. 'Gold treasure, Master?'

Lu notices that Mr Strawbridge lifts his face to the sun when he smiles or is relating something interesting. She soon discovered that Mr Strawbridge knows more about everything than any teacher she ever had. 'Did you know that Hampshire is an old, old county? Did you know it's Hampshire where we live, Bar?'

Bar nods; whether she does or not isn't important. Bar likes to listen to him telling about the really olden times.

'People have been living here, you might say, since time began; all of them building somewhere to live, growing things like we do at Roman's, really not all that much different from how we do now. They had pots and colanders, and fireplaces; not like ours, more like yours is, Bar. And wherever people live, they leave traces of themselves, even people who lived as far back as the dawn of time itself . . . '

The sound touches whatever part it is that makes Lu thrill to certain words and phrases. 'As far back as the dawn of time itself.' '*Dame anglaise.*' She would like to find a reason to use or say such words herself, but can imagine the snorts of derision if she put them in a composition at school.

It is not just the words, but the significance his expression gives them.

She has been gradually grasping the idea of space since she encountered it in the landscape; perhaps now she can get to grips with the grand scale of time, and the inhabitants of time. As in the landscape, they are not immediately visible or knowable.

As far back as the dawn of time itself. The phrase sings to her mind, and a green bud of an idea of the immensity of time swells. There were people here all that long time ago.

They had pots and colanders, they cooked and ate food. On another level of consciousness she is still listening to Mr Strawbridge's fascinating story. '. . . Of course, eventually all the crumbled houses with their broken pots get buried, and new ones are built on top. Sometimes not, sometimes people moved on to other places just like we do now, but the houses and broken pots are still there, buried deep now, and we know about some of the places . . . the land close to Howton's Farm is one place.'

Lu doesn't know whether he can see her and Bar, but as he is telling them the story, he leans towards them gesturing with his hands as though both eyes are working properly.

'Later on, there's going to be what is called "a dig" going on there. That means taking off the top layer of earth and then digging down to try to find those places where people used to live.'

'People who lived as far back as the dawn of time itself?'

He looks as pleased as though she has given the right answer to a hard question. 'Yes, Lu, there are hundreds of places like that, all over Hampshire.'

'Is that what the treasure-hunt is?' Bar asks.

'Something like that. We're going to see if we can find bits and pieces that might have worked up through the soil in these fields before the dig starts.'

Duke says, 'Main queer treasure if you asks me, Master Strawbridge.'

'If it's gold doubloons you are after, you're right, Duke lad, it's main queer.'

The cart rumbles to a stop at a field-gate, the girls and Gabriel get out. Beneath a large oak tree, where there is a pile of rucksacks and coats, two women and three men are gathered. Mr Strawbridge waves his stick in the direction of their voices. The five appear surprised but offer a flurry of jolly greetings. 'Is that Mr Strawbridge?' 'It *is* Mr Strawbridge!' 'Dear fellow, how unexpected, we haven't seen you for months.' 'Ah no . . . alas, it's these blessed eyes of mine . . . but never mind, I have brought along some young ones that are as sharp as a blackbird's.'

Lu and Bar follow Mr Strawbridge's beckoning hand as he makes his careful way into the gathering, using his stick as he does so in an attempt to discover any obstacles his goodish eye misses. Duke, with his snares in his pocket and his ferret in a bag, takes Pixie from the shafts and rides her back through the gate and into the farm-track to hunt the field edges whilst she grazes. Villagers believe that the Barneys can make money better than anybody, which may be true; for all the family, with the exception of the youngest, waste none of their waking hours idling. Even Bar, who is getting paid something for helping out Mrs Wilmott, plus anything extra laying straw and collecting slugs in the fields if Lu falls asleep in the sun.

Lu stands close to Bar as Uncle Gabriel shakes hands all round and then indicates Lu and Bar as 'temporary members of the expedition'. A gentleman with a beard says, 'Good-oh! Your eyes are probably the best of all of us. Come with me and I will show you some of the pieces we hope to discover.'

He squats down and opens a cardboard box which contains a mixture of pieces that look to Lu like a ha'porth of broken mixed biscuits. 'These are pieces of broken pots and jars. Pick up a few, hold them, feel them. Do you think you could spot pieces like this in the field?' Lu and Bar, dipping into the box, look at one another. Bar says, 'I should think we could. I found a sixpence in some long grass once.'

The shards are mostly of a nondescript brownish red clay, but a few are a gritty white, some blackened, some holed like a sieve and others crimped at the edges. There are small and large handles, and several discs which were once the bases of vessels that are not much different from a present-day broken jug except that these have no glaze.

Lu stares at the pieces in her hand. The man picks out one. 'This,' he holds it up between finger and thumb, 'before it became broken, was part of a strainer, you know, like your mother uses to strain vegetables.'

'A colander?' Lu says.

'Right!' His beard opens and he smiles, all red lips and white shining teeth. 'Who knows, maybe thousands of years ago, some young girl just like you two was helping Mother with the dinner when she dropped it.' He pulls a face. 'Or maybe it was old and cracked, so when the family decided it was time to move, they left it behind with all their other rubbish.' He looks up into their absorbed faces. 'Would you like to help look for some?'

Bar says, 'Mr Strawbridge said it was treasure.'

The man raises his eyebrows. 'More precious than mere ordinary treasure, these were once things that people like you and me made and used every day. They have stories, like the girl straining the cabbage and dropping the colander. Sometimes we can find pieces that fit together and make a jug perhaps. You should get Mr Strawbridge to tell you about some of the things we have in the museum.'

Lu says, 'We got a museum back home.'

'Where's that?'

'Portsmouth.'

'Oh well, you've jars and pots in your museum that have been found unbroken. That's because you have mud and sea there. When things fall into mud, they often don't break, so that if a fisherman hooks one, it comes up whole.'

'Things from the dawn of time?'

He smiles warmly. 'Could well be.'

Lu lets out the common backstreet expression of wonder, 'Waah.'

In the sectioned field, the bearded professional, the five amateur archaeologists, and the children, Gabriel between the two, go line abreast each in their allotted section. They walk upright, step by step, heads bowed, each carrying a little cloth bag, eyes intent upon every stone and piece of chalk in case it is a remnant of a life once lived close by Howton's Ford. Although the bedrock here is chalk, it is not known to give up fossils, ammonites and the like, but it is well known that earthworms and ploughing bring to the surface every year plenty of evidence of former inhabitants. The present-day Howtons are reputed to be possessors of a large collection, even the kind of treasure that Duke would have appreciated.

The field-walkers do not walk fast, so Gabriel is not outpaced; perhaps he sees nothing more than his own feet appearing and disappearing with each step, but his face shows his pleasure and satisfaction at taking part in a field-walk, something he expected never to do again.

The first find is signalled by one of the women. It is noted and put into a haversack; after this, finds come thick and fast, and once they have 'got their eye in' as the archaeologist says, Lu and Bar's sharp eyes find no difficulty in doing nearly as well as the experienced adults. Each time, Mr Strawbridge says, 'Well done, well done,' and fingers the piece, peering at it through his powerful magnifying-glass.

Lu is spellbound, her imagination working overtime. After the first sweep, there is a pause whilst somebody hands round a bag of boiled sweets, and Lu, reluctant to take her eyes from the ground six inches in front of her toes, pokes a knob of earth which crumbles and reveals a white stone. It is not a shard, she knows that, but it is smooth and white. Like her own lucky pebble which she brought back from Southsea beach, this stone is pleasant to hold in the hand, to fondle and stroke and, like the lucky pebble, it has a hole the size of her little finger.

Bar says, 'Let's see,' and pretends that it is a magnifying glass, looking through the hole at her fingers. As she is returning it to Lu, the woman with the sweets says, 'Martin, I say, look what the girl has turned up.'

'May I?' He holds his hand out for Lu's stone, rubs off soil with his thumb and says, 'Well done, the girl with the chestnut curls.'

Lu and Bar watch intently as Lu's stone is passed around. When it reaches Mr Strawbridge he inspects it closely. 'I'll tell you what you have found, Louise, you have found a loom-weight. Whoever made this could have found the stone in the stream we call Howton's Ford now, or he or she could have brought it with them when they settled here. Feel the hole.' Lu and Bar each feel in the way that he had done. 'A person made that. They picked it up and said, "That's just what I'm looking for."'

The man, Martin, asks, 'D'you know what a loom is?'

Neither of the girls does, so another absorbing bit of information comes their way, illustrated by looking closely at the weave of Mr Strawbridge's tweed coat. To the other field-walkers, Martin says, 'As far as I know this is the only example in this sector . . . of course, Howton may be hoarding others . . . but who knows what Howton may be hoarding?' They agree by their expressions that they are helpless to know the answer to that. He says to Lu, 'I'm afraid I shall have to take it.'

'Oh, that's all right,' Lu says, 'I've still got my Southsea pebble on the mantelpiece.'

'Tell you what', Martin says, 'sometime, when the dig is over, there is bound to be an exhibition, and a loom-weight would almost certainly be displayed. It may not be for a year or so, but I will see to it that you get to know. What is your other name?' He pops it into a bag and writes a label. 'See?' He shows her what he has written. 'LOOM-WEIGHT. LOUISE WILMOTT, HOWTON'S FORD, FIELD-WALK, APR. '29.'

On the jog back to Roman's Fields, Gabriel Strawbridge feels gratified at the girls' response to the outing. What is it the Jesuits say? 'Give us a child and it's ours for life'? It would be very gratifying to take Louise and give the world another woman like May, at one with herself and the world. Not young Bar Barney, she was already there. She was growing up, knowing a kind of freedom that enabled her to be herself, that is given to very few girls. 'Louise, have you ever given thought to keeping a journal?'

Lu looks at Bar, hoping to discover whether this might be a pet or something else. It is obvious that Bar doesn't know. 'I don't know . . . what is it?'

'It is a kind of diary, a book in which a person writes down, perhaps each day, or week, the happenings of the day, or week.'

Bar says enthusiastically, 'Like today she could write she found a white stone with a hole and it was a loom-weight.'

'Yes, and more than that. A daybook is a private thing in which the keeper may write their thoughts. For instance, Louise might write down what her feelings are about finding something that is so very old . . . and about Martin and the others and the things they found . . . in fact, anything at all. Perhaps even recording your dreams, and things that you dream of doing when you grow up, or promises you make yourself.'

'Like New Year resolutions?' Lu suggests.

'Like that and anything else that comes to mind to put down. I have kept a journal since I was your age. I call it my daybook,' he laughs, 'though it's not just one book; over the years I have filled a good many.'

Bar, never shy, asks, 'What did you put down first go?'

'I remember word-for-word, I've read it many times. "Went to Wickham Fair. Rode on merry-go-round. Watched the gypsies trading horses. Won coconut, had cloves and humbugs, spent sixpence. Saw a fair fight. It was a very merry occasion."' He turns in Duke's direction. 'Much the same today, eh, Duke?'

'No fair fights, Master Strawbridge, only dirty ones outside the pubs. I knocked off three coconuts last year . . . one was dry, I took him back, they didn't want to swap it, but I made them.'

'I won't ask how, Duke.'

'You can ask. I promised to upend their crate of wooden balls. And I would've.'

Turning back to the girls, Gabriel Strawbridge says, 'If it takes your fancy to do so, I dare say I could find a couple of notebooks and a few pencils.'

Bar says, 'It wouldn't be no good me taking it home, our little'ns would only just tear it up, they tears up everything. You could keep it for me, couldn't you?'

'All right. How about Lu?'

'I'd like to write it all down, then I shan't forget anything, and I could give it to Mum and Ray and they could read everything I done in the country.' Her eyes are bright with anticipation.

Back at Roman's Fields, Lu runs ahead of Mr Strawbridge and Bar. As she reaches the house, the smell of frying bacon greets her, and for the first time in many weeks, her mouth is awash at the anticipation of eating. She feels marvellously hungry. She races into the house, breathless with eagerness to tell Aunty May everything, then, as she reaches the kitchen door, is stopped in her tracks.

'Ray!' she flings herself at him. 'Oh Ray, Ray, you said if you came it would be on a Sunday. I never expected you.'

Ralph pressed his face against hers, rubbing her with his bristly chin as he sometimes did when he came home from work. 'Well now, and who is this bold miss flinging herself at me? I'm sorry, but I been spoken for. Only last week my sister said as how she would a liked to marry me.' Picking her up under her arms, he swings her round. 'Lord love me, Lu, whatever's Aunty May been feeding you, you're a ton weight.'

Bar, one foot tucked behind the other knee, stands by the dresser watching the animated Lu hugging her brother, ruffling his hair and laughing. Bar laps up every detail of him. She has heard enough about Ray, but had expected that he would resemble Lu, but he does not. His eyes are bright blue like chicory flowers, his teeth are nice, one of the front ones just crosses the other, but that seems to make him even better looking, and although he has shaved close, you can see where his beard grew.

She imagines him with a dark curly beard, like the one her father wears: he would look lovely. His dark hair is all little waves like Mr Wilmott's, but it is short and shines and, where Lu has ruffled it, a wavy lock hangs over his forehead. She can smell the lemony smell of his hair-oil. He has on a proper suit, blue with a fine stripe, the jacket is hanging behind the door, his white shirt hasn't got a crease in it, he has red armbands which hold up his sleeves which are puffed up above the elbow, most impressive are his stiff white shiny collar and red tie. Bar would love to know him well enough to jump into his arms as Lu did. Yet when Lu says, 'Look, Ray, this is Bar, we're best friends,' Bar can only say, 'Hello.' He shakes her hand and beams his lovely smile at her. Ray . . . the sound of his name has changed now that she has seen who Ray is. Bar had imagined he would be as uninteresting as Duke. He isn't; he is the loveliest man she has ever seen.

May, standing at the range turning bacon, watches the scene between brother and sister with pleasure, for she has never seen Lu in such an exuberant mood, or so rosy-cheeked. And look at Bar, she's blushing . . . she's growing up and I've hardly noticed, thought May. She says, 'Looks as though somebody had a good morning,' and as they all sit round eating bacon and eggs, Lu launches into a report on the expedition to Howton's Ford. Ted says that she seems to have lost her appetite and found a lion's. Gabriel praises Lu and Bar and says what grand helpers they've been, and how well the field-walkers' group thought of them.

* * *

They went out into the garden to have a cup of tea, and Lu dropped off to sleep. Ray said, 'Is she all right?'

'She's fine. She takes a lot of cat-naps, which is good for her. That way she don't out-run her strength.'

Ray said, 'I think she wants to stop on. I'm glad, and I'm grateful to you and Ted. I can't believe how quick she's picking up. I think I'll tell her about Mum, not that I know what to say – she's sure to ask what's up with her.'

'I'll tell her later on if you like. She's not a little girl any more, she's coming twelve. Girls that age are a lot more knowledgeable than people give them credit for. I never liked people to keep me out of what was going on in the family, it don't matter what you're told after, you can't forget that there were things going on and you were treated as though your feelings weren't important.'

Ralph said, 'I never thought of it that way. If she asks, I'd be grateful if you'd tell her.'

When Lu awoke, her extended stay was settled. 'If you can manage without me, I would like to see what it's like in summer. I can't hardly tell you how nice everything is. And now me and Bar are going to start writing books about it. It's going to be Wickham Fair in May . . . do you think I could stop on that long?'

They spent the next few hours looking at the strawberries already forming, and the piles of sticks being delivered for the stick beans, and the goat, and the bees and Cowslip. Bar went everywhere with them, her impishness and giggling and her usual chattering stilled, her eyes darting away from Ray every time there was a danger of him catching her watching him.

'If they'll have you, seems a shame not to use that nice room now that she's put all the work into it. Tell you what, I'll leave half a crown with Aunty May for you to go to the fair, then you and Barbara will have enough to ride the dodgems.' He smiled at Bar but had no idea that it was the smile that would set the seal on her ideal of masculine desirability.

She felt almost as though she was trancing into a spinning spell. In future, the elation which she summoned while dervishing, she would not see in her mind's eye as an amorphous white light, but it would have form: male, potent and white-collared. Her first entry in the journal Gabriel Strawbridge started her on read, 'I was going to write about Lu's brother coming to see her. Only when I thought what to say about it, I didn't want to. Writing it would only spoil the pictures in my head and the feelings. But I like to write his name which is Ralph Wilmott.'

When Ralph reached Portsmouth that night, he celebrated his good mood, his nice Wilmott relations, with a night on the town with Chick and the boys.

April melded into May, the good weather held up and improved, drawing out June butterflies – the meadow browns and small heaths – ahead of time to join the flittery, black-dotted garden whites. Woodland trees – plane, beech and oak – flowered profusely, with tiny fluffy tassels that floured the air with pollen, and from the miles and miles of hedgerows, a delicious scent of vanilla drifted from the may-blossom.

Bar had to go to school, but she still came in before and after school and at weekends. She stopped going to Mrs Catermole's; her dad said she didn't have to put up with anybody, least of all vicars and high-hat old faggots. They wrote their daybooks. Bar's was more sparsely entered than Lu's because nothing happened at school, but Lu's filled because there was so much going on. She described her first attempt at milking Cowslip; her fear at watching bees swarming; the size of the yellow slugs that invaded the garden at night; collecting eggs from the hen-house; and, matter-of-factly, the strange courting and coupling of the one cock and several hens. And she wrote in great detail about Bar taking her to see where she lived. This account took her most of one showery afternoon.

'Do you want to come over our place?'

'Is it all right?'

'Ma says why don't you come?'

It was easy to see that when Ann Carter and Eli Barney had set up together, their two cultures had either clashed or collided, for they lived in a kind of encampment surrounding a very cottagey-looking 'house' made from a reconstructed stone stable. In good weather, all their food was prepared over a brick-built open-air fire.

Ann Carter must certainly have shocked the village when she took up with a gypsy for, if there is such a thing as an average young village woman, then – except that she wore a heavy gold ring threaded through one ear – she was it. She was short-haired, pixie-faced, heavily bosomed, broad-footed, and she wore a cotton dress with a cardigan and a cross-over flowery overall. Her arms were deep in a tub of soapy water when Bar led Lu in through a gap in the hedge. When she turned to greet them, Lu saw that she was expecting, and was surprised that Bar hadn't even mentioned it. 'Well then . . . so you're the visitor. We heard a lot about you . . . sit on that stool if you like. Bar, fetch the tea-caddy and some sugar. I dare say Lu could do with a cup, couldn't you, love?'

'Ma will tell your future, won't you, Ma?'

'Don't you be so pushy, miss. It's not everybody wants their future.'

'I do, Mrs Barney. My mum had her teacup told once, and it was all true she said . . . There was a sailor in the bottom, and that's who she married.'

'Well, there you are then. Do you want to marry a sailor?'

Lu shook her head.

'What then?'

'I don't know yet. Somebody important. Somebody they'll say, "Look, that's her."'

'Rich then?'

'I suppose you have to if you're going to be important.'

'I'll have a look at your cup when you've finished. You don't have to call me Mrs Barney, I'm Ann.' She smiled and nodded in a general direction. 'Their name's Barney, mine isn't. I'm still the same Ann Carter I always was, always will be. Nobody tell you that?'

Lu shook her head.

'That's because you haven't been down the village yet.'

Although her scandalous act had taken place seventeen years ago, and the Carter family's shame had become mere occasional embarrassment, Ann was convinced that she was still the hottest subject of village gossip, when in fact these days it only caused comment when she went there with Eli, or when the gypsy clans spent their three days trading at the time of Wickham Fair. What still lingered was not that she had taken up with a gypsy, nor that she had never married in church; what lingered was indignation that they had not taken themselves off to another country, and that they kept breeding children who were expected to be taught alongside proper folks' children in a church school.

There were two other children: Ephraim, who Lu had already seen riding double with Duke, and a baby, Harry, Ann had named for her father, who wasn't as pleased as he might have been. Harry, all eyes and with dark curls down to his ears, was a two-year-old replica of Duke.

'This one's another boy,' Bar said, patting her mother's mound.

The stone walls of the old stable gave the Barney family's house a grim look, but Lu thought the inside was very cosy. There wasn't much furniture, but then neither was there in Lampeter Street. Mattresses were rolled up and put back against the walls, seats by day, beds by night.

It seemed to Lu to be a really easy way to live. There were only two cooking pots, one for stewing and one for hot water. The whitewashed walls were full of ledges and cubby-holes from the days of the horses; on every ledge was a marvellous display of china ornaments, cups, jugs, and plates in rows. There were pretty things everywhere.

Ann Carter picked up a teapot covered in gold and flowers and dusted it gently with her overall. 'You like my things, Lu?'

'They're beautiful, I've never seen so many plates.'

'Aren't they? No two the same. They're all antiques, mostly rare.'

'That means old.'

'Old and priceless.'

'That's why we have to drink out of mugs,' Bar said.

'Ah yes . . . what about that tea then?'

Mr Barney was out with Duke. 'Coppicing,' Ann explained. 'Getting bean-sticks for Strawbridges next door,' and the two young children were playing with a box on home-made wooden wheels. 'Just us women then,' she said as they sat at a wooden table on heavy stools, drinking tea stewed over the fire. It was the strongest, hottest tea Lu had ever drunk, black and clear. At first drinking it in little sips, she gradually began to like its strange taste of smoke.

'When you finished, Mum will tell your future . . . oh, go on, Mum, please.'

'I'll tell your hand if you like.'

'Can you do that?'

'In the lines, Ma tells the lines,' Bar said. 'She won't tell mine. She looked at it once but she wouldn't say. I expect I'm going to die, that's why.' She peered at her own left hand, running her fingernail down the crease that ran around her thumb.

'Don't talk silly, Bar. I just looked to see how many grandchildren you are going to give me; the rest can be a surprise.' She picked up Lu's hand and ran her own palm over Lu's, as though brushing away dust. 'If you're one of those who don't believe, or are scared to know, then I won't do it.'

'Oh, please. I want to learn about things they don't teach you in school.'

'What things is that?'

'Different things . . . like I learnt since I been here.'

Bar giggles. 'Like that strawberries don't grow on trees and bushes.'

'That was because I just never thought about it before . . . Like how to aim right when you pull to get the milk in the pail, and the sort of things Mr Strawbridge told us when I found that old stone. And I'd like to know about telling lines.'

'There are people who think it's wrong to read hands, so I say that's all right, nobody's going to make them. Look, this one's your life-line, it's a real good strong one, only there's a little crack right here at the beginning . . . see? That's over and done with. It was your diphtheria, and now it goes on very strong. You'll live to be a hundred. Well now, this here's interesting . . . see this one's your heart-line.' She looked up and into Lu's eyes, peering right into them as though she was looking through a keyhole, then back at the hand. 'How old are you?'

'I'll be twelve next month.'

'Ah, that's a good month. I'm a September, too, and here's another.' She patted the unborn baby.

'No, my birthday's in June.'

Bar said, 'Ma means you was got in September. Your dad must have got you on your mum in September, so you could be born in June. They planted me in March, so I had to come out a her when it was cold winter, din't I, Ma?'

Her mother smiled and tucked a stray lock of hair behind Bar's ear. 'March was good enough for the Holy Virgin, and December was good enough for the Christ child, wasn't it? And I was so glad you was a girl I kept you cosy as a duckling, you never knew you was born. I carried you about next to my heart till it was spring. So no complaints. Now shut up and let's look at this interesting line here.'

Mrs Barney wasn't like any mother Lu had ever known. She talked to them as though they were grown up.

'It don't look to me that you will be thinking of getting wed. Not that there isn't men in your life, my dear Lord no . . . there's a deal of loving here, but remember love isn't always a primrose path, real love . . . I mean *real, real* love can go hand in hand with hurt. A long life and a lot of men to love you, that isn't bad for a start, is it?'

'What about babies?' Bar asked. 'Look, fold your hand over.'

'Get off, Bar. Who's doing this, me or you?'

'Well, you wanted to look at my babies lines.'

'Have you got your flowers yet?'

Lu had never heard the word. 'I don't think so.'

'Your monthlies.'

That was not a question Lu ever expected to be asked. Last year, those girls in their eleventh year had been given one talk by a visiting school nurse; it had sounded like a warning. The rest, the truths, half-truths and inventions had been learned in the playground. 'Oh,' she said, 'that. The Curse. No, I haven't.'

'Well, I reckon you soon will. Before you do, you just get that word out of your head. It's not a curse. To my mind it's more a thing to feel pleased about. It's us women in our prime gets it. It's what makes us women, makes us special; nobody else gets it, only us. There was a time when women were made into goddesses because of its mystery, so don't never mind it, and if you don't mind it you won't ever get any aches and pains.' She gave Lu's hand a brief squeeze. 'Bein' a woman is just fine. Anyhow, enough of that . . . let's get this done. You have a lot of men here, but your babies won't show up until you start getting your flowers. And see this here?' She prodded the cushion at the base of Lu's thumb and smiled with satisfaction. 'It's Venus's Mount and, according to how plump it is, that's how much you can enjoy being loved. It's something you have to wait for. It's a good thing to have a high Venus's Mount.' She slapped Lu's hand playfully. 'Now off you go, or May will want to know what you've been up to all this time.'

The weather has changed, there are squalls and high winds. Ted is glad that he wasn't tempted by the early spring to get his runner beans in ahead of time. May's strawberries need rain, but she frowns at the winds gusting across the fields. Bar comes and goes. Lu tries her hand at baking bread; the mysteries of the action of sugar on yeast, the balloon of dough, falling and rising again, never fail in their interest. Ted gives her a handful of rape to grow on a piece of towel, and in days he has taken her first crop for sandwiches. The pale ghost who left Lampeter Street a few weeks back has come to life. And, as spindly winter twigs will burst into pink blossom in the spring sunshine, so Lu, nourished and away from the smoking chimneys of a score of staymaking factories, has recovered her vitality. Her hair shines and bounces, her complexion is clear and her eyes bright. She now seems to be much taller than Bar, and she looks very pretty. She seldom falls asleep in the day, but is up and brimming with ideas of what she will do today.

The great event in the month of May was Wickham Fair.

Once the police had pulled barriers across the main road through the village, the fair sprang up in hours. May and Ted Wilmott, like most villagers, gave themselves a half-day holiday and let themselves go. Lu, having been given fair-shillings by Ted and Mr Strawbridge, had a pocketful of money. She was allowed to go with Bar and be free to do as she pleased.

The transformation of the quiet village was spectacular. Overnight it was made into a place of thrills, flashing lights, wind-organ music, proud horses with flaring nostrils prancing up and down and round and round on brass poles, sparking dodgems, and swinging-boats. Licensing hours were abandoned, the school closed, and shops and houses around the square became hidden behind stalls that glittered and twinkled with prizes, booths that offered contests, and structures which offered rides that rocked, whirled, rose up, plunged and rotated. There were skills to be tested and male muscle-power to be measured, there were things to do, to see, to eat, to drink, to win and to buy.

For a couple of hours in the first morning, village children were given free rides on anything moving, so that even quite early in the day there was noise and excitement. Bar knew the ropes and pulled Lu here and there, on and off rides and then all over again. She wore the same black clothes she had worn at the field-walk. When she was out of her shapeless work dress, it was easier to believe that she was the dervishing girl.

At one end of the square, the roadway is taken over by gypsy horse-traders. Bar says, 'Come on, let's go and have a look, see if Duke's bought Pixie.'

Although many of the sideshows and stalls are owned by gypsies, it is the men with their horses and the women who look on in a laughing, chattering group that look the part. Most of the older women wear dark skirts that reach below the calf, some have woollen shawls. The men all wear felt hats or caps pushed to the back of their head. Lu and Bar stand on their own watching as the men take their horses back and forth along a stretch of the road at a fast trot. The horses wear no tackle except a bit and a short length of rope, as they run they prance and flick their heads, the men call, 'Hip–hip. C'me on then . . . Yip!' The women take no notice.

Lu sees Bar's father with Pixie. Although she has seen him coming and going many times back at Roman's Fields, he has never said more than, 'You all right, girl?' and Lu has never replied other than, 'Yes, thank you.' Several times he has made her wonder about her own father, and what it will be like when he comes home again. Duke looks a lot like Mr Barney, thin and brown-skinned, long, dark curly hair, wide-spaced teeth, always busy loading or unloading something. But Duke is not straight-faced and silent, though; Duke makes sure people see him, standing up to drive a cart, cracking a whip on the air when riding a horse, he whistles at dogs, and whenever there is a bit of silence in the open air, he calls out something to break it up. Today his chin is clean-shaven, but he has the beginnings of a moustache growing; he wears black trousers with braces and a collarless striped flannel shirt with several of the top buttons undone. The two girls watch him, tossing and spinning a golden sovereign over and over again, showing off in front of some girls.

'Is your dad really going to sell Pixie?'

'I expect so.'

'Won't Duke mind?'

She shakes her head. 'He'll buy her.'

'That don't make sense. Why don't your dad sell her direct to Duke without showing her to other people? Somebody else might buy her.'

'If Duke wants her, then he'll have to go the price she gets to. They both got a good idea what she'll fetch.'

'What if somebody else will pay higher?'

'Then Duke'll pay a bit more. He won't let her go. He's already got a stallion in mind for her. It will be Duke's first foal . . . Lord, won't he just show off then?'

'Has he got a lot of money then?'

'To buy horses, yes. He'll get Pixie, he'll pay whatever price she runs up to. None of my dad's people will bid her up above what she's worth, so Dad and Duke both get a fair deal don't they? There isn't no reason why Dad should let her go for less just because it's Duke, and Duke wouldn't want no favours.'

They drift away, buy bags of chips and sit on a doorstep eating them. They watch as May drives Ted in a dodgem car, May leaning forward eagerly to see who she can crash into next, Ted being jolted around laughing, and paying again and again because May loves the dodgems so. Lu tries twice to win a coconut; she is about to try again when, without a word, Duke gives her back her money, pays for the balls, has three misses and one coconut. When Bar asks him to get her one, he says, 'Go on, you got muscles of your own.' For a while he continues going with them from stall to stall. He makes the bell ring on the 'Try Your Strength', and gets a 'Strong and Handsome' on the 'Tell Your Character' grip. He shoots a bullseye with a rifle and gets a little china pig which he says he'll take home for his mum.

Bar said, 'She won't want that old thing against all her nice things.'

'You want to bet? She'll want it because I won it for her.' Which Lu suspects will be true because, although she doesn't even know if she likes coconut, it felt like a real prize when he pushed it into her hands. Before he goes to take Pixie back home, he tries the darts and wins a black kewpie-doll with a feathered skirt which he tosses to Bar with a lofty air.

Lu's opinion of Duke is that he is really nice when you get to know him.

'That's because you're pretty.'

'Don't be daft.'

'You are, you're ever so pretty. He's always hanging around pretty girls. What do you think he got you that coconut for?'

'Because I couldn't even get a ball near.'

'No, it wasn't . . . he wanted to show himself off to you. He likes you, I know he thinks you're pretty.'

'How?'

'I won him at arm-wrestling and we had a truth or dare on it. I made him tell truth what he thought of you.'

'Well . . . what?'

'I'll tell you if you tell truth what you think about him.'

'I just said, he's nice.'

'Tell truth, go on.'

'He's good-looking . . . I like his hair.'

'It's like a girl's!'

'I know, and I like it tied back like he's got it today.'

'Shall I tell him?'

'No! Don't you dare!'

'I won't . . . don't you worry, he's swelled-headed enough already. He'll dip his whole head in his hair-oil if he thinks you like it. You could be his girlfriend.'

'Don't be daft! I'm not old enough for him.'

'My ma was twelve and my pa was twenty when he first come to Wickham . . . *that* was Fair Day, too.'

'Anyway, I don't want a boyfriend. Go on, I told truth, what did he say?'

'He said he liked your hair, and one day he would get himself a thoroughbred Arab stud horse the same colour, and he would put you up front and gallop you up over Corhampton Downs.'

'Did he say all that?'

'Honest. And he said he'd give me a Chinese burn if I ever told.'

Lu's impending womanhood arm-wrestles her receding girlhood and the woman wins. Had it not been for the devastation done temporarily to the woman in her, she might have noticed Duke weeks ago. She tightens the waist-tie of her dress, drawing it in so that it shows that there had been young breasts there all the time, as yet only

134

budding but there, swamped by the loose bodice Aunt Elsie had made with allowance for growing.

It was late in the evening when the girls walked up the long lane with Ted and May, Lu chattering and giggling as much as Bar. Ted said, 'You done a good job, May, she's a different child. What do you reckon about her stopping on till the end of the school holidays?'

'You saw what Ray said in his letter. If Lu's happy, then Vera will be only too glad. That job always takes some getting over. She's going to be laid up for weeks yet.'

'Do you reckon they'd be covered for the hospital?'

'I was only talking to Pa about that yesterday. Ray said they paid in a Doctor's Club, but I don't know about hospital.'

'If it was his wife, then I dare say the union would cover the whole family, but I doubt if they stretch to mothers.'

'Hardly seems fair, Ted. I mean, like Pa said, we could help out, but it's a touchy thing offering your actual money.'

'Well, think about it. There might be a way. It's a real bugger an't it, not being able to afford to be ill and worrying your guts out over doctors' fees.'

'I wish I could believe my pa was right about there being a government sickness insurance for everybody before long.'

'And I wish I could believe in Father Christmas.'

'It don't seem such a difficult thing, and it's only what the unions are already doing, and the Doctor's Clubs . . . everybody paying in a few pence a week to one big insurance scheme, and you don't have to worry about how to pay the bill if you have to have an operation.

'Perhaps Ray might feel better if it was a loan. I sent Vera a couple of night-gowns from Joycey's, but you don't want to look as though you're being patronizing. I mean, Vera's had a terrible hard enough life as it is.'

'Well, we done one good job, May. She's a grand girl, we're going to miss her.'

'Oh, Ted, don't go and put the damper on things after we had such a good day out.'

Walking ahead of Ted and May, Lu told Bar it had been the best day she had ever had. 'I spent all my money. But I still got Duke's coconut.'

'And the slab of toffee in a tin from your uncle.'

'And it's got its own hammer to break it. If it hadn't been for all the free rides this morning, I wouldn't have had enough to buy all the presents.' Lu had had money to burn, to lavish on presents. It was a heady feeling pondering, choosing, discussing with Bar what to buy. Loving every moment of the spend up, she was carrying home a painted paper sunshade for her mum, a knot of white heather on a ribbon for over the Roman's Fields door, a lucky black cat for Ray's pocket and a whistling bird for Ken. She and Bar bought each other threepenny rings, each with the appropriate birthstone. Her best bargain was a heavy wooden pencil into which was burned, 'A present from . . . ' The pencil, intended for Mr Strawbridge, was a penny, and for a ha'penny the name of the place could be added, but Lu didn't want the pencil to be a present from Wickham, so she paid the ha'penny for 'Louise' to be burned into the space.

About Lu's flowers coming soon, Ann Carter was right. It was hardly anything really. She told May, who was very matter-of-fact about it.

'Of course, it's a private thing, women talk to each other sometimes when they're on their own, Lord knows there's times when we need to talk to one another, but it's not the kind of thing men like to know about, goodness knows why, it's only nature at work. Thank the Lord, we don't belong to any of the religions where they put you out of the house once a month. I will write a note to your mum later on. She'll want to know.'

Lu is surprised to receive a letter and small booklet of pictures and verses, entitled, 'Thoughts, by a Mother'.

'Lu, my dear, If I had been up and about I would have just sent you an ordinary card, but I had to get Dotty to choose it, and she got carried away in the Christian bookshop, but she's proved to be the best neighbour you could hope for. She thought it was wonderful and sat here reading the verses aloud. The words are very sentimental but what they say is that the recipient is a daughter loved by her mother from the minute she was born.

'I have been thinking about you a lot whilst I've been laid up in bed, and you couldn't be in better hands than May's. Hector and Ray say that you are back to your old self, and you are grown quite a lot. May says she hopes that you will stay on till the end of the school holidays, and that you can visit them any time you like. That says to me that you must have got pretty good marks for good behaviour.

'My twelfth birthday, I seem to remember as being a milestone. It was the one that was the bridge that went from girl to young woman, and of course that is what you now are. I should like you to have something nice on your birthday, so Ray has given Hector five shillings to pass on to May, and I have asked her to get you a new dress from a shop. I have also sent you the only thing left over from when I was a different woman from the one you have always known. It is the cross and chain given to me by my mother on the day I was confirmed. It is gold. Disregard the bad verse, my dear Lu; my words are simpler but more sincere: I love you and am proud of you. Vera Wilmott – June 1929.'

Bedtimes now are later. Ted's bedtime reading has stopped and it is now Lu who reads aloud whilst they all sit outside the back door, May shucking peas or scraping carrots, Ted and Mr Strawbridge smoking pipes, puffing out clouds of smoke to keep the midges away. On Fridays she reads to Mr Strawbridge. Aunty May puts pencil rings round the columns that will interest him most, and although the *Hampshire Chronicle* looks dreadfully dull with its dense, unrelieved print, the items always turn out to be interesting. A court case where somebody is sent to gaol will start Mr Strawbridge off about prisons, asking Lu if she thinks it is a good idea to have prisons and which people should be sent to them. Lu, of course, has never given any thought to such matters. Prison is for criminals.

But he makes her think. Is it as simple as that? He never talks down, although he often punctuates what he has to say with, 'D'you understand what I'm getting at, Louise?' In his quiet voice in his quiet, book-filled room, he is gradually getting her to question every established notion. 'No law is carved in stone so that it can't be changed. Ask yourself why things are the way they are, and then ask yourself if there's a better way of going on.'

Gradually she begins to question him back. 'All right, then, what would you do if a thief stole something from you? Why shouldn't he get sent to prison?' and he throws a question back. 'Why do people steal? Will prison stop them? If it works, then why are there still thieves about?'

And Lu is left with big questions.

Why are some people more important than others? Why are some people rich and some very poor? How did they get rich? How did the land become theirs? What are soldiers for?

May, listening, sometimes says, 'Father, you'll have the poor girl's brains addled.'

'Are yours addled? I am only asking her the same questions I asked you.'

And May says to Lu, 'Questions, questions. My father's been asking questions for sixty years.'

'Oh, longer than that . . . ah, yes . . . '

May tells Lu about Gabriel's quest to find the truth behind the newspaper reporting of the Boer War. 'He couldn't get a straight answer, so he got on a boat and worked his passage to South Africa to see if he could find out for himself.'

'And did you find out?'

'I did. It was how I discovered that in newspapers there are half-truths, lies, deceptions, falsehoods, whitewashes and treachery. Which means that if we take things for granted and don't ask questions, we shall never know the truth of anything.'

With June came settled sunny weather; suddenly the fields were flowing with strawberries. From the moment the dew has dried until dark, Uncle Ted and his two casuals, plus Eli Barney and some of the village women, squat over the rows and pluck ripe 'Sovereigns' to fill the hundreds of punnets, woven in winter by the Barneys from thin wood strips. Lu, and Bar when she is not at school, lay supplies of empty punnets along the rows, the filled ones being packed in crates by Aunty May and Mrs Barney.

Lu, who had rarely eaten strawberries until now, could never tire of the sight of the exciting profusion of fruit with its bright red skin, and juicy flesh surprisingly white within such glossy scarlet.

When the day is over, Lu eats ravenously anything that comes her way, and drinks plenty of the Jersey cow's yellow milk. Her skinny arms are gone, along with the bruised, hollow eye-sockets; her long legs are becoming shapely and firm, and people in the village who saw her during the first weeks at Roman's tell her, 'Look at her, she's a different girl.' She can see it for herself in the long mirror on Aunty May's wardrobe. The waistband of the skirt Aunty Elsie made has had to be let out, and Aunty May has bought her, from Joycey at Clark's, two new cotton tops, some strong leather sandals like her own, and some new knickers.

Uncle Hec takes messages back and forth between Lampeter Street and Roman's Fields, a cheery report on Vera's health for Lu, and a more realistic one for May. 'I don't like to say this, but like my Else says, she's seen other women go the same way. She can't see Vere making old bones. They let her go home, but she's not the same woman . . . but there, Vere hasn't been the same woman for years, humped up in that chair trying to get her dozens done for the factory. Outwork like that's the ruin of many a woman, but there, what can they do if they'm married to a man like our Arthur? I know he's my brother and your Ted's, but, speak as you find, he never had no responsibility to his family. He shouldn't never a got married, we've said that many a time, he never *had* to marry her, it was as though he couldn't a-bear leaving her for some other chap to have. And of course, you know Arthur, he always was a ladies' man . . . oh yes, I'll say. But Vere Presley was a cut above the rest. The Presleys was quite a posh family compared to ours – a course they're all gone now. Like I said to Else, if our Arthur's a rotten husband when he's at sea, he don't improve ashore.'

May frets about what Lu will find when she goes home. The best that she can do for Lu is to continue making her as healthy and resilient as is in her power to do. She also determines to give her a small amount of savings in the Post Office for when she returns. She says that Lu must be paid something for working out in the fields, to keep for when she goes home.

Midsummer Day, the day of Lu's birthday. Some of her experiences of this day would be trapped in her memory like flies in amber.

Bar was no longer needed to see that Lu made a good breakfast, and since Lu's recovery was complete, she continued to come in before leaving for school and the two girls would sit and eat together. Although when she came today it was still very early, the kitchen at Roman's Fields was busy with preparations before starting another day of strawberry picking, Ted pulling on his field boots, Gabriel

Strawbridge eating a dish of porridge, May, packing a rush bag with cheese and chunks of bread said, 'Morning, Bar, you're early. You look nice . . . been making up remnants again?' Bar wore a black sleeveless dress with a gathered skirt, much like the one she had worn for the fair, except that it had rows of brown ricrac sewn around the hem.

'Good Midsummer, Mis Wilmott.'

'Oh . . . I'd forgot . . . Good Midsummer to you too, Bar.'

'It's your birthday, in't it, Lu? I got you these.' The sheaf of flower spikes in a jar of water gave off a fragrance that filled the kitchen.

Ted said, 'Wild orchids, that's nice, you must have gone a long way off to find the "butterflies". I haven't seen one of that kind around here in years.'

Lu, having often listened to Bar on the subject of wildflowers, guessed that these were special. 'Thanks, they've got a lovely smell.'

'It's not the "butterflies" that have the smell, it's these ones with the little flowers. Their proper name's "*spirantes*" but I think "summer tresses" is the best.'

Ted ruffled Bar's hair. 'Proper mine of information, an't you, Bar?'

'Teacher don't think so, she says I've got a rag-bag of worthless information, and I'd do better to learn to take dictation without so many spelling mistakes.'

Gabriel Strawbridge said, 'No information is ever worthless. But you'd do well to learn to spell . . . last thing I heard, you were going to start writing everything you know about nature, so that when you're grown up you can write a book. You'd need to be able to spell to do that.'

'I should come and ask you, Mr Gabr'l. I had to go out to Warnford for them, but I lent Pixie.'

Lu, knowing how possessive Duke was of the little mare now that he owned her, said, 'Duke let you borrow her?'

Bar flashed a grin. 'Yes . . . he borrowed her to me all evening. He didn't know though, not till he caught me bringing her in over the field way. Anyway, when I told him I had to go to Warnford to look for "butterflies", he never said anything, only next time I should ask first. You see, I said he liked you.'

Lu blushed, not really wanting May and Ted to know about that.

May said, 'I'm off out to see to Cowslip. You two help yourselves to what you want. You coming down to the fields later on, Lu? And don't forget we've got to go down to Joycey's and get that frock your mum said you were to have.'

'Could me and Bar go on our own?'

May considered. 'I don't see why not. After all, you're the one has to wear it, and we all have to learn at some time to make our own decisions. All right. Why not go down there first thing, then there's time to take it back today if you change your mind.'

'We was thinking of going over the woods first. Can I take a towel?'

'You best not go in till the sun's well up, that Swallitt can strike cold. And take your hat.' May had great faith that Lu's good hand-me-down Panama hat would prevent any chance of renewed fever by protecting the top of her head from strong sunshine.

Lu made no promises, but nodded.

'No school then, Bar?' Gabriel Strawbridge asked.

'I never goes to school on Midsummer.'

May smiled. As Duke had made his own rules about what was and what was not worth wasting time on in classrooms, so Bar too was getting through her school years, treading the path between rules that applied to village children but did not apply to Romanies. It was not often that the School Board wasted its time trying to make gypsy people abide by the rules laid down for children who were settled and conventional.

Bar's shaking of the head about getting something to eat was imperceptible except to Lu, who already knew that they were not to eat yet, or in Bar's own way with a secret language which Lu loved to hear, 'No morsel shall touch our lips till the Sunwising be done.'

How Bar came to be aware of those things she knew but which were not taught in school was a mystery. Perhaps as much a mystery to Bar as to anyone else. At best she might have explained, 'Things just come by me.' One might say that rituals, and the ecstatic spinning, were of her own invention, except that she did appear to have some sense that what she did was nothing out of the ordinary, and that there were other people who wouldn't think her queer for what she did and what she knew. Certainly in the village school there was never a mention of anything spiritual, except what was orthodox Church of England teaching in a C of E school, and anyone knowing the circumstances in which the Barney family lived, would find it hard to believe that this mystic side to her nature had come from anywhere except from the air around her. But then, how had Ann Carter come to read cups and palms? Certainly not from Eli who, as a male gypsy, would not have been taught the art, and she had most certainly not learned it from her own respectable family, who would have no truck with any of it.

The prospect of Sunwising and learning to dervish both excited and alarmed Lu, much as sitting in church and watching teachers take Holy Communion did. On those occasions she had always been thrilled to watch the way the teachers, kneeling at the altar rail, were transformed. From the back of the big church, where schoolchildren were consigned, she saw them transformed into biblical characters, kneeling before somebody more powerful than themselves, the only time they ever appeared to be humble. The robes and precious objects, the solemn tolling of the bell. Then the language of mystery which could send more than a mere frisson of alarm running from the pit of her stomach to a place between her legs. 'Take, eat, this is my body.' Did the bread really become meat? Did the jug of wine contain blood?

However, the alarm was only in small proportion; it added importance to the occasion. Perhaps there was danger in gaining access to mysteries, but it would be worth it.

'First thing we have to Sunwise the house, which is walk round it east to west.' This accomplished, they Sunwised a yew tree, and the bee skeps, then set out for the woodlands, at the centre of which was The Swallitt, the site of Bar's Midsummer observances. 'We can't cut across the fields, because we have to follow the pathway of the sun.' So they set off along the tarmac road and then made their clockwise approach into the birch woodlands and then on to The Swallitt. By the time they reached the wide pool of clear water, the sun was penetrating the quivering leaves of the birches. 'Say this: We make a vow to come by the well, and tour all about it thrice times . . . Now take a mouth of water from the bottle and hold it till you have done your tour all about, then you open your mouth and let your water out into the well.'

'The Swallitt's not a well.'

'It don't matter. We can't do it round the well, Pa forbid me after last year. Don't swallow the water, give it back to the mother.'

Bar's rituals were entrancing, truly so, because as the morning progressed, Lu did become overpowered with delight as she was carried ever further into the world Bar had created, or had somehow discovered. Their first search was for empty snail-shells, which seemed a hopeless task, until Bar showed her how to use her eyes.

In a clearing on the bank of The Swallitt where the water was shallow, there was a pan of gravel just above the waterline where Bar made Lu lay out the snail-shells in a spiral. 'Go them sunwise, like the shells theirselves go.' On the snail-shell base, Bar then built up a small pyramidal cairn of stones.

'What's it for?'

'It's Soil's clock.'

Lu didn't question what Bar meant, or how Bar knew; she accepted that it was so. Much of the time Bar seemed preoccupied, her eyes searching, seeming constantly on the alert. From time to time she counted silently on her fingers as though ticking off from a list of items to remember. Lu squatted and watched. When the cairn was finished, Bar sat back with her arms about her drawn-up knees. 'That's the best one I ever made. Did you ever know in Portsm'th that you was a Midsummer child?'

'I never even knew about a Midsummer anything.'

'It's one of the most important days in the year. I wished I knew what time of day you was born.'

'Why?'

'Because of how important it is. If you was born Midsummer Day, then it makes you partic'lar special to it, and I'd like to know where in the sky Soil was when you came out of your mother. Days of the week is named after old spirits and Sunday is named after Soil. I do wish I could find out what time of day you was born.'

'I can easy tell you that. It was when the fact'ry dinner whistles went, my mum said it was like they gave me a twenty-one-gun salute.'

'What's that?'

'It's when a ship goes by and somebody important's aboard. They fire off some guns down the dock, and it's according to how important they are how many they booms off. Seven's lowest, and top of all is twenty-one guns. You have to be the king or admiral or somebody to get that.'

'Then what time of day is it when the dinner whistles go?'

'Same time they always do, twelve o'clock for dinner-time and half-past for going back. Does it mean something to be twelve o'clock?'

Bar smiled. 'I'll tell you when we've got it all ready.'

The morning grew warmer and the sun more sharply piercing through the birches; their earlier business slowed until they eventually sat beside one another looking into the pool. 'Are you still scared to jump off the bent willow?'

'I don't know.'

'I'll bet you wouldn't be if you did it. You can swim all right now, and there's nothing you can hurt yourself on. Just hold your breath.'

'Is it important?'

'You keep on asking is everything important.'

'Well, is it?'

'Of course. Everything today is important. We have to get bound together everlasting.'

Although Bar had talked about it, Lu was still unsure of what 'bound together everlasting' was meant to be. Bar said it was a kind of marrying, only it was better than that because a man and woman being wed, or coupled like her ma and pa, meant that you couldn't have anyone else, but the sort of binding they would do was that you were true to each other for ever until you died, but you could be true to other people as well, except that the first person you were bound to was more important than the rest.

Lu said, 'There was this film at the Tu'penny Rush, and a young cowboy boy and a young Red Indian boy both cut their left thumbs and pressed them together so that their blood mingled and they were brothers.'

Bar drew her brows. 'Boys always have to do things like that, showing off . . . Anyway, they should a cut their wrists. Shall I tell you now why it's important, and why you got to try to jump in off the bent willow? You

146

know what I said about today being one of the most important days . . . ? Well, the other one is Midwinter Day. D'you know Midwinter?'

'Only the carol.'

'When did I tell you is my birthday?'

'Twenty-first December.'

'Well . . . ?'

'Is that it? A course, it's exactly six months from today, so it must be Midwinter.'

'Before you came, I asked your aunty when your birthday was, and I knew it was an omen. Then, when I saw you, it was that exciting I near told you right out.'

'You just stared and said you thought I was asleep.'

'I stared because of your colour, your hair. I couldn't believe it, you was Midsummer *and* the colour of summer- . . . see? I'm black, the colour of winter. We was both born at a solstice . . . oh, never mind what it is now . . . but see? the two of us together makes a whole one, it must have been foretold that we should meet, so I've been working out everything for today.' She threw a stone far out into the pool; it plopped and the rings began to spread out. 'See the middle of the rings where the stone went in: we have to jump in dead centre. We have to keep facing each other, and hold on to one another so we don't get parted, and so we go deep enough for our whole selves to be right under the water. That means we shall have to jump off sideways and keep holding on till we have come up again. Then we are bound, winter and summer together.'

Now that she knew how the ritual was to be done, and the meaning of it, Lu found the whole idea of having their own ceremony so thrilling that her heart seemed to be beating very fast. She imagined the stone making an opening for them to enter the pool, she visualized the frogs and fish and the dabchicks bouncing about as the rings reached their floating nests. Lu, for all that she had been schooled in Old Testament burning bushes and pillars of salt, plus New Testament resurrection and the feeding of the five thousand from one lunch-basket, had never seen much relevance to life in Lampeter Street, nor had she known any kind of spiritual experience. But this was *real*, it signified something she could understand. 'It's *wonderful*! How did you think it? I shan't be afraid to jump . . . I want to. When can we do it?'

'When Soil is overhead.'

Shielding her eyes, Lu looked up. 'It is now.'

'Not quite. See? We can't go until there's no shadow from the stick on the cairn.' The tall flower-stalk that topped the cairn of stones by the water's edge was now very short. 'We have to let our hair loose and take off our clothes.' They stood together hunched, their fingers knotted nervously, pale- and dark-skinned, golden- and black-haired; delicate, vulnerable, unformed, embryonic women, shivering a little in the air at the water's edge, and watching the shrinking of the last inch of the shadow of the stalk. Bar looked up, squinting her eyes, 'Soil's looking full down on us. It's even better now we know this is your true birthing minute.' She picked the topmost stone from the cairn and took a step out on to the bent willow. 'Come on then. When we get to the diving part of the branch, face together and catch a hold round each other's waists and when I say jump, don't let go of me, don't close your eyes.' They stood for a second, then Bar let the stone plop into the water just below the branch; the circles on the surface of the pool began to form around the turbulence. Lu felt Bar's hard fingers grasp her tightly by the waist so that their chests and bellies touched. She gave Lu a broad smile and whispered, 'Now!'

Lu didn't close her eyes, even so she could see nothing but disturbed water as they went in, and then nothing except their own hair swirling around them as they touched bottom and were pulled round by their own impetus. For a second, as her toes clutched at the silt, she saw Bar's still-smiling face close to her own. Then Bar, clasping her tightly, pushed off from the sludge and gravel. They soared upwards. When they broke surface, Lu drew in a gasp of air. Bar, paddling with one arm, made them twirl, then they released one another and Lu turned and floated on her back. The water was fresh but not cold. Lu looked up at the sky and thought it had never looked as blue as this before, nor the trees as green, nor the air as clear, nor anything as anything as it had been before. Bar, her hair like a crêpe cloak, paddled water. They looked at one another and giggled. Bar said, 'It was good, wasn't it?'

Lu grinned. 'Really good. Did we go down in the right place?'

'Yes. I think I felt my stone, I'll see if I can find it.' She flipped over, her bottom, legs and feet broke the surface of the water and disappeared as she dived down, then in seconds reappeared holding the round stone which she lay between her breasts as she sculled gracefully along on her back, her hair now streaming like a silk scarf in a wind, her body scarcely making a ripple.

Arms stretched wide, Lu lay still, feeling the small movement of the wash made by Bar lapping her body. A few weeks ago she would never have believed it possible that she could ever feel so safe in water; it was as though she had always known how to swim, as she had always known how to walk and run.

They rubbed down with Lu's towel and sat in the warm sun drying their hair. 'I'm getting hungry,' Bar said, 'let's leave the dervishing till another day; then we can get a bite to eat and then go down to Joycey's and get your new dress.'

Their experiences at the pool affected the girls' mood for the rest of the day. They went about hand in hand, their hair flying loose, self-aware of the impression they supposed they created. Joycey looked over her glasses when they entered the shop, clanging the bell as they jostled and giggled. 'You not at school again, Bar?'

'No, it's Midsummer holiday, didn't you know?'

'No – nor, do I reckon, does the School Board. Everybody else has gone.'

'That's because it's only me that gets today off.' She winked at Lu.

Joycey wagged her head. 'Well, have you come to buy something, or are you just visiting?' As she said later, you really couldn't help liking Ann Carter's two eldest; they got the cheek of Old Harry, but they never gave no offence, it's just that they were a law unto themselves, *and* . . . they never seemed short of a bob or two.

'I've come for my dress,' Lu said.

'Ah yes . . . your aunty said you'd be in. It's a present from your mother, she says. Well, Happy Birthday, dear. These ones are your size, your aunty says you are to choose, and she'll come in and settle.' One by one, she extracted six from their tissue paper. 'Shall I leave you to choose?'

'No, I want this one.'

'Yellow? I'd have thought you'd go for the green with your colouring.'

Lu fingered the pale lemon cotton printed with darker yellow buttercups. 'No, this one.'

'Very well, dear, your aunty said you was to choose. A bit different from Bar here; never wants anything except a length of black since she took to making her own. I never knew a girl choose black before, not many twelve-year-olds got that sort of taste. Mostly it's widows buy black.'

Bar never responded to the little digs people thought it all right to make at youngsters, especially herself. If Joycey couldn't see that she looked better in black than anything, then it would be no good trying to explain. Not that Bar had bought more than two or three lengths.

Lu said, 'I think she looks all right in it. I wouldn't.'

Joycey gave her a well-you-know-best-dear smile. 'Do you want to try it on?'

'I want to wear it.'

'Out of the shop? You don't want to show Mrs Wilmott first? Very well, there's a mirror in the back room.'

'Do I look all right?'

'It's really pretty. You should get some yellow ribbon to go round your hat.'

Peering closely in the mirror, Lu smoothed the thin cotton bodice, and whispered, 'What about . . . ? It shows them, don't it?'

'That's all right. You can't hide them, can you?'

'I didn't hardly have any after my Dip.'

'Well, now you're getting some,' she grinned, 'and one day they'll grow as fat as my ma's.'

'Ssh!'

Joycey, having caught whispers and hushes, put her head round the curtain-and-box arrangement. 'Well, have you decided?'

'I *do* want it. And can I have some hat ribbon the same colour?'

Feeling very conspicuous in newness and colour, Lu, carrying her hat, hand in hand with Bar and suddenly feeling quite grown up, went back up the lane to Roman's Fields where Ted and May were taking a break on cold tea and bread.

'Well! I *must* say, you two make a picture. That's a real pretty dress, colour of sunshine. Ted, go in the house and fetch your camera.'

'Good idea, go down to the meadow where we're cutting, that's the place to take pictures.'

The meadow where Ted and the casuals were cutting hay was full of poppies. There, Ted, who considered himself something of a good amateur with film, took photographs of the two girls standing in tall grasses and massed poppies, then one of May, then each of them separately. May took Ted with the girls, and Ted with Lu. Bar had no doubt how she wanted to appear in her photograph. She let her hair loose and swung it around until static electricity made it stand out like black froth. She got Lu to help her stud it with ox-eye daisies, then, with fists on hips and her legs straddled, she laughed into the camera. Lu reacted quite differently, feeling shy at being the focus of attention.

'Wait a mo, Lu,' Bar ordered, 'and I'll get you some flowers like a bridesmaid.' She gathered a bunch of poppies which Lu held shyly, and put others all round the brim of the Panama hat.

These were the first photographs either girl had ever had taken. Later, when they had been processed, Ted had some of the black-and-white prints tinted, pale bluey-green in the background, a lot of summery gold in the dry grasses, Lu's dress and hat, which contrasted with the brightness of the wild red poppies. May sent one to Vera, gave another to Ann Carter, one each to Lu and Bar to paste into their daybooks, and one for the Roman's Fields mantelpiece. Ted had the two portraits in a twin frame. A beautiful frame with silver twining lilies and wheat.

'You must be hungry after all that. Come on, I made a special treat, seeing how you aren't twelve every day.' The treat was a deep open tart filled with strawberries set in red jelly, which May, Ted and the girls sat at the edge of the field and consumed to the last crumb. Lu had seen such treats in the window of the Swiss patisserie and tea-rooms in Southsea. The taste was as luxurious as the look.

'What's the programme for this afternoon?' May asked.

'We're going up to show Bar's ma my dress, then I expect we'll go back over the woods.'

'I should be careful of it then; that yellow won't be much good for climbing around over there.'

'Oh, we shan't go climbing, Mis Wilmott. I expect we're going to get flowers to press for Lu to take back home.'

'Off you go then,' May said, 'enjoy the day. I'll go back and put something out for your tea and Father's, but I shan't be in that early: with this heat and sun, the fruit's ripening as you watch it. You be all right?'

'Yes, Aunty, it's the best day in my whole life.' She began to follow Bar, but then turned back to May and struggled out with, 'All the time here is the best day in my life . . . thank you for letting me stop with you,' and rushed away, covered in the confusion of her attempt at expressing what was not really expressible.

Slowly, slowly the sun went down into the afternoon. Lu showed off shyly to Bar's ma, who said she looked a treat and the bloom on her cheeks was all credit to May. 'I know what day it is, because *she* hasn't talked about hardly anything else lately. I don't know what she gets up to half the time. Anyway, I got a keepsake for you.' She drew from her shirt pocket a small lozenge of smooth wood with a small hole bored in it through which a leather lace was threaded.

It appeared to Lu that it was made to be worn around the neck, so she pulled it over her head.

'You don't have to wear it if you don't want. It's called a pocket-piece. It's ash, which was known in old times as "sympathetic ash" for its virtues. I once did a trade for a whole box of them, and, as it was told to me, they came direct from a man who cut thousands and went about giving them to anybody he could. This was more than two hundred years back, so that's a good old piece.'

Lu listened; no one could help but listen when Ann Carter leaned enthusiastically into her subject.

'The thing is, this man knew what he was doing, because ashwood is at its most potent at Midsummer, so if it is cut then, the piece is partic'larly special. You mustn't ever sell ash for cures, it has to be give away, so when I heard you was a Midsummer child, I thought you should have one.'

'Thank you, Mrs Barney. Is it an amulet? There was a hero in one of the stories had an amulet.'

'I suppose you could say it is, except that amulets was often worn against witches, which was wrong, for there was never a witch born that would do harm to any creature that come to live on this earth.'

'I never knew that. I thought they were bad.'

'Ach! That's men saying lies. You want to remember that: witches were the wise ones and the birthers till men couldn't stand playing second fiddle, so they started this tale about magic and spells . . . Well, if you think about it, bringing a baby or curing a sickness is a kind of magic, but it was never anything but good magic. When you hear any bad thing being said about any creature female, you just ask yourself if there's any truth in it, and who says there is. Anybody ever calls you a "bitch" you say thank you, for bitches are gentle and caring, 'tis dogs that goes after each other's throats.'

'Oh come on, Ma, don't keep on all day, we want to go back down to The Swallitt Pool.'

'All right, you go on and sport yourselves about a bit. You going to swim?'

'We did already.'

'It's the best sort of weather for it. A pity more don't want to go to the old Swallitt.'

'No! We don't want nobody else, do we, Lu? It would just be spoilt.'

The woods are still and the warmth in them seems to have quietened birds, small animals and rustling leaves alike. As they make their way back towards their earlier spot by The Swallitt Pool, the fresh smell of new-grown moss, dog mercury, violets and other floor-covering plants kicks up as they walk. Lu's towel and their bottles of water are still where they left them by the pan with the cairn.

Lu, who has grown confident that The Swallitt Pool is secluded and unused by anyone else, is becoming quite accustomed to taking off her clothes and walking into the pool, which no longer feels cold, but fresh and clean. As she paddles on the margins of the water, she likes the feel of the meadow-sweet and purslane upon her bare skin; then, as she goes a bit deeper, quillworts and frogbit brush her legs beneath the waterline. With her yellow dress, ash amulet and hat safely hanging from a branch, she wades in and swims with her head held above the water and gathering armfuls of water to her as Bar had shown her. She looks across to see if Bar is watching, but Bar, still dressed, is seated on the bent willow, leaning forward and looking down at the place where they jumped in and became bound everlasting.

At the far side, she turns on to her back. From 21 June, the days grow shorter; in a few weeks she will have to go back to school. She would like to stay floating in this magical world in The Country, the place that had a few weeks ago been empty and frightening but has turned out to be amazing. She sometimes misses home, but if she's honest, only when she wants to tell Ray something she has discovered. She has forgotten how Ken sounded. It seems awful not to be able to remember something like that.

How badly she is going to miss Bar. She thinks again of those few seconds when they stood on the bent willow, clinging to one another, just before they dropped into the centre of the rings. The experience of closeness to a girl of her age is totally new. Her best schoolfriend is Kate Roles; they had started school together and stayed friends, yet she would never have been able to wrap together naked as she and Bar had done. Kate would have giggled or tickled and said they were being rude. With Bar it had been serious and really lovely, and except for their heads and their eyes looking at each other, it had been almost as though she couldn't tell which was Bar and which was Lu.

Bar's voice breaks in, 'D'you want to try the dervishing?' They sit, Lu in front as Bar winds Lu's hair into six or eight long, thin plaits.

Lu's first attempts make her giddy and she topples around.

'It's because you're not thinking inside yourself. Be as if you're a conker on a string, only be a seed of thistledown spinning on a spider's thread, round and round.'

It takes a good many attempts, but at last, with her arms stretched, Lu is able to keep her feet on one spot as she pirouettes, east to west, sunwise. Slowly at first, but then faster. She closes her eyes and gets the rotating rhythm. The sounds of the woods and the water fade until they have become small disturbances within her ear. Faster, until she feels that she has started to whirl east to west, with the earth, with the sun and the heavens, with her plaited hair. Whether her movements are graceful and flowing she can't tell, only that she hears Bar say, 'You got it . . . that's it, that's lovely.'

There is no slowing down, but suddenly she feels that she is in a brilliant light and the spinning has stopped, yet when she slits open her eyelids, she sees the trees, the pool and Bar whirling around her. Then it does slow down; she opens her eyes wide and finds that she is standing still, as steady and as rooted to the spot as the birches around her. Her arms are stretched above her head as, hands laced, her two forefingers steeple skywards. Waiting for a conclusion. Bar, standing only inches away ready to catch Lu if she topples, says, 'Now you know.'

Lu, surprising herself, puts her arms around Bar's neck and gives her a hard kiss on the mouth. The elation from her experiences with Bar today, together with the daily joy and pleasure of this summer, is summed up in that warm kiss.

Suddenly, there is a yell and a loud splash and they jump apart. Lu crouches down behind the sedges on the margin of the pool, hiding her breasts with her arms. Not so Bar: she has picked up stones and is hurling them out into the pool where strong arms are pulling a swimmer along in the direction of the bent willow. Once there, Duke hauls himself out and stands dripping on the branch, his long black hair plastered to his head and shoulders. 'Don't take no notice,' Bar said, 'it's only because he thinks we're watching him. He just likes showing off. Nobody's interested in him.'

But Lu is interested. Duke's face and arms are so brown and his feet always so dirty that the whiteness of the skin ordinarily covered by the dungarees is astonishing. He looks lovely and smooth, like a statue.

'I can't come out, he'll see me. Give me my towel.'

Bar raised her voice. 'Have you been watching us, Duke Barney? You clear off. We was here first.'

'No! You don't own it!'

Lu, immersed in intimate silence as she waits for Bar to throw her the towel, is intent on Duke Barney standing on the willow, the first mature testicles, the first black body-hair, the first partly turgid penis, the first completely naked man she has seen.

This image of youth, male beauty and virility standing unashamed of its potent state, was surely bound to be a standard by which a mature Lu must measure all men who would come later.

With the regularly renewed approval of Vera, relayed by Hector Wilmott, Lu stayed on at Roman's Fields until the end of August, when it could no longer be said that she was still recuperating from diphtheria. If she didn't appear on the register for the new term, the School Board would be after her mother.

Upon the morning of her departure, she teemed with so

many mixed emotions that at times she felt her heart would jump out of her chest and that she would burst into tears.

It was hard having to part with Bar, and the relations at Roman's Fields. And with her bedroom, its peachy walls, daisy toilet set, and view over to the strawberry fields. She went into the village wearing her new dress and said goodbye to the shopkeepers, and then to Ann Carter, who held her hand and kissed her on the cheek. Ted gave her *The Children's Golden Treasure Book* and said he was sorry there had been so many stories in which the boys were the heroes, but before she came next time, he would search for something where girls had the adventures. 'But then, you're reading so well now you're ready for some of the classics: now they're an education in themselves.'

Mr Strawbridge gave her the leather bag he had taken on his journey to South Africa in which to put the many possessions she had acquired since her arrival, and asked her to try to keep up her daybook, on the first page of which he had written *'Question, question, question and, when there is an answer, ask, Why? Why? Why?'*

'Will you write us a line, Lu?' Uncle Ted said. 'Let us know how your mum is going on. And listen, if you ever need anybody . . . you know . . . if there's a time when you'd like me or Aunty May to do anything, you know you've only got to ask.'

Lu noted the serious tone of his offer and thanked him solemnly.

Aunty May shed a few fat tears, and said the door of Roman's Fields was always open and her room would be always ready. 'Next time you'll be a head taller.'

Uncle Ted said, 'Next time she'll know her way around.'

Lu said, 'And I shan't be worried, now I've seen both sides of the hill.'

Charlie Barrit handed back his tea-mug and Uncle Hec came back from the outhouse. 'Ups you get then, Lu my lovely.'

As the lorry drew out of the gate, Lu felt suddenly a moment of apprehension at going back to the city, almost equal to that of the outward journey.

Although Uncle Hec had made his delivery at The Bells on his way in, he said he had promised Peg they would stop a minute on their way back, about when afternoon 'Time' had been called, just so she could say hello. Lu, wearing her sandals and yellow dress, was unhesitating in jumping down from the lorry when it stopped. She had tied up her hair and put the diamond shooting star on top.

Peggy, wearing an off-the-shoulder 'gypsy' top and full skirt, came out, followed by a man wearing an open-neck shirt and tennis shorts. He was a happy-looking man, as big as Uncle Hec, with black hair and a bunch of dark hair showing where his shirt buttons were open. Peggy waved as though Lu was an old friend. 'Well, will you just look at that! Your Uncle Hec said that you were better, but I never expected such a young woman. That frock! You look a real treat . . . lovely. Didn't I tell you Louise was a star, Dick?' Dick Briardale, landlord of The Bells, stood back, nodding and smiling affably, drawing on a cigar, whilst Peggy patted Lu and clasped her hands. 'Your holiday's done you a lot of good, I can see that. Did you enjoy it?'

'It was lovely . . . there was so much happened. I got a new friend – Barbara. We're going to write to each other, and I've got loads of things to take home.' She patted her diamond star. 'I decided to keep this for special days. I'm wearing it today because I'm going to see Mum.'

'Well now, just you promise to come in next time you're passing. We'll be wanting to see, won't we, Dick?'

Dick Briardale felt in his shorts pockets. 'Here, Peg, give the girl a "stiver" to spend when she gets home.'

The stiver turned out not to be a sixpenny piece, but a florin, which Lu later slipped into the pocket of Mr

Strawbridge's bag in which were her accumulated earnings from strawberry picking, her bag of gifts, slippers and new clothes.

Seated in his big armchair in the living room at the back of The Bells, Dick Briardale pulled Peggy down on to his lap.

'I thought you were supposed to be up at the nets this afternoon.'

'I am. There's time.' With one hand up her skirt and the other feeling her belly, he said, 'Well, I suppose we'd better put this chap on a proper footing.' He looked pleased enough as he pulled down the easy-going top of his barmaid's gypsy top. 'Not that I reckon it's a good deal for me having somebody else horning in on these.'

Peggy – who had always surmised that expectant women wouldn't want that kind of thing, and was surprised at the intensity of her own sudden and strong needs since she had become pregnant – eased herself into a position where they could be comfortable for half an hour. The hell with his cricket, they'd have to wait for him. Perhaps it was ditching the cap, or maybe ditching the gin bottle that made her like this. It didn't much matter, things were looking up, and Dick was beginning to learn a thing or two about holding on and making the fun last, and he had been pleased as punch that they had had the accident. She had told him it wasn't safe, so it had been his own fault for keeping going anyway. He knew that, but he was pleased anyway.

'Peg Briardale sounds all right, don't it?'

'It sounds lovely, Dick.'

'Best get on with it soon as we can, then.'

Hec stopped his lorry for a minute on the top of Portsdown.

'Well,' Charlie Barrit said, 'do you still hold to the fac' that there's nothing between here and World's End?'

Lu grinned. 'I don't know whether it's me or the country that's changed.'

Charlie Barrit, inarticulate and unimaginative, without children of his own, seeing something of note in the ripening cornfields and the girl's plump golden arms which he would have liked to put into words, said, 'Queer old world.'

Lu, having recently become aware of the different ways in which words could be arranged, had taken great care with the birthday entry in her record book. 'My old child's self has not gone, but has gone into making the girl who is me now. This one is like the dragonflies at The Swallitt Pool, the new self climes out of their old self, but leaves that old self still there clinging to the rushes looking the same. Perhaps when/if I come back next summer I shall see me crouched down in the shallows watching Duke Barney and, I think, him knowing I was there on Midsummer Day when I was twelve.'

Such reflections flew from her mind when she arrived home. She had imagined that her mother would be standing on the pavement, probably talking to Dot next door, she had expected to jump down and astonish them with her new frock and looking so well.

The real scene was that Dotty next door was waiting in the doorway of Number 110 and saying gravely that Lu wasn't to worry or take on, but her mum had had a bit of a set-back and wasn't up to getting out of bed at the moment. 'She's not ill or nothing, Lu, but she's weak. But, Lord love us, you'll be a tonic to her and that's no lie. I shouldn't a hardly known you except for your hair, and that's grown a foot.'

Lu raced upstairs and discovered her mother in bed propped up by pillows, her eyes dark and deep, her cheeks hollow and her arms pale and thin. 'Oh, Lu,' she said, 'I have been looking forward to seeing you. We were all like peas rattling around in a bucket without you.'

For a moment, Lu was transfixed at the sight of this woman who she knew to be her mother, but who looked so frighteningly ill and who was wearing a proper night-dress and a pretty bed-jacket. Then she recovered and gave her mother the kind of hug and kiss she had learned to give from a thousand given and received by May. 'You'll be all right now, Mum. I learnt from Uncle Ted and Aunty May and Mr Gabriel what you have to do to build people up. I've got a box downstairs with bees' honey and Cowslip butter.' She grinned. 'You don't know what that is, I'll tell you later . . . but I'll keep giving you what they gave me till you're as better as I am. I've got that many things to tell you. And before you go to sleep at night, I'll bring you warm milk with bees' honey, and I'll get out my *Children's Golden Treasure Book* and I'll read to you every night so you will have lovely dreams.'

Vera Wilmott looked at her changeling daughter and smiled. 'Oh, Lu, what a stupid I was to wonder if I was doing the right thing sending you to a place right out there in the country.'

'I'm sure Aunty May would have you there and make you better.'

Vera, for all the assurance given by the gynaecologist that she would soon pick up, felt certain that one miracle per family was about all that would be given.

'That won't be necessary, Lu, for it feels as though you have brought a breath of the country right into this room.'

Lu had seen enough of the ailments and diseases of poverty to know that her mother was very ill indeed. So, she wrote to May and Ted and asked them if sometimes they would send some butter and honey by train and that if it was all right with them, she could come and work off what she owed next strawberry picking. 'But please, Aunty,' she wrote with great perception, 'don't send it by Uncle Hec; it will only make the aunts be jealous, but none of they are ill.'

As May said when she received Lu's note, 'That operation wasn't ever going to do her any good if you ask me. She was probably suffering from anaemia, it's going to take months for her to get on her feet again.'

May guessed that she was whistling in the wind. Vera had been a sick woman for years.

1931

Two years have passed, it is summer, and the weather has grown heavy with threatened thunderstorms. Trees are stilled, their leaves drooped. People are crabby and children restless. Lu Wilmott left Lampeter Church of England Girls' School for the last time at the end of the summer term. She has had a last girlish fling with Bar Barney in the fields, woods and ponds around Roman's Fields.

But that stands out like a full-colour illustration in a book of dark lino-cuts.

Not that Lu has been doleful; she has been too busy for that.

On her return to Lampeter Girls', to the surprise of her teachers after her long absence, Lu surged ahead with her lessons, so that by the time she reached the age of thirteen, the headmistress, Miss Lake, was sure that she at last had a girl capable of winning a place at the grammar school. However, when she entered the living room of 110 Lampeter Street, to discuss the prospects with Louise Wilmott's mother and her elder brother, and saw the state of health of the girl's mother, she wondered if, yet again, she would be told that the girl must leave school and go to work because the family couldn't do without the girl's pay.

But Miss Lake did not know Vera Wilmott, or her early history. Vera had put on a little make-up, pearly earrings and a brooch, and got out her one good dress which, although it hung about her spare chest, was clean and well pressed.

Ray, in his working suit but with a clean shirt collar,

opened the door at the first knock. 'Come in, Miss Lake. I'm afraid my mother don't find it too easy to get up out of her chair.'

Cynthia Lake never ceased to be surprised at what she discovered lay behind the rows and rows of slum houses in her 'parish'. Often the shock was at the degradation and poverty in which the Lampeter Girls and Infants lived out their lives, but in Number 110 she found what she perceived to be the last remnants of the knowledge of a better life.

'I'm sorry not to get up, Miss Lake,' Vera Wilmott smiled apologetically, 'I'm afraid I'm a bit of a crock at the moment. Please take a seat. Ray, shall you get us a cup of tea? Ray is my elder son, he is a clerk with the Southern Railway.'

Miss Lake, taking the thin, pale hand politely offered, thought, she can't be much older than I am. 'I understand that your husband is in the Navy?'

'Yes, it's a long time since he made Portsmouth. He sends us cards.' She pointed to the small collection of picture postcards slipped into the frame of a mirror. 'Actually, he is due home . . . but of course we need to get this thing with Lu settled before then.'

The room of four cracked walls, a splintery floor coloured with dark woodstain, and an ill-fitting door and window-frame, was poorly furnished, but, like many of the houses in the area, the tell-tale boxes of piece-goods and made-up items for the corset factories told the story of sweated-labour outworkers. Cynthia Lake thought that this woman hardly seemed capable of making any kind of living. How could any child of such a household hope to keep up in a grammar school? But Louise was not just any child. She was a girl who, when she had gone down in the diphtheria epidemic, had seemed to be an average child constantly in trouble for scrapping like a boy with the pathetic Grigg girl, but who had returned after some months with a quite astonishing application to her lessons, and an apparent desire to learn anything and everything. Which she did at great speed.

When Cynthia Lake had questioned the girl in a friendly way about her lessons, she had replied, 'Well, I'm not far off fourteen, so I haven't got much time left, have I?'

And when she had hesitantly pushed the matter further by saying, 'There are, of course, scholarships to the grammar school,' the girl had seemed to hold her breath.

'You mean girls out of Lampeter Street?'

'Yes . . . girls from anywhere. The entrance examination is open, which means it is for anybody to try.'

Without hesitation, the girl had said eagerly, 'Yes please, miss.'

The elder son returned now with a wooden tray that must have come from a school woodworking class, and some tea and biscuits which he offered with a nice politeness, not forced. 'Thank you . . . should I call you Raymond?'

'Ralph.'

'Ah, thank you then, Ralph.'

'It has to be Ralph who decides, because if Lu gets a scholarship, it is going to fall a lot on his shoulders. I'm afraid my husband is just an able seaman.'

Cynthia Lake knew this to be as near to useless as pay can go – no fat for grammar schools – and although she would have no truck with the idea of a deserving and an undeserving poor, she felt that there was something admirable about Mrs Wilmott and her children. There were those who would have considered that here was a woman imprudent enough to keep an entire house of living room, scullery and one and a half bedrooms and not rent out at least one or take in lodgers. Miss Lake knew that, had she been in Mrs Wilmott's situation, she would have done anything to cling on to her remnants of decent family life. Overcrowding of the sort that went on in this slum area was what was killing to both body and spirit, to decency and respect.

Ralph said, 'It's not *if* she gets it, Mum. She *will* get it. She's capable, isn't she, Miss Lake?'

'Oh, yes, she's perfectly capable. She is a very clever girl.'

'All my children are.' Miss Lake saw the pride gleaming from within the hollow of the mother's dark eyes. 'Ray got a white-collar job, and my other son is apprenticed at the Co-operative, the funeral directors – he's just learning to drive.'

And Miss Lake saw too the affectionate look the smart young clerk gave his mother. These were nice people. Why shouldn't they be? Poverty was a state, not an inborn characteristic. She had always believed that the country's greatest talent was in its working people, who were being scandalously wasted because the capitalist system was so blinkered, and the class structure too self-seeking to share anything with families such as these. Wasn't it for this very reason that she had applied for the headship of one of the least promising of the Church's many schools?

'Louise's academic capabilities are not in question. My reason for asking to see you to discuss whether the application should be made is . . . well, a free place means that there are no fees to pay, but there are expenses.'

She noticed Mrs Wilmott flick a look at the son, but he kept his eyes upon herself and said straightforwardly, 'The thing is, even with my money, we aren't too well off. Kenny's money will go up in time, but now he hardly gets enough to keep himself. Could they amount to a lot, the fees?'

'I'm afraid that they are often the reason why scholarships are not taken up, even by better-off sections of the community; but in Louise's case I very much hope that she will receive a full bursary. What we have to think of are the extras: sports equipment, items for use in the science laboratories, aprons and caps for domestic science for girls.'

Miss Lake saw the pain of disappointment in the mother's eyes. 'Those are the very things that go to make the education a whole thing.' She smiled almost apologetically, 'I went on to school myself . . . I was to have been a teacher . . . ' She stopped herself. 'But now Lu might have the same chance. Have you any idea how much would be involved? It wouldn't matter too much to have some things second-hand . . . I mean, a tennis racquet is a tennis racquet, and I could probably run her up aprons and such. There might be ways . . . '

Miss Lake had decided that, if it looked hopeless, then she herself would pay for the girl. But here, confronted by their pride, she could see that their independent honour would be damaged by a crude sum of money. They would accept for the girl's sake, but Cynthia Lake did not wish to see them humiliated, so she plunged into her lie. 'There is a fund. If you would agree then I could apply as Louise's head for a grant to buy all her uniforms and equipment.' Again the son exchanged a slightly embarrassed glance with his mother, who said, 'Charity, you mean?'

'Think of it as being in receipt of a legacy, Mrs Wilmott. A grant is a gift from someone who likes to share their good fortune.'

'Oh, I don't mind, Miss Lake, you get used to it. Nobody in these parts can get far without a bit of charity. It's just asking for it that is hard.'

Mrs Wilmott minded all right. The more proud and sensitive the person, the better the face they put on things.

'You wouldn't need to ask. I would make the automatic application through the school. You need not be involved.'

Mother and son nodded at one another. Perhaps they had been over this ground in anticipation of her visit. Mrs Wilmott smiled at her son. 'Well, that don't sound so bad, Ray.'

'I did make enquiries whether there was any fund I could apply for through my union. If Lu had been my daughter, I could certainly get things like free travel if the school was out of the area. Unions are very good, but of course, she's my sister.'

'Ray's a big union man, aren't you, Ray?'

'Not exactly "big", Mum.' He turned and Cynthia Lake had her own gaze engaged by his proud one. 'I'm a shop steward, and usually get to represent the branch at conferences.'

'Which union?'

'The NUR – National Union of Railwaymen.'

'Of course. A good strong union. Were you a member at the time of the 'twenty-six strike?' Unexpectedly, she smiled. 'I'm sorry if that sounded like a trick question . . . I am interested. One doesn't often get the opportunity of getting an opinion direct; even the most honest journalists are given to bias.'

His look was very direct. 'To be frank, Miss Lake, I think if my union had held on, things would be very different now.'

'You mean the laws making general strikes illegal?'

She saw that he was intrigued at her interest; she knew it must be surprising to him because of the very nature of her position as head of a C of E school.

'Yes, Miss Lake – that, and depriving the unemployed who were not "genuinely seeking work" of benefit. How can a man genuinely seek work when there is none to be had?'

'Or woman.'

'Women won't be unionized.'

'I don't agree. It is bad employers and the huge surplus of women workers that don't allow them to be unionized.'

She watched his sharp eyes weighing her up, then he said, 'I have only attended one congress, and I felt that the railway unions still have a long way to go before they are forgiven by the other unions.'

'Then, in my opinion, if you don't mind me saying so, the other unions might do better to look for enemies elsewhere than within their own family. Oh dear . . . we are supposed to be considering Louise's future, and here I am carried away. Shall we say, yes, then, Mrs Wilmott . . . Ralph? We agree that when the time comes I shall do my best to see that Louise gets what extras are necessary?'

'That would be very kind, Miss Lake. Thank you.'

Ralph conducted her the few steps to the front door and held out his hand. 'Miss Lake, thank you for giving Lu the leg up she's capable of taking. You know what I think? Her thanks are going to be in the example she will set for other children from round here. One day people are going to realize all the talent that is going down the drain.'

'I realize it, Ralph. I see it every day.'

As Ray said later to Ken, 'You could have knocked me down with a feather. You don't expect a headmistress of a girls' school to have any politics, but she's red hot.'

'Do you think it's on then, our Lu going to the grammar?'

'Miss Lake don't think there's much doubt about her getting a full scholarship.'

'I'd help if I could, Ray. A bit later on I'll be able to. You'd think the Navy would do something for sailors' kids.'

'They do, but I don't reckon they're going to give Lu a place in a boys' college.'

Kenny laughed. Kenny laughed easily. 'Our Lu'd give them a run for their money.'

Ray nodded, pleased that Kenny at last seemed to be growing up and understanding that the world wasn't all football.

Lu, started at the grammar school, feeling conspicuous in the uniform that her mother was so proud of; she left early in the morning and came home with it hidden as well as she could. She knew that she would get used to it, but at the moment it felt as though she was doing a 'duchess', which was something no Lampeter girl would wish upon herself. But, hardly had she been there long enough to sort out her timetable and her way about the huge school, than it came to an abrupt halt.

One day, she came out of the school gates to see Ray waiting at the corner. At first she thought that their dad was home and Ray had come to tell her. Then she saw his face.

'What's up, Ray? You look white as a sheet.'

'It's Mum, she had a bad turn this morning. I came off early turn, I didn't want anybody else telling you . . .' He faltered.

'Ray! Is she . . . ?' She knew. 'She died, didn't she?'

Stopping for a brief moment, he put a tentative hand round her shoulder. 'Yeah . . . I'm sorry, Lu, she passed away this morning.'

'Oh, Ray, thank goodness you were on the ten-to-six turn, otherwise she might have been on her own.'

He nodded, not able to say that Vera *had* been on her own. Once again, it had been Ralph's misfortune to suffer the shock of finding his mother in a state of bloody saturation. He had made her a hot drink and some toast, gone quietly upstairs and discovered her slumped down in bed. Asleep, as he at first thought, but she was dead. He would never tell Lu that.

No one happening to glance in their direction would have suspected that the young man with oiled hair and wearing well-pressed blue serge, and the uniformed schoolgirl with a thick copper plait hanging below her felt hat were experiencing a great crisis. Vera's children were not like that; they did not make a poppy show of themselves.

'Is she . . . ? Where is she?'

'In the Chapel of Rest.'

'I don't have to see her, Ray, do I?'

'Our Kenny's been marvellous, you'd never believe. Dr Steiner got him at work and Ken came home and saw to everything. I've never seen him like that, he just took over – no wonder they think so much of him there. There didn't seem any point in getting you out of school, you couldn't have done anything.' There had been things to be done that he and Kenny could not have borne she should see. Dotty took away the bloody washing bundle, and Ray burnt the mattress and went out and bought another from a trader who sold bedding, guaranteed fumigated.

In death, Vera became almost celebrated in the Wilmott family. Not only had she died suddenly, but she had died dramatically, just as her husband's ship was sailing into home waters.

On the day when he was due in Portsmouth, the older Wilmotts gathered at 110 Lampeter Street to welcome their brother Arthur to his house of mourning. May had come down from Wickham and was staying in Portsmouth until Vera's funeral was over. But Arthur did not come.

He had already been delayed because, before the *Augusta* reached Portsmouth, she and fourteen other vessels of the Royal Navy had been ordered to change course for Invergordon, a port in the north of Scotland, several days' sailing time from home.

Vera, already very ill and anaemic, in bed on Dr Steiner's orders, liked to catch half an hour when all her three children were in the house. News of the delay came when Ken had brought home a newspaper he had found on the tram. The story was told in dramatic headlines: STRIKE! TWELVE THOUSAND MEN OF THE ROYAL NAVY WALK OFF. FIFTEEN SHIPS OF HIS MAJESTY'S FLEET UNABLE TO SAIL.

Kenny had said scathingly, 'Look at that, "Leftist and Communist speak against RN cuts." They've always got to blame the Reds.'

The story continued for several days, about scuffles breaking out at strike meetings, fights breaking out, windows being broken and an officer being injured, and each evening one of the boys brought home a newspaper. Lu was not greatly interested, but liked it when they were all together for half an hour. Lu had been quite surprised that her mother had opinions such as she expressed. 'Whoever would have thought of the Navy striking? Who would have thought people in this country had it in them?'

Ray said, 'With all this unemployment, I should think they're afraid for their jobs.'

'No,' Kenny said, 'it's because the men's got a quarter cut off their pay and the officers hardly anything.'

Kenny had said, 'It's the *Potemkin* that's got them going – that's what the government's afraid of.'

'What's that?' Lu had asked.

'The Ruskies had a battleship called the *Potemkin* and the sailors came out – that was even before the revolution.'

Ray had said jokingly, 'Our Ken and his revolution.'

'Our people aren't like Russian peasants.'

'No,' Vera said. 'We make excuses to ourselves why we shouldn't stand up against what's wrong. We take the easy way.'

Thus Arthur Wilmott was still at sea when he heard of his wife's death.

The *Augusta*, which had been Arthur Wilmott's only real home since he was a boy, was a stirring sight as it sailed towards Spithead. Dressed overall, pennants flying, a full complement of men lining her decks, looking from a distance like a newly-painted picket fence, the *Augusta* whooped signals of her arrival in the home port, and received a salute from the shore guns. This was the sight and sound that stirred British hearts, inspired nationalistic sentiments, and persuaded Portsmouth's young men to sign up to spend a large part of their lives away from home for very little pay.

Vera Wilmott's husband had been one of the men standing legs astride and hands crossed behind, eyes fixed on the shore. His home town had slipped past – Hayling, the sandbar, Southsea shoreline, castle, pier, sea-front hotels, houses, gardens. Steaming on along the deep narrow channel that divides Portsmouth from the Isle of Wight, ploughing steadfastly through the deadly, swirling, sucking fast current that ebbs and flows there, past the town pier, the ancient fortifications, harbour-master's tower, old dockyard buildings, and on more slowly into the great crane-lined dockyards.

The Wilmott family waited all day. Hector went down to the ship, and then asked around the dockland area. A matelot who could have been him had been seen in one or two pubs. He had left his kit-bag in one, and in another a hat with an *Augusta* ribbon had been found. A barman remembered a sailor sitting on his own doing some pretty serious boozing, 'like he was drowning his sorrows'.

Hector thought it looked serious, so the police were informed.

Arthur was missing for a day and a night. Two fast tides had sucked him into the harbour mouth, and two more had swirled him back out before his body was grappled by the crew of one of the pilot tugs. The coroner had not had much option other than to issue a death certificate stating death by drowning and institute an inquest for a later date.

The complications over his death delayed the arrangements for Vera's funeral. Lu couldn't bear the thought of her lying there so long waiting and waiting, so she suddenly decided to go and visit her mother at the Chapel of Rest. Because it was Kenny's place of work, the mortuary chapel did not make her feel at all apprehensive; in fact, when she encountered the combined smells of wood, polish, scent, disinfectant and slow corruption, they were the familiar ones Kenny carried about him. Because Kenny was in the trade, as he would insist on calling it, Vera was laid out in the kind of coffin not often seen in the Lampeter area. Kenny said, 'She's had a lot of visitors. I never knew so many people knew her.'

'What do they do when they come here?'

'Same as all people do. They just stand for a minute, say, don't they look young or something? People said she looks peaceful.'

'That's a blimmen lie, Kenny. She don't look peaceful. Why should she be, she had a rotten life.'

'It's no good blaming people, they don't know what to say. It's always seemed to me like talking behind somebody's back.'

'Where have they put him?'

'Dad? Not here.'

'Is that because he's . . . ?' She wanted to get out the words, 'Because the fish got at him?', but it wasn't Kenny's fault that she felt so angry with their father. He couldn't even come home when he *did* have the chance. He had drunk himself silly and fallen over the sea-wall. She wanted to do some violence to him, but he had escaped. He deserved to be dead, but her kind, gentle mother did not.

And it was Arthur who was in her head as she stood in silence pouring her resentment over the remains of Vera.

I'm not sorry he's dead. He's never been here, he never cared about the boxes of work everywhere. He never saw you ill, or worried about money. He was always at sea when there wasn't money for the rent. I hate him. He never wrote to us, just a few cards saying nothing. Did he think that was being a father? I hate him because she felt guilty because she didn't want to take in a lodger. I hope that we haven't yet sunk that low, she said.

Ray had often told about how he used to come home from school and feed Lu bread and milk from a cup, and give her rides in the basket of the errand-boy's bike on

Saturdays. What was Ray doing working on Saturdays when her father was enjoying himself out there in those beautiful, sunny places on the postcards? Join the Navy and see the world. He shouldn't have been seeing the world, he should have been looking after their mum and them. I hope the fishes had a good meal.

Her thoughts were disturbed by a group of aunts and neighbours who came shushing and whispering in. Lu did not acknowledge them. She knew that people were saying that she was taking it badly. She didn't care. From time to time, she would look out from within her mind where she had spent a lot of her time since it all happened, and find Ray looking at her as though it hurt him. Aunty May was keen for her to keep busy, even Kenny would keep giving her a bit of a hug and saying things like, 'We'll be all right, Lu. You'll get over it. Get the funeral over.'

I'm not taking it badly. I'm not even taking it well.

Dotty cried buckets. The aunties all had cheeks widely wetted with tears, her cousins had trickled and sniffed and wiped. When Lu herself again looked down at her mother, the only emotion she could conjure up was anger, a strange anger that had seemed to fly in all directions looking for somewhere to settle, but had found it impossible to do and had consequently gone on trying to alight upon everyone who came within her range. Eventually the anger hovered over her father and settled upon him. Around her, in the chapel, she had heard the sincere platitudes. 'How peaceful she looks.' 'You could imagine she was just asleep.' 'She don't look no more than thirty.'

Lu had stayed chewing the lining of her mouth until it bled. Her mother looked neither peaceful nor asleep. She looked as she had looked for years: hollow-eyed, sunken-mouthed, worried and haggard. And ill. Even though it was over for her, she still looked as though she suffered. Even with her hair tied in a ribbon and dressed in one of the night-gowns she had had in hospital, she looked bad. Lu pushed her way out of the chapel not looking at anyone.

Somebody had tried to press a handkerchief into her hand, but she had pushed it away. Somebody whispered, 'She's taking it bad.'

On the morning of the funeral, before all the aunts and cousins started pouring into the house bringing plates of sandwiches, the three of them had sat in the scullery, silently drinking sweet tea and eating bread and dripping whilst Ray spat and polished his black shoes – his only shoes. They had been speculating about whether any of the Presley relations would come. Ray had said, 'Don't count on it', and 'I wouldn't know one if they did', and Ken had said, 'They never cared about her alive, we don't want them coming now she's dead', and Lu had been wondering whether she could ever do anything so bad that Ray and Kenny would cut her off from them. It had never occurred to her before to wonder whether her mum missed her family.

When the Co-op hearse had arrived, Lu half expected to start behaving like any normal girl and burst into tears and sob unashamedly as Dotty had done. 'Poor Vera,' Dotty had said, 'she never deserved this. Poor Vera . . . poor thing, she was the best neighbour anybody ever had. I'll be lost without her. I can't imagine her not being here any more.' She had put her arms out and drawn Lu into her shoulder. 'Go on, love, have a damned good howl, get it all out of your system. Don't be ashamed of it. If you can't cry when your own mum goes, then when can you?' Ashamed of her dry eyes and even drier emotion, Lu had run upstairs, hoping that Dotty would think her misery too hard to bear.

But the desired and natural grief had not come. Ray had cried, every day, silently, when there was no one about to see him. He would go out the back door, into the lavatory, and ten minutes later come out with red-rimmed shining eyes and a stuffed-up nose. Even Kenny, who nobody expected would, had cried there in the room over his mother's body. He had walked around the coffin, smoothing the waxed finish of the wood, rearranged a lock of her hair and smoothed down the collar of her night-gown.

Lu stood between Ray and Kenny. The boys had wanted her to turn out in her new school uniform, but she stubbornly refused, saying that they would all think she was showing off. So she was wearing Granny Wilmott's hemmed-up funeral coat which had grown too small for the old lady, over a black skirt of her mother's, a blouse bought on the Co-op card, and an expensive black bouclé Tam o'Shanter that Miss Lake had loaned her. Ray, being chief mourner, had had to lay out money for the occasion. He'd paid cash for a black suit from a Fifty-shilling Tailor's and wore a Dunn's bowler-hat. Kenny, because of his job, hadn't had to lay out for clothes.

Lu fixed her eyes on the gleaming toecaps of Ray's shoes.

Kenny's workmates, beautifully turned out to the great satisfaction of senior Wilmotts, bore the coffins to the deep grave. Lu stared at Ray's feet, allowed her eyeballs to become dry, and refused to let herself blink. At last, and with some discomfort, her eyeballs were sufficiently dried by the air to make her tear-ducts automatically trigger off enough moisture to brim over, run beneath her lower lashes and down her cheeks. Perhaps now they would all stop watching her.

Her mother's coffin was lowered first. Crumbs of earth rattled on its lid. Then, when Kenny's workmates took the strain of her father's coffin by the straps and began lowering carefully, Lu snatched off Miss Lake's Tam o'Shanter and ran out of the cemetery.

Later, a policeman seeing her sitting on a bleak shore at Southsea, took her home. It hadn't occurred to her that people would be out searching. When she got back to Number 110, she was filled with remorse and ready to go along with whatever anyone said, especially when Ray and Kenny said that they would feel better going back to work if they knew she was at Roman's Fields. Lu needed no persuading.

It was dark when Ted's little van rattled through the gates of Roman's Fields. May said, 'Don't you worry yourself about anything, Lu. If you don't want to speak to anybody, you don't have to. Bar will be over in the morning; she won't know you're here, but I won't let her come rushing upstairs. I'll give you some valerian to help your nerves, and some marigold to help you get a good night's rest.'

'Let her come up, Aunty. Bar always makes me feel better. I'm not bad, there's nothing wrong with me.'

'Of course there isn't,' Ted said. 'You just needs a bit of peace and quiet, like Ray and Ken.'

'I expect they'll be glad to go out to the pub without having to worry about me.'

'That's just what I told them would do them good,' Ted said. 'We can be proud of them two in the Wilmott family. They looked like proper gentlemen.'

'What d'you mean, looked like – there's more gentlemen in those two lads than in a wagon-load of the likes of them in red coats that chased the fox over my strawberry beds last winter. Offered me five pounds to put it right. Five pounds! I told them to clear off; five years of their time planting new stock there would be more like it.'

Gabriel Strawbridge's voice echoed down the passage from his room. 'Was that Louise's voice I heard?'

'Yes, Mr Strawbridge. Do you want me to come and see you?'

'Do I? My eye, I do.'

'Go along and see him, pet. I'll put the kettle on and then make us all something to eat.'

He was seated in his usual high-backed winged chair, upholstered in a tapestry-like fabric, which Lu used to think looked like a throne. Peering as she came in at the door, he held out his arms in welcome. 'It is you. Dear love, come close and sit here.' He put a cushion on the stool upon which he rested his leg, and took both her hands as she sat down. 'Let me see you, I haven't been able to get you out of my mind. I'm so sorry that you've had to face dreadful events so early in your life . . . but you're strong and you're intelligent. Louise, my dear child. If only I could do something . . . I would do anything.'

'You could put your shawl round me, like you did before.'

'Good Lord, I'm all fingers and thumbs,' he said as she settled at his feet, leaning into his knees. He enveloped her in the shoulder blanket.

'I couldn't cry.'

'No?'

'I don't think I even feel sad.'

'What do you feel?'

She looked up at him. 'Angry . . . I feel so angry. That makes me ashamed.' It was like confessing directly to God, as though his milky eyes were clouds through which he could see her clearly and she could look directly into them.

'Honest anger is nothing to be ashamed of, is it?'

'Yes . . . because she couldn't help dying, could she?'

'Why are you so angry at her?'

'I don't know.'

'For leaving you? It's always frightening when parents die . . . quite terrifying, even for older people.'

'No. No, I was going to make up for everything. Now I can't. She's spoilt everything I was going to do.'

He pulled her head against him and gently caressed the side of her face where his hand rested. God's hand, impersonal and involved, giving but not taking. 'Of course she has. Death is the worst spoiler of all.' His dry, fine-skinned old-man's hands brushed tendrils of hair away from her face, as Ray had done during the nights when she was so ill and he had sat up with her. 'None of us has any business dying. It hurts those who love us most, messes up their lives and leaves them with feelings of guilt that they are not responsible for. They want to please us, give us their achievements and love, and if we die we are rejecting all that. Anger and disappointment seem very natural responses, wouldn't you say?'

May came in bringing wine in long-stemmed glasses. 'Tomato. It's powerful strong but it'll warm you through. You drink that whilst the supper's cooking.'

'Aunty May, I just remembered . . . there was a man at the service carrying a wreath.'

'The one in the grey trilby?'

'Yes.'

'He was a shipmate of your dad's. I said to Ted, how much he was going to miss Arthur. His name was Sid something. Ray and Ken will know, he came back to the house but only had a cup of tea. I only met him a minute, but I thought what a nice man he was.'

'Oh. He must of thought I was terrible running off like that.'

'Never. I said he was a nice man.'

Preoccupied, Lu fiddled with the fringe of the shawl. 'I thought he might of been . . . '

May and her father waited.

' . . . might of been somebody from Mum's family.'

Lu swallowed a mouthful of wine which made her cough. 'I had some brandy once when I was little . . . this is better. I expect that's who I'm really angry with.'

'Your mum's family?' May asked.

Lu looked puzzled. 'No, I don't expect she's got anybody except us, but I just wondered. It's him I feel angry about . . . Dad. They buried him on top of her.'

Gabriel said, 'It's quite usual, Louise m'dear.'

The pressure that had caused her to run away had been building for weeks. It had started one day when Lu, sitting in the lavatory, found herself an unwilling eavesdropper on Vera and Dotty talking over the back fence about the prospect of the *Augusta* returning home, their voices low but carrying. Her mother had said, 'I don't know what to do, I can't go through all that again.'

'Now you had the operation, you're safe.'

'I don't mean falling . . . I mean the rest. I don't want it any more . . . I dread it. I'd as soon let him into my grave as let him into my bed. Last time he was home, he wouldn't leave me alone.'

Dotty had said, 'Ne'mind, maybe he's past it. Why don't you tell him?'

'I don't know. We've got grown-up sons, Dotty. I wasn't brought up like that. I can't stand all that going on with them about. Last time Lu had to sleep in the armchair. She's fourteen this trip.'

Lu had sat there with her hands over her ears, longing for her mother to go indoors so that she could escape down the back garden without her mother knowing that she had been overheard.

May said, 'Married couples are often buried together, whole families sometimes.'

'When they put him in on top, I ran away. It was like my mum was trapped there.'

She didn't see the pained expressions on May's and her father's faces.

Gabriel said, 'Try not to think of it in that way. What was buried today was the physical remains of your parents, not people with awareness, or sensitivity.'

May said, 'Your mum was a lady with a very strong

spirit, you know that yourself, Lu. That spirit wouldn't hang around once it was free to fly, now would it?'

The mundane smell of frying bacon drifted into the room.

'You're going to fry that supper to a frazzle, May. Louise must be hungry, I know that I am,' Gabriel said, rising from his chair. In the two years since the time when she had first met him, he had shrunk in direct ratio to her growth, so that now she could give him a firm kiss on the cheek without stretching up.

The marigold and valerian, or perhaps the relief of having got something off her chest, gave her a night of deep sleep. When she opened her eyes, Bar was in the room. She came to lie beside Lu on the bed.

'Hello, Lu. I knew you would come out here.' She got under the bed-covers, they put their arms about one another and lay as close as lovers. 'Bar . . . I'm so miserable. I never realized . . . I know I didn't cry but I did love her . . . they probably think it's queer, not crying over your mother.'

'I don't, I cried a lot when my old rabbit died, but my Ma . . . ? that'd hurt my heart a lot more than a cony. Perhaps there's some things that's too sorrowful for just crying. Do you think that's it? Poor Lu, I could just cry because of you.' She raised herself on one elbow and kissed Lu's eyelids. 'What say we go and sit by Swallitt. You can cry if you want to – if you don't it don't matter. I'll make you a candle-boat; you can light it and send her a message in it. Or you can just know you loved her without it being anybody's business.'

Later they walked down the lane towards the woods. Bar, wearing a tweed cap, old riding breeches and a man's hacking jacket rolled up at the sleeves and the hem down to her thighs, might have looked like a stable lad had it not been for the black ringlets cascading down her back, and with Lu, in Granny Wilmott's funeral coat and a pair of field boots, they might have been little girls dressed up for a game of grown-ups, except that they walked slowly, engrossed in one another.

'They letting you off school then, Lu?'

'I shan't go back to school.'

'You will.'

'No.'

'But it was the thing you wanted – you been on about it ever since I met you, about learning everything, and going somewhere nice to work.'

'I know. Mum wanted me to, I think she would have done anything to get me to the grammar school, she used to get on to me every night to learn stuff at home. Her and Miss Lake. But I can see now: people like us can't afford to keep on at school after fourteen.'

'I wouldn't of anyway. But you got all them clothes and stuff. Will they take them back?'

'I don't know. They came from charity, so I expect they will.'

'Your Ray will be sorry.'

'He'll get over it. Anyway, we've got big debts over the funeral. I don't want them to be lumbered with me. Ray don't have much as it is, and Kenny likes going out. What's it going to be like having to keep me for years after I should be out at work?'

'You going out to work then?'

Lu nodded. 'I'll get the aunties to speak for me at Ezzard's.'

'What's that?'

'It's a corset factory, all the Wilmotts work there. Granny Wilmott used to, and my cousin Mary has just started. She won't half laugh up her sleeve when she knows I'm giving up the grammar.'

'You hate them factories.'

'I know, but there isn't anywhere else. You can earn more than in a shop, but it's hard work, kills you when you get on piecework.'

'Are you going to tell this aunty?'

'I'll tell Mr Strawbridge first. He won't try to persuade me one way or the other. If he knows I'm serious, then he will help me say it so that it doesn't look as if I'm being daft or ungrateful. And I'm not doing it because I've took things bad because of Mum. I must go out to work and earn my keep. I really need to. I expect they will offer to help out with money, but that would just be another debt to be paid back.'

Bar helped her communicate with her mother in the flame of a candle-end sent floating across The Swallitt on a tin lid. No one except them would ever know. You couldn't talk about that kind of thing – except to a half-gypsy girl who seemed wiser than anybody. Lu still didn't shed any tears, but what with having let her mother go with the floating candle, and having let her chance of being a scholar go, she was soon ready to go home.

Ray, of course, insisted they could manage, but she told him, 'Don't treat me like a kid, Ray, you know we can't. It's going to take months to pay off the funeral.'

'But it's such a waste. Miss Lake says you've got a really good brain.'

'What makes you think I'm going to waste it? Look, Ray, I wanted to go to grammar school because I saw it as the first step towards going to university. I wouldn't be satisfied with just a taste of it. I'm greedy, I'd want everything. You can't keep me for the next six or seven years.'

Kenny didn't join in the discussion, except to say, 'It won't be long till I'm earning a bit more, Lu.'

'And what happens if either of you decides to get married? I'm sure you'll get a lot of girlfriends if you have to tell them you can't afford to marry them because your little sister is still at school at twenty.'

There was no answer to the logic of her argument. When Ray went round to see Miss Lake, he asked her to leave Lu to make her own decision. 'She's got some idea she worked out with an old friend of ours, my aunty's father. She's going to keep on reading different subjects, and later on maybe she'll go to evening classes. I thought maybe you could guide her a bit too.'

Miss Lake was obviously bitterly disappointed. 'I suppose it was something of a dream, Ralph.'

'No, I don't think so, Miss Lake. It was just bad luck that we happen to have been born poor.'

'Things will change.'

Ray smiled, 'You should tell our Kenny that, and he'd tell you that the seeds of destruction of the system have already been sown.'

'Who knows, perhaps we have too narrow a view of what our academic institutions can do? Perhaps there is some truth that the university of life produces graduates who are of more use to society than those with letters after their names. Certainly there are very many brilliant minds that have never been near a conventional institution.' She held out a hand and took Ray's warmly. 'I wanted Lu to be the first of many, but the Lord works in mysterious ways. Please, do promise that you will allow me to help in any way I can.'

'Perhaps you could give her a recommendation to take when she applies for a job?'

'Willingly.'

Leaving Childhood

Louise Vera Wilmott, the child who had once felt that she changed after she had seen both sides of the Portsdown Hills, had grown up to be, at fourteen, shapely and tall.

Having burned her grammar-school boats, she will now need to go humbly to her aunts for help, and then cap-in-hand to ask for work in a factory. All that Lu has to offer, that a factory manager might want, is the Wilmotts' reputation for hard work and docility.

In Britain, in these years of the early thirties, large-scale unemployment makes the whole country uneasy. It shows up most particularly in factory areas like the Lampeter slums with its 'beached' women providing such an enormous pool of dirty-poor female labour. Here, it is important to know somebody who knows somebody who might be taking on a novice.

Eileen Grigg was one fewer girl in the labour pool.

She had disappeared overnight, and it was rumoured that she had been sent away to a Home for Wayward Girls, but nobody seemed to know the truth of it. Not that that stopped people talking.

The school doctor, on his annual visit, had asked the first question which started Eileen on the road to the Home. Mrs Grigg had been told to come up to the school. Mrs Grigg had sworn at the vicar and the vicar had threatened her with the police. Mrs Grigg brought men home and took money to let them go with Lena. Lena Grigg went with her brother, Brian, who had got a disease that had made little crabs grow on private parts and then Lena caught them.

Lu disbelieved most of it, particularly about the crabs, until she went down to the library and read it up in the section that had given her most of her information about human biology and disease.

But there was no reference book to consult when it came to what knowing what Lena herself had said about it all. Lu had asked Dotty if it was true that Lena Grigg had been sent to a Home. 'Yes, she's a dirty little bitch like her mother.'

Lu had thought about Lena and Brian Grigg until she could stand it no longer, and went knocking at Miss Lake's front door at home. When Miss Lake had said for her to come in, Lu had shaken her head. 'I just wanted to know if it's true about Eileen Grigg? Is it true she's in a Home for Wayward Girls?'

Miss Lake, her eyes level with Lu's, with her bun unwound and wearing a kind of robe tied with a cord, stood saying nothing. This was the first time Lu had come face to face with her headmistress since the funeral. Lu's knowledge that she had disappointed Miss Lake over the grammar school did nothing to lessen her aggressive air.

'I have a right to know, Miss Lake. You know how it used to be between me and her, but that don't mean I think it's fair what people are saying about her.' Lu's voice was croaky from the restraint she was trying to show.

'So you may, Louise, but you do not have a right to stand on my doorstep and demand that I tell you.' She held the door wide, with a command that drew Lu into the hallway, then went on leading her into a small room in which there was nothing but a desk, a couple of chairs, a lamp and whole walls full of books. It had the same smell as the library which Lu loved. Her desk was piled with school exercise books.

'Please sit down.'

Lu hesitated. She was stimulated by her anger and did not want it to be drained away by Miss Lake's lesson in the proper way to behave. 'Good manners stem from consideration for others, Louise, so if you do not wish to sit then I shall have to stand too, for you are the visitor here.'

Lu sat. 'They're saying a lot of dirty things about Eileen Grigg. I didn't like her and she did mean things and she liked hurting people, but if it was her brother who did what people are saying, then I don't think it's fair that it should be Lena who's the one sent away. Lena is only my same age and their Brian is nearly as old as my oldest brother. If he made her do it, she wouldn't have been able to stop him, would she? He's a man, a big dockie. If anybody was going to be shut up it ought to have been him.' She paused, her heart seeming to beat fast and loud. 'Is it true, Miss Lake?'

'How can I possibly answer such a question, Louise?'

'Because they say that you were one of the people who decided.'

'Unfortunately that's true, but in a position like mine, there are a good many things that I can never discuss. I hold confidences regarding my Lampeter Street families, and if I were to discuss them with every person who came knocking at my door and demanding that I should, do you think anybody would trust me? Would you?'

'But miss, this is different. People are saying that their Brian . . . ' Now that her anger was being deflected into reasonable discussion, she found it difficult to say the shocking things she had intended to fling at Miss Lake on her way here.

'I know full well what the gossips are saying, Louise.' Miss Lake opened a box and took out a cigarette which she pressed into a short holder and lit up. Who would ever have supposed that Miss Lake smoked cigarettes? 'Louise, you are one of the most intelligent girls I have encountered since I took up teaching, which means that I have too great a regard for you to offer mere platitudes. I am impressed that you care so much about wrong having been done that you have come to confront me.'

'I wasn't meaning it was only you, miss, but I don't know who else to ask, or what to do about it not being fair.'

'What is it that is unfair?'

'Brian Grigg should be locked up, not Lena.'

'Do you know what Brian Grigg has done to Eileen?'

Lu saw the catch. 'No, of course I don't actually know, only they can actually know . . . but it wouldn't be likely it was Lena who forced him to mess about with her, would it? And she wouldn't get a . . . vernal disease on her own.'

Miss Lake blew out a long stream of cigarette smoke and tapped her holder on an ashtray. 'The word is venereal.'

Lu watched as the headmistress began to change into a woman. She said a sex word without being embarrassed. The dictionary had said it was associated with lust. Vernal disease wasn't something you talked about.

'Your friends call you Lu, don't they?'

'Yes, Miss Lake.'

'Would you mind if I called you Lu?'

'No.' Miss Lake had always surprised you with things like that, speaking to kids as though they were real people.

'Thank you. Well, Lu, let me put this to you. If you felt certain in your own mind that a friend of yours had been harmed, what would you do?'

'Tell the police.'

'Then what could you do if, having gone to the police, your friend denies the whole story – probably because she is scared out of her wits that if she tells the truth then she might be hurt much worse in future?'

Lu did not answer at first, but sat looking steadily at Miss Lake. 'Is that what Lena said?'

'If your first concern is for your friend, then mightn't it be best to get her away from the source of the trouble?

Wouldn't that be the best you could do in the circumstances?'

Lu looked up at the rows of books. Rows and rows, all different sizes and shapes and colours of binding covering the walls better than distemper, a bit like being in Mr Strawbridge's room. 'Is a Home for Wayward Girls safe? I thought it was like a prison.'

'There aren't always perfect solutions. Maybe there is a better way and I just haven't seen it.'

Lu didn't know how closely Miss Lake had watched her clever girl's innocent anguish as she struggled to find another way out of a dilemma where there was none. 'But it's not fair, miss. It's just not.'

Miss Lake removed the cigarette from its holder and blunted the burning end until it went out. 'You're absolutely right, Lu, and I'm glad that you think so. When the choice is between something bad and something worse, it's hard on those who have to do the choosing.'

'I suppose it is.'

'Perhaps we should not be so willing to accept situations which involve making decisions which affect other people's lives.'

Miss Lake continued to watch the girl: such potential.

'I'm sorry, Miss Lake.'

'For what?'

'For coming here and saying those things . . . I didn't know.'

'You still don't. We talked only about a hypothetical case of a friend being abused and afraid to tell.'

'I didn't like Lena Grigg, Miss Lake.'

'I know, and that is why I am so pleased that you have stood up for her.' She smiled. 'I remember you two being parted on the first day you came to school. Did you know that it was my first day there too?'

Lu shook her head. 'I might have given her my hair-ribbon if she hadn't tried to snatch it off me,' Lu grinned, 'or maybe I wouldn't. She thought I was too soft to fight her back.'

'I don't really approve of little girls scrapping in the playground, but you were right to stand up for yourself. We can't just go about the world taking what isn't ours.'

'But that's what people did to Lena, isn't it, miss? They've took away her ordinary life.'

'Do you smoke yet? It's all right, I know that most of my girls do by the time they're thirteen.'

Lu looked rather abashed. 'Sometimes . . . not much, sometimes Ken give me one of a Saturday or Sunday.'

Cynthia Lake offered a box of cigarettes and watched Lu take one and accept the light skilfully. 'It's inevitable, it's harmless and pleasant – we all do it eventually. But, Lu, if you are going to smoke cigarettes, take a tip from me and do it with a bit of style . . . not stuck in the corner of your mouth with the smoke trailing up your face.' She folded her arms across her chest, twisted her mouth and half-closed one eye, and became Dotty leaning against a door-jamb watching the world go by.

Lu grinned.

'I should go.'

'Finish your cigarette. Listen, Lu, no one knows it, but I am keeping in touch with the institution where Eileen has gone, and I shall do my best for her when she is no longer under the care of the authorities. The family is moving to a council house where there will be more room.'

Cynthia Lake had been glad to get the headship of the Lampeter Street school because she was a socialist and so against the takers of all kinds. The docks, the Navy, the sweated-labour factories and breweries, the shops that stayed open till midnight, all in cahoots with the system bent on keeping workers ignorant and plentiful. She watched this one as she walked away from the house, the girl of whom she had very high hopes. Lu Wilmott wasn't a victim. Surely she would not become one. She had a fine, bright mind, and she wasn't afraid of speaking it. If that girl, and a few others like her, did not clamber away from this smothering, dulling cycle of marriage and poverty, then Cynthia Lake thought she may as well give up now and spend the rest of her life exploring in some remote regions of the world.

Lu is no longer one of Miss Lake's girls. She has jumped her last rope, chalked her last hopscotch squares, scrumped her last vicarage orchard, had her last school holiday at Roman's Fields. Perhaps she has not bought her last ha'penny bun and sat eating it on the doorstep, nor perhaps picked her last penn'orth of chips and scraps from a hole in the newspaper, but these occasions will not be so appealing when she is a factory girl. If a factory girl has time to play, she will choose quite different games.

But Lu is not a factory girl quite yet; she has first to confront Mr Ezzard.

Mr Ezzard, as seen from the factory floor, is harsh, and nose-grinding.

The majority of school-leavers' jobs in the Lampeter area of Portsmouth are in the gift of Mr Ezzard.

There are very few jobs and many girls out of work, but the aunts have put her name forward, and Miss Lake has sent a supporting letter for a place at 'Ezzard's Royal "Queenform" Factory'.

Outwardly self-possessed, Lu's stomach turns with anxiety as she walks smartly along the road to present herself before the great Mr Jacob Ezzard. When she reaches the factory which is within high walls, the main gates are shut as they always are after the hooter has sounded; thereafter entrance and exit must be sought from the gatekeeper's hut. He was too slow by half for Lu's eagerness. Having said who she was, she waited patiently whilst he looked for her name. 'Another of the Wilmotts? Lord love us, we shan't be able to move for you before long.' He smiled genially. 'I shouldn't have thought there were any more of you left.'

'There aren't. I'm the last of the cousins, the youngest.'

'Ah well, it's a good solid family. I doubt you'll come away empty-handed. But you're lucky, they aren't really taking on any more girls. That way, across the yard and up the stairs. There's a little cubby-hole office at the top, ask there and they'll tell you where to go.'

The 'Queenform' factory is one of the largest in the city. Built three storeys high of reddish-grey brick, its small, squared, gothic-style window-lights are set in regimented rows. It is probably these window-lights that give the building the appearance of a church rather than a factory. A rather gloomy church, too, for what with the colour of the brickwork and the mean lights, one immediately has the impression that the interior must be dismal. There are various buildings corralled within the walls; although Lu has never been beyond the gates, she knows of course that this is box-making, this is packaging, this is the old stables where the vans are kept, and these are the stairs up to the offices.

She has never seen Mr Ezzard, but his reputation as a hard, feared and unpleasant man has gone before him. But with luck, after the first interview, Lu is scarcely likely to be in his intimidating presence again.

When she is shown in, Mr Ezzard, without looking up, says, 'Stand there.'

His ears are large and stand away from his head, further than any Lu ever remembers having seen; or perhaps they are just ordinary and she has never been kept standing for so long studying a person's head from this angle. They are long minutes during which the only sounds are Mr Ezzard's scratchy pen, the loud ticking of a pendulum wall-clock and the rumbling of her own nervous stomach.

Lu, remembering the drilling she has received from the aunties, stands exactly there and has not moved or even fidgeted. He has not looked up once, not even when he opened desk-drawers to take another sheet of paper and a paper-clip. Wilmotts – mostly the women, but Grandpa Wilmott was a cutter – have worked at stay-making for the Ezzard family since the original Ezzard set up in a small back room not far from where he stepped off the boat as a refugee. Generations on now, the Ezzard factory has grown to a great corset empire. It is still run by Ezzards and for Ezzards. The pool of unemployed female labour is still full.

Mr Ezzard laid down his pen and turned over some handwritten pages. He frowned and pursed his lips as he read them to himself.

Dear Mr Ezzard,

I enclose herewith a character reference regarding the ex-pupil I mentioned to yourself and Mrs Ezzard at the annual dinner of the Dickens Society. You were kind enough to say that you would interview the girl. I am sure that you will find her a most willing worker.

Yours most sincerely,
Cynthia Lake

Re: Louise Wilmott

I am pleased to recommend this girl for consideration as an employee. She has been an exemplary student, and has gifts which, I sincerely hope, may some time in the future be developed to their full potential. She was perfectly capable of continuing her education but it has not proved possible for her to do so.

I am aware that she is applying for factory work, but I know her to be capable of a clerical or secretarial position. She is honest, trustworthy and gives her full attention to any task given her.

Cynthia J. Lake

Miss Lake had said Lu might read it before she sent it off. It was the first character reference Lu had seen, and she was impressed by the language as it applied to herself. She could have recited every word. Now, submissively standing looking at Mr Ezzard's ears, she felt gratified and proud. Even so, she continued to stand respectfully before Mr Ezzard's desk.

As the office clock struck the half-hour, her prospective employer threw down the pages and at last sat back and looked at her. His eyes, which were surprisingly blue and hedged by thick, black lashes, held Lu's attention there.

'So, you are another of the Wilmotts?'

'Yes, sir.'

'However many of you have we got already?' He probably knew, and so did Lu, but she perceived that it was not a question.

'And your mother is dead?'

(Don't do none of that lah-de-dah talk.) 'Yes, sir, she used to be one o' your outworkers, she put 'and-stitched lace and bows on "Queenforms" and I used to help her.'

'And now you want me to give you a job.'

'Yes, sir, please, sir, if you will take me on.'

'I'm told that you are clever, a bit of a brain-box, that right?'

Lu fixed her eyes on his tie-pin – perhaps it was a real diamond. 'Not particular, sir.'

'Come now, come.' He picked up Miss Lake's reference. 'I'm sure you know what this is?'

'Is it a letter from Miss Lake, sir. She said she would give me a character.' Call him 'sir' till he takes you on, then you start calling him 'Mr Ezzard'. George Ezzard, his brother . . . don't never let yourself get in a corner with George Ezzard: he takes advantage.

'Yes.' He peered up at her, with his head on one side, looking her up and down. 'You're tall . . . rather developed . . . you're only fourteen?'

Lu felt herself begin to blush. 'Last June, sir.'

The sudden thrust of his stiff forefinger as he leaned towards her across the desk made her stiffen and start back as he probably intended. 'Miss Lake says you could be clerk material.'

Aunty Glad said, 'Don't think that Mr Ezzard's going to be impressed by anything except how fast you can work a treadle. He won't care if you can talk double-Dutch.' Like the mistake of showing off the pink slippers, it had been a mistake to give a rendition, at Granny Wilmott's Christmas party, of the French national anthem she and Bar had learned from Aunty May.

Lu's heart sank. 'Um . . . yes, sir.'

'Well?'

'I'm not bad at sums, and my writing's neat enough.' She hated doing this to herself, but it was safer than letting him think she was a smart-ass.

'And you think you're good enough to be a clerk?'

She longed to say, 'Yes, yes, I could do it standing on my head. I can add up and do decimals and long division and say up to my sixteen-times-table, and I know all the capitals of Europe, I know who Circe and Ulysses are, and Quasimodo the hunchback, and about the girlhood of Beatrice and Hero . . . and in a glass case in Alton Museum there is an Iron Age loom-weight labelled, "Howton's Ford Field-Walk 1929 – Presented to the Museum by Miss Louise Wilmott".'

Instead, she cast her eyes deskwards. 'I really don't know, sir.'

'Miss Lake seems to think that you might, but I have no vacancies in the offices. But I'll take you on as a button-threader. If you prove yourself quick-fingered enough not to keep the pieceworkers waiting, you can go on to be a runner – you know what a runner is?'

'Yes, sir, my mum started as a runner with old Mr Ezzard.'

Nodding impatiently, he said, 'Good, good,' and scribbled something on a pad of yellow paper.

The interview had gone on quite long enough; he had only prolonged it because Alma and Miss Lake belonged to the same society. He liked to please Alma. Perhaps, after a few months, when he saw how the girl shaped up in the factory . . . Alma was his second wife – young, pretty; and in five delightful years of marriage had added four new children to the eight bequeathed her on the death of his first wife. In total he now had five sons, all of whom would be needed in the expansion of the 'Queenform' factory he envisaged now that big London stores such as Swan & Edgar were looking for specialists to undertake high-quality, made-to-measure work. Expansion was imperative – twelve Ezzard offspring all needing to be fed, clothed and educated.

Ripping the sheet from the pad, he held it out to Lu. 'Take this to Mr George . . . you know Mr George?'

'Yes, Mr Ezzard.'

He gave a brief smile. 'Right, I guess the Wilmott regiment has been briefing you. In the factories I'm Mr Ezzard, my brother is Mr George and my father likes to be referred to as . . . ?'

'Mr Queenform.'

Mr Ezzard nodded. 'And that's no joking matter. My father created the famous "Queenform" pattern, and it's patented . . . you know "patented"?'

Ingenuousness in her gaze, she denied knowing.

'It means that the pattern is ours under the law. If anyone tries to copy it, then they can be taken to court – indeed *would* be taken to court. It was my father's father who instituted the tradition that no one other than the head of "Queenform" takes on its workers. This is a family concern, up here and down there on the factory floor. Owner and worker come face to face, we now have a common interest: the well-being of "Queenform". Now go.'

'Thank you, Mr Ezzard . . . thank you for the chance.'

Clutching her passport to the great 'Queenform – Stay-makers to Royalty' empire, Lu turned to leave.

'Stop! Your time will start from when you clock on after dinner. It's already going on for nine o'clock, and by the time you've found Mr George, and he's given you to your overseer, half the morning will be gone. Understood?'

'Yes, Mr Ezzard.'

'I haven't finished. Don't think that this letter gives you any privileges. And don't think you will ever get into these offices until you have worked at every job and on every machine in the factory. I have taken note of what Miss Lake has said, but all that means is that I shall be keeping my eye on you. If you don't come up to scratch you haven't got an ice-cream in Hades' chance of getting your backside on a clerk's stool. Understood?'

None of the aunts had mentioned that the great Mr Ezzard used words like 'backside'. Never mind what they said about Mr George, Lu had seen the way this one's eyes had roamed over her. 'Yes, Mr Ezzard.'

One and six a week. He wasn't doing her any favours: that was the lowest pay anybody started on. Mary, who had already started in the same machine room as her mother and Aunty Phil, had started on two shillings. Uncle Ted had paid better than that picking and packing stick-beans, and although she had been tempted at first to go back to Roman's Fields, she felt it was necessary for her and Ray and Kenny to stay together.

There were times when she longed to be back there, seated at the kitchen table after a day in the fields, listening to Uncle Ted speculating on the chance of rain before the beans went stringy and beany, or to Mr Strawbridge painting a word-picture of Zulu 'rondavels' built of dried mud, or the vastness of the 'high veldt' and the awesome-ness of the mountainous regions. Or to be with Aunty May, out in the fields, early morning on a good day, pegging down the runners to grow new strawberry plants, squatting over the lines, keeping up with the skilled 'casuals', and with Bar chattering on telling the latest village gossip: Brown's the Butcher bought the Smithfield champion and hung it in his cold store a month; the Co-op's going to open a shop in the village; Warwick's has got their daffodil bulbs in; the flagpole on old Cat's tower fell off. Bar and The Swallitt Pool. Duke breaking in his own bred gelding. Duke giving her long looks and flirty winks.

Bar had already got herself a job on the Boarhunt Estate. Stable-hand. A boy could have called himself a groom, but Bar's job was not dignified by a name. Bar hadn't thought this any kind of a problem; she was strong, good with horses, and unlikely to cause indignation in the village by taking the job a village girl could have done with. No village girl would want a job mucking out stables and exercising horses, and these days the village lads wanted something a sight better than mucking out horses when there were towns within cycling distance. So no one raised any eyebrows at Bar doing the job.

Lu crossed the gravelled yard between the office and the factory. This famous workplace where the famous 'Queenform' stays and corsets were created. The antithesis of open bean-fields. No blade of grass, petal, or leaf of tree intruded here; the only thing God-given in this whole area of industrial Portsmouth was the sky; even that was veiled with smoke from factory chimneys, from workers' homes, from railway engines, road traffic, firing ranges and naval vessels.

The noise that came from the factory was a familiar one to Lu – not only to Lu, but to most of the inhabitants of the poor areas of Portsmouth. Here, many staymaking factories had sprung up generations ago and expanded into every available space. It was a huge industry.

In the building for which she was making, there were at least one hundred machinists passing work beneath the needle-foot of one hundred machines. Some machines had four or more needles. Each needle-foot gave out a sound like no other – not like the spinning or the cotton-looms of Lancashire, the stocking machines of Derbyshire or the knitting machines of Nottingham. The first sound to catch the ear of a stranger passing by on the pavement outside the walls of the Ezzard factory was the regular beat of the forty-horsepower engine rotating a great iron wheel, then the ear caught the flip-slap of the driving bands, then the whir of spinning drive-wheels and the unique sound of hundreds of precision-made sewing machines at work spearing closely woven Courtiel or twill fabric.

Although Lu had been born and bred into one of Portsmouth's staymaking families and had grown up familiar with the language of that huge industry – 'seaming', 'fanning', 'binding', 'flossing', 'flat binding', 'boning', 'slotting' – she had never seen the inside of a factory.

At the side-door of the sewing room she paused a minute to quell her fears. She was about to start work in a corset factory. For a moment she was forced to confront what that meant. The lives of her sour grandmother Wilmott and of the aunts who had married Wilmotts showed in the hard lines of their faces, their petty jealousies and the caustic tongues. Please God, don't let me get like them . . .

Her mother had gone on working for Ezzard's even when she must have guessed she had a growth in her. Rage at such unfairness was never far from the surface, made her want to hammer her fist into something. Somebody must be to blame for keeping them so poor that her mother had had to hand-sew lace and bows for a few pence a dozen. If it hadn't been for Ray, what would they have done all those years when her father was away?

'Oi, what do you think you're doing there?' The security

man's voice made her jump. He took the yellow paper from her hand. 'You're the other new Wilmott girl. Mr Ezzard sees you hanging about like that, you'll be out on your ear before you even start. You come to find Mr George? Well, come on then, buck up, I'll take you to him.' As he led her through a side–door he said in a more kindly voice, 'Don't take no notice, sweetheart, me bark's worse than my bite. Here you are. Don't let 'em know you're scared, they can't eat you.' He gave a short laugh. 'Only suck out your marrow.'

The noise was terrific! She could only surmise what he said by his quick march and beckoning finger. At the far end of the sewing room was a glazed mezzanine office giving the occupant full view of the work room. The security man knocked once and put his head round the door, handed over the yellow paper, said, 'New girl, Mr George,' and left Lu to it.

Mr George. Dressed in tweed jacket and trousers and no tie. He was not bad looking, younger than Mr Ezzard. But you could tell that they were brothers. He looked at the yellow slip. 'You're to start as a button-threader then. What do they call you?'

'Lu, Mr George.'

'And you are only fourteen? Big girl for your age.' He cocked his head sideways in just the way Mr Ezzard had, and kept her talking, presumably to pass the time. Again, as in Mr Ezzard's office, Lu answered in her best Ports-mouthian whine which her mother used to detest. 'Have to look at your hands – no good if you've got old breaks that have knit badly.' He picked up her hand and inspected it. 'You'll do,' then, indicating with his head, 'this way.' He led her down the length of the sewing room. Eyes flicked a glance at her, but not for long enough to slow down the flying shuttles and thrumming needles. He raised his voice to be heard. 'You'll be under Mrs Tuffnel. You know Mrs Tuffnel?'

Lu shook her head.

'She's overseer in this room. Nellie!' he yelled, and a woman stood up from one of the worktables separate from the rest. She had big breasts straining her white apron, and shapeless ankles that seemed to brim over her shapeless bar-button shoes. She walked on very bad feet, worse even than Lu's aunties'. A room filled with hunched backs and bowed heads, all bent close to the point where the needle pierced the fabric, so as to watch that there was not a hitch as the pink seams were sucked under the needle-foot.

Lu's introduction to Mrs Tuffnel was brief and conducted in shouts, ending with, 'All right, Mr George.' Lu followed the overseer into a room off the machine room. The room, lit with a couple of old-fashioned oil-lamps hanging from beams, had walls of old, dark, bare brick, along which were gloomy recesses; windows of frosted glass were barred with iron and the floor had a cobbled surface like some of the old streets.

'This is where you'll be . . . I know it looks bad when you first come in, but you get used to it.' She gave a brief, wry smile. 'I started in this very room as a button girl. It an't changed; I have.'

Mrs Tuffnel sank gratefully on to a bale of something. Now she looked at the yellow slip. 'Which of the Wilmotts got you in?'

'My Aunty Elsie spoke for me.'

'That's her married to Hec who drives the beer lorries.' Lu nodded.

'Knew Hec Wilmott years ago.' She slapped her high stomach. 'When me and him both was a bit lighter than we are now . . . Mine's not beer, though. Know your granny too, poor old soul. Can't hardly see now, can she? Corsets gets us all in the end, one way or another. I expect you know what button girls do. Nothing much to know. One reason why Ezzard's likes to take on girls who has family is that they don't come as strange to the work. Your ma went before, if I remember right?'

'Yes, she passed on a few weeks back.' Words like 'dead' were taboo.

'She couldn't have been no age, what took her?'

Cancer was a word equally taboo. The disease might almost be caught by hearing it said. 'Growth' was acceptable: it had the drama but not the dread. 'She had a haemorrhage.'

'Oh, the poor dear . . . but there are worse things. Anyway, you'll be getting over it by now.' There was no questioning inflection in the sentence, rather it was a positive statement: you are all right, you have to be; no use moping, you just have to get on with things.

Lu nodded. Mrs Tuffnel was right: nobody really wanted to know.

'You'll be run off your feet, I can tell you that for a fact, but you're young. When anybody calls for buttons or straps you'd better move – you hold up a pieceworker and she'll put her scissors in you . . . Not really, but nobody on piecework can afford to stop.'

'Am I stopping you now?'

Now that she was here, Lu wanted to get going, to learn whatever she had to. 'It part of my job training up new girls. Didn't he tell you, Mr George?'

'Only that you are the overseer.'

'Well, it goes like this. While you're learning the job, you're supposed to hand over to me best part of what you earn. That way it don't cost the firm anything and you learn quick.'

It quite pained Lu to see her first wages disappearing before her eyes. She had given up everything to get a pay-packet. 'Mr Ezzard told me I won't get paid for this morning.'

'I know. This is a place where you don't get summat for nothing. It's hard work, the pay's bad, but we survive.'

Lu thought briefly of her mum and the endless boxes of work. 'My aunty said a girl can earn more in a factory than serving in a shop.'

'Ah . . . factory girls are pretty much down the ladder, but I reckon shop girls come below because, no matter how hard they work, they don't take home any more. On piecework, it's the more you do the more you earn.'

'I don't mind hard work.'

'That's the spirit. And about the money you're supposed to pay me. I know how it feels to earn your own bit of money, and I expect yours is needed now your mum's gone on before. I never have taken money for learning a girl.'

'Honest?'

Mrs Tuffnel smiled. 'Honest. But what I expect is that a girl takes notice of what she's told first off so it don't waste anybody's time. That's what it's all about here: time. You've got to fill every minute you're on the factory floor with Mr Ezzard's work. He's the paymaster, and there's few enough of them about.'

Into Lu's mind flashed the image of Mr Ezzard in his big office, seated behind his big desk keeping her waiting till it suited him to look up. The paymaster. She hadn't heard the word before, but it fitted just right.

The door opened suddenly and a young woman in an apron and cap came in. 'Straps, Nellie?'

'Well, you know where they are, Katy.'

'Hello, Lu, I haven't seen you in weeks. Sorry to hear about your mum and dad. You give up going to the grammar? Can't stop, see you dinner-time.' She grabbed a box and made a stroke on a tally-board and gave Lu a wink. 'Well, don't let them catch you at it, Lu,' and was gone.

Mrs Tuffnel smiled. 'You know Katy Roles then? I suppose you'd have been in the same class as her.'

'She used to be one of my best friends.'

'Oh, well, that's nice, I dare say there's other girls you'll know. A lot of your Wilmotts work upstairs. I expect you'd have liked to have got in with them; but still, it's a nice bunch we've got down here.'

Lu wondered whether it made any difference because when she had come through the factory all she saw of the machinists were their figures hunched over machines concentrating, not talking, moving only where the stitching took them.

'Let's get the training done with then, Lu.'

She made her painful legs and feet take her round the room, and as she went she tapped many different boxes, thankfully all labelled. 'Trimmings for the bust-tops and corsets, laces, ribbons, hooks and eyes, needles, made-up straps, boning, springs and cottons – make sure when somebody asks for "Sylko" it *is* "Sylko", and when a fanner asks for a different colour, get the right one. Know what that's for?'

'Stitching fans over the ends of bones?'

'That's it! Being a Wilmott will be a help to you. Wilmotts, Samphiers, Tuffnels and half a dozen more families have been making stays in Pompey since Adam was a lad. You won't need to touch any of this stuff till you're a runner, but you might as well know now, save time then. All you need to know to start is the buttons, and how to prepare them. Really, a trained monkey could do it, which is why they won't pay anything hardly, but it's a job that's got to be done and there's more girls wanting to do button-threading than there is buttons wanting to be threaded. So you just get on and get it done: the sooner you learn, the sooner you'll get on a machine.'

This time when Mrs Tuffnel rested, she supported her sagging stomach from below with linked hands, just as Vera used to do. Lu looked around at the grim walls and wondered whether her mother used to come in here. She had never been curious about the time when her mother worked in the factory. It was impossible to imagine her seated on a stool bent over a machine. Lu's image of her was seated in the low, sagging armchair, as close as possible to the light, doing hand-finishing. One day, she thought, I'll work out how many . . . No. To think of all those piles of finished work endlessly replaced by piles waiting to be finished made the walls seem to close in on her.

'What's he paying you?'

'One and six, till I learn the job.'

'You've just learnt it. Well, best get started.' She hauled herself to her feet, still holding in place her women's bits and pieces. 'Things to remember . . . If you see a rat, don't go panicking and throwing things at it, just bang hard on something so George can let Nig get at it. Go to wee before you come in because the WCs here are more often than not choked up. Don't drop your scissors or you'll have the whole shop floor on your neck. You'll want to buy your own scissors – try not to get yourself into debt over them, but if you do come and tell me.'

Lu was still thinking of rats, her eyes searching the gloomy corners. None of the aunts had ever said there would be rats.

As Nellie Tuffnel often said to her husband: You could cry to see little bits of girls straight from school running their backsides off for a couple of coppers a day. Nellie was an angry woman, but it seldom showed. Certainly not with her girls.

'Our Ray is good with money, he wouldn't let me get into debt. I'll probably get them on the Co-op card.'

Poor little kite, Nellie Tuffnel said to herself. Same poor little kite I used to be myself, and that don't seem so long ago either.

Out in the main factory, the noise was overwhelming, but she quickly learned to interpret her orders and run back and forth, seeming to have to do a dozen things at once to keep the needs of the women she served supplied. There were other girls doing the same job, but they were ahead of her in experience and speed; Katy was one, and it was Katy who, on the run, would point at what Lu was supposed to fetch.

What fascinated her most was the speed at which the machinists worked, and the skill. Straps and binding zipped through so fast that she wondered how they could control what they did. She would have liked to stand and watch the different kinds of operations, but there was never a minute to spare, and she was very aware of Mr George watching everything that went on from his office. There was something about him she didn't like. Whenever he left his office he had with him his black whippet on a piece of rope which he played out so that the horrible bony dog could sniff around under the benches for scent of vermin.

Although there were scores of women and girls, there was nobody she could talk to until the hooter went when, almost as one, they shut off their machines and made for the exit. There Kate Roles was waiting so that they could hurry along together. Kate, having started work whilst Lu was still at school, knew everything worth knowing. 'I'm glad you decided to come to work, Lu. See you when the five-minute hooter goes. Don't be late or you'll get locked out.' Katy's dinner would be ready, but Lu would have to grab whatever was there and do a bit of shopping, which they had agreed would be one of her jobs. She determined that in future she would be more organized and try to make a sandwich before she left in the morning.

And so Lu worked her first day, her first week, her first month. Her whole day was controlled by the factory hooter. She would never be late, never risk having money docked. And whilst she was waiting to become a machinist, her life was the factory and the factory her life. She longed for a machine of her own, to have control of the speed, to learn to make seams pass under the needle so fast that it was impossible to see it move. Then at last Mr George called her in and said she could start on a machine. Soon she would be on piecework. George Ezzard said, 'Any mistakes, dirty work, stains, crooked seams, spoiled work – in fact anything that isn't perfect – Nellie will send back to be done again. You only get paid for perfect work. If it's too bad to be salvaged, then rejects are deducted from your pay. Understood?'

'Yes, Mr George,' she said, her face sweetly grateful. 'Thank you very much.'

'You'll find that Ezzard's always looks after its promising girls.'

Hurrying home, Kate said, 'You want to watch that George. Now he's give you a leg up he thinks you owe him a favour.'

'I know,' Lu said.

'When I started, I was warned about him, so I was careful, yet he still found a chance to catch me when I was getting stuff from the store. I never even knew he was in there.' She gave an exaggerated shudder. 'It was horrible, I was getting a heavy box off the top shelf, both hands, and there he was behind me, pressed up close. "Oh," he says, "that's a bit heavy for you, Kate, let me give you a hand." Give me a hand! He did that all right, he squeezed my titty.' She nudged Lu. 'Know what I did? "Oh, Mr George," I said, "you did put the wind up me. I never heard you," and I turned round quick and cracked his nose with my elbow, and dropped the bloody box on his feet. You know how heavy plywood boxes are. I never told my dad or he'd have murdered him.'

Lu laughed at the imagined scene. 'You was pretty smart.'

'Presence of mind, Lu. It's surprising how it comes to you. I always carry me scissors with me since then. You do the same.'

December 1933

At Roman's Fields, May was preparing for the arrival of Lu, Ralph and Ken for Christmas. She cleared out the box room, painted it, put in two camp beds, trimmed the house and baked, excusing her abundance with the excuse that, 'It never seemed worth it for just us, so I thought I'd have a bit of a splurge.'

Everybody had to be back at work on the morning following Boxing Day, so they piled everything into the two days.

Lu mostly spent her time beside the fire, curled up hugging her knees, in one of the big chairs, absorbed in a novel. Ted took Ken out with a gun, who suddenly found a sport more enthralling than football. Ted didn't mind: he thoroughly enjoyed trudging over the frozen fields with his talkative young nephew. 'Young Ken's all right, May. I've took to him. You should have seen him – a natural shot. I wished for a minute I had two good arms so we could have had a proper shooting match. I should have liked that.'

Ray suddenly took to horses, and Bar, who had never got over her first sight of him back in that first summer, had a heart overflowing with love for him and a soul filled with joy at having Lu again. She had become a woman. Even wearing her usual breeches, shirt and man's cap, one could see that. At seventeen she carried splendid round breasts high on a wiry, spare figure, which seemed almost too slender to support them. Her uncut, black curly hair, when she let it free to blow in the wind as she exercised a fast horse, made her look as untamed as she probably was.

Bar spent whatever time she had free from the stables in their company. On Christmas morning, before their coats could become spoiled by the Boxing Day chase of the fox over winter fields, she took Ray to see the hunters. They were beautiful animals and she was proud. She was on duty much of the time, but on Christmas evening she came in wearing a full black skirt and a knitted top, this so shrunken that both Ray and Ken found it hard to stop watching her all the time.

May said, 'Didn't Duke want to come?'

'I told him I was coming over, but he never said. You can never tell with Duke, can you?'

Gabriel Strawbridge said, 'He said he didn't hold with Christmas, so I told him that the Yule log and the holly and mistletoe was pagan and nothing to do with Christmas. I thought he quite took to that idea. Hark . . . I think that's his tread.'

At that point, Duke makes his appearance. Lu, who has been curled up cracking nuts, jumps up and brushes the debris into the grate. He is a grown man now and is beautiful. His boyish chin has squared off and his hollow cheeks show off his fine, high cheekbones. He has still not cut his hair, but wears it oiled and tied back and bound in a kind of black stocking tube. In spite of his boots, black trousers and a knitted fisherman's jumper, nothing can stop the image of him standing on the bent willow from leaping into her mind.

'Right on cue, Duke,' Gabriel Strawbridge says. 'I was just about to say you were on your way to making your fortune. You've got some nice horses up in the field.'

'I have, Master Gabr'l, main good bloodstock. I reckon I'm ready to ask the estate to let me rent some of their spare stabling.' Although he is speaking to Gabriel Strawbridge, his unwavering gaze is directed at Lu.

May says, 'D'you know Ray and Ken? Well, you do now. Why don't you take a plate, Duke, and help yourself to what you want whilst we go on clearing a bit of space?'

'I shall, Mis Wilmott.' He takes a plate, fills it with meat and bread and goes directly to where Lu is and seats himself beside her. 'You've grown up.' His eyes roam over her from ankles to breasts and back again, as men's eyes do. 'You out to work?'

The unabashed appraisal doesn't make her bridle as it often does with men at the factory; instead it makes her unconsciously breathe deeper and raise her rib-cage, provoking his interest. 'I'm a machinist.'

'What's that when it's at home?' He opens his mouth to the bread and Lu watches his teeth as they bite through the crust and then his tongue as he cleans his lips of powdery flour. Without thinking, she brushes a stray crumb from the corner of his mouth, and a fleeting sensation like a sweet, pleasurable twitching, almost a pain, flashes between her thighs.

'I work a sewing machine in a corset factory.'

'I thought you was going to college.'

She shakes her head. 'I gave it up.'

He laughs. 'Fancy that. And there's me thinking about you all dolled up in one of them posh uniforms. What d'you wear to be a corset girl then?'

He sits just a couple of feet from her, and she is more aware of his presence than she has ever been, even more than on the significant day at The Swallitt Pool. She still can't stop herself from thinking of that image of him ready to dive. Lean, white body with patches and lines of growth of dark hair, brown arms, feet and face, black hair plastered to his head . . . and the thing that was the focus of her attention, the unforgettable thing – which as yet doesn't have a name because playground words are too silly and the others she doesn't yet know.

'You're making fun of me.'

'I'm not. What's wrong with asking?'

'Nothing, but it's just any old skirt, and an overall.'

His direct gaze and direct way of asking what he wants to know puts Lu in mind of her aunts' blunt manner of questioning. The corners of his mouth lift a little and his eyes incite. 'Do you go swimming?'

There! Now she stirs herself and looks directly back at him and, keeping her voice so that it doesn't carry to her brothers, almost snaps, 'Yes. Do you?'

'When the mood takes me. Do you go in the sea?'

'When the mood takes me.'

'In your skin?'

She knows that she has flushed and is annoyed with herself. 'Not since I grew up.'

'That's a shame. It's the best way.' Half smiling, he bites into a slice of tart. 'I don't see what growing up's got to do with it, anyway. I enjoy myself in any natural way I can. So should you.' He sucks a bit of stickiness from his fingers. 'I'll come down your way and see you one of these days.' Without a further glance in Lu's direction, he puts his plate on the hearth and goes. 'Thanks for the supper Mis Wilmott. I've still got the horses to water.'

Ray is sitting easily, smoking a cigarette and talking about his union work, Bar listening quietly. Bar, who hardly knows what a union is, let alone a shop steward, is absorbed in the workings of that earnest world.

Ken is listening to Ted explain the distracting tactics of some game birds.

Gabriel has nodded off.

May is filling hot water bottles.

Lu sits with her knees drawn up to her chin, gazing into the burning log fire recalling that he said – there's me thinking about you all dolled up. Did he mean her to know that he'd been thinking of her? The unsuspecting virgin has been visited by one of the darker gods, who has left her with an exciting image of potent unconformity.

In the new year, Lu, putting up her hair in a tidy bun and her age from sixteen years to eighteen, enrolled in a WEA class in local government – not because she was particularly interested in the subject, but because she had made up her mind to do something to educate herself, and local government was the only evening class that wasn't dressmaking or cookery – which wasn't her idea of education. Mr Matthews, the tutor, said he wasn't supposed to take anyone under nineteen, so he bent the rules – and rather more than he realized.

The prospect of not being accepted for a class she hadn't been particularly keen on in any case made Lu determined they should take her. 'It's supposed to be the *Workers'* Educational Association, isn't it? I'm a full-time worker, so why shouldn't I be able to join?'

Mr Matthews being a man who gave all his spare time to educating workers in civic affairs, thought that no such arbitrary rule should keep a youngster so eager for his subject out of his classroom.

On Friday evenings, until Kate started going out with a regular boyfriend, Lu and Kate went to the cinema, the 'Royal' or the 'King's' for a show, no matter what the programme. Sometimes they went to the cinema again on Sundays. They bought *Picturegoer*, and argued over their favourite stars. The boyfriend put paid to those outings unless the Pompey team had an away game, in which case the girls could have that Saturday evening together.

Whenever she could manage to fit in the cleaning and ironing during the week, she went out to Roman's Fields on Saturday afternoon and returned on Sunday evening. By running to the station after she had taken her machine to pieces, cleaned and oiled it on Saturday morning, she was just in time to catch the train to Fareham, where half an hour later she would arrive to find Uncle Ted waiting with the new second-hand pick-up truck that was big enough to get the strawberry crop to the station more quickly than waiting for the unreliable carrier's cart. It also proved invaluable in getting about for pleasure. Mr Strawbridge loved a trip a few miles out to a country pub. And so, throughout the year, Lu became such a regular visitor to Roman's Fields that she kept a change of clothes there, and took to wearing breeches and a shirt like Bar.

Bar had taught her to ride without a saddle on her father's work-horse – a strong, fluffy-hoofed mare; and Ted had taught her to drive the van. As with her work as a machinist, the synchronization of foot and hand was paramount, and she worked hard to become a competent driver.

She kept her two worlds quite separate. Kate tried to pump her about what she got up to when she went away, but Lu would only say that she went to stay with her aunty and uncle. The fact that she could ride and drive now would have made her different from the girls she worked with, especially now that she had lived down her short episode as a scholar.

When the WEA course finished after the spring term, Mr Matthews suggested that the class should go for a fish-and-chip supper. The course had been surprisingly interesting, and she had never missed an evening of listening to him describing how a council worked, how the electoral system worked, what democracy was.

Over the chip supper, he asked, 'Have you ever attended a meeting of the full council, Miss Wilmott?'

'No. I didn't know we could until you said.'

He leaned forward, his glasses glinting with enthusiasm. 'You should go. If you're a bit apprehensive about going to a place like the Guildhall for the first time, I'd be pleased to show you. Could you get time off?'

She grinned, 'I could probably be sick enough to go to something like that.'

'But you'd lose an afternoon's pay.'

'They say you have to pay for experience. It might even be better than going to the pictures.'

The Guildhall, which as a child she supposed must belong to somebody important, was a revelation, as was the council in special session, the mayor and aldermen in robes, the mayor wearing a heavy gold chain; the polished wood panelling of the council chamber reflecting the blaze of lights.

Mr Matthews was, it appeared, quite well known to many of the council officials. He gave her a short conducted tour along some of the many impressive corridors.

'You said the ratepayers paid for all this, is that right?'

'Yes, in a way it is the official home of the mayor, and he's Portsmouth's representative.'

'But what's it for? Why does it need to be so big and grand?'

As so often over the past weeks, this questing girl had put him on the spot with her simple questions. He did his best to give her a reasonable explanation about civic pride and its effect on the population as a whole.

'It doesn't work though, does it? How can people be proud of paying for a place like that when half of them are out of work? People where I live can hardly afford paint for their walls or lino for their floors. The council could run just the same without spending all this money on robes and cars and stuff that doesn't matter, couldn't it?'

She had learned well over the months. Mr Matthews did not have an answer that would sound convincing to a girl who lived in a place like Lampeter Street. 'I'm afraid my answer will be too lame for you. But it is traditional, and such trappings give dignity to the office, wouldn't you agree to that?'

'No. It just seems silly. It's all right for children making each other into princesses with daisy chains; I don't think grown-ups ought to. If I was a councillor, I'd put a stop to it.'

For the tutor, it was one of those moments that made all the winter evenings spent in stale, cold classrooms worth while. 'Perhaps one day you will be.'

'Me? No, I don't think so. I expect I shall go away when

'I'm a bit older, there's so many other things to do.' Until then, she hadn't known that this was what she intended.

He offered to buy her tea in a café, and she accepted with the kind of pleasure that made the occasion a pleasure for him. She intrigued him. She had the kind of eagerness for learning that he used to have when he was her age – still did have for that matter, the only difference being that he had found a channel into which he could guide his enthusiasm, whilst hers appeared to be uncontained and ready to break out in all directions. That was how it should be in the young.

In the tea-shop she still questioned him closely about the ethics of spending ratepayers' money on pomp and luxury. Stock answers were not for her: she taxed him, made him question what he had not questioned for years, put him on the spot, until almost in self-defence he asked her about herself. She told him about having won a free place at the grammar school, which did not surprise him. What a bright light she must have been in that backstreet school amidst the terraces and factories. What a bright light she was in his class.

'I know it's too late now, but I do sometimes wonder how I would have got on there.'

'There are more roads than one to education.'

'That's what I thought, and why I started your classes. I've learned things with you that I shouldn't ever have learned at the grammar.'

The ageing tutor admired the girl's confidence . . . wisdom even. She shouldn't be lost to factories and babies. 'But they do give you that piece of paper that opens doors to opportunity.'

'That's all right if they're the sort of doors you want opened. I mean, would I want to be a teacher? It's what everybody said I could be. It's what my mother would have been if she hadn't met my dad.'

It suddenly occurred to him that she was even younger

than the age she had given to get into his classes. She was simultaneously innocent and wise. A young woman teacher with a Lampeter Street background would be exactly what poor schools could do with. Much better than the usual tired teachers with nowhere else to go, or the modern, idealistic products of private education and university.

'What job would you like?'

'I don't know, I really don't. I only know that I couldn't bear to stop around here. I'd like to go everywhere. When I told Ray – that's my brother – he said I'd got itchy feet, which perhaps I have because I sometimes just want to run and run and run.'

'Where?' He watched as her eyes searched inside her head.

'Where? I remember in geography we used to have tests about places: names like the Russian Steppes, Guadalajara, Minnesota, and then there was this poem about Xanadu, and another that went, "I will arise and go now, and go to Innisfree . . . " And there's the place where they thought all the gold was – El Dorado. I used to say names like that to myself, over and over, I just used to wish that I had a magic carpet to go to places with names like that.' She came back, smiling, looking a bit shy that she had opened up like that. 'Then I'd wake up and still be in Pompey . . . I mean, Pompey!'

He could have said, The world is full of Pompeys with names like Minnesota; instead he encouraged her. 'When I was about your age, I saw an illustration of the Acropolis . . . you know? I longed to go there, but to travel back in time and see it when it was gloriously new; sadly that's something I can never fulfil. But I *have* travelled in the region of Guadalajara myself.'

The revelation seemed to quite take her breath away. 'Guadalajara? Have you really?'

'So you won't stay and change things here? Do away with the mayor's funny hat and spend the ratepayers' money on better schools?'

'I don't think things like that could be changed.'

'Why not?'

He watched her face reflect the goings-on in her thoughts. 'Because it would take too long. You said yourself that a lot of that stuff goes on because it always *has* gone on.' She grinned mischievously. 'Anyway, men like big funny hats, don't they? You know, like admirals and the king?' She giggled, quite out of character for the young woman with the upswept hair and the ever-ready notebook. 'All those feathers. I expect it's because of the hats that they have to travel about in posh cars.'

As he walked with her to her tram he asked, 'Will you be enrolling next term?'

'Of course. I've only just started.'

When the new term started, there she was, her eager pencil poised over her ready notebook. The prospect of hearing her views on Parliament and national government cheered Mr Matthews. So, on the first evening of term he proposed that there should be a debate to consider whether the luxurious trappings were essential to good government.

For a while after she had started at Ezzard's factory, whenever she'd passed by the grammar school, or seen a girl wearing the uniform, a satchel of books slung over her shoulder and carrying a tennis racquet or hockey-stick, Lu had felt a hot pang of jealousy to be one of them. But now she began to think differently. The curriculum of a grammar school was planned to cram the brain but not to broaden the mind. Here she had a real chance to extend her knowledge *and* think for herself.

With all this new experience, it might have been expected that she would neglect to keep up the journal Gabriel Strawbridge had started her on five years ago, but she did not. In fact, most nights she quite looked forward to sitting at the scullery table with a mug of cocoa or packet soup before bed, writing whatever came to mind.

Inevitably many of her entries were to do with her working day.

Ezzards is a very old building, with whitewashed walls. These get done every year when they close down for the first week of August which is when we take our holiday. Factories that close down the last week in July get an extra day because of August bank holiday, but if anybody was to suggest that Ezzards give an extra day, he would just say as he always does, 'If you don't like it, you know what to do.' Which I don't think is fair.

We are all glad to get away because the place gets as hot in summer as it gets cold in winter. It wouldn't be so bad if the heat from the boiler room came up through the floor to warm our chapped ankles when it's cold, but it seems to wait till the sun is belting down before it does that. The running belt and the treadles make the spindles and wheels warm, and the belt seems to carry the heat right through the room. The windows have all got bars and don't open, so that the only air that comes in is from the end door which is propped open. It might let in a bit of air, but it is warm air. Upstairs in the offices, they have got ordinary windows that open and blinds they can pull down. I don't know why people who come to work in suits and dresses need better treatment than us. If it wasn't for us, they wouldn't have jobs, but I don't expect that they would see it like that.

If it wasn't for us losing our wages, shut-down week would be a nice break. But still, seeing as there is nothing we can do about it, I try not to let it stop the fun I get out of going to Roman's Fields. I can't hardly wait to be on the train there. Bar said she would ask if she could borrow one of the horses – 'hacks' she calls them – so we can go riding together. When I am sitting at my bench with sweat running down my sides, it is as though this is all happening in a different world from where Roman's

Fields exists. But I like being with the other girls, we have a lot of laughs.

Ezzards factory isn't a lot of laughs though. It is a really harsh place. Perhaps if I never got away to Roman's then I wouldn't be able to judge, but I do, so I can. Factory owners live comfortable because we do not. Sometimes a girl will say 'I wish somebody would put a bomb under this b——y place.'

[Later] Mr Ezzard knows he can treat the girls like that because there are so many women and girls desperate for work no matter how bad the money. As Ray says, the bosses hold all the cards in this game as well as making up the rules as it suits them. It's like the houses we have to live in, nobody would live in places huddled together and falling apart and having to be fumigated if there was anywhere else to go. Dotty has applied for one of the nice council houses in Portsea, but she won't get one, nor will we because Lampeter Street is not as bad as a lot of other streets. It's only when I sit down to write that these things make me angry, it's best not to think about it but to enjoy yourself as much as you can.

I didn't used to know that I was Lower Class. Now I know what it means I hate it that there are people who think I'm that. When I walk past all the big houses on Southsea Front, I get so bitter I would like all of them to get bugs and cockroaches and bad drains and damp under the floors. Yet another part of me wants to have one of the houses and a garden with a wall round so nobody could see in. I would have a high gate with 'Beware of the Dog', and red tiles on the roof. *I really hate being common and working class*. I won't always be. I'm going to be *Somebody*! I have made myself a promise.

I was telling Kate Roles how I felt about wanting to get out of Pompey and do something exciting. She thinks getting a good-looking husband and a home of your own is exciting so she doesn't really know what I'm talking about.

It's ironical that I should be earning my living making things that restrain and control women, when I spend half my time thinking how I can break out. When I'm making up 'Grand Duchess' corsets which are all bones and hooks and laces that can be pulled tight, I sometimes think how lovely it must feel to get released from one of them. Kate laughs at me. Nothing much bothers Kate. She's a good person to have around. She makes me laugh.

It snowed today and is still snowing. The machine room is so cold everybody put on double clothes, but that doesn't help your feet and hands. We aren't allowed to wear mitts in case they make smudges on the pink 'Courtiel'. We have all got chilblains, the same as we all have corns on our thumbs from using scissors on heavy twill, which must be the toughest material going. There is a four-inch hot pipe running round the walls about a foot from the ground, and as we have to squeeze by to get in and out of our 'lanes' (the rows we sit in), most of us have got some sort of a burn on our shins from it. Some older women have leg ulcers from these burns not healing up.

I don't know why Ezzards don't make a bit more room for us to move about – yes I do, it would mean taking out machines and they would only do that if it meant they could make it pay. Like the burning pipe, it could easily have a guard of some sort put over it, but guards don't make money.

Scissors. They supply us with scissors, but they are cheap and don't cut which spoils the material and then we get docked wages. So we buy our own. It's right what Ray says, everything is one way.

There was a real to-do today. Something went wrong with the boiler and it sent out black sooty clouds. Later on all soots started to rain everywhere, all over us, and our machines and our work. We tried to keep going, but when Mr George saw what was happening, he turned off the machines. Everybody was as mad as hell because no matter

222

what the cause, we only get paid for what is passed by Nellie and put down on each of our tally-boards.

Mr Ezzard came into the factory, something he hardly ever does, and a big row started between him and George and the mechanic who keeps the boiler running. We could all hear this because the engine was stopped and we could hear through the glass. Mr Ezzard said George should have told him about the boiler ages ago. George swore he told his brother but Mr Ezzard shouted that if he'd been told then the work would have been done. It was a bit of a laugh watching the bosses have a stand up row, but at the same time we were sitting on pins wondering how long we were going to be kept with our machines cut off, and what would happen about the spoilt work. They could hardly dock us for spoilt pieces we hadn't spoiled ourselves.

But they did, at least they docked our pay because of idle time. It was awful, some women broke down because they didn't know how they were going to face their husbands. Most of us are in debt one way or another, things to pay off at the Co-op or the tallyman and there's always the rent man. Most women in the shop I work in are in debt up to their ears, always borrowing from Peter to pay Paul. I know what it was like when I was little, Mum sending me to the door to the rent man to say she had gone down the town.

Ray is very good with money. We get everything we can from the Co-op because of the Divi. Divi pay out is about the most important and happy day of the year. Ray keeps a tin with slots for different things that have to be paid and he puts that by before we see what is left to buy fancy things like soap and hair oil. Right from when he first took over he said he guessed there was things a girl has to have he wouldn't ever think of, so he always gave me a few pence of my own. He meant buying Dr White's and sanitary belts which we can't talk about. I love Ray. I love our Kenny too, he's a lot better looking than Ray. Kenny and I never spent much time together which is funny really, because he's nearer my age. Ray is ten years older than me.

I like Kate Roles, we both look forward to our night at the pictures. I read in *Picturegoer* that they are probably going to make a film out of *Jane Eyre* which is now my favourite book.

D.B. puts me in mind of Mr Rochester, I can imagine him keeping a mad wife shut up. Sometimes I have dreams about D. In some he looks hard and cruel and I try to hit him, but he just laughs because he has a magic circle round him. In other dreams he is smiling yet I still want to hit him, and when I do my hand goes right through him. Sometimes D. turns into Mr E. when I hit him. I hate dreaming about Mr E.

Kate likes musicals and romance, I quite like some romance. We both like Fred Astaire's dancing and Gracie Fields' singing. Kate is really good at imitating her and sometimes she gets everybody in the machine room going.

George's dog 'Nig' (which is short for 'Nigger' because he's dark brown) caught a rat today, right in the machine room. That is two this month. Mr Ezzard had a large notice pinned up saying that anyone caught bringing food into the machine room will get instant dismissal. We all know it's not allowed, but we get hungry between eight-thirty and dinner-time. There are no breaks at all so what we do is to have a bit of something in our pockets, nothing that would mark our work. Sometimes one of us will bring in a lemon or an orange and share it out along the bench, this freshens up your mouth, but you have to be careful because of getting juice on your work. My cousin Mary told me that in their shop they sometimes have mugs of Bovril or Oxo, but she wouldn't tell me how they managed the hot water, or how they get away with it without being seen. She wouldn't say because somebody would be sure to give the game away. (I think it's just because Mary hasn't ever liked me. She's still on about Aunty May making me a favourite.) It's probably not true about the Oxo anyway.

That's how it is here. Everybody working to see they come off best, and every shop working against every other shop. Ray said that's why he is so keen on unions. He said All right, so the bosses hold nearly the whole deck of cards except for the one workers hold which is their labour, and nobody can play the game without it, and sometimes they should take their card away and refuse to play. That would soon sort out the bosses. Though it seems to me that bosses like Mr Ezzard would find it easy to make the married women in my shop play *their* card, because being in debt or having hungry children and no coal can make them do whatever the boss says. Ray says that is because they are all playing their own card separate and that the garment factories should get unionized. I don't see why railway workers should be allowed to start a union but not factories like ours. Ray said it has always employed female labour. I've been thinking a lot about that.

Jeana, one of the fanners in our section is getting married. To a sailor off the *Augusta*, my dad's old ship. We made a collection for her, nobody must give more than threepence because even that is hard for some women to find. We all came to work with our hair in pins and done up in a turban, and a spare skirt in a bag which we changed in the machine room. After work some of us went on the tram to the pier restaurant and gave Jeana a send-off party.

For this sending-off party, the twenty girls went to a café and had several tables put together. Lu looked down the length and saw nothing but happy faces. Girls laughing, all talking at once, giggling, pulling Jeana's leg, gusts of laughter – what she would see on the marriage night, was there much to see? – more whoops of laughter, teeth demolishing ham sandwiches, with mustard/without mustard, pickled onions, chutney, piccalilli, sausage rolls, pork pies, cream cakes and iced fancies, port and lemon.

How different it would have been if I had gone to grammar school. Sometimes Lu thought like this. I would probably be just starting out as a junior clerk in some solicitor's office.

I'm one of Ezzard's experienced hands. There's no part of a garment I can't do: seams, slots, fans. I can work single-needle machines, twins, triples and four-needlers.

Would I want to be a clerk? Would I?

Do I seem to be hard and unfriendly, too, when I'm hell-bent on getting in a good week? When I was a runner I vowed I'd never shout at a beginner.

'No need to swear at the girl, she's doing her best but she's only got one pair of hands.'

'Sorry, Nellie.' I'm not really sorry. The girls have to learn to keep their machinists going.

Just imagine . . . twenty grammar school girls enjoying a wedding party. But then, if I had been to the county grammar, I'd be a different person.

Why did Jeana choose an electric iron? Lord! Imagine actually *wanting* an iron of any kind. A pretty bed-cover would be something, but to choose such a useful thing seemed awful.

What would I choose?

I wouldn't!

Can you imagine taking an electric iron home to Duke?

Since Christmas she had been in love with Duke. Whilst she bent over her machine, she daydreamed scenes wherein Duke would suddenly appear. He wouldn't say anything. They would just go off somewhere and have fun. 'I'll come down your way and see you one of these days.' But Duke at the pictures? Duke shop-window randying? Duke wanting to go for a walk after WEA class? Duke standing on the corner eating chips? He didn't fit into many of her ideas of having fun. But she could picture him at the funfair. He stood up in the swinging boats and took no notice when told to sit down, he won fluffy rabbits, shot off all the clay-pipes and knocked off coconuts. He was all right on the beach, too. He skimmed stones. She tried to make him run with her into the waves – he would have unwound his club of hair – but the idea never got far because of being arrested for indecent behaviour and getting her name in the paper. Duke wouldn't care.

'You awake, Lu? Just look at her, Daydream Number One . . .'

'She's a dark horse.'

'That's why she's always running for the train on Saturdays.'

'Can't wait to get to him, a country boy with hair on his chest and big muscles . . . Been learning you to milk the bulls. An't that right, Lu?'

'I'll bet he takes her off to the Wild Woods, don't he, Lu? Or is it in the cornfields?'

'What's he like behind a haystack?'

Lu grins, it's a bit like being back in the classroom, acting the fool behind the teacher's back and being the focus of attention. 'You don't think I'd tell you lot that, do you? There wouldn't be a haystack left standing.'

After all I said about the steam pipes and old women having ulcers on their legs from burns, today I got a really bad burn on my arm. As George kept telling me, I should have known better than to try to push by the steam pipes, but we do it all the time because the tables are pushed so close to the walls, we have to if it isn't going to take us all day to get out to go to the WC. This time I caught my apron on something and fell with my arm caught between the wall and the hot pipe. I let out a scream which brought George out. Nellie gave me a couple of sugar cubes for shock and ten minutes to recover in the stock room.

That happened six hours ago, my arm really hurts. Nellie said try not to let the blister burst, but I think it has. I'll have to wait for Ray to come in to put some fresh rag on it.

Nellie is our guardian angel. We're always saying we don't know what we'd do without her. She is supposed to be on Ezzard's side, checking that we don't turn in bad work – she makes sure we don't. But she knows staymaking inside out, as well as all the short cuts and wrinkles to unpicking and re-doing. Work has to be really bad to get thrown out and docked. She seems to know everything about our floor (the factory is divided into floors, different work carried out on each floor, and an overseer like Nellie to each machine room with George and his rotten dog over the lot, and Mr Ezzard over us all like a cherry on an iced fancy). I think that Nellie could run the factory better than George.

Ray says, until female workers (when he's got his union hat on, he don't seem able to say women workers) get organized, they will never have their skills recognized. He said that if Nellie was foreman of a shop in the railway works and belonged to the NUR, she would probably be picking up twice or three times what she does now, plus cheap rail travel, a works canteen, first-aid room with a nurse, and a shop steward to negotiate with the bosses. 'No boss is going to offer you better pay and conditions. Unity is the only way you get anything out of them.' In our house then, Ray belongs to a union, Ken belongs to an association, Lu is not allowed to belong. When I think of it, it makes me feel very peevish.

Two days after the accident, Lu's arm was hot and swollen, so much so that she found it difficult to feed into her machine. When she stopped for a minute, George came out of his office to know why.

'Hells-bells, some of you girls do know how to make a

fuss. It's only a hot pipe, you didn't set fire to yourself. You're lucky it hasn't happened to you before, it's your own fault for trying to take a short-cut.'

As the factory cleared out to the dinner-time hooter, Nellie beckoned Lu. 'What was the trouble with George?'

'He thinks I'm making too much fuss about this burn.'

'Let's see.'

Lu gently pulled the strips of rag away and revealed a red and weeping patch above her inner wrist.

'Nasty. Pity the blister busted.'

'It's just in the place where I have to keep moving it backwards and forwards feeding the machine.'

'I can see that. If I was you, I'd go round and see Dr Steiner in your dinner hour, let him have a look at it.'

Dr Steiner rolled Lu's arm back and forth, humming with pursed lips. 'When did you do this?'

'Day before yesterday.'

'Why didn't you come straight away?'

'It didn't seem anything – '

'A burn is always something. Cold tea or cold water straight away, and then let somebody take a look at it. Septicaemia isn't unknown if wounds are neglected. Where do you work?' As he talked he was carefully cleaning the festering wound.

'Ezzard's.'

'Ah well, no hope of tea there, hot or cold, eh? (That hurt? Sorry, but I have to get it clean.) Salt and water cleans wounds. No need to buy antiseptics. Tea, bicarbonate of soda . . . use boiled water if you can. Always bathe any wound and cover it at once. Is there anyone trained in first aid in the factory?'

Lu shrugged. 'Not that I know of.'

'You should at least have some dressings. Go to the dispensary when I've finished with you. Mrs Steiner will make you up something to clear this up, and I'll get her to give you a few things in a box to keep in the factory.'

'Somebody was just saying that the factory ought to have a first-aid box, but it don't hardly seem fair that you should give it.'

'If we wait for fairness, we are in for a long wait, I'm afraid.'

He ran his practice from his own home, which at one time had been a backstreet bakery until the Co-op came with cheap white bread. The surgery was in the shop part, and the dispensary was where bread had once been put to rise. A smell of cooking pervaded the medical area, a spicy aroma quite strange, but not so strange that it didn't stimulate Lu's ravenous hunger. He broke out a wide gauze bandage from its blue paper wrapper, a size that cost twopence in the chemist's, which was equivalent to Lu's share of the family contribution to the Doctor's Club. Why did he work in the slums when he could have been in Southsea and lived along the sea-front and been doctor to people who could pay? Perhaps he was like Miss Lake who had come to work here because nobody else would. Lu didn't understand.

He fastened his neat bandaging with a small gold pin. 'There you are, wounded soldier. Would you like a sling?' His long, sad Jewish face was always surprising when it smiled.

'Thank you, it feels better already.' She offered him her Doctor's Club card. He looked at the name and handed it back thoughtfully. 'I remember, 110 Lampeter: you lost both your parents tragically.'

'When I was fourteen.'

'And before that you came through that bad diphtheria epidemic, didn't you?'

Lu nodded. 'When I was twelve.'

He changed to another pair of spectacles and read a record card he had selected from a cabinet beside his desk. She had always imagined him to be a lot older; at the time when he was treating her for diphtheria she had thought him an old man. It was the glasses. Between one pair and another she caught a glimpse of a man in his forties. 'Well, young lady, you seem to have bounced back pretty well. It looks as though you haven't called upon my services since you were twelve.'

'I don't get much wrong with me, Doctor.'

'Do you look after yourself? I mean, now that your parents are gone?'

'We live together, the three of us, my two older brothers and me.'

'You have relations around, don't you.'

'Oh yes . . . there's lots of Wilmotts about.'

'Good . . . good. Take your card and the club card to Mrs Steiner. She's my right-hand man in the dispensary.'

Lu rose to leave; he held up a finger to stop her. 'I suppose this is your dinner-time. Will you find time to eat?'

'I'll grab something quick on my way back to work.'

He pressed a buzzer and Lu heard it ring in the next room.

'What are you now? I see, nearly seventeen. Have you got a good sensible woman you can talk to?'

'What do you mean, at work?'

'At work or in your immediate family . . . a neighbour?'

'I spend quite a bit of my spare time with my aunty at Wickham. She's sensible, she runs strawberry beds.'

'What about sexual matters? What to do, young men, how to look after yourself in that way . . . '

'She told me a bit. I was staying there when I got my first – you know, when I started.'

'Your *periods*. Nothing to be ashamed of, you can say that word, it is a normal function of women to menstruate. No problems in that direction?'

Lu remembered Ann Carter and what she said about it being natural and normal. The fact that he was a doctor didn't make it any easier to look at him – he was still a man. 'No, I never do.'

'Being your family doctor gives me some sort of duty to ask personal questions. I play a part in your general good health, so if I allowed you to go without doing what I'm paid to do, then I wouldn't be a very good doctor. But you don't have to answer.' Mrs Steiner, her generous body in a starched white dispensary coat came in, smiled, and raised her eyebrows questioningly.

'You might not recognize her now that she has become such a grown-up young woman, and so blooming, brimming with health, but this is Miss Wilmott, Sarah. Louise Wilmott, from further along the street . . . both her parents died within a few days of each other.'

'Of course, I remember. Your mother was ill for a very long time. I liked her, I used to call in sometimes. I remember how pleased she was when she got you away to convalesce after you had been ill yourself.'

'I didn't realize at the time how ill she was. I suppose I was too young.'

'I'm glad to see you looking so well. You are right, Aaron, she's absolutely blooming – except for your poor arm, but healthy bodies soon heal. I hope it's nothing to keep you from your work.'

'Sarah, Miss Wilmott is thinking of rushing back to work with a crust in her hand. We can do better than that, I'm sure?'

'Do you like vegetable curry, Miss Wilmott?'

'I don't know, but if that's what I can smell, I expect I do.'

'Ha, Aaron, an adventurous eater, now that's something you don't come across every day in Lampeter Street. Come through, my dear, I was just putting out a bowl for myself. If you like it, I'll tell you how it's done.'

It was funny, suddenly the Steiners were ordinary people who asked you if you'd like a bowl of food. Until now, he'd been the tall man with a sad face seen in and around

Lampeter Street every day, who opened doors without knocking and went upstairs two at a time, and Mrs Steiner was usually just a head and shoulders looking out of a little trapdoor and a hand that gave out bottles of medicine wrapped in stiff white paper and blobbed at the ends with sealing wax.

They had a living room crammed with everything. Odd and strange and different in a score of ways from anything Lu had come across. The brightly woven shawls thrown over old chairs, as well as shelves of books and collected objects, reminded her of Miss Lake's room. That there were Jews anywhere but in the Bible was information that had not so far come Lu's way, no more than the fact that there were European Jews and that Mr Ezzard had descended from them.

'My husband is probably concerned that you are in danger of not knowing as much about yourself as he knows, Miss Wilmott. That isn't why he suggested the vegetable curry (by the way these are matzos if you haven't had them, a kind of bread), but I know he'll feel easier in his mind if I ask you whether you have any problems. When I was your age, I had my mother. Girls do need their mothers when they are growing into full womanhood.'

She put down her spoon, smiled, and folded her arms across her large bosom. 'Do you mind if I ask you about yourself?'

'Not really, but I told Dr Steiner that I didn't have any problems with . . . periods and that.'

'And I'm sure you don't. Have you got a boyfriend?'

'No. Just sometimes I go to a social with one.'

'Have you gone all the way yet?'

Lu did her best to appear unfazed. All the way was something girls whispered and giggled over when one of them had had a solo date.

'No. And I wouldn't anyway with a boy from round here.'

'Do you know about protecting yourself? Preventatives . . . contraceptives?'

'I know about boys getting Durexes from the barbers.'

Mrs Steiner said, 'Did you know that women don't *have* to rely on men? I don't mean that it is safe to stand up, or afterwards to cough, or pass water, or jump around. What I mean is that women don't have to rely on men to provide the protection; they can provide their own.'

Lu shook her head.

'Not everybody would agree with what I propose doing – which is to give as many women of child-bearing age the knowledge and means to protect themselves. Now this is not something new. There are clinics in London that have been running for ages, but not here. Yet it is here as much as anywhere where there should be one. Sometimes Portsmouth appears to overflow with soldiers and sailors, doesn't it?'

Lu had finished her stew and, without asking, Mrs Steiner served her a slice of sticky cake. 'Oh, honey . . . lovely: it reminds me of my aunty's place.'

'Would she mind me talking to you like this?'

'No. She told me to be careful, that it's easy to say you won't let anything happen with a boy, but sometimes you can't help it.'

'Then I hope she will be glad if I tell you that you can be prepared for that eventuality. Society is very touchy about unmarried women and girls obtaining information, as though we don't fall in love until it is our wedding night.'

Lu was fast losing her embarrassment. 'So why don't Portsmouth have a clinic?'

'Prejudice, religion, ignorance, money. Maybe one day, that's the idea. But, until then, people like myself have to do what we can where we can.'

'I reckon you'd have women lining up at the door if you started one.'

'Understand, I am in no way offering or encouraging

you to accept contraceptive advice. All I would say is that, if and when you ever want to come and see me, then I hope that you will. I neither condone nor disapprove of pre-marital sexual love, or casual love – we all have to sort that out for ourselves, don't we? But it would be nice, wouldn't it, if all children who were born were wanted, instead of so many by accident?'

'What is it . . . I mean, how are the babies stopped from coming?'

In the dispensary, Mrs Steiner opened half a dozen of the assorted little boxes and rowed up their contents. 'Simple, aren't they? The eighth wonder of the world.'

'What do you have to do with them?'

'Once you know which one fits, it is slipped in and taken out. Clinic nurses explain these things.'

'They look too big to – '

Mrs Steiner joined the tips of her left finger and thumb, pressed the sprung rim of the largest device with her right hand, slipped it into the space between the finger and thumb. It shot through like a freed animal, bounced on the desk, fell on to the floor where it rolled and wobbled across the linoleum. The dimpled smile appeared again. 'That's the general idea, but it was never intended to be inserted between finger and thumb.'

Lu left with only five minutes to sprint back to the factory before the gate was drawn and she was shut out for the rest of the day.

It was amazing how much better her arm felt when she got back to her machine. So much to think of. Every day there was something new. She felt blooming, she was blooming. She hummed quietly to herself as she fed strips under the foot and quietly burped memories of the tasty spicy new food.

1934. Today is Midsummer Day. I am seventeen, the age I have always wanted to be. Ray is trying to get me a ticket

235

to go with him to a big union meeting he is going to – a visitor's ticket. I am so excited. It will mean stopping overnight in a hotel for bed and breakfast. He says behave the same as you would at home. They will probably serve up soup before dinner, and a roll to eat with it, but you don't put your bread into the soup. I hope I won't let him down. I have lanolined my hands every night for a fortnight and slept with gloves on. I have promised myself to have long painted nails by then. I overheard him telling Kenny not to take any women in their bed. Kenny laughed and said, OK he would make do with the settee. Then he said, I got better things to do than get caught that way.

I don't know what to think about that. I know they are young men, but don't want to think about my brothers going with girls.

Eileen Grigg. Lena Grigg has come back. She has grown fat. At least fat for Eileen Grigg who I remember as the skinniest girl with rickets in our street which is full of thin rickety children. She just appeared in the factory one morning, sat at a machine near Nellie and started work as though she had done it every morning for three and a half years like I and Kate Roles have. Lena is acting very strange, a bit like my Gran Wilmott is these days, it's as though a bit of her brain has gone or been shut down. I never thought Lena would forget who I was. I would have sooner she had come and shouted and put her fist up to me than to see what somebody has done to her. Tomorrow I'm going to see Miss Lake about it. Somebody must be to blame for what has happened to Lena. One thing, Lena is a good machinist.

Kate hooked a thumb in Eileen's direction and mouthed, 'What's going on?' Lu shrugged and indicated, 'Search me.'

Lu almost hungered for the money to save for dress fabrics, clothes and hairdressing appointments, but she was never reckless in the work she turned out; she made sure she made no rejects or let anything distract her.

Eileen Grigg attracted her attention all morning, so that she felt more than the normal relief when the dinner-time hooter sounded.

Kate nodded in Eileen's direction and they chose her aisle to get out of the machine room. It must have been the sudden cessation of the machines that attracted Eileen's attention. She looked around her as though trying to fathom out where she was, then slid from her stool and made her way past the other machines in her row.

'Hello, Lena,' Lu said quite affably. She had no reason not to be. 'Nice to see you back again.'

Lena dragged her eyes in Lu's direction. 'Oh, hello . . . Katie, isn't it?'

'No,' Kate said. 'I'm Katie, Katie Roles, that's Lu . . . Lu Wilmott. We was all at Miss Lake's together.'

'Oh yes, Lu. I get mixed up . . . It's been a long . . .' She never finished, but went off touching the wall at every step, as though she might be counting the bricks.

'Blinking Hell!' Kate said. 'She's off her rocker.'

Lu thought it was more as though she had had the stuffing knocked out of her. She watched her with curiosity over the next few days and found that, although she was changed, she wasn't off her rocker. She was sort of loose and baggy – not so much physically, but in the way her focus needed a moment to catch up with her gaze, her speech and her actions.

If anyone had asked Lu, she would have said that the last person she would find herself drawn towards would be Lena Grigg. Something about Lena's whole demeanour was an affront. To whom? Lu couldn't possibly have said. But somebody had done something to stamp on Lena's old spirit. The deeper her studies and classes carried her along, the more certain Lu became of her opinions. She wasn't above changing them frequently, but her mind was always alive and coming to conclusions about everything.

There was no such thing as bad luck; most situations had a root cause created by the men who made the rules. In a word, things happened to people – such as with Lena – because other people created the circumstances in which they were bound to happen.

Lena had no hand in what she had become.

This had been done to her.

Why? Why should any person have such power over another?

Who were they, the Theys who had decided what should be done about her? Who chose them? Who gave them the right?

From her evening classes she knew how the magistracy worked. Magistrates chose other magistrates. In secret. They chose their own kind. The same with Boards of Governors; how could that sort of person know anything about girls from Lampeter? And the same people kept on choosing one another for every position going in the city.

It was people like those who must have had something to do with changing Lena.

As soon as Cynthia Lake opened the door to Lu, she said, 'It's all right, Lu. I know exactly why you're here. Come in. Sit down, pour yourself some coffee, take a cigarette, and tell me. What do you think?'

'Kate says she's off her rocker.'

Cynthia Lake rubbed her eyes. 'Oh, dear. Is Lena really bad? I really hoped she'd find something there with a few of the girls she used to know.'

'Oh, she's all right at her work. She's been a machinist a long time – you can tell the way she reaches out for her pieces without looking.'

'Yes, she's been in a similar factory in another town. But she had . . . she was quite ill.'

Suddenly her behaviour made sense to Lu. 'She had a nervous breakdown,' she said intuitively.

'Come along, Lu, you know I can't break a confidence.'

'And you come along, Miss Lake, you know I would never either.'

'Touché. Yes, she did have a slight breakdown. Of course, she hasn't been under the care of the authorities for some time. However – ' she paused and blew out a long stream of smoke, then took a drink of coffee – 'there was a move to send her for treatment in a mental hospital.'

'Bung her in the nut house, out of the way.'

'I don't know why you do it, Lu. If you don't know by now that factory talk doesn't shock me, then you'll never know. I've taught here for twelve years now; do you think there's anything I don't know about Lampeter Street? In fact, I could probably quote you a few choice dockyard words you've never heard. But if it suits you . . . Yes, there were people who thought that she would be better off being "bunged in the nut house".'

'Was it you stopped them?'

'No. Actually, it was Mrs Steiner and the Reverend Crompton. It was I who asked Mr Ezzard to take her on.'

'What did he charge to take her?'

'Lu! Your cynicism doesn't do you justice. Have you ever thought that you may not know Mr Ezzard well enough to make such judgements upon him?'

'Speak as I find, miss.'

It looks as though Eileen Grigg is back for good. She has got lodgings in Lake Road. Miss Lake thinks she will be all right because Mrs Grigg has taken the pledge with the Salvation Army. I don't know what it is makes me talk to Miss Lake the way I do. It's as though I'm back in Standard Four and think it's clever to say rude or shocking things. Cheeky. Sharp as a tack to get a laugh from the class. Afterwards, I feel so stupid. I admire Miss Lake above all women I know, except perhaps Aunty May, but they are admirable in different ways. I'm never rude to May, why do I have to be to Miss Lake?

The meeting which Lu had been hoping to attend as Ray's visitor was not an NUR meeting, but a big conference with other organizations about the future of public transport, and was held at Bournemouth.

It was hard to see whether it was Ray or Lu who was the more excited about the event.

Ray said, 'One day, and maybe it won't be that long, this country's going to be run by the socialists, so we've got to be ready. People with vision will be there, Lu. Good public transport can change people's lives.'

Lu wouldn't have minded had the conference been to discuss wooden blocks, provided she had a visitor's ticket and was going away. 'Is the Seaview Hotel big? Will we be staying near where the big shops are? Shall I take all my three dresses? I'm going to wear that new two-piece I made. Katie is making me a blouse to go with it. Oh, Ray, I can hardly wait. Fancy sleeping two nights in a hotel!'

Lu took a half-day off on the Friday and went to meet Ray at the station dressed in a new two-piece suit in the latest café-au-lait shade, worn with a cream Peter Pan blouse, silk stockings and high-heeled court shoes. She felt a million dollars. Because it was an object of real class, she carried Gabriel Strawbridge's well-labelled leather grip with her overnight things. At Southampton, where they changed trains, Ray introduced her to a group of other NUR men, all a lot older than Ray, all going to the same meeting, who treated her with great awkward politeness and joviality. When the Bournemouth train drew in, Ray said he'd see them at the other end. 'Why can't we sit with them, Ray?'

'Well, talk gets a bit well . . . you know.'

'For goodness' sake, Ray, go and sit with them. I'm not a kid. I go to and fro enough by train when I go out to Roman's. I'll find a seat on my own and read all the way. I'd rather, so go and sit with your old union blokes.'

But Lu didn't read all the way. When a well-dressed woman sitting in the opposite corner couldn't get her cigarette lighter to work, Lu offered her own box of matches, and they dropped into easy conversation about how good Ronson lighters were, how neat, how slim, how reliable – if one just remembered to put some fuel in. Although the woman sounded like a real lady, she was friendly, and questioning, and to Lu's surprise she found herself talking about life at Roman's Fields as though that was her home, and Ted and May her parents. She didn't actually say they were, but when the woman referred to Lu's 'people', Lu responded in that way.

Another small falsification was to do with her accent, which Lu had been gradually modifying whenever there was a chance to do so. Many of her WEA classmates were worth listening to and copying. She could have mimicked radio accents, but they were so crack-jawed that she would never get away with that. She practised her better way of talking when buying goods in shops where she wasn't known, asking for a tram ticket, and quietly reading aloud to herself on the sea-front. She didn't try too hard with this woman, she just concentrated on vowels, word endings and aspirants in the right places. Because her mother had been Vera Presley, a dentist's daughter and trainee teacher, there had always been a home way of speaking which was more careful than the outside way.

In her role as Louise, she was glad that she had been working hard on getting her hands and nails into some sort of shape so that they did not immediately announce her as a factory girl.

'Are you holidaying in Bournemouth?'

'My brother is meeting some people down here, and I'm just going along for the fun of it.'

'Lucky you. It's work for me. I've got a meeting. Transport! The Comrades, no less. The Brothers. Hundreds of them all under one roof. Talking about unions, underground trains and buses – and steam-engines too, I shouldn't wonder. Can you imagine?'

Lu's false heart sank. What a fool! 'Oh?' Is there a more lame-sounding response?

'I'm a reporter, you know. Malou.' She spelled it out. 'Malou. French. I do fashion pieces.'

At this information, the third occupant of the compartment, a bowler-hatted, stiff-white-collared, dark-suited, grey-haired man who had been either asleep or deep in his newspaper gave the woman a glance of curiosity.

Idiot! A reporter. Lu did not know. Of course she did not know. Had she known she would have never dreamed of becoming Louise, the nicely-spoken girl whose home was in a lovely setting in rural Hampshire. It was so completely embarrassing. The weekend was ruined.

'The thing *is* there are so many *lady* comrades these days, that my editor thought we ought to do a piece on their fashion sense . . . their *style*.'

This was the first Lu had heard of any women tradeunionists. Not that it mattered in view of having made such a fool of herself. Showing off to somebody she would probably meet again at the conference. A reporter!

'I said, Can you imagine: double-breasted suits, navy blue, with an inch of petticoat showing; lisle stockings; crocheted jumpers and hair shingled half-way up the back. I said . . . '

She lost Lu, who could see no way out except to make her way along to the toilet compartment, then stand in the corridor until the train reached Bournemouth. It could not be too long. The last station had been Boscombe. She tried to remember the order of the stations, but could not.

She picked up her handbag and scarf and made a move to leave the compartment. The man shuffled his irritable feet and untidy newspaper. Lu smiled a brief apology and slid back the compartment door. Was he smiling? Or smirking? Had he seen through her sudden elevation in class?

In the toilet compartment, she stood for a minute looking at herself in the mirror, seeing what the reporter had seen. Louise Wilmott, a young woman invented by an ambitious factory girl from the slums of Pompey. She smiled slightly at her own reflection. That woman thought that I was her own sort. Then she looked into her own eyes and quickly looked away, concentrating on the tip of the lipstick as it outlined her mouth. Who am I, then?

For so long now she had been switching from one Lu to another, trying out various roles. I could invent a whole fictitious background, she thought.

She combed her new bouncy hairstyle and wondered how the two of them appeared to the man who had been sharing their compartment. Did he see two fashionable modern young women of the same class? He probably couldn't care two tics whether I'm working class and she's middle.

What was that performance all about then? Who was it for? Not for the man. Not for Malou French – she was the worst sort of snob, ridiculing women who are more concerned about getting better working conditions than about fashion. She would probably ridicule Ray because he didn't wear the right tie or something and wore his work shoes to meetings.

Suddenly, she felt quite ashamed, then angry. There was nothing wrong with making the most of yourself, but nobody had the right to poke fun at people who had better things to do. She was the sort who would gang up with her snobby friends as they had done at the grammar school and ask, I say, you're the charity girl, aren't you? Her shame at not having stood up for herself then – and just now – was revealed to her in the reflection of her eyes. To let yourself be put down by some posh cat who's never so much as seen the inside of a factory. You rat!

Lu brushed her shoulders fastidiously, sprayed her ears with 4711 and went to stand in the corridor deep in thought. I don't want to be like my own sort, and I certainly don't want to be like them. How does Miss Lake manage it? She can be on the side of poor people, yet she still talks lovely and she's not ashamed of being interested in clothes and fancy things like painting, and she doesn't think reading is a waste of time. She's just herself.

But then, she didn't start out being born in the slums; nobody can be proud of that. Hanging on to the window rail, Lu watched the steam from the engine stream past, much like the thoughts that were streaming through her mind. Can I be myself? No. The world's set up to keep top people up, and low people down. Therefore, if people at the bottom want to get heard, we have to be like them. No, we have to appear to . . . we have to fool them by talking and dressing like them, but we don't have to think like them. Join them and beat them at their own game, Kenny had once said that. He probably didn't think like that now, but it was the way to do it. She was sure that she was worth two of Miss Malou Whatsit. Miss Lake had explained the great difference between compositions and essays, and Mr Matthews had encouraged his classes to practise debate, discussion and discourse. Mr Matthews loved his three Ds. Her two mentors would probably be quite pleased at how she was learning to sort things out for herself.

What am I doing skulking in a corridor?

Malou French was inspecting her own features in a powder compact mirror. When Lu returned to the compartment she looked up and smiled briefly at Lu standing, about to reach for her grip. A little cough was the only sign of Lu's lack of confidence. 'Miss French, can I ask you . . . Do you think my style is all right?'

'My dear, love it. Holds together beautifully. I just love that new coffee colour with the cream. Ach, and so totally *right* for your lovely auburn colouring.'

'Oh, good. Ah, you said you wanted to write about lady comrades' style.' She held out her hands in an attitude of presentation. 'This is it!' As Lu went to retrieve her grip from the rack, the man in the corner threw down his newspaper, jumped up and took it down for her, but Lu was hardly aware that he was carrying it until he stopped outside an empty compartment and asked, 'Will this do?'

'Oh, yes . . . thank you.'

He put the grip on the rack, raised his bowler-hat and said, 'Thank *you*, miss. Bucked me up no end you have. Should you mind if I joined you? I gather we're going to t'same place.'

Lu was almost gushing in her gratefulness for his friendliness. He offered a hand to shake, and with amusement in his eyes, said, 'Aye, a brother . . . one o' the *comrades*.'

'Oh. Louise Wilmott, and I'm not really one of them, I just said that . . . I'm only a visitor.'

'Aye, I thought you might be.'

'You did? Why?'

'You'll likely not remember me.'

'I'm afraid I don't.'

'Sidney Anderson. I were at sea with your dad. I lost a good shipmate. When I came to the funeral, I had not a notion that there had been a double tragedy. A terrible thing. I were right wrung out for you all.'

'I do remember you. You're the man who carried a wreath and put it by the graveside.'

He nodded. 'Aye, I shan't forget that day in a hurry. I stood there thinking how proud Art would a been to see the three of you like that. A credit to the Wilmott family. I said to my sister later, I've seen more dignity in Art's children than you'd find in a carriage-load of dukes and duchesses.'

'I've never met anybody outside the family who knew my father, except for neighbours and that.'

'I've often thought how hard it must be for the wives and children of a man always at sea.'

The grey-haired man and the golden-haired girl sized one another up and wondered what was going on in the other's head. What did he mean, he thought how hard it must be? Was she as hurt as her eyes showed?

'It was hard . . . it certainly was hard. If it hadn't been for Ray, I don't know what we would have done. I didn't realize it when I was young, but I see now that my mother had been slowly dying for years.'

Yes, she was even more hurt than she showed.

He decided to take the plunge: after all, it had been on his mind for long enough. 'I dare say you won't have a deal of time for men who join the Navy and leave their families?'

'If there's no work sometimes it's the only thing they can do.'

'That's true.'

'What I don't have time for are sailors who don't write home, don't ever send their children a message, let alone a letter. I'd have given anything to have got a letter from him.'

What could he say? He remembered odd, tawdry toys that Art had bought from some downtown market when he was maudlin drunk. A fan, a paper-knife, a kite; nothing that travelled well. He remembered a little silk baby's bonnet embroidered lavishly. Art had held it up on his fist. 'Look, it's for my little Lu.' 'Art, your little Lu is going to school now.' Sid Anderson could have told it amusingly if it hadn't been such a tragic little story. He felt that he had to do something, say something to help her to have some kind of a father. Children needed that. He remembered years ago thinking, Most men make damned poor fathers, yet families needed them in the same way that a bit of canvas needs a pole if it's ever going to be a tent.

'It's a shame you didn't get a chance to know him.'

Lu noticed that he was leaning forward, his fingers laced, his knuckles white, as though he was straining to prompt her to remember something. I might have *really* hated him if I had had a chance to know him. Yet, instinctively she liked this man in much the same way as she had grown to know and like Mr Matthews. Mr Matthews, whose radical ideas were hidden behind old-fashioned glasses and a stammering way of speaking. Mr Anderson spoke quietly in his northern way, but he had what Pompey people would have called 'sea-dog eyes' that could see over the horizon. If her dad had been anything like this . . .

'Tell me something about him.'

His blue gaze wandered to the steep banks as the train ran into a cutting. I must give her something. She's so splendid herself that she needs to know that her father was not weak and neglectful. She must sometimes wonder about herself, how much of him she has inherited. There was no doubt that she would have quite as devastating an effect on the opposite sex as Art had always had. Would that be a plus for a young woman of this modern age? For sure he wasn't going to test that. 'I reckon my last memory of him was the best in a way. Aye. We'd been together since we were lads, and as far as I knew, Art never had a political bone in his body.'

He saw her eyes widen with interest. 'That's the last thing I'd expect anybody to say about him. I thought you'd say he was a bit of a lad, like his brothers and sisters do. I know he had that reputation.'

He smiled, 'Ah well, all sailors have that hanging round their necks. Take it from me, lass, most of it's talk. There's good and bad in sailors, tall and short, hard-workers and loafers, same as men everywhere. Now there's something

Art Wilmott never was – a loafer. He was as good and reliable a sailor as you'll find in the British Navy. People these days laugh, but a good job well done is still something to be admired, in my book.' He expected that she would turn that back on him; instead she said, 'Tell me about that last memory you had of him.'

'Oh, I can tell you about that all right. Look, is it all right if I call you Lu? Good, thanks, I spent a good many years practically knowing you, as you might say. Look, Lu, there's a refreshment carriage. Should you like to have a spot of tea?'

They made their way to the refreshment car. Sidney Anderson watched her as she delicately sipped her tea and used a cake fork. Funny how things can happen. If Art hadn't died when he did, how would this girl have turned out? She caught him looking at her and smiled.

'We'd stand there for hours keeping each other company for a spell, me and Art drinking Bovril, the old *Augusta*'s bow dipping and rising. When it was dark, you could imagine you were alone in the world.'

'Did you do that on your last trip?'

'We did. We'd both been a bit quiet like. I was trying to break it to him that I was thinking of packing it all in. You see, I wanted to get into this lark.' He pointed to his briefcase.

'It had been a long tour, that last one, we'd been too long away. We both knew we were running pretty close to t'finishing tape. I knew that if I didn't get out, it would be too late.

'We were sailing north, and with luck would be in Pompey before October. He was on watch, and as usual I fetched us both some Bovril.' His gaze went inwards, and unconsciously he took a sip of tea. 'You know about the Invergordon strike?'

'Vaguely. It's why the *Augusta* was late home that year.'

'They were going to cut our pay, only three per cent for officers, but a twenty-five-per-cent cut for ratings.'

'A quarter reduction, I didn't realize.'

'Well, it was obvious that the country was going down the pan fast. All those Navy ships whose home ports were in the south were diverted to tie up alongside in the Ivergordon dock. I always reckoned we were as near to a revolution then as we've ever been since Cromwell. There were over two and a half million out of work, and the dole was being cut. The Stock Exchange was in one hell of a mess, and t'government about to chuck its hand in. Aye, there could a been revolution, it was touch and go.'

'How did my father react to that?'

'Well you know, it was strange. He'd never taken the slightest interest in politics or current affairs, but he seemed to change overnight. All the way until we reached Scotland, he was asking me a lot of stuff. It was as though he was trying to catch up on twenty years of ignoring what was going on. He seemed to soak it up like a sponge. I tell you one thing about Arthur Wilmott, he was nobody's fool. His head was screwed on the right way.' He knew that she was watching him like a hawk, ready to pounce if he said something trite. 'The trouble with Art, as I always saw it, he was a bit of a sybarite.'

Lu seemed to relax, probably because she knew that at least was the truth.

'Only a bit?' she said.

He made a gesture, rocking his hands. 'Well, by the time we reached Invergordon we were really steamed up. I mean how, on ships at sea, can you dissipate the resentment of thousands of sailors? We all streamed ashore. The commanders were caught between the devil and the deep blue sea. You see, if we'd have been kept on board ship until new orders came to sail, they'd have been hard put to contain their crews, yet if they let us ashore, we would be bound to feed one another's hostility to the admiralty. The worse evil of the two was to keep us aboard – like as not they'd have a mutiny on their hands. In the event, the officers didn't have any choice; we simply walked off.

'Arthur and I attended a meeting being held in a canteen. Men were standing shoulder to shoulder and overflowing through the doorway. The atmosphere was that explosive, a spark could have set it off.

'Ah, there were some good speeches made there, bar none. We had a good leader: he went to Russia after he got out of the brig. There was a lot of wild talk too. Well, at this particular meeting we were all standing there listening, fired up to anything, then out of the blue your father jumped up on the rostrum. Now I have to admit this about him, there were times when he could go off like a penny fire-cracker, sometimes get himself into a scrap, but never over politics. But that day . . . I don't know . . . it just seemed to come to him.'

Lu did know. 'Looks like I got one thing from him then. I could go off like a penny fire-cracker too when I was at school. You needed to know how to use your fists.' She smiled. 'Not so much now, I'm trying to be lady-like.'

He smiled warmly. 'I can believe that, seeing how you set about our reporter friend, but I'm glad you've given up fist-fights.' He watched with pleasure as laughter bubbled up in her. My, she was a cracker and no mistake. If I had a daughter, that's the one I'd choose.

'What makes you think I've given up? It would have been difficult to have given her a right-hander to the shoulder. Best done standing up, it throws your opponent off balance.' She held her hand over her mouth to stifle her laughter. 'I'm sorry, please go on.'

'Art was good, I have to give him that . . . I reckon you'd have been proud of him. I was.'

'What did he say?'

'I can remember it nearly word for word, because I was so amazed. It's like the old story about a dog walking on its back legs: the surprise is not that it does it so well, but that it can do it at all. I've thought since that he must have caught politics in the same way as those Holy Joes who catch religion. You can hear them in Hyde Park, spontaneous and natural because they speak from their guts. Not like me, I speak from reason and my head.

'Any road . . . He said, "I'm no speaker, I'm just an ordinary seaman, but I just feel I've got to say something. What's happening at home isn't of our making. How many of us got a vote in the last election? I didn't, I was down in Hong Kong, obeying orders . . . some of you were some-where off Sydney, or patrolling off the Med. None of us got a say in anything. Did you? Right! Yet we're expected to suffer for the mess made by a bunch of nincompoops elected without our say-so." (I'm just saying it as I remember.)

'He said, "Maybe it wouldn't be quite so bad if we were treated equal. Or if we worked under officers who had scrubbed a deck or slung their own hammock. Do the gold lace know what it means to live on a rating's pay?" he said. "Is the wife of an officer expected to keep house on fourteen shillings a week?"'

Sid Anderson made a long pause. Lu watched him frowning as though searching for something. 'I'm afraid there's no climax to this story . . . well, it's not a story, it's the truth: I suppose that's why it doesn't round off as it would if it *was* a story. It's a queer thing, many a time I've thought about it. There he was, in full flow as you might say. He had them in the palm of his hand; you could have heard a pin drop. Then, just as sudden as he jumped up and took over the meeting, so he jumped down and pushed his way out of the canteen. I never had a chance to ask him, because it was just after that he got the message about Vera.'

Bournemouth turned out to be as Sidney had promised, 'a nice sort of place'. Lu need not have worried about not knowing how to behave at the hotel. The first meal, dinner, turned out to be easy to handle; even the soup, which at home they always drank from mugs, was served exactly as she had seen it scores of times in films. The hotel was full of delegates, so when they gathered in the bar, Lu slipped away, changed into a floral dress she had made from the cheap remnant of an expensive fabric (spoiled by an easily-dealt-with pulled thread), and went out to take a look at Bournemouth on a summer evening.

It was wonderful.

The beautiful public gardens, the ornate streetlights, people in holiday dress wandering on the promenade, some men wearing dinner-jackets with women in filmy dresses, the imposing sea-front hotels, and the Winter Gardens where the conference was to be held, a modern building glittering with lights. She was seventeen – the age she had always wanted to be – in the kind of glamorous setting she had always wanted to be in, and with some spending money in her purse. In the window of a tobacconist, some of it was wooed from her by a Ronson Ladies' Special, a pretty, slim little cigarette lighter, and a little more when the shopkeeper offered to engrave her initials on it. She settled on a curly 'L'.

It was just so wonderful!

The sound of dance music spilled out on to the promenade and she suddenly longed to be in there. She had been going to quite a few dances recently, and Sonia, Kenny's hairdresser girlfriend, who after work was a professional partner at a ballroom dancing school, had taught her a lot of new steps which Lu had practised at every sixpenny hop in town. She was drawn to the brightly lit foyer of the dance hall. She would love to go inside. If only Kate had been there.

Suddenly, she was inside, had bought a ticket, and was seated at a table ordering ginger ale from a foreign waiter, her heart turning over with apprehension and her skin tingling with excitement. She would not stop long. Just long enough to use her new lighter. Just as long as it took to drink the ginger ale. Ginger ale in a very tall glass chinking with ice. She had no idea what the little bamboo stick with frayed ends was for, so she left it until she noticed a young man twirling one in his own fizzy drink. It was a sophisticated thing to do in such a gleaming, glittering place full of hot foot-tapping music from the sprung floor to the rotating mirror ball. This was such an experience.

There was no clock that she could see, and she didn't own a watch but, judging from the ice in her drink, she guessed that she had been there for about half an hour, and ought to get back before Ray started worrying.

'Excuse me, could I ask you for a dance?' His accent was very top-drawer. His skin was tanned and his fair hair sun-streaked. His teeth were white and perfect. He was tall and long-legged. He was dressed in light fawn trousers, a cream-coloured casual shirt and a coffee-coloured linen jacket. All this Lu took in as his hazel eyes looked at her questioningly.

'I was about to go.'

'What a pity. I'm here on my own, and I thought you must be too.' He smiled. 'I noticed your feet were tapping. Mine too. Brilliant band.'

'I love them.' She desperately wanted to dance.

'Well then, just one dance? Listen . . . a tango. Do you?'

Oh yes, Lu tangoed. She had learned from Sonia and later had a marvellous experience at a tango session of being twirled and caught by an olive-skinned naval officer who hadn't known a word of English, but who danced like a dream.

'I'll have to go directly afterwards.'

'Come on then.' He held out a hand. 'David.'

She shook his hand. 'Louise.'

Although he was much taller than the Latin naval officer, he was just as good a dancer. Lu followed without even a minor fault. The music slid into a slower tempo, and hardly aware that the tango had finished, he drew her closer as he led them into the more leisurely dance. They didn't speak, but the silence was not awkward. She was aware of her breasts against his thin, unlined jacket. One hand, warm and firm on her back, pressing her close, the other enclosed around hers. It was so romantic, dancing with a handsome stranger. The music stopped, there was a roll on the snare drum indicating an interval, and they stood pressed close for a moment. He looked down at her, pressed his lips to her fingers, and led her back to her table. 'Thank you. You dance beautifully, put me to shame. Do you really have to go?'

'Yes, I do. I really do.' She picked up her purse. 'Goodnight. It was lovely.' She hurried out into the evening which had now grown dark, her heart thumping with excitement. Wow! She had never even dreamed of such a romantic adventure. They didn't even know each other's names properly, yet he had held her close on the dance floor and kissed her fingers like a lover. He was fast!

Kate loved fast workers; Lu was glad now that Kate was not with her. She would have gone on and on. What about his hair, Lu? Didn't he have a tan; where do you think he's been? What did he say . . . are you going to meet him again? Kate didn't really know what romance was. She knew about dates and boys, and French kissing, and butterfly kissing, and love-bites and how far to go, but she'd never understand in a hundred years how romantic the quiet men like Duke and David were.

Back at the hotel, Ray was seated in a gathering of about twenty soberly dressed men who were loud with beer. Lu waved to him over their heads and slipped upstairs to her room, where she flung herself on top of the unblemished bed-cover and gave herself up to being totally happy and as much in love with David as she had been with Duke. The Malou French episode was entirely forgotten.

Next morning, although she breakfasted with Ray, he had to be off long before the conference started. 'Just show your pass and you can come and go as you like. If you get bored, then you can get off down to the beach. I probably won't get a chance to see you till after the last session, so it'll be supper-time, I expect.'

'Dinner.'

Ray smiled. 'Right. We'll meet for dinner, then.'

When she arrived at the Winter Gardens, there were a number of other people with visitors' passes being directed to part of a balcony reserved for them. As part of her WEA courses, she had attended a full meeting of Portsmouth council, but this conference was different. Nobody here had any gold chains or fancy robes, nor was there any fancy language. The man who was speaking when she took her seat was talking about toll bridges; then a woman went to the platform and spoke for about five minutes about the need for a plan to give old people free tickets on public transport.

From where she was seated, the delegates looked tiny, so she had to count the rows and seats to distinguish which was Ray. He was there. He must have seen her before she saw him because he was looking up at her smiling. She waved two fingers at him.

A man on the platform pulled a microphone stand towards him. 'Right then, comrades, shall we move on to Item Four?' She at once recognized the voice that came through the loudspeaker system as Mr Anderson's. She would have loved to tell somebody that she knew him, and that he had been at sea with her father since they were boys.

The balcony opposite was filled with people who kept coming and going, talking to one another, exchanging bits of paper, passing messages, and generally seeming to take very little notice of what was going on, except for certain short spells when they gave the speaker their full attention.

It was just dawning on her that they might be from the newspapers, when Malou French made her way down the steps to the front row. Lu slunk down until she was well hidden behind a broad man and a broad woman who kept their heads close as they commented on everybody and everything. She was quite shielded now, but as there wasn't much going on that seemed of interest, she decided to slip out at the first opportunity.

When she looked up from checking the agenda, and peered between her shields to check on Malou French, her heart missed a beat; more than one, perhaps, for brushing the journalist's cheek with his lips was the man the scent of whose spicy shaving soap had stayed on her cheek all night. Her tango man with the top-drawer accent and soft voice. A dreadful vision arose of the reporter looking across, recognizing Lu, pointing her out and telling him her version of the factory-girl-on-the-train story.

The best thing Lu could do was to get out of here, go back to her room, fetch her book and swimming costume and sit on the sands until supper-time. The next time Lu looked across, her dancing partner was loping up the steps two at a time towards the exit, making little signs of acknowledgement to several people as he went. She left the Winter Gardens cautiously, and was glad that she did so because from within the foyer she glimpsed him, David, the man she now wanted to avoid, tossing a canvas bag into the back of a small green open tourer and driving off.

As she lay on the pale sandy beach, which was much more seductive than the shingle shoreline at home, her mind constantly wandering from her reading, she came to the conclusion that the episode in the dance hall would have its place in a modern novel. Strangers meet by chance and part without either knowing the other's full name . . . perhaps one day they would meet again, when they were married to other people. They would remember that brief romantic experience that only they shared . . . they might fall deeply, passionately in love, a mature true love that would destroy two families but was too strong to resist.

That evening, Lu and Ray were invited by Mr Anderson to have dinner with some of the official guests. Ray was buoyed up with his whole experience of this weekend, and kept apologizing as if she might think that he was neglecting her.

'Ray, I should hate it if I had to drag around on your coat-tails.'

'Fancy you meeting Sid like that. Of course I knew his name, but I never put two and two together, and there was never a hint in his letters about what he was doing. I mean, it wouldn't occur to anybody that Sid, the sailor who was Dad's pal, was one and the same as Sidney Anderson who was chairing a transport conference. He's asked me if I'd like to serve on a couple of local committees, and to write a report. Have you got something to wear to dinner?'

'I've got that dress I went out in last night.'

'Good, that's just right. Sir Walter Citrine, Lu. Did you ever imagine eating your dinner with a Sir?' Or imagine entering a dance hall alone, or falling in love with a stranger in a single dance?

Sir Walter Citrine was a quiet, white-haired man. Lu wouldn't have picked him out as a Sir, but then her mind was humming 'Jealousy', her legs still dancing the tango, her back held by a warm hand, her breasts conscious of being pressed in the slow waltz, smelling the shaving cream from her partner's cheek pressed close, hearing his soft voice: 'Thank you. Do you really have to go?'

A remark made during the evening, 'We'll be all right tomorrow, the harpies and vultures are away back to Fleet Street', told Lu that she could go to the final session and hear Mr Anderson's speech without fear of meeting Malou French. In a jovial goodnight to brother and sister, of whom he felt proud without any good reason for doing so,

Sid said, 'I'll not keep you long about with my speechify-ing, and I'll not have a deal to say about high-speed roads and public ownership, but I'd be honoured if you'd be there.'

It was true, he was not long about.

'If a thing is wrong, then it is wrong. No good saying otherwise. Wringing our hands is no good. Bitterness is no good. Cynicism is worst of all. It's up to people to stand up and say, No! And if nobody listens we have to get out in t'streets and shout, No, this is wrong! If a thing is wrong, it is wrong!

'Not one of us is let off the responsibility for what goes on in the world.'

His words, when Lu came to record them in her journal, seemed uninspiring, until she recollected his voice and accent. His manner of delivery had been so impressive, and his idea of the future so visionary, that Lu, at the impres-sionable age of seventeen, was not likely to forget easily. What it all had to do with the future of public transport, she had no idea.

With three single people bringing home wage-packets, 110 Lampeter Street began to look up. Since Lu started earning they had bought a settee, and four kitchen chairs, front curtains, and a mirror over the mantelpiece. Not all at once: they paid weekly into a club; then there was the Co-op dividend which came in useful for new linoleum and a few frivolous items – a clock for the mantelpiece, a picture in a gilt frame and a silk bedspread for Lu's bed. They got on pretty well together, except when they got on to politics, in which they differed in means to ends, but not the end. Since the Bournemouth conference, Ray had been wrapped up in committees and sub-committees. Kenny had emerged from the Labour League of Youth – which he had joined for its football team – and become a full member of the Labour Party. What with Ray and his union and Ken with his politics, there was sometimes a bit of table-thumping.

Lu had been in the Labour Club and the NUR meeting hall. What sort of people were they who enjoyed such places? Deadly dull places that she would never have entered but for those occasions when a visit formed part of Mr Matthews' course. Even their social evenings seemed to Lu as tedious as a Good Friday church service compared to the glamour of the dance halls or the modern cinemas with beautiful soft pink lights and gold-sprayed walls. Lu closed her ears and looked at *Picturegoer* or the instructions on a dressmaking pattern.

By the time he reached his early twenties, Kenny's life outside Lampeter Street seemed never to leave him enough time to throw out his shaving water, or help with clearing out the fireplace or riding his bike to take the washing to the bag-wash. Lu did the ironing when it came back from the bag-wash, but she hated it. As she hated all housework. But then, she had been brought up to do it, and who else was there, now that her mother was gone? Ray and Ken might think that stripping beds and scrubbing out the lavatory wasn't man's work, but they slept, didn't they? And they peed, didn't they?

Lu did a lot of angry crashing and banging about on Sunday mornings when most of the cleaning was done. It was true Ken always brought in something hot at Sunday lunch, but Lu suspected that was only because he didn't like bread and cheese. She absolutely refused to cook a meal, though, when she had just put the gas stove back together after soaking off the grease in hot soda-water.

Ken had finished his years as a junior, and now wore a black coat and acted as one of the pall-bearers at funerals. Lu thought he looked good in his pall-bearer's clothes. He had grown tall, lean, like Duke, and handsome. Large brown eyes fringed with long lashes; a mild expression that, when not set in his professional mould, smiled readily.

Girls liked him. The general opinion of the Wilmotts was, like father like son. Not that he had much chance of a fling on his home ground, because for one thing he didn't like girls to know what he did for a living, and for another the sight of a pall-bearer flinging himself around a dance floor wouldn't be good for trade. So he went to Southampton for the gay life. If they wanted to know, he told the girls there that he worked at the Co-op. Where at one time he had spent his weekends on earnest rambles with the League of Youth, he now found the big Saturday dances and modern bars of Southampton more his style.

From time to time he would meet a girl off the train at Portsmouth station and bring her home for tea, take her to the pictures and see her off again on the last train. There was a whole series of different girls. Usually they were about twenty and, although older than Lu, it was from these modern young women, who all seemed to work in hairdresser's or fashion departments (Southampton being a greatly sophisticated city compared to Portsmouth), that Lu began to be interested in the very latest fashions and beauty styles.

Sonia – the girl who had taught Lu to tango and had cut her lively locks so that the line of her hair swirled from ear to ear, curling under and dipping to the top of her spine, bouncing as she moved – lasted longer than most. Ken was quite proud of Sonia and her glamorous work, but when she and Lu became absorbed in hair and clothes he got ratty that he was not the focus of her attention. 'Come on, Sonia, or we won't make first house.' Sonia took no notice, but continued to comb and snip Lu's hair until she was satisfied. 'You need some earrings. Here, try these.' She gave Lu her own large, imitation pearl blobs. Lu felt transformed. 'Keep them as a present for the nice tea you made. Any time you want to come shopping in town, let me know. You can ring me at the shop. I love buying clothes and things.' This infiltration into the family was not what Kenny had intended; next time he would not be so hasty to bring a girl home.

But it was Sonia who had catapulted an eager seventeen-year-old Lu into a more glamorous world than she had hitherto inhabited. Lu and Sonia were shopping and dancing companions long after she and Ken had broken up. Lu developed a passion for fashionable clothes and, whilst she was good at turning out good copies on her mother's old treadle sewing machine, she loved the whole mystique of buying from a proper gown shop: the groomed and snobbish saleswomen, the curtain changing rooms, the flattering approval of the manageress, the tissue paper and the exit with the smart box which discreetly indicated that it held something from a very posh shop. This desire to go out with Sonia, both dressed to the nines, drove her on at work to keep topping her own piecework figures.

At times when she was working, day in day out at the same task, doing dozen after dozen, she could work up a speed. It was very hard work, with no time even to look up; she kept her head down and her rhythm going hour after hour. The same thing again and again until she felt herself to be an extension of the machine, of the fan-belt, of the driving wheel, of the boiler turning the wheel, and the wheel running the band, and the band powering the machine and so on, round and round with Lu's skilled hands pushing hundreds and hundreds of seams under the needle-foot. The only part of the entire operation that could not be done by a machine. Ezzard's needed her. Her runner and button girl were kept going. Every so often, a pile of her work went to Nellie for checking for flaws which she never found. Lu's estimate of herself was right: she was a good, skilled machine operator.

In all her years, Nellie could remember no one able to keep up the speed at which Lu Wilmott worked. Girls would sometimes go flat for a week if they were going to buy their wedding dress, or if the 'bums' were coming round to settle a debt, but not just to keep pushing up weekly wages. On one occasion, memorable to every woman working in the same machine room as Lu, the girls had a lottery on her tally for one day, with Lu trying to beat her own record.

A Tuesday was chosen because her machine would still be clean after the Saturday dismantling, and nicely run in from the Monday. It was several weeks since the burn to her arm, so that had healed and was no longer a handicap. The lottery was to guess how many pieces Lu would produce on this Tuesday. They paid a few pence for each guess, which was written on a sheet divided into numbered squares. The winner would be the one whose guess was nearest to Lu's tally for the day. Sixpence was usually more than anyone could afford to lay out on a bit of fun, but a kind of fever seemed to build around the idea, particularly as it would have to be done under the eye of George Ezzard. By the time it was all set up, there was over seven pounds in the kitty: half would go to Lu and half to the winner. A lot of money, more than a second week's wages for an average pieceworker.

Although the place seemed to crackle with excitement when they clocked on, once the treadles and fly-wheels started moving, the machine shops settled down to their usual noise. The idea of fast machining was catching, so that in the entire room there was little movement except to grab scissors and start off on another pile of seaming pieces and tapes. When Mr George walked through the shops, he felt uneasy. Something was up. He tried to pump the security man, but he shook his head and said he couldn't see what Mr George meant: things looked all right to him. The security man had had two goes on the lottery.

When the dinner-time hooter sounded it was as though the girls themselves were letting off steam with their sudden burst of loud chattering and rolling of stiff necks and shoulders. No one was even a minute late back, certainly no one risked being five minutes late and being shut out for the afternoon.

At three o'clock when there was usually a bit of coming and going for a pee and a puff in the toilets, there was very little disturbance. George kept looking up from his tally-sheets. There was something up. He'd been here a sight too long not to sense when something was up. He loosened Nig's rope, which usually meant that, as soon as the dog saw the door open, he would scoot off out of the office and down the length of the factory like the whippet he was, causing the girls to look up and laugh. Nig went off as though coursing a hare, but nothing happened in the machine room. At four o'clock he went over to the main office and said, 'Something's up on the bottom floor today.'

'What are you telling me for, George? Sort it out.'

'I can't put my finger on it. But they're up to something.'

'Somebody getting married?'

'No, no. It's nothing like that. When that's happening, they get giggly and fidgety, and they come with their hair in curlers, same as when they're going out randying. No, it's just all quiet and the machines are going like merry hell.'

'What do you want me to do then, go over and stop them working?'

'All right, have it your way, but I tell you, there's something going on.'

When his brother was gone, Mr Ezzard pushed his glasses up on to his forehead and tried to think, but couldn't imagine what might be going on. The thing was, George knew the factory, and he knew female labour. God knows he should, he'd been in trouble with them often enough.

About fifteen minutes before the five-thirty hooter, Mr Ezzard tidied his desk, put on his Melton cloth coat, picked up his briefcase and said to his secretary that he was just going to have a walk over to the work shops before he went home.

At five-twenty the security man opened the factory door and ushered his boss in. Mr Ezzard stood for a moment. Nothing amiss, an industrious workforce doing what it was paid to do, keeping its head down, and earning its keep. He started, as he usually did when visiting the work shops, at a slow, determined pace, his tipped heels ringing on the concrete floor. As he progressed he sensed rather than heard that he was observed. George was right, there was something going on. The sound that went ahead of his progress was the whispered sibilants of 'Watch out . . . Missster Esssard . . . Missster Esssard.'

It was only when he reached the row of machines that the fastest seamers always claimed as their own, that he realized that whatever was going on, was going on here. The girl was oblivious, and there was no doubt that she was the disturbing focus of attention of all the other workers. Even in her white head-cloth and with her head bent low, he knew who she was. He remembered her at first because Alma would ask him how Miss Lake's clever little girl was progressing, then he had begun to notice her sometimes as she went out through the gates talking nineteen to the dozen, laughing, gesticulating. Several times recently, he had found himself standing at the window actually trying to pick her out. It was not difficult; she had a habit at the end of the afternoon shift of, as soon as she reached the gate, ripping off her head-cloth and shaking her bright chestnut hair free and running her fingers through it. Even in the rain. Against his will, he found her attractive – he would not let his mind admit to finding her desirable – but undoubtedly she had developed into a striking young woman.

'Wilmott! What's going on?'

Lu jumped out of her skin and her thumb went under the needle-foot. So fast was her machine working that it had made two stitches before it jolted to a stop. She sat there, pain streaming down her face in tears.

'Don't stand there, George! Fetch the mechanic.'

The mechanic was not always as swift in answering a call to free a machinist who had run over her fingers, but the news that Mr Ezzard was on the shop floor reached the whole factory almost before Mr Ezzard himself. Although the mechanic dismantled the machine-head quickly, Lu was pale and fainting by the time she could free her hand with the needle still embedded.

There were four outlets for her blood to flow: it dripped over her worktable, over the unstitched pieces, down her skirt and across the floor as she dripped her way to George's office.

'Get out your brandy, George.'

Lu was dazed, and allowed the spirit to be tipped into her mouth.

'Fetch Nellie.'

'I think she should go to the emergency at the hospital.'

Lu sat looking weak and pale; not so much from the injury to her thumb – although that wasn't pleasant – but from eight hours of working flat-out at top speed, but Mr Ezzard wasn't to know that. Through the glass partition she saw Kate, her machine still running, trying to see what was going on in the office. The hooter sounded, but tonight there was no rush to cover the machines and run for the door; instead they diligently tidied away every thread and brushed off every bit of lint. Nobody would know who had won until Nellie had counted the pieces Lu had been working on, and added them to her running total.

Nellie said, 'It looks nasty, Mr Ezzard. I'll send out to the chemist's and get some sal volatile and something to put round her finger, and then I think somebody ought to see she gets to the doctor.'

Lu said, 'Kate will. Ask her Nellie, please.'

The whole episode discomfited Mr Ezzard, and he wished to be away from George's stuffy little office, away from George, away from the factory women with their secrets and that kind of silent, sullen exchange that they went in for. And he wanted to be away from the Wilmott girl, who had sat in George's chair, straight-backed and looking as arrogant as any of the spoilt daughters of county mothers he had had the misfortune to meet – and infinitely more interesting. During the entire dismantling of the machine, she had hardly said a word. She had not even cried out or sworn at the mechanic like any normal factory girl. He had no wish to walk back through 'the factory of a thousand eyes' as he had once described it to Alma, but dignity, and not making mountains out of molehills, ensured that he must do so.

'What happened Wilmott?' George said. 'Did you nod off at your machine? Do you pay into a hospital scheme? You should. Always be insured for doctors and hospital treatment.'

Kate, indignant and blaming Mr Ezzard all the way, and Lu, her hand still with its needle covered with a piece of reject cloth provided by Nellie, walked through the streets to the hospital where the needle was removed.

As he drove out through the factory gate, Mr Ezzard was still puzzling about what had been going on. George was welcome to spend his time down there with hundreds of females. Always trouble, always mischief going on; women were so secretive. He never knew what was going on in Alma's mind, even when she pulled up her night-dress and put her arms around him, he was never certain what she thought about it. A man had physical evidence that he had had pleasure, but neither of his wives had shown much response, even after five or ten minutes of his attentions.

'TWO HUNDRED AND THIRTY-FIVE WINS' chalked on the

factory wall meant nothing to Mr Ezzard. But, the following week, when George saw the tally Wilmott had totted up last Friday, he guessed what had been going on. Wilmott was one of the fastest seamers he could remember; he guessed that she had been trying to break some sort of record.

When Lu came in with her thumb bandaged, she was greeted by a cheer, which brought George to the window and started Nig barking. Pam, who had kept the board and money, handed Lu three pounds and eighteen shillings.

On the weekend when she got her big pay-packet, she took what was left after her contributions to Ray's box, plus her winnings, and caught the train to Southampton to meet Sonia; they went round the shops. Lu bought cosmetics, had a bright chestnut colour put on her hair, and bought a beautiful swing-back coat. They had tea in the art-deco surroundings of the Odeon café, and then went into the cinema. Afterwards Sonia signalled a taxi as though they did it every day and, as they parted, Sonia said, 'I say, Lu, you're more fun than your Ken.'

Lu's life was becoming more interesting and complex, but she kept each component separate from the others. Glamorous interludes in Southampton – window-shopping and dancing – contrasted with and – because there could *be* Louise as well as Lu – added spice ·to the other lives at Ezzard's, at Roman's Fields and at the WEA classes. Mr Matthews was now running a course on International Affairs, so she began to gain insight into people of different origins and different classes from her own, if not Miss Lake, then Jews generally and the Steiners in particular, and to learn that there were worse origins than those of an illegitimate child of a sailor born in the Pompey slums.

Eileen Grigg came into the factory day after day, plodding and unobtrusive, then sat industriously working until the hooter sounded. Lu, against her will, often found herself drawn to looking at her, always trying to catch a glimpse of the old Lena behind the expressionless face. It was the very placidity of her old antagonist that poked and prodded at Lu. On rare occasions Eileen would look up and catch Lu's eye and at once jerk her attention back to her work. It bothered Lu that she could not see beneath the layer of fat that now overlaid the once jagged little skull that the fighting Lena used to thrust into Lu's face.

Sometimes Lu hung about waiting whilst Eileen methodically tidied her table and cleaned lint from her machine. She would then fall in beside her to walk out of the factory and along the road to the corner. Kate Roles, irritated with Lu, said, 'What you starting palling up with Lena Grigg for? She's just a fat, boring old daftie.'

'She's not daft.'

'Well, you can't say she's not boring.'

'We–ell, I know, it's a lot more fun with you, but don't you feel sorry for her? I do.'

'There's a lot of people I feel sorry for, but that don't mean I have to start palling up with them.'

'You can't just chuck people to one side.'

'Oh, Lu! Sometimes you're such a goody-goody.'

Lu flushed with resentful crossness and embarrassment. 'That's just stupid. How would you feel if people said I only went to the pictures with you because I'm sorry for you?'

'It wouldn't be true.'

'Well, somebody's got to mind about her. She used to be one of us.'

'Speak for yourself.'

'You know what I mean, you can't get away from all those years we sat in the same classroom, can you?'

Kate wouldn't see Lu's point of view; perhaps didn't suffer the same kind of guilt at how things had turned out with Lu and Kate having everything and poor old Lena nothing. 'It's not asking much just to be a bit friendly.'

'I wasn't never unfriendly . . . you were the one always falling out and fighting with her.'

'We were just kids then.'

Kate went sulky: she resented her friends having other friends. 'She probably likes her own company anyway; she don't make much effort to talk.'

'And it don't take much for us, either.'

Kate flounced. 'Do as you like, Lu, if it makes you feel any better.'

Even if trying to get some response from Lena wasn't going to make Lu feel better, she felt compelled to try. Lampeter girls might be hard, touchy and belligerent, and develop into sullen, obedient workers, quarrelsome wives and harsh mothers, but they never withdrew into blank acceptance, nor removed themselves from their workmates as Lena appeared to have done. Two things especially troubled Lu: one, it scared her that such a young person could have had the stuffing knocked out of her; the other, nobody seemed very bothered that she had. Her old belligerent self was at least a girl you took notice of. Lu smiled to herself. If you didn't, she'd smash you in the teeth.

Embedded somewhere within Lu's mixed bundle of thoughts was that an injustice had been done. The Grigg family were certainly a nuisance: they didn't fit in, they didn't even seem to care. Nobody had ever had a good word for them and it seemed as though somebody had to be punished for being a Grigg. It had been easy to pick on Eileen.

'Kate? Do you think it's OK what's happened to Lena?'

'You don't ever give up, do you, Lu? Look. Eileen's quietened down and the Grigg family have been cleared out of our area into a council house. I can't see what there is to keep on about.'

'What's to keep on about is that Lena's a scapegoat.'

'I tell you this, Lu Wilmott, if anybody's changing out of all recognition, it isn't only Lena Grigg.'

Kate was right; there were times when Lu couldn't leave things alone. She waited for Lena one evening and asked her what she did after work.

'Nothing really.'

'Don't you go out?'

'Sometimes on the beach.'

'Don't you go to the pictures?'

Lena shook her head and turned off to where she lived without another word or look in Lu's direction.

Lu ran after her. 'Do you want to come to the pictures?'

'I don't mind.'

'You could come with me.'

'If you like.'

'We'll go in the cheap seats.'

'If you like.'

'Shall I call for you?'

'All right, then.'

'First house or second?'

'I don't mind.'

It was like stirring custard powder with insufficient milk. 'First house then, straight after work tomorrow.'

'All right. Which one?'

The first spark of interest. 'There's one with Frederic March, do you like him?'

'I don't mind. I like musicals.'

'All right then, shall we go and see the Ginger Rogers and Fred Astaire?'

'Yeah, all right.'

They sat side by side in the cheap seats, viewing the screen at a neck-aching angle, Eileen solidly in her seat eating her way through a bag of broken biscuits which she offered to Lu from time to time. When the lights went up at the interval, Eileen watched the progress of the approaching girl selling ice-cream. 'Are you going to have one, Lu? They sell Eldorados here . . . better than Walls's.' Lena rummaged in her pocket.

Lu said, 'I'll treat you if you like.'

'All right . . . can I have a tub?'

At twopence, a tub was an expensive treat, but Lu felt quite pleased that Lena was at least acknowledging her presence. Lu devoured a water-ice whilst it was still frozen and hard, but Eileen was still methodically dipping her wooden spoon into the tub well into the start of the big film. When the lights came up and the organist playing a Wurlitzer rose from the depths, Eileen sat on. 'Are you going to see it round again?'

Lu felt that to say no would be like taking a treat away from a child; even so she said, 'I ought to get home really. Anyway, I'm quite hungry.'

'All right, then.'

'Did you enjoy it?'

'I like a musical.'

'Are you going straight home?'

'I'm going to get my chips.'

'So will I, save me doing anything. Ray's out tonight.'

Eileen was obviously well known in the chip shop. 'Two penn'orth with scraps, open, same as usual, Eileen?'

'Closed, I want them closed.' Eileen's eyes followed every movement of the shopkeeper as he scooped up two large portions of chips and three scoops of batter scraps in a separate bag wrapped in newspaper. Lu had a threepenny fish and a pennyworth of chips. At twice the price, Lu's supper was a quarter the bulk when wrapped.

In that part of town where Lu and Eileen Grigg had grown up, scrap pudding, scraps with bread and vinegar, chips and scraps or simple scraps in a bag had in some families been part of the daily diet from the time when there were chip shops to provide it. Towards the end of the week, when the money had run out, scraps were in demand. Children would hang around chip-shop windows and watch for the fryer to sieve out the bits of fried batter from the hot oil and then build them into small mounds on either side of the stove. Fried flour, salt and water, still not drained of delicious hot lard and oil, called to hungry children. Some fryers would not give scraps unless chips were bought too, so sometimes a penny needed to be scrounged or lifted, or winkled from a chocolate vending machine.

'Don't you like fish, Lena?'

Eileen shrugged. 'It's all right, but it's threepence.'

On the following Thursday morning, Eileen waited for Lu at the factory gate. 'There's Shirley Temple on tonight, first house starts at quarter to six. I don't want to see *King Kong*.' Lu had some reading to do for Mr Matthews' class, but because Lena had strung two sentences together and spoken before being spoken to, Lu decided to postpone her first plan.

'All right then, Lena, but I shan't stay on to see it round.'

'That's all right, I don't mind.'

And so Lena and Lu, still in their working clothes, started to go together to first-house pictures on Thursday evenings, the pattern following the first outing. Lu didn't tell Kate, but as Kate was going out with another new boyfriend, they were going through one of the periods when they saw very little of one another outside of work.

Ray said, 'You lead a funny old life, Lu. The pictures and chips with Lena Grigg in your work clothes, and then posh shops and shows with Ken's girl all dolled up to the nines.'

'I know, I was just thinking the other day, it's like having a row of little boxes and each one's got a different Lu inside. When I get up I have to think which one has to come out today.'

It was only at Roman's Fields that she felt completely herself; nobody expected anything of her.

But who was this person Herself?

On the return journey from the comforting and undemanding atmosphere of Roman's Fields, and the often silent affectionate hours with Bar, she could see clearly the changes in herself and in Bar; yet there was no question that they were still basically the same people of six years ago.

But Bar's family were not the same deviating family they had been then. Eli now owned Gabriel Strawbridge's field and stable, and had converted the buildings into a more permanent home; as a consequence, they had become slightly more acceptable in the village.

Duke had never come to see her, and had now gone off to make his fortune at Newmarket.

His mother said, 'He *says* he's going in for breeding and training, but I don't know, I reckon that'd cost a deal of money. There, you can't never tell with our Duke. He's always been a law to himself.'

Now that the stables were partitioned inside, windows put in and a wood-burning stove installed, Lu felt a loss of some of the magic a visit to Ann Carter's had been. They were still not 'respectable' people. Eli made his money in ways that were too mysterious and nonconformist for that – knackering, breeding and dealing generally in horses, on the hoof or as flesh. The villagers proper still believed that what Ann Carter had done was scandalous – to 'go' with a Gyppo who wore a gold earring – but the two youngest of the family, Ephraim and Mary, attended the village school with much less aggravation than Bar had experienced.

The more her family became part of the village, the less Bar seemed able to adjust to it. She could not accept the greetings of such as Mrs Catermole: 'Well, if it isn't Barbara. I hear from Mrs Stickland that you are proving a star with the horses.' Mrs Stickland was an Honourable, so Mrs Catermole was bound to concern herself with any comments made by such a personage. Nor did Bar find herself able to reciprocate the smiles of some of her erstwhile playground bullies when they were forced to serve her in the village shops.

273

As her skill with horses developed, she withdrew into her life at the stables, relieved only when she could visit Roman's Fields where, as May Wilmott expressed it, she was as welcome as the flowers in spring. When Lu paid her visits there, May would sometimes tell Ted, 'Did you see our two girls go off together? I never knew two girls take to each other like they did.'

Through the strawberry fields towards the woods or The Swallitt Hole, or any one of the secret places of that first summer they had spent together. When Ralph visited, May would say, 'Do you think there's going to be a romance there?' Ted would cast his eyes upwards and say, 'Why do you women always want to marry everyone off?'

It wasn't that May particularly wanted that, it was more that she wanted the people she loved not to have problems, and she supposed that if Ray and Bar were to fall in love then she could feel sure that they had each found a good partner.

When Christmas came round again, May invited the three of them for their two days' holiday at Roman's Fields. Early on Christmas morning, Bar, eighteen years old now that the winter solstice had passed, came to tell Lu that she was allowed to borrow two of the Barneys' horses to take Lu riding; but Lu was full of a head cold and decided to stay by the fire with Mr Strawbridge. Ken was off out with Ted to take a look at the pack at the estate kennels before the great Boxing Day hunt.

'What about taking me on, then?' Ralph said.

Bar's eyes brightened. 'Riding, d'you mean?'

'Why not? I'd do my best not to fall off.'

'Then I'd best get a saddle for you.' And within fifteen minutes she was back with just one horse, saddled ready for Ralph.

May and Lu watched from the window whilst Ray, refusing to try to mount with them watching, waited for the privacy of the yard before subjecting himself to any indignity. 'I think we'll go round my pa's field a bit first. I'll have to lead you.'

Ralph, who had never had so much as a kitten for a pet, was, even though Bar had insisted that it was only a docile little animal, suspicious of a creature of this size and, looking down from the saddle once she had helped him to mount, it seemed to him that he was much further off the ground than he knew to be the fact. Looking down too, he caught glimpses, between watching his own hands on the reins, and watching where his horse was being led, of Bar's head, which had more than once entered his thoughts since that occasion when he had realized that she was no longer a girl. At the moment her long, black hair, which had seemed to him so much at odds with her short, slight figure, was bundled in a coarse net, and he wished that she would set it free.

'Go as limp as you can . . . not floppy, keep your knees in. Get your head up, look ahead. Keep your back straight, loose off the rein. That's it, good . . . that's it.' She began to quicken her pace, urging the horse to a gentle trot. 'Don't grip the reins so hard.' Round and round and back and forth over the frost-hardened grass where there was a pig-sty and where goats were tethered. Ralph, out with Bar and no Lu, became aware of the intimacy of this fortuitous circumstance. Thought of it, led to arousal by it.

She had led the horse out of the field where her father kept his own few animals, and into a small meadow which was lying fallow, the seed-head ghosts of last summer's poppies, winged pepperwort and cornflowers protected from the crisp wind by an ancient, high hedge. The hedge, providing its own protection, still held here and there flames of dog-rose hips, dark crimson haws of the thorn bushes, mummified crab-apples, and a few sagging strings of shiny black beads of the nightshade. Having shut the gate, she said, 'Now, slowly forward on your own. Knees together, straight back, forget your ass, it knows what to do if you let it.'

Twice, three times he went slowly round the field, with Bar sitting astride the gate calling encouragement to both horse and rider. When she was on the back of a horse, she was totally at ease, in command, an extension almost of the animal. She made it look easy, and although he felt that he was slowly getting the hang of it, he felt rigid and awkward. Sixth time round the field, he called for the instruction about 'pulling up'. Bar laughed, 'Try the hand-brake, or just shout "woah".' The horse stopped close by where she sat straddling the gate.

'Now I'm stranded, how do I get down?'

She smiled at the silliness of his situation, and he smiled back. Ralph knew that she idealized Lu, almost hung on her every word; more so now that Lu was becoming quite the fashion model. Bar wore no cosmetics, but her skin, having known only rainwater upon it, was clearer and finer than any that had been daily laved with cream and lotion. Her cheeks were reddened by gentle exertion and the winter chill. He would have liked to see her hair unloosed, 'gypsy hair like my Dad's' she had once said it was, and later he had realized that she often referred to that side of her ancestry. Which was surprising, remembering all that Lu had told him about the villagers' prejudice against the Barney family.

Ralph thought, 'Whoever would have thought I'd fall for a gypsy girl?' He knew, of course, that this was not altogether correct, but he liked it, the colour and romance of a railway clerk and a girl who had been brought up as hardy as a red Indian, and had seldom been out of her home village. Yet, as he suddenly became aware, it didn't matter who or what he had been, who or what she was: he was in love with her.

In love with a girl only Lu's age and himself ten years older.

In love with a girl who had been a barefoot urchin when he was already a man. He had first seen her, standing in May's kitchen, one leg tucked into her thigh. At that time the difference in their ages seemed great. When she was twenty-five, he would be thirty-five. When she was sixty he would be seventy. Not until then would the age-gap appear reasonable.

'You froze up there, or do you want me to lift you down?'

He returned her challenging smile. 'If I thought you could, I'd let you.'

'Don't you worry, I could. Swing your right leg up and over. I'll see you don't fall.'

He looked down at the diminutive figure, boyish in her breeches and pullover except where her swelling breasts and hips showed her femininity. As he swung down, he twisted too much; his left foot did not leave its stirrup so that he hung there helplessly.

And it was in that situation that he received a long and ardent kiss upon his mouth.

A kiss he quickly returned. Then exchanged again when he took off the riding net that offended him and laced his fingers into her long, black locks.

Lu and May were about to chaff him for his dalliance in frosty meadows, when they exchanged glances at what they thought they perceived in Ray's frivolous and boyish manner.

A working-class Christmas was short but was packed with as much pleasure as could be had in two days. Except that this year Duke was not there to make an enigmatic visit, which was disappointing in view of the impression he had made upon Lu last year. But Duke had gone off, Mr Strawbridge said, 'to seek his fortune in the manner of all young men with romantic notions'.

Until then Lu would have scarcely associated Duke with romantic notions, but as she had discovered over the years, Mr Strawbridge had the ability to see into people. It was he who had said that the two eldest Barneys hankered after things they wouldn't find round here. 'You've only got to see young Bar on fair day, she becomes her true self in the crowds and bright lights.' Until then, in Lu's imagination, Bar was forever a fey, mystical girl who belonged in the woods, or riding hard on big hunters. But Mr Strawbridge was possibly right. Lu remembered from that very first visit that Bar's dream had been for a proper house with a cooker indoors, and the way she had dressed up for the fair. And remembering Duke's noble pose with Pixie's reins running through his fingers, it became clear that he had no future in the self-contained little village.

Early in 1935, and quite out of the blue as far as Ray and Lu were concerned, Kenny suddenly announced that he and two of his oppos were going to pack up their jobs and go on a hike through France and then into Spain. 'We've all got a few quid; we shall sleep rough and get what work we can.'

'What brought this on so sudden, Ken?'

'Not sudden, but we decided to do it instead of keep talking about it. Three of us from the old Labour League football team. I was going to say about it when we were at Aunty May's, but I still wasn't sure then whether I was being a fool giving up a safe job. I told Ted I was thinking about it. He said, "Young men out of universities do it, so why not?" It was Georgie Hoffard that started it.'

'Georgie's dead,' Lu said. 'He jumped off the tram right into a lorry.'

'Don't tell me something I know, Lu. Wasn't it me laid him out? And that's it really. Georgie started school the same day as me, and there he was gone. So I thought to myself, you'd be better seeing a bit of the world and end up falling off a mountain or going under the wheels of some lorry in China or India as never do anything.'

Ray said, 'There's trouble brewing in Spain.'

'I know, Ray.'

Ralph said, 'So it's Spain you're really aiming for then? It's not just a hike through France. I never thought you were that serious about hiking off abroad.'

But he had been. 'Why not? What is there here for us? There's no chance of us getting another Labour government in for a hundred years. Yes, I do want to see Spain, I want to know what it's like living in a republic.'

To see Spain. From half-remembered geography lessons, she created a place of sun and blue skies and the warm Mediterranean sea. Castles . . . olives and oranges . . . or was that Italy? To go there, to be there. To walk out of the house as Kenny was going to, with a bit of money, some friends. The idea exhilarated and excited her. She was envious. She wanted to be Kenny. 'You don't know how to speak Spanish.'

'*No entiendo . . . ah lo que quieres . . . decir,*' he stammered. 'How will I get on? With a dictionary to start off. Terry Black's one of the others going. He's a teacher, speaks good French. And I'm the Spanish expert.' He grinned, '*El pan* – bread, *el té* – tea, *por favor* – please. *Gracias* – thank you. Nobody thinks twice about all those French onion-sellers who come over here and can't speak English. It can't be that hard getting around in a foreign country.'

He left in early spring. The letter he wrote home was composed in fits and starts over the days that followed. Lu devoured every word.

Dear Ray and Lu,

The night crossing was so cold that I wondered if the climate on the continent really was going to be warmer than home. Then we arrived in Paris. It was early morning, the sun shining warm and bright and sparkling, steaming the wet pavements.

At first it was disappointing to find that the trees and

winter flowers were no more exotic than those in Portsmouth parks, but the buildings were very different. So was the way in which groups of small tables were put out very early. The four of us who started out from England together are forced to be mean with our money, but the pastry rolls and plentiful coffee are nicely filling and stimulating. Over breakfast I watched Terry Black reading a French newspaper, can you imagine being able to do that? But I will learn. How would we manage without Terry? He even took us on the Paris Metro. You should see it, the ticket cost twopence and we could go anywhere the trains went.

'The night crossing.' The words leapt from the page and into her daydreams, embedding themselves in the great pool of fertile imaginings that sustained her during her long hours of repetitious machining. She saw the decks lit up, light streaming from portholes and smoke streaming from the funnel as the steamer's prow cut into the dark waters of the English Channel. Lu had suggested to Ray that they should buy an atlas and mark up where Ken went. She didn't know what to make of Ray since Ken left. Certainly the house seemed a lot emptier than she had anticipated, but Ray and Ken had never been in one another's pockets, except when they went together to watch the Pompey team play. Ray thought Ken, when he was away from his sober work, to be too rackety, and Ken thought Ray too much of a sobersides.

For the first time in their lives, Lu and Ralph began to fall out over trivial matters. They were irritable with one another. Once, Lu bolted the outside doors and went to bed, forgetting that Ray was going to be late, leading to a wrangle that lasted days; another time they each said that the other had promised to bring home something for supper. Nit-picking arguments, until on one occasion Ralph actually raised his voice to Lu when she launched into an angry tirade against the Ezzards. 'Give over, Lu, you've only got yourselves to blame.'

'Don't be so ridiculous!'

'You'd soon sort him out if you formed yourselves into a damned union!'

'It's all right for you in your safe railway job. If anybody at Ezzard's joined a union, they'd just sack them and take on some more hands. I can't do without my wages, can I?'

'He can't sack you all. Where would he get three hundred trained hands overnight? If all three hundred of you switched off your machines and walked out together, he'd soon learn. He wouldn't want to lose a day's production.'

It was the same at work, snapping people's heads off, arguing, burying herself in the mind-numbing slog. She had no patience with the unnecessary rules, whose only purpose was to keep factory girls in their place: rules about starting time, peeing too frequently, walking in the factory without permission, talking, singing; so she took pleasure in rubbing George Ezzard up the wrong way.

That same disturbing unsettlement had a wider focus. Massive rearmaments in Germany. Counter-arming at home. The country was said by its leaders to have eighty per cent recovered from the Depression. It did not show on the streets. Unemployment was nationwide. Signs of poverty and deprivation did not appear to lessen. A housing bill was passed outlawing overcrowding. It had no effect in areas like Lampeter.

Then, in May 1935, the whole country was given a prolonged whiff of laughing gas in the form of the king's Silver Jubilee. A great show of pageantry, wealth, privilege and abundance was put on to calm the unsettled nation.

It was from this time that there began a sequence of events that sent Lu hurtling into a whole new realm of experience. She often needed someone to talk to to make sense of what was happening, but of the people close to her, there was none she could trust not to treat her as a child to be protected. Ray wrapped her in cotton-wool, May would probably have liked her to settle down and have lovely babies, Sonia and Kate judged on the amount of pleasure or fun to be had. Bar was inexperienced and would want Lu to do what Lu wanted without judgement. Which left Ken. He seemed an ideal person on whom to test out her ideas, so she often wrote to him. She never expected him to comment, and usually he did not.

The trouble is [she was forced to confess when she wrote to Ken about the Jubilee celebrations] Miss Lake asked me to be one of the helpers to go on the train taking Lampeter Street schoolchildren on an excursion to London to see the big parade. I didn't like to refuse, because she is very good to the people round here. The factory was closed down for the day, and she said she had hand-picked some of her old girls to go with her because she knew they were reliable. (I know what you're thinking, but girls like me and Katie are reliable when it comes to Lampeter kids because we talk their language, not like the Sunday school teachers who are so soft they let even the tinies run riot when they take them on outings.) I'm like you and don't agree with royalty and, like Ray says, we ought to be wondering why we keep on putting up with them, but most people don't care, and I don't see why children shouldn't have a bit of a treat now and then, Lord knows there's few enough of them round here.

So, early on Monday morning, a special train full of schoolchildren went up to London. I have to say it, the three compartments full of Lampeter Street Mixed Infants Kate Roles and I travelled with were proper little angels. The third 'aide', as Miss Lake called us, was (you'll never guess) Mrs Ezzard! I thought I would die when Miss Lake said, but she turned out to be nice. I can't imagine how she ever came to marry *him*. But then I could never understand how Miss Lake was friends with *her* – until now. Perhaps underneath *he* is nice too (ha-ha).

You won't want to know, but I'm going to tell you about the parade. His Remoteness in a scarlet uniform wearing all his medals (for bravery in marrying Her Haughtiness, Kate said her dad said) was in a carriage with Her H. Everything was plumes, horses, jingling harness, swords, peals of bells, scarlet uniforms, busbies, bands and a dog that got in the way of everything and couldn't be caught even by soldiers with swords and policemen with truncheons. Miss Lake said 'Britain at its best'. Mrs Ezzard agreed. I thought they were being ironic (the dog). I hope they were.

In the evening there was a street party. Ray says he can remember the Armistice party when the street was all decorated with flags and there was a supper in the middle of the street. Can you? The kids loved it. If I'm honest, we all did. Do you remember Eileen Grigg (who used to fight me)? She doesn't have any friends, so I asked her to come. Her only pleasure in life seems to be food, so I thought that she would love all the jellies and cakes, but you'd think I had asked her to enter a lion's cage the way she reacted. Something happened to her between the time she was sent away and the time she came back, it's as though somebody pulled the heart and spirit out of her. When she speaks it's a bit like she was talking in a different language from her natural one, just short sentences, no conversation, almost childish (no, childlike).

Even Ray condescended to come and have a dance when it was dark. I'll tell you something, Kenny, our Ralph's a bit of a dark horse, he's a really good dancer, so I suppose when he goes off on his old union 'dos' it isn't always work. It did us both good. We've been like bears with sore heads lately. We miss you. Really. Forgive our lapse into monarchy (or is it royalism?). There's a lot to be said for Maytime in England. Back to work on Monday (when I shall take a close look at Mr E to see if I can fathom what a nice person like Mrs E saw in him). Love, Lu.

When she returned to work the day following the day off, Lu felt restless. Meeting Kate Roles at the factory gate, she said, 'Come on, Katie, how do you feel about running away from home?'

Kate Roles asked, 'What's up, you got the hump?'

'You used to be the one who wanted to run away from home.'

'I know, that was when I didn't get my own way with my dad.'

'I don't think I can stand this place much longer.'

'What you going to do then?'

'I don't know . . . something. I feel like a balloon that's been blown up too much. If I don't do something I'm going to explode.'

'You shouldn't go mixing with the nobs. What was she like, Mrs Ezz? Did you like the procession?'

'It was quite good, the kids loved it.'

'Quite good! You get a free trip to London to see the parade and all you can say is it's quite good. There's times when I could slosh you, Lu Wilmott.'

They punched their time cards and walked down the aisle between the rows and rows of machines. Bright sunlight beamed through the barred windows, illuminating the disturbed motes of lint. 'See, Kate, we breathe that all day. I expect our chests are full of pink fluff.'

'I don't know about yours, but mine isn't.' She jiggled her breasts up and down with her hands just as George Ezzard stepped out of his office. 'Watch out, it's Goodtime George . . . Trust him to get his eye full.'

'When you two ladies have finished your little chat . . . The boss wants to see you in his office, Wilmott.'

'What's he want, George?'

'How should I know? I just run the place.'

'Somebody else got the hump. Must be catching.'

'Get to work, Kate, and you get on upstairs.'

'Why does he always call you by your first name and me Wilmott?'

'Because he's afraid of you.'

'You must be joking.'

'Has he ever tried to touch you up?'

'And he'd better hadn't.'

'There you are then. Makes you pretty unique in this place. You scare the pants off him.'

All the way across the yard and up to the main office, Lu tried to think why she was being called upstairs. She wasn't the most careful employee when it came to factory rules and regulations, but George was the one to give the dressings-down. The only contact she had had with Mr Ezzard was when he had made her jump out of her skin and stitch her thumb. She had often felt eyes boring into the back of her neck when she was in the yard, and had looked up knowing he would be at his window, but she never crossed his path. Perhaps she had said something she shouldn't have to Mrs Ezzard; but Mrs Ezzard had seemed nice, not the kind to go complaining. She hadn't been much help with the children, especially considering she had so many of her own, but she had been quite friendly and thankful for Lu's help.

It was four years since she had last stood before his desk. Full of anger and anguish I was then. He seemed so old then, yet I don't reckon he's much more than his mid-forties. This time he didn't keep her standing long. 'Well, Wilmott, is your hand mended?'

'My hand . . .? Oh, yes sir . . . Mr Ezzard. It is . . . ages ago.'

'I suppose you nodded off . . . Not a clever thing to do.'

'I was working very fast, and it is not easy to hear footsteps in the noise of the machine room.' Lu felt that she could almost read his mind. She sensed that she made him uneasy, as apparently she did George also. He didn't seem able to look directly at her. But, no matter how much she despised him, he had the upper hand. She needed the job, for a while longer, until she had enough savings to do whatever it was she eventually decided to do. He knew well enough that he had been the cause of that accident.

He looked at Cynthia Lake's clever girl, as Alma had referred to her at breakfast. 'Jacob, what do you think, one of Cynthia's aides with the Jubilee outing was that clever girl who gave up the grammar scholarship. You know who I mean?'

He did indeed. Often, when the hooter sounded, he would go to the window where he had a full view of the main gate. He could always pick her out, surrounded by her acolytes, chattering enthusiastically, flinging her hands, often laughing with a display of those strong wholesome teeth. She seemed unable to talk without gesturing. He did indeed know her.

Sometimes she wore her hair knotted on top, showing off that long, slender neck, damp wisps and tendrils escaping, giving the primness of such a neck a confusing touch of amorality. Occasionally, as she was walking along, she would unleash that hair and allow it to flow round her shoulders like molten bronze. Her lively breasts were not shaped by 'Queenform'; they moved, they swelled, they seemed too full and mature for a girl of eighteen. She wore her working apron tied tightly about her slender waist. The swing of her hips swayed her cheap, thin skirt into a rhythm of movement. She showed humility and respect that day in the factory, but she was not humble and the respect was false. If she had been a man, he would have suspected her of being an agitator and dismissed her. As it was she was an intriguing young woman, out of place on the factory floor, and he could suspect her of anything.

What he didn't know for sure of Cynthia Lake's clever girl, he guessed at. The silkiness and length of her upper thigh, the density and colour of her pubic bush, the tight roundness of her behind and whether she was bare beneath her skirts. George, in explanation of a sudden temptation, had once said most of the younger girls wore no underclothes. She was an irritant, a touch of sweetness, an enigma. Twice recently she had turned and stared up at him, as though she had expected him to be there. That look had caused an arousal of a proportion that would have been a pleasure had it not had such a whore-touched origin. How could any man not sense when she was near? How could a man in his position not feel guilty at finding himself watching a common girl from the Lampeter slums?

'Jacob? Did you hear? I met Cynthia's protégée.'

'Yes, Alma, I heard, she helped with the Jubilee outing. It must have been quite an occasion.' He continued looking at his newspaper, giving the appearance that her breakfast-time chatter was distracting him from important affairs.

'I shouldn't be at all surprised if Cynthia's liberalism (with a small "l") hasn't brushed off on her. When a child asked what does the king do when he gets home, she (Cynthia's girl that is) said, "Search me, perhaps he gets popped back into his box till the next time he's needed." She didn't know that I had overheard her, perhaps I should have said something; but it was such a spontaneous reply and the child saw that it was a joke . . . and it was amusing. She has a brother who is exploring the Continent on foot. I don't think she found that at all a strange thing to do for people of their sort. She is really an extraordinary young woman; she has views on everything. I felt quite unread and ill-informed at times. Cynthia says she attends evening classes – you should take her into the offices, Jacob.'

He had already intended to give the girl a try-out in the filing department before Alma had mentioned it. Now she would believe that he had taken her advice.

'How old are you, Wilmott?' he asked Lu.

'Coming eighteen, Mr Ezzard.'

'And how long will it be before you are off getting married and leaving "Queenform"?'

'Married! I haven't even got a regular boyfriend.' The 'Mr Ezzard' came a second too late to stop her reply being an indignant retort.

'I won't have young marrieds in the office. As soon as they are trained up and worth their salt, they start families. Factory work is best suited to married women.'

'It's best to be a young man, then.'

That innocent little smile couldn't hide the look in her eye. She knew exactly what she was saying behind the harmless words. Cynthia Lake and Alma were right, she was no ordinary factory hand. Any other factory hand, male or female, would be struck dumb at having been called up to the top office. He had been right himself when he had put a touch of arrogance into the character he had created for her when watching from his high window. What he should do was to get rid of her. That had been his same instinct when he had become interested in Alma. The last thing any employer needed were factory hands who believed in egalitarianism. One couldn't even say that she *believed* that she was his equal; this young woman was *certain* of it. This was a mistake. Yet it could work, as it had worked with Alma. No one had believed that such a young widow with small children would be the best wife for a widower with his own established family to take on, but it had worked out very well, and he had had a life infinitely more interesting than he might have had with a safer woman nearer his own age.

'I am prepared to give you a trial period as a trainee clerk in the filing department.'

Lu was astonished but wouldn't let him see it.

'You know the kind of dress required?'

'Do I have to decide straight away?'

Mr Ezzard was astonished. 'What is there to decide? The opportunities to work in the "Queenform" offices are few and far between. We have *never* taken a girl off the factory floor. Miss Lake thinks you are capable, and I am prepared to try this experiment. Yes, you do have to decide straight away. The filing department needs a clerk at once.'

'I haven't any idea how much clerks earn.'

'If you live up to Miss Lake's assessment of you, then you must see that money is not everything. Lady clerks have status; a girl like you could move up in the community. The salary is twenty-five pounds.'

Ten bob a week! Is that all those stuck-up office girls got? Walking around in their cuffs and collars, filing bits of paper, typing letters. A girl off the factory floor in the office would put their noses out of joint. Apart from that, would the girls in the factory speak to her if she became a clerk? Office girls and factory girls lived in separate worlds. Office girls didn't come from Lampeter Street. It would be nice to come to work in a decent skirt and blouse, though. Ray and Ken always left the house looking respectable and a cut above the rest. Why was working a typewriter posh and working a sewing machine common?

'Thank you, Mr Ezzard, but the thing is . . . my brother and I have got our budget worked out, and I can't see how we could manage.'

He had never counted on her rejecting him. In his mind he had dressed her in a grey flannel skirt with white collar and cuffs, tied her hair in a black velvet bow, and set her walking in and out of his office in silk stockings and polished shoes, taking away papers and bringing him customers' files.

'There would be an increase of five pounds a year after six months if you prove satisfactory.' That was a top-rate starting wage for a girl out of commercial college. 'Reasonable sick pay, and one week's paid holiday.' He had never intended offering her so much. In a minute she would see how close to bargaining this was becoming. That was how Alma had come so close to being master in his own house – she had seen how pathetically weak his need of her was. George had no such nonsense. When a girl caught his fancy he didn't offer to take her into the offices, he used her fear of losing her job. But he was not George, and this girl wasn't one to be intimidated. Had she been then he would never have even noticed her. 'There is also a bonus scheme based upon the profitability of the factory as a whole. It is intended for senior staff, but I am considering including more junior members.'

'Don't think I don't appreciate the offer, Mr Ezzard, I do, but I think I'll keep on with what I'm doing now.'

'Very well.'

As she made a move to go, he said, 'You understand that everything said here is confidential?'

'Yes, of course.'

'Then I have your word that you will not talk in the factory about this?'

Her colour rose. 'Why do you need my word? I agreed it was confidential, that means I won't talk about it – except for with my brother. We don't keep things from each other.'

'So much for your Miss Wilmott, Alma,' he said later. 'She prefers the factory floor.'

'Really? I should have thought she would have liked to work with her head.'

'She said that she needed the piecework.'

'Do factory girls earn better money?'

'A girl like that one can.'

'What is the machine girl's wage then?'

'Factory hands don't receive a wage. Their payment is by result, by piecework. A girl is paid according to how many pieces of work she turns out.'

'And Miss Wilmott can earn more that way?'

'Because she is one of George's fastest and best workers, yes, she can.'

'I wonder that she can stand such repetitive work. I really wish that we could do something for her. I liked her very much.'

Jacob Ezzard continued to keep his head down in his newspaper. He too would have liked that. She had turned him down. Had even had the audacity to insinuate that he doubted her understanding of confidentiality. He had felt intimidated, half-ashamed of having watched her, guilty of the sexual thoughts she had caused in him; yet he was still unable, or unwilling, to do anything about them.

When Lu told Ray about the offer of the job as a filing clerk, his response was, 'Is that all Ezzard's pay them? I reckon office workers need a union as much as the rest of you. What did you tell him?'

'That I needed piecework money.'

'We could manage if you wanted to be a white-collar worker.'

'You know we couldn't.'

It was a two-minute wonder. Having discussed it briefly they were soon lost in their food and reading. They still missed Ken, especially at their one meal of the day. Ray was no longer on shiftwork, but was working the same hours as Lu, and they would sit eating whatever the day brought: knuckle-bone ham, shop pie or fritters or fried fish or peas and faggots, or sometimes enormous potatoes left baking in a low oven whilst they were at work. As they ate they leafed through a shared daily paper, reading out any news items that might be affecting Ken in Spain. Much of it was disturbing news. When Ken wrote, it was usually not about the threats to Spain's stability, but about the people: how primitively they lived in rural areas, and how advanced they were in the cities. He had become enthusiastic about the history and architecture of the country. He was especially taken by the Moorish buildings of the south. 'I shouldn't mind settling down here, but there's still a lot more to see. And then there's Italy, I shouldn't mind going on there eventually.'

Lu said, 'Do you reckon he'll come back?'

'Of course he will, people always want to come home.'

'I don't think I would, if I was in his shoes. I can't imagine anything more exciting than to wake up one morning and be able to say, I'm leaving! To go and see elephants in the wild, or watch glaciers floating along, or get a job on a newspaper. It wouldn't really matter what you were leaving for, just that you had decided to go and you went.' At that moment something about her father flared up like a match-head, but she doused it before it had the chance of illuminating any similar desires in him. 'Of course,' she said, 'it's different if you've got responsibilities.'

Ray kept his head in the newspaper and didn't respond.

Suddenly, she felt unreasonably irritable. 'What are we going to do, Ray?'

'What are we what?'

'You might at least listen, Ray. I might only be a factory girl, an unimportant woman, but you could listen sometimes.'

'I'm not going to let you pick another argument, Lu. Just say what's up.'

'You and me. What are we going to do? We're just here, look at us, we're like some old married couple when their children have gone. We sit here, one each side of the table, then we wash up and then we sit one each side of the fire, then we go into the scullery and get things ready for work, then we both have a cup of cocoa.'

'For God's sake, Lu, do shut up. What's the matter with you? You're always picking a row these days. When are we ever here in the evenings? More often than not, you're flying round going off somewhere or other, and I'm getting ready to go to a meeting. How many evenings have we sat one each side of the fire?'

'Well, we probably are going to.' She had a sudden glimpse of something which panicked her. 'I don't want to live in this hole for ever.'

'You'll get married.'

'Married! I should hate being married. Besides, where in this dump would I meet the sort of man I would marry, even if I wanted to – which I don't!'

'What about all these tango merchants in their Burton's suits you're always meeting in Southampton?'

'To *dance* with, yes, but I should be bored to death in two days with somebody like that.'

'Come on, stop being so quarrelsome. If you are going to snap my head off, then I'll stop talking.'

'Well, they are about as good at conversation as Lena Grigg. They're just for dancing.'

'You make them sound like a special breed of dancing chap.'

'Well, they are really. We meet there, we dance, and we go home. For all I know, the band brings them in special men-shaped cases, like they do the drums and double-basses.'

Although they had more quarrels now than before Ken went away, no argument between them ever lasted for very long. Now she saw Ray's usual kindly self re-emerge. She liked to amuse him and see him respond.

'I reckon that sometimes they unload the vans and find they've brought all fox-trotters and left the waltzers back in the store room. That accounts for all the dancers with two left feet. Have you finished with that plate? I want to get washed up.'

He grinned. 'You are a fool, Lu.'

Jacob Ezzard should have known that his wife would not leave the matter there. She had that streak in her which made her want to take up causes.

A day or so later, she had raised the matter again. 'I have been thinking, Jacob. Do you think Cynthia's girl would consider modelling? I thought about that beautiful little corselette you will be taking to Paris to show Monsieur Lascelles – '

He interrupted her. 'This will not at all be like one of our usual factory showings: this will be something of a fashion show in the Parisian manner.'

In normal circumstances, when a new style needed to be shown, one of a few 'suitable figures' was selected from among the Ezzard's employees. The item would be shown in the factory demonstration room being worn over undergarments. Very respectable, and nothing that warranted more than a passing comment on whether the figure was suitable. It meant a shilling or two extra, but none of the unmarried girls would have wanted that bit extra if they were asked to model one of the boned and plated battleship styles.

'I am aware of that, Jacob. You said that you would engage a professional model. Why not give Cynthia's girl the opportunity? I'm sure she would be very suitable; her stature and bearing are very fine. I do think that we should try to foster the talents of our own local girls. Jacob? Are you listening?'

'No, Alma. I went along with your filing clerk idea, but this is altogether different.'

Had she but known it, 'Cynthia's girl' had been his inspiration for the new corselette. Watching her from his window, there was no doubt that lithe figures such as hers had no business confined in the usual 'Queenform' styles, but that was between him and the drawing board. He would never have gone so far as to suggest that she model it. It would not do to show enthusiasm. 'Alma, she is a factory girl, not a professional model.'

'Was it not for the young working woman that you designed the new lightweight? Such a pretty design, Jacob.

294

You are so talented in that direction. Just imagine how marvellous it would be to be able to say, I have designed this for the young modern, working woman, and here it is actually being worn by a true working woman. My instinct tells me that this would be an excellent selling point.'

'It is not merely a matter of showing it, it is the manner in which it is shown. A girl not used to it would be embarrassed and awkward.'

'Wasn't I right about producing a white corteil version of some of the "Queenform" styles instead of always making them up in the pink?'

'It would mean going over to Paris, to show Monsieur Lascelles.'

'Heavens, Jacob, do you think the girl would die of fright being in Paris?'

'It might have some currency in terms of publicity in the trade . . . but it's a crazy idea.'

'Haven't I heard you say that it is the innovative man who gains the lead in the market?'

'Working-class people are easily scandalized. The Wilmott family have been with us for generations; they are highly respectable.'

'This is 1935. There is nothing scandalous in modelling lingerie, especially corsetry: it's so modest that it's almost stuffy. I'm certain Monsieur Lascelles' dresser would drape her as decorously as they do your "Queenform" queens.'

'I meant they might not like the idea of her tripping off to Paris. In the working-class mind, Paris doesn't equal business or even the Tuileries and the Louvre; to them Paris is low life and the can-can.'

She would win him over. Alma considered herself an enlightened and modern woman. 'That is easily overcome. I will ask Cynthia to act as chaperone if you like. No one could ever connect Cynthia with anything scandalous. In fact, I am sure she would think it a wonderful idea to expand Miss Wilmott's experience.'

'Would you let one of your daughters do it?'

'Of course I would not, but my daughters don't have to earn their keep. They visit the Continent almost as a matter of course, and I sometimes wonder whether they get anything at all from the experience except a knowledge of the most expensive new fashion. However, a girl such as Miss Wilmott might benefit very much from a visit, even if it was just there and back. You don't know her, Jacob, but as I keep telling you, she is no ordinary factory hand.'

'You seem very keen on the girl, Alma.'

'She is eighteen, Jacob, well read and intelligent. I was much like her at that age, except that I was a pregnant bride. I like the idea of this girl getting the opportunity of having a little wider experience before she finds herself in the same situation. She's a splendid young woman, she's bound to be snapped up before long.'

'As I snapped up you?'

'But as a widow, older and wiser than when I leapt into my first marriage.'

Somehow, Alma's undoubted faith in his faithfulness to their marriage protected Jacob Ezzard from any doubt about how he came to be won over by her idea. If a bronze-haired girl in a white, lacy 'Princess' corselette crept into their marital bed, she only served to confirm Jacob and Alma Ezzard's continued assurance that they had a very good relationship still.

It was Nellie who called Lu aside and put to her the idea that had come from the top office via George.

Lu could scarcely believe it. 'Paris? I'd get to go to France? Nellie, please tell me it's not a joke.'

'It's no joke, Lu, but it's work. You won't be going up any Eiffel Towers, you know.'

'But I'll have to get there, won't I? Going on a journey anywhere is exciting. I'd have to go on a ship, even a plane! Do you think I'll have to fly? I'd give anything to go through clouds. Just fancy, going abroad, and I won't even have to pay my own fare. I'll be scared to death, I know it, but I'll love it. France!'

Nellie smiled, 'I take it that you'll do it?'

'Like a shot.'

'I don't know what your Ray will think.'

'He'll be proud. And he'll be green it's not him getting a chance to go abroad.'

Nellie's unspoken doubt was nearer the mark than Lu's certainty about Ray's response.

'You forbid me! *You* forbid *me*? Who the hell do you think gives you that right? I'll do as I please.'

'You're not twenty-one yet.'

'And you're not my father!'

'I'm responsible for you.'

'*I'm* responsible for me. Jesus, Ray! What do you think I'm going to get up to in Paris that I couldn't get up to here if I wanted to.'

'I'm not suggesting anything like that.'

'What then – that Mr Ezzard has designs on me?'

'Don't be ridiculous.'

'He might . . . why wouldn't he? Why wouldn't he take one of his factory hands to Paris just to get his way with her? Isn't that what you're thinking?'

'No!'

'Don't you trust me?'

'Of course I trust you.'

'Then what is it, Ray? What is it that worries you so bloody much that you're behaving as if this is Victorian times instead of the twentieth century?'

He didn't respond. She felt let down and miserably disappointed that he was being so mean-minded. This was not how she expected her brother to react, her brother who was always on about equality. It was just equality for men he wanted. If he meant real equality then he'd take turns to cook the Sunday dinner and scrub the kitchen

297

floor. Oh no, men couldn't ever be that equal. She fell sullenly silent. Crushed and furious, she said to herself, I shall go. I don't care what he thinks. This is a chance of a lifetime and nobody's going to stop me taking it.

Even so, in spite of this silent protest, she really wanted him to be pleased. Half the pleasure would be gone if he wasn't.

She looked across at him staring at his unfinished meal. The loud ticking of the clock began to widen the gap between them. This was a serious row.

He looked desolate and perplexed, and Lu sensed that if they did not settle it now, then they would become so distant that their life together could easily become intolerable. She loved him too much to throw away all those years of care and happiness he had given her, yet she could not allow him to continue to think that he had the right to make decisions for her now that she was an adult.

She put down the knife and fork she had been holding on to but not using, and went to his side of the table and put her arms around his neck. 'Ray, listen. I know you've only got my best interest at heart, and I love you for it, and I don't know how I would have got on without you. I can't bear hurting you. Please, Ray . . . I'm sorry I said those things. I'm sorry I swore. I know you trust me and you wouldn't ever think I'd do anything to make you ashamed. But modelling is a proper profession, Mr Lascelles is one of the most respected buyers of lingerie in the trade, they have proper dressing rooms with women dressers, and nobody sees the garments, only Mr Lascelles, his manageresses and top assistants. It's all very proper, I wouldn't do it otherwise. You know that, Ray, don't you? Ray, look at me. You know that, don't you? Please don't be miserable about it. I shall go. It's too good a chance to miss.'

He took her hand and pressed his lips to her knuckles, in the way that he sometimes said goodnight when she was preoccupied with her reading. 'It's not about any of that,

Lu. You're growing away, you're leaving your own kind. You have been for months now: this is just one more step.'

He was right, and her respect for him was too deep for her to leap in at once and deny it in order to placate him. 'But it's not the end of the world, Ray. We were born in a slum and nobody's to blame for that, but I've no intention of staying in it.' She kissed his cheek briefly, hoping that he was not too hurt to mend. 'The way out of here is up, and that's the way I intend going.'

When, quite by chance, Lu met David, her dancing partner from Bournemouth, again, she did not tell Ray. David was better than middle class; he was top-drawer – accent, manners, dress, confidence.

She and Sonia, at one of the tables set back from the dance area, were sitting drinking cool drinks, criticizing the dancers, enjoying themselves, giving marks for deportment and dress, when Lu suddenly felt that she was being watched. When she looked across to the other side of the balcony, she saw him. David, the man she had met in the Bournemouth dance hall, whose manners and style were so casual and modern. In a Hollywood film he would have said even less, just 'Hi', then held out a hand and she would have followed him on to the dance floor. She was suddenly struck by the notion of how ineptly she had behaved. She had run away. It had amounted to that. She had seen him speaking with that snobby journalist woman and lumped them together.

Just as she remembered him. She could imagine that, even from across the open space between them, she could smell his shaving cream and hair oil, that she could see greenish-gold eyes. He had wheat-coloured hair and eyebrows, and a lot of the same rough hair on the backs of his hands and fingers, but on his hands the hairs were almost invisible. His nose was straight and long and blunt as she thought a good-looking man's should be. And he *was* good-looking. He was about six foot tall. This time he was not wearing the linen jacket, but a navy blue blazer, a pale blue shirt such as would never be found in Portsmouth, and grey flannel trousers.

She had often thought of him and day-dreamed of a second meeting, but not as it was happening now. Her heart raced. She panicked. Even though this was a second chance, she still could not bear for him to know that she was a factory hand. Nice as he had seemed to be, he was posh, and probably had as distorted a picture of what working-class girls were like as that journalist. If she told him about herself, saw so much as a flicker of distaste, it would be mortifying.

He touched his forehead in a one-finger salute. Sonia, noticing her inattention, followed Lu's line of sight.

'Hey, is he trying to pick us up?'

Trying to keep to their usual flippant style of talking about men, she said, 'Actually, he's trying to pick me up.' She raised her hand and he began threading his way between the tables towards them.

'He's coming over. He's a fast worker.'

'Sonia, listen to me . . . *listen!* I'm serious. I know him. Don't you dare call me Lu. *Louise.* I mean it, I'm not joking. Don't you dare say anything about me at *all*. I don't want him to know anything about me, not even my surname. Do you understand? I'll tell you later.'

'All right, keep your hair on. How come you met an absolute bear like that and didn't say anything?' Sonia's greatest of compliments to masculine desirability was to call him a bear. She sipped her drink nonchalantly and watched the handsome chap as he smiled down at them, at Lu.

'Hello, Louise.' His hand was strong and firm and dry and warm and Lu liked the feel of it very much.

'David.'

'You remembered my name.'

'Well, you remembered mine too.'

'What a fantastic coincidence. I never believed it would happen, but I've carried this about with me just in case.' He placed on the table the little lighter she had lost in Bournemouth. 'It was on the table after you had left. I ought to have handed it in, but I lived in hope that I might come across you somewhere during the weekend.'

Sonia picked up the lighter and inspected it. Lu was certain that she must be consumed with curiosity, but was equally certain that Sonia would never reveal her true interest, common curiosity being considered unacceptable. 'I didn't know you had this, Louise. It's so pretty.' She slid a smile between Lu and David. Lu thought, She thinks he gave it to me. 'And it's got your initial.'

'Sonia, this is David. David, this is my friend Sonia.'

Sonia held out her white, well-groomed hand. 'You don't have to stand there, come and sit down. Louise is such a dark horse keeping you to herself.'

'You remember, that weekend I went to Bournemouth . . .?'

'I do.'

'I met David at a dance.'

He smiled warmly. 'We were pretty good together, weren't we?'

Lu smiled back, suddenly very light-hearted and happy. 'Sonia should get any credit; she's the one who taught me.'

A tenor sax ran up the six notes that led to the dramatic note that led into the most popular tango music of the day. 'I say, right on cue. Shall we?' He held out a hand and nodded a little acknowledgement at Sonia.

In Bournemouth, Lu had been uninhibited and relaxed. There they had been complete strangers, neither of them expecting anything of the other. She kept her fingers crossed that this time, in a hall where she knew people, it would be the same. She need not have worried; as soon as they slid their shoes on to the silky floor, they were carried forward by the passionate rhythm. It was not the kind of dance for conversation, but from time to time they caught one another's glance and smiled with pleasure. When they returned to their table, Lu saw Sonia showing off her fox-trot with Marco, the male teacher from the dance school where she spent many of her evenings.

David brought fresh iced drinks to the table and said, 'Cheers.' The short silence seemed longer, then he said, 'Go on, say something.'

'I can't really say, "Do you come here often?" I know you don't. Do you have a regular dancing partner?'

'No, do you?'

'Sonia and I come together. She usually leaves with Marco.'

'Her boyfriend?'

'Her dancing partner . . . he's married.'

'Ah.' That 'Ah' expressed the same polite doubt that anyone seeing Sonia and Marco dancing together might have expressed.

'What about your equivalent to Marco?'

She gave him a crooked smile. 'I try not to have one. Serious dancers are deadly dull once they are off the floor. I like different partners for all the different dances.'

'Was deadly dullness why you flew away last time?'

'Of course not, I was really enjoying myself. What I said was true: I had promised to meet my brother.'

'What a good thing we have brothers or we might never have met. This time it is one of my brothers who has brought me here.'

'How many brothers have you?'

'Two, my twin, and then a much younger brother, Dominic – he's at school here in Southampton. Being a bit of a tyke at the moment. I have to placate his headmaster. I come in for the dressings-down when Dom threatens the good name of the school. I'm sort of Dom's guardian, parents live abroad much of the time. One in America, one in Brazil. It's not surprising Dom gets a bit too anarchic for headmasters: it's his third school in two years. He wanted to leave, but . . . No! that's enough about me. Tell me about you.'

Lu's daydreams had prepared her for such a question. 'My parents are both dead. Two brothers, I live with one, the other is travelling on the Continent at the moment. Last time we heard, he was in Spain.'

'I was there in January. An astonishing country. Have you been?'

'No, never, actually. I'm about to cross the water for the first time. Paris.' That sounded wonderful. She would never invent or tell a lie about herself, especially to a man like David who seemed so open, but she had such good truths now. She would be enigmatic. Allow him to draw what conclusions he liked. She hoped that one conclusion would be that a young woman who could converse well in a classless voice, whose hair had been styled in Southampton's best salon, and who was about to travel to Paris, could not possibly be a factory hand. He said, 'Paris in spring. I wish I was going too. How long will you be there?'

'A few days.'

Sonia returned and he stood up at once. 'I just want my bag, Louise. Marco wants to leave now. What do you think?'

'It's all right. You go with Marco.'

'What about you, Louise? Should I leave you with this handsome stranger?' She smiled at David.

Damn you Sonia. I can manage this myself. 'I'll get a taxicab as I usually do.'

When David discovered that her taxicab was to take her to the railway station, he asked, 'Where do you live? Couldn't I drive you? My car is just down the road.'

'My brother will be waiting at the other end.' Naturally she did not say that before she reached her waiting brother

303

she would be catching the terminus tram and that he would be waiting up for her at home, sitting by the fire with cocoa ready mixed and some fish and chips keeping warm in the oven.

'Right. Could I write to you?'

'I'm not sure where I'm going to be . . .' She was teetering on the edge of having to lie to him.

'The thing is, I'm trying desperately to make sure that you won't run away a second time without knowing that we will meet again.'

She couldn't think. She too didn't want that.

'How about this?' He produced a small card from his breast pocket. 'It's an invitation to a buffet dance. At the Royal Navy dockyards in Portsmouth.' He laughed. 'Well, no need to look so alarmed – officers' mess affair, lots of gold buttons, very nice food and drink.'

'Are you Navy?'

'No, I'd never stand the discipline. Look, I'll be staying in Southsea, at the Queen's Hotel. I'll write it on the back so you'll know. If it suits you, we could meet there. It's not a bad place, on the sea-front. We could have a drink first, if you like. It's not until mid-July, so you'll be back from France by then.'

What flashed through her mind was, did she know anyone who worked there? If she did, then it would be a chambermaid, or someone in the kitchens. An opportunity to go through those splendid doors and into that world where the other half lives was worth the small risk.

'I'd love to come. I'll be back from France ages before that.' When she heard herself say that, she could hardly believe this was her own real life, and not something she was dreaming as she machined her way through a morning at Ezzard's.

When she got off the Lampeter Street tram, every one of her senses was heightened. Light breezes drifted across at the many intersections of the grid of streets, her heels clicked rhythmically on the pavements. As she passed the great façade of St George's, the church that dominated the factory area where she worked, the Guildhall clock struck twelve. Cinderella! She twirled as though still dancing. The smell of lilac, drifting over a vicarage wall, added an unbelievable glamour to the night and her thoughts about her prospects.

The way out is up! Yes. Up in an aeroplane to Paris, and after that up the grand steps leading into the Queen's Hotel. Up in the world. Her future was lilac-scented, strewn with rose petals, a stairway to the stars.

Ray, as usual, had waited up. Recently, they had been in a state of truce. When she had come home and said that she had been picked out to be the figure for the new model and would be going to Paris, instead of being thrilled for her, he had behaved as though he was one of the aunts saying that she was too young, it was not a proper thing to do. He had called it a jaunt and that had made her furious. They had rowed, then lived in an atmosphere of chilly politeness. But Lu was determined that she was not going to let him dominate her. When he learned that Miss Lake would be travelling with her, he made an effort to put things right. But Lu had been hurt that he should have thought that she would have anything to do with a mere jaunt to Paris with the boss.

Slowly the chill had gone out of the atmosphere so that when she saw that he had waited up and was mixing her some cocoa she decided that she had made her stand for long enough. She smiled at him as though nothing had happened. 'Oh, lovely, I can just fancy that.'

'Nice time?'

'Lovely.'

In his usual careful way, he put the newspaper he had been reading back together and folded it good as new. 'Is that your new dress?'

She turned round to show him the dark gold satin calf-length frock.

'You're really clever with your needle. You look like you stepped off the front of one of your fashion magazines. Nobody would ever think you worked for a living.'

'I hope they don't. I don't want people to know that I'm working class.'

'You don't have to be ashamed of your class.'

'Why not? They're rough and coarse and small-minded.'

Oh, no, here they were, off again before she had hardly got into the house. She hadn't meant Ray, he must realize that, but she had called him narrow-minded when they had blazed away at each other over the modelling job.

She watched his fingers as he ran them along the folds of the newspaper; familiar, practical fingers that she took for granted until suddenly they seemed terribly special and precious. She would have liked to have caught hold of them, but to do so would have made her so full of emotion that she would probably have cried. It had been Ray's hands as much as their mother's that had tended her as a baby. She had told Lu how he used to dip his knuckle into the milk to test the temperature. It had been his hands that had wrung out cloths to keep her temperature down when she had been in crisis with diphtheria. She wanted to tell him that he was such a nice man. Nobody said those things until the person was dead. Everybody was good after they were dead. 'I didn't mean you, Ray.'

'Oh, good. Am I just the one exception, or are there others who get your seal of approval?'

'You mean well-mannered, broad-minded, well-read people like Uncle Hec and Mary and the Wilmott aunts?'

'I thought you might approve of Sid Anderson and some of the delegates you met at the Bournemouth conference.'

'They're different.'

'Oh yeah?'

'They've risen above it. They're not like the people who live around here.'

'So, what are you going to make yourself into? You can't go on for ever with one foot in the coarse world and one in that one you've got when you're out with Ken's girl.'

'Don't let's fall out again, Ray.'

'What do you expect when you seem hell-bent on joining the middle classes?'

'What's wrong with them? They don't hang around chip shops and billiard halls. They speak nicely, and wash, and do more interesting things than us.'

'Of course they do, they're the ones with the money. They can afford bathrooms and tickets to orchestra concerts; they can travel, and sit in the sun.'

She wasn't going to let him be cross, so she quoted his own words. 'Because they've got people like me turning out millions of aprons and corsets and brassières for the smallest pay-packet they can get away with.'

'We'll make a union member of you yet.' He gave her a token peck on the cheek and went to lock up, leaving her with an apron over her gold dress and her hands in soap-suds washing the supper things. What sort of future could she possibly have? The weight of responsibility for his young sister hung heavily on Ray Wilmott's shoulders.

She called him back. 'Ray?'

'That sounds like you're going to sweet-talk me into something.'

'I was thinking, how about if we asked Bar to come here for a few days?'

'If she'd want to come to Pompey, go ahead, it's up to you. I've got a district meeting next weekend.'

'That's the week I go away with Miss Lake.' She no longer spoke of it as going to Paris. 'I thought the weekend of my birthday.'

'That's nice, but just don't go making your arrangements

around me. I'll be really pleased to see her, but don't go making any more of it than that.'

Bar came on the Friday of Lu's eighteenth birthday, laden with foxgloves and flags from around Swallitt Pool, Roman's Fields strawberries, Cowslip cream, and a jelly tart that May said would remind them of Lu's twelfth birthday, their first Midsummer Day. Ray, who had been to the barber's and changed into grey flannel trousers and an open-necked shirt after work, took chairs into the back yard and shared the tart with them. Later, the two girls took a punnet of strawberries to eat on the beach, after which they wandered round the late-opening shops and market-stalls. It was such fun that Lu wondered why she had never thought of asking Bar before this. Bar showed her enjoyment at everything. Her questions made Lu look twice at things she had taken for granted. Walking up the impressive steps to get a close look at the stone lions guarding the Guildhall reminded Lu that it was not so long ago that she had been as much in awe of the place as Bar now was. And again, when sitting in a booth at Palccino's Ice Parlour, as they consumed parfaits with long silver spoons, she admitted, 'I used to think that this place was too posh for the likes of me.'

'I never even knew there *was* such places. Southey's sells Sno-fruits and choc-ices, but fancy having ice-cream in glass vases. Ma would laugh at eating out of a vase.'

They took tram rides all over the city, sitting on the top deck; they walked on Southsea Pier and had refreshments there; then they walked the sea-front and had afternoon tea prettily served in a café, and then on to first house at the Theatre Royal, where Bar could hardly believe the velour curtains, chandeliers, murals and gilded plaster. To pack in as much pleasure as possible, Lu had even ordered refreshments for the interval.

Bar's ingenuous pleasure made Lu feel very sophisticated,

and dwelling on that thought during the boring second half of the performance, she saw that, compared with all the girls she had known since childhood, she *was* sophisticated. She had set out to be and it was working. Slowly, bit by bit, she had learned the tricks of 'doing things right'. Some of her confidence had come via Mr Matthews' classes on local affairs, knowing that even the grandest and most intimidating buildings were on the whole quite ordinary places inside, containing rooms and curtains and chairs and tables and lavatories, and realizing that even the grandest palace had been made by human beings for human beings. There were really no 'special' people in the way that she had seen them as a child. Kings were only kings because other people said that's what they were, the same as mayors were only mayors. Since Kenny had started writing about republican Spain, Lu had thought a great deal about the monarchy. When Lu asked Mr Matthews, 'What are they for?' she found his reply about tradition, stability and order very inadequate. Even so, at the end of the show she stood for the National Anthem, which Kenny had vowed never to do again: 'If we've got to have a national song, then "God Save the People" will do for me,' he'd said.

When the girls came out, Ray was waiting. 'I just thought you might like to go somewhere else.' It was Bar he was really asking.

'Where?' Lu asked.

To Bar: 'How about the funfair?'

Lu said, 'When did you last go to the funfair, Ray?'

'Too long ago. Would you like to, Barbara?'

'If Lu wants to. I love fairs.'

Lu said, 'Just don't ask me to go on anything that goes fast or goes up high.'

Which left the side-shows, cars and rocking-boats for the three of them together, and the switchback, big-wheel, and all the other spinning and whirling rides for Ray to ride with Bar, who clung to him, thrilled and bubbling over with enjoyment. On the long walk from the sea-front to Lampeter Street, Ray walked between them, linking arms. He stopped to buy three bags of chips, and when they crossed over the railway bridge, they leaned on the parapet whilst Ray pointed out to Bar the office where he worked, and answered her questions about what he did there and about the other men. He told the traditional railway stories about horrific accidents, head-less corpses, crashes prevented by some brave soul in the nick of time, trains that jumped the lines, and the dodges people found to travel without paying. Lu thought that she had never heard him talk for so long about the railway without once mentioning his beloved union.

Back at Lampeter Street, where Bar couldn't get over how many people were about at night, and how light it was on the streets, the three of them sat with their feet on the fender and talked about Ken, and Roman's Fields, and Bar's favourite horses and the ones that were devils. 'I kept my eyes about me today, just in case I might see Duke. I keep thinking he might come over to Wickham Fair. I always ask them, but they're a close lot, my pa's people. He says, if Duke wants us to know, he knows where we live. And that's the trouble. Dad don't want to roam. He's took to living on the Strawbridges' land.'

Later, when Lu and Bar were in bed, Lu pinning her hair down and Bar plaiting hers into a long fat pigtail, Lu said, 'I shouldn't worry about Duke. I expect when he's king of the gypsies he'll have to tell you.' Lu too, whenever she heard the clop of horses pulling drays and floats in town, without being too conscious of the con-nection of that sound with Duke, would look to see who the driver was.

'He never could, because he's only a half-breed. Duke couldn't ever be a king, he comes from the wrong sort of family.'

Lu said, 'My teacher at evening school reckons that if people really want to change something, and if enough people decide it must be changed, then it will be changed.'

'Do you believe that?'

'I don't know. I'd really like it to be true.'

'What would you change, then?'

'I . . .' She paused then went on vigorously, 'Oh, there's so *much*! Wherever would I start? I'd do something so that people who had to work in factories got a say in what goes on there. I'd make bosses talk to us like we were human beings. They think that if we had windows we'd be forever looking out, but we wouldn't, we'd just have more fresh air so that we didn't get half dopey with fumes from the boiler and the stuffy air.'

'Why do you put up with being treated so bad?'

'Why do you?'

'Because of who I am. At least on the estate they leave me pretty much to my own.'

What must it be like to be Bar? Her life straddled two camps as well, but nothing like the two Lu inhabited.

'If I lived here, it wouldn't matter being a Barney. Towns are exciting, you can't hardly walk down a street without finding out something you haven't ever seen before. All the stuff you've got – trams so you can get about anywhere, you just wait and it comes along and it takes you where you want to go. You got pavements to walk on everywhere. You know what it's like out our way, if a van or a wagon comes tearing along, sometimes you have to jump in the ditch or up in the hedge, and when it rains it kicks up mud. And there's all these different places to look for work.'

'Different, but factory girls are factory girls everywhere. They pay you what they like, and if you don't like it then you can leave, and you won't get more anywhere else because the owners get together and fix piecework rates.'

'So why don't fact'ry girls get together? There's a lot more of you than them.'

Lu laughed, 'Ray would love you saying that.'

Bar blushed. 'Why would he?'

'Because he thinks trade unions solve everything. Of course, he might be right, but I don't see how we're ever going to find out.'

'Why?'

'Too many women with kids to feed.'

'Ray told me once that girls like you could do it. You haven't got kids to feed, you wouldn't starve, you got Ray and your aunty would send you down boxes of food on the train.'

Lu laughed. 'Strawberries, Cowslip butter and stick-beans.'

'Your uncle's got a couple of porkers now, and another sow about going to farrow. Good ones, they'd send you bits of belly pork. You wouldn't starve, Lu.'

'Who'd pay the rent and gas and coal?'

Bar lay back on her pillow, gazing at the ceiling, smiling at her foolproof plan. 'I could get a job here and be your lodger, and I'd put in share and share alike.'

Lu leaned on her elbow and looked tenderly at her friend. 'Bar, you working in a factory? You wouldn't last a month away from your horses.'

'Why not? You're all right.'

'Are you serious, would you like to live in Portsmouth?'

'Like a shot out of a gun. I'd give anything to live like you. You go to all those classes, you got girls your own age to talk to all day, you can go out at night . . . look at it, streetlights still on – you can buy chips when it's near midnight – and look at the shops . . . Everything in the whole world anybody could want.'

'And not enough money to buy it.'

'Oh, Lu! You should just hear yourself.' She jumped out of bed and opened Lu's cupboard where her swing-back coat and two dance dresses hung over gold dancing shoes and a pair of high-heeled patent courts. 'You earned enough for these.'

'It took me months of slog and going without . . . and I won a bit of money. Factory work is terrible, I shan't stop there for ever.'

'But you *got* them. I couldn't get things like these, it wouldn't matter how hard I worked or how long. I only got my coat to come here because I got some field-work with your aunty and she helped me make the skirt and this night-shirt on her machine, and Joycey got some cheap shoes off the traveller.'

'Your pa would never let you go.'

'He let Duke.'

'Duke's a man.'

'He couldn't say anything. My ma did as she liked, so did my pa. It wouldn't hardly be fair if he said I couldn't.'

They lapsed into silence. Lu lay imagining what it would be like with Bar here every day. Three people in the house again, except that it would be a sister who would live there instead of Kenny. She envied girls who always had some tale to tell about one or other of her sisters. They could go together for weekends at Roman's Fields. But she could not visualize Bar in a dance hall. As she drifted into sleep, Lu wondered why she had always supposed that Bar must be happy working in the stables. When Lu visited Roman's Fields they spent hours trying out hair-dos and practising dance steps. Why wouldn't Bar enjoy those things too?

Next morning she awoke early, her mind still buzzing with what Bar had said last night. She had been disturbed by Bar when she put her coat over her night-dress and went downstairs and across the yard to the lavatory. She'd heard the lavatory flush, the back-door latch click, the kitchen tap squeak and water gurgle through the pipes, stairs creaking, Ray's voice, Bar's voice, the kettle being filled, cups being set out, scullery chairs being pulled out from the table. There was not much privacy in the jerry-built terraces of Lampeter Street.

An element she hadn't considered in her fantasy of Bar living here as her sister was Ray. Not just Ray, but Ray and Bar. Ray with Bar. With Bar as a lodger . . . Bar could never be a lodger, but living with them, she and Ray would meet like this every day. It would be throwing them together. Ray said he was much too old, but it wouldn't be long before he stopped thinking about that. Lu sat on the side of the bed unpinning her hair. Good God, what the hell am I thinking about? It's not my affair if Ray and Bar . . .? If they what? If they fell in love and got married. Bar would still be a sister. Lu and Bar and Ray would all be closer; they all loved one another.

But Bar would be Ray's wife. Ray's wife would not go to the Pier Ballroom on Saturday nights. Ray's wife would not jump on the train after work on Saturdays and spend the weekend messing around at May and Ted's, would not go riding on Mr Barney's horses, not venture out on to the quiet Sunday lanes in the van. Ray's wife would sleep with Ray, and Lu would have the single back room to herself. Not the same thing at all as the original fantasy.

Ray shouted up the stairs, 'Tea, Lu!'

With her big baggy working cardi over her night-dress, she went down. Bar was seated at the scullery table, her coat demurely buttoned. Ray fetched a chair from the other room. He was dressed as he usually was first thing on Sunday mornings, in his working trousers and yesterday's shirt without a collar.

He had put some bread under the grill and, as he was taking it out, he said, 'Barbara was just saying she'd like to live in Pompey.'

Bar twisted her pigtail round in a bun and fixed it with a bone pin on top of her head before she added, 'I don't want to stop a stable-hand for ever.'

Lu said, 'We could give it a try. It won't be easy getting a job, but there's got to be something.'

'I know where there's one going if it hasn't been took already.' Her cheeks blushed red with excitement.

'Where? How do you know?'

Bar smiled. 'It was plain there for all to see where we went yesterday. If you're sure I could be your lodger, I'm going after it.'

Lu protested, 'You can't go on your own. You don't know Portsmouth.'

Bar shook her head. 'Of course I do, we walked all over the town yesterday. I've been finding my way around since I was three.' She rearranged the long twist of her hair, and encircled her head with it. 'Do I look all right? They won't want anybody who don't look nice.'

Lu said, 'For goodness' sake tell us where you're going.'

'No. If I get the job it will be a nice surprise.'

It was six-thirty when she returned. Lu was just making a pile of dripping toast for tea when Bar tapped the front door and came in. Her prim coronet of hair had gone and her long black mane hung beautifully around the shoulders of her cheap coat. Her eyes shone, her cheeks were flushed and she greeted them with an open-armed twirl. 'I got it! I got it! I started straight away. And look,' she delved into her pocket and brought out a handful of assorted small coins, 'a down- payment on my first week's lodging money.'

Lu had never seen Bar demonstrate such exuberance.

'Tips!' Bar said. 'I don't know how much there is, but it don't matter. I got the job, ten-and-six a week. It's long hours, but I already work long hours at the stables. Plus tips. A bit extra for summer work because they open late. I get a bit of a snack during the day when things are slack. If they're pleased with me – and they were, they said I was just what they was looking for, they said it was really good getting a girl with long black hair, because that's what their daughter has got, and customers will think I'm family . . . it's a family business. I start proper on Tuesday. That gives me time to go home and get my things. Is that all right with you?'

'For goodness' sake, tell us what the job is.'

Bar threw off her coat and took a drink of the tea. 'Guess.'

Ray said, his face showing the pleasure he was experiencing watching this lovely display of ebullience, 'Waitress in one of the cafés?'

'How did you guess that?'

'Couldn't think of anything else that opens Sunday and gets more custom in the summer months. Which one?'

'Palccino's.'

Lu said, 'They're famous, you know.'

'I know. Mr Palccino (he's called Papa) told me that they supplied ice-cream to the old king when he visited the Navy. They had some other girls went for the job last week, but Mrs Palccino (she is always called Mama Palccino), she said she wouldn't take any of them because they wore powder and scent. She didn't say it like that (she speaks funny like "door-to-door Indians" but not the same).' Bar tried to mimic Mama Palccino. ' "They all a-stink like a-bath salt. People not like a-bath salt with ice-cream." She told me that half a dozen times. She said Papa Palccino is very fussy about the way his ice-cream is served up (he can't hardly speak any English). I won't be allowed to do the scoops straight away, only take the orders and carry them to the tables. She said she liked my hair, because it smells fresh. I smell "like a-girl".' Bar giggled with delight. 'She says a lot about how things smell. I didn't tell her that last Friday I smell-a like a-stable.'

'What are you going to do about that?' Lu asked. 'You are supposed to be back at work on Tuesday.'

'I'll go back as early as I can tomorrow morning. Go up to the stables and tell them I've left. They don't owe me any wages, and they docked me for the two days off, so I don't owe them anything. Go and tell Ma and Pa, and your aunty, and then catch the train back and start on Tuesday morning. I told Mama Palccino – don't that sound silly, I expect I'll get used to it – she said she would keep the notice out of the window till Tuesday afternoon. And if I go back, she will take me to the store and buy me two white overalls and some caps and aprons – I said I liked red, and she said she did too. I told her, "Mama Palccino, I said I would be back and I will; I don't never say things I don't mean." I just wanted to get things straight right from the start. She said all right, she would throw the notice away. That's how I knew there was a job going . . . the notice, it was in the side window when we went there yesterday afternoon. Didn't you see it?'

Lu shook her head. 'It wouldn't have registered if I had.'

'It did with me. "Young girl wanted to wait on tables." All the way on the tram I kept wondering whether I was young, and then thinking what you said about there being a dozen girls for every job going, so I kept my fingers crossed. I think I was meant to get the job, don't you?'

Ray said, glancing at Lu, 'You realize Lu won't be here for a couple of days next week.'

'I know. I won't get in your way. I expect you won't hardly know I'm in the house.'

Lu expected Ray to have something to say about that, but he didn't; what he did say was, 'You and me might be able to get back on our old footing with somebody else in the house.'

'She's a bit like Ken in that respect: they're not such earnest people like you and me; they don't want to change the world like we do.'

That gave Ray something to think about. He thought Lu wanted to be in a different world, not change the one she was in. If she did, he didn't see much sign of revolutionary fervour in the kind of fake Hollywood life she seemed to live when she could.

* * *

Bar moved in to Number 110 the day before she started her job at Palccino's Ice Parlour. The busy summer season had just begun. She found it all so stimulating that for a few days she never seemed to stop talking and laughing. There was no doubt she refreshed the crumbling little terrace house and the jaded relationship of its two occupants like a cheerful new coat of paint.

'I brought my picture, Lu. Can I put it up with yours?' The well-remembered first photos in the meadow with the poppies were put together on the mantelpiece, Lu with poppies in her hat looking out timidly, Bar, her wild bush of black hair starred with ox-eye daisies, grinning fearlessly, directly into the lens of Ted's camera.

'Just look at us, Lu. Who'd have thought then that you'd be goin' off to Paris and I would be living in a big city? Pa give me five gold sovereigns for a rainy day (would you look after them for me, Ray?), and my ma sent two of her ornaments to remind me that I must go home and see them sometimes on my day off. And she give me the gold earring she'd been saving for if I got wed, but she said I should have it now so I had something nice to wear to show I'm not just anybody. Duke's got the other one, he got it on a chain because he said it was too fancy to wear, so Pa gave him his out of his own ear. That meant a lot to Pa, you know, it was the last bit of his old ways. Ma said she would buy Pa a new one for a wedding ring.'

The earring was fancy, but very distinctive and beautifully embellished. The heavy gold in one ear and her hair tied back in a ribbon, as she took to wearing it now, gave her a particularly feminine appearance. She believed that her new appearance made her blend in with the modern city girl; she was wrong, she stood out as an exotic exception. When men's eyes were upon her as she walked towards them, and after she had passed by, Bar did not notice, she was interested in just one man, and she would see him every day.

* * *

There were mixed feelings amongst Lu's workmates when they heard that one of their own sort had been chosen to go abroad with the boss to show the new 'Princess' line. It wasn't surprising that there were some who thought it was just a better way than George's of trying to get a girl's clothes off, but nobody who knew her was foolish enough to say that to Lu's face. Some thought that having a common factory girl modelling the latest style would bring 'Queenform' down to the level of Woolworth's, and Old Mr Ezzard would turn in his grave. The majority, especially the ones working on the prototypes being made exclusively for the Lascelles store, thought it was modern and a kind of Hollywood thing to do. Kate said, 'It's real rags to riches, taking a poor girl and making her into a princess. "Princess", see? You might get your picture in the paper even.'

That had never occurred to Lu. Miss Lake said, 'Kate Roles was always able to carry anything to the nth degree. There will probably be something in the trade journals – the garment, not the model.'

Lu and Cynthia Lake were booked on the night crossing. Mr Ezzard had flown over ahead of them. The train to London was ordinary passenger, except that they travelled second class, which was quite superior and roomy compared with the normal third class by which working-class people ordinarily travelled. She eyed the splendour of first class, but did not wish that for herself, at least not for the moment. Second was enough for now.

Once on the boat-train, Lu, in a window-seat opposite Miss Lake's, leaned back into the plush comfort and rested her head against the fresh white linen antimacassar and felt so thrilled she almost felt sick.

Outside on the platform, the last-minute stages of preparation for departure were going on: passengers hurrying, porters running with bags, others pushing baggage carts, carriage doors banging, hissing steam, and indistinct voices echoing in the vaulted roof of the station. Within the comfortable compartment, Lu felt both a participant and voyeur of the drama in which only she and the other travellers on this expedition, on this particular boat-train, were involved. It was a unique set of circumstances which she felt sure she would never forget.

Gradually her sick excitement subsided into a warm, pleasurable elation and she could relax.

Over the last few days she had felt unable to eat, and at work had had to force herself to hold in her excitement, not wishing any of her mates to think that this meant more than an extra duty imposed by the Ezzards. Insincerely she agreed with girls who said it would be horrible having to eat frogs' legs and stuff like that, and with others who said that she must take her own flannel because their dads knew for a fact that French people only used all that scent because they didn't like washing. Now, though, having left all that behind, plus the stand she had to make against Ray, she could give herself entirely to the experience. This was a chance to leave Lampeter and the factory behind for a couple of days. The more she read of Kenny's freedom and experience in foreign countries, the more she longed to find a way of doing something equally adventurous, and this was a start.

At last the long train began to pull out with great ceremony. Only then did she become conscious of Miss Lake watching her. When she drew her eyes away from the scene slowly passing and gaining momentum, she met her chaperone's eyes which, like her mouth, were smiling at Lu. Miss Lake leaned forward, slightly resting her arms on the table and her chin on her fists, and said quietly, 'Well?'

Lu, equally discreetly, said, 'It's like a dream. I've seen scenes like this loads of times at the pictures. I feel a bit like an actress.' Her attention was caught again, this time by the snatches of London as it rapidly changed from the great capital of the Commonwealth to stretches of blackened houses and factories not much different from their own smoke-grimed streets.

Miss Lake removed her velvet beret and laid it beside her. Lu, feeling nicely dressed herself, observed every detail of her dress and her actions, and decided that, if she modelled herself on Miss Lake – when she wasn't being headmistress – then she couldn't go far wrong. Long ago she had copied her way of speaking, sounding aitches in the right place, putting ts and gs where they belonged. Now she could observe the correct way to travel. 'You never expected to find yourself leaving England on a boat-train, Lu?'

'Oh I did, yes. Every film I see where there's somebody leaving, I always imagine that it's me. I've left on stage-coaches, aeroplanes and big liners. Have you ever been on a liner?'

'I've travelled by air several times, and I've been as far as the Mediterranean on a steam-ship.'

'If I was a boy I'd do the same as Kenny. Do you remember that poem we had to learn in Miss Nash's class? "I will arise and go now, and go to Innisfree". That used to give me goose-bumps, that idea of just "arising" and "going".'

'Ideas like that do have great driving force. Gives one the impetus to do what one wants – without let or hindrance, as they say.'

Lu was surprised at the tone, the enthusiasm with which Miss Lake concurred. 'If that's the case, then how did you come to arise and go to Pompey? Lampeter of all places?'

Her reply was interrupted by a waiter serving refreshments and taking orders for dinner. Not recognizing a single item except beef – boeuf – on the impressive menu, Lu nodded at Miss Lake's suggestions, trusting her not to order frogs' legs. 'You might say that Lampeter was my

Innisfree.' She pursed her lips, and smiled wryly in anticipation of Lu's expression.

'You're pulling my leg.'

Thrusting her fingers into her thick waves, and combing them back from her broad forehead in a gesture that Lu now recognized as a prelude to directness, Miss Lake went on, 'This may sound rather patronizing, but I had an idea that I could do some good for children in Lampeter. I was born into a family who had a lot of everything. My father was, still is, a mill-owner . . . Lake's of Shirebrook.' She lit a cigarette. Lu followed her gaze to the new passing scene of suburbia: green, spacious, leafy and clean. 'My father had this quality: he saw no harm in allowing a daughter to be educated. By the time I had obtained a degree in teaching, I knew what I wanted to do.'

'A mill's a factory, isn't it?'

Cynthia Lake nodded. 'Though people who live in the south of England hardly ever think of them as other than the ubiquitous cotton mills of fiction – Mrs Gaskell's *North and South*, you know? Eh lass, there's trouble at mill.'

Lu could have laughed aloud hearing Miss Lake talk like that: 'Like Gracie Fields in "Sing as We Go".'

Miss Lake nodded. 'Lake's is a knitwear mill: they make stockings, jumpers, cardigans and suchlike.'

'Are things better in that sort of factory?'

She blew out a long stream of cigarette smoke and shook her head. 'So why did I not arise and go to inflict myself on some school closer to home?'

Although the question was in her mind, Lu shrugged non-committally.

'Because I would have always been Alfred I. Lake's tommy-opposite daughter and I wanted to get as far away from that as was possible. Had I chosen a village school nearer to home, I should have had my father against me, and that would not have been easy.' She smiled. 'And I am sure that my mother would have felt compelled to send me over nourishing broth and pies. In my first job as a teacher, I went as far south as I could without falling off the edge: a hamlet near the Tilly Whim caves in Dorset, and worked my way eastwards until I obtained my headship in Portsmouth.'

'And you like it?'

She stubbed out her cigarette with an air of finality, but added, 'You have seen *my* small cabin built there, of clay and wattles made . . . Yes, I find work in Lampeter entirely to my liking.'

The waiter brought a fresh pot of tea, which gave Lu time to consider this experience of being treated as a friend rather than as a charge. 'I suppose I must have been more of a disappointment to you than I realized over the scholarship.'

Miss Lake considered the tablecloth, then looked up. 'I was – yes, to an extent I was. But then, the girl who I had thought to mould into something had ideas of her own, and stood up for what she wanted against everyone with great strength of character. That was not disappointing. She was doing what I would have done, in fact what I did do, saying, No, I'll lead my own life, thank you very much.' She put out her hand and briefly touched Lu's fingers. 'And look where it has got us. Leaving England on the boat-train and heading for the Continent. Would this have happened to a grammar school girl? Who knows? As my mother is fond of saying, "There is more than one way to skin a cat."'

Lu supposed that this meant approval. 'Why a cat?'

'A cat? Oh, heaven only knows. Perhaps my mother's nourishing pies are not rabbit after all.'

Lu made a face and Miss Lake smiled.

Something had happened between them, Lu felt. Their relationship had become more that of equals; she seemed at last to have left Lampeter Street school behind.

The rest of the journey was filled with new experiences

which she stowed away in short cryptic notes to be translated into her journal later – the boat, the crossing, strange, almost public sleeping arrangement, Calais and at last Paris.

Paris. Paris. I am in Paris. Those are French people and I am a foreigner. None of the little French she knew was of any use – she could not understand the quick, run-together words with odd inflections – but Miss Lake spoke the language fluently.

She sent a letter *poste restante* to Ken, wishing that she could see his face when he received it.

I'll bet that puzzled you, seeing my handwriting on a letter posted in France. Well, yes, it is me, and this is the life. Even after this short while I understand why you always sound so enthusiastic about being out of England. I knew that somewhere there must be some trick exit through which people who grew up in the sort of places we did could escape. Here in Paris, I'm having a peep through. Do you remember the story in that science-fiction magazine you used to take about there being a fault in Time and Space and people from the past and future and other worlds kept falling through? I think you fell through something like that and landed in Spain. Now I want to. I would come looking for you and then keep going with you. Oh my, Ken, the prospect of such freedom and adventure. To be where no one knows you, to be whoever you want, to be anybody or nobody, to be just passing through, or stopping off.

I don't know what I shall do from here on. 'How're they goin' to keep 'em down on the farm, now that they've seen Paree?' Now that they've had a carriage ride, now that they've visited the Louvre, been to see the Tuileries. Did you go? Goodness, Ken, what extraordinary things kings did with the money they stole from their people. I suppose it's the same at home, except that palaces in England aren't open to the public. I can imagine you and your Marxy friends there.

Miss Lake is with me (I shan't go into detail of how it all came about. Suffice to say that it is a business trip – don't that sound grand? – to show a buyer a new style that 'Queenform' is starting off in Paris), and of course being Miss Lake we had to go to the Louvre, not to see (as she put it) 'pictures that are on every calandar and in every popular art book ever made', but to look at one or two works of real importance. I think I could really get very interested in the 'Impressionists'.

While I'm at it, I should tell you that I have been invited to a posh dinner-dance at the shore base in the docks. No, not the usual coach-load of factory girls invited to entertain the sailors, but a long dress affair in the officers' mess. Miss Lake says she will lend me a dress, black, I've never worn black. *Très chic* (I think that's right). I would like my own, but beggars can't be choosers. I am meeting my escort at the Queen's . . . yes, *the* Queen's Hotel on Southsea front, and am being taken on from there.

Don't ask, Ken, because I'm not going to tell you, only that he is a very nice man, and an exceptional dancer. We are great show-offs, and there'll be no one to touch us in the officers' mess. Forgive me, Father, for I have sinned against the working class. Oh, but Ken, life is so exciting that I hardly care. Ray doesn't even know this much, so don't mention it, he just thinks I'm going to a dance at the base. I have to do this sort of thing these days, because he doesn't seem to realize that I'm grown up and quite capable of looking after myself. I told you all about Bar coming to live with us in my last letter – I'm hoping that with her there Ray isn't going to be picking at everything I do. I'm really looking forward to her being there. I only hope it all works out and she's happy living in Lampeter Street. Imagine what her life must be now if her magic door opens to *Pompey*.

I have no idea where I am going, but I do know that I am going *somewhere*. I have to, I am a plant that has taken all the available nourishment from my original plot. If I don't move away, then I shall never bloom, but will wither in the bud. I feel that it is the same for you. How much better I seem to know you now. Keep going, Kenny, your journey inspires me.

Lu wrote to Kenny on the night of her arrival, before she went to Lascelles'. She probably wouldn't have told him about the episode anyway; he might quite likely have been as censorious as Ray. Lascelles' was a store that prided itself on the exclusivity of its clients (not customers) and the quality that went with a Lascelles' label. It glittered with crystal hanging lamps and whispered with carpets and refined assistants. Her own part in convincing M. Lascelles himself that the 'Princess' had the quality and style fit for his store lasted about an hour and was surprisingly unstressful, and involved no embarrassment to herself. For the purposes of modelling, the corselette was worn with a modesty skirt of filmy georgette pinned to the hem.

M. Lascelles' chief sales-lady, Mme Manet, a beautifully groomed woman, helped her step into the boneless corselette, pulling and tweaking until it was like a second skin, then arranged Lu's breasts in the brassière of the 'Princess', adjusting them with a finger until Lu's nipples were pointing directly ahead. Finally the modesty skirt was attached.

Miss Lake looked on, absorbed in the procedure. 'Heavens, Lu,' she whispered when the fitting seemed to have been done to Mme Manet's satisfaction, 'I hope working girls are going to be able to jump into these things a bit more quickly than that.'

Lu, who had been standing on a plinth watching herself in the many mirrors surrounding her, said, 'It is pretty, though. I expect it won't be long before every bride will include one in her trousseau.'

'And we shall all be rich.'

Lu didn't miss the irony. 'It will give us factory girls a lot of work, though, won't it?'

'You must learn to sift the propaganda. I'm not saying that you won't find a grain of truth, but don't swallow the thing whole. The purpose of the exercise is not to keep you all in work – except only incidentally.'

In an odd way, although dressed only in undergarments and wisps, Lu felt invulnerable. Perhaps it was Mme Manet's expression of approval at the position of Lu's nipples and the smooth curve of the elastic panel over her buttocks which gave her confidence. She looked at herself in the mirror and saw a Lu she hardly recognized. Mme Manet had tied Lu's hair on top with a white ribbon, allowing the bundle of curls to fall down over the right temple. If I saw myself in a painting, I'd think, She's really beautiful. I am. At this moment, if never again, I am beautiful.

As she smiled faintly at herself she caught Miss Lake's eyes watching her, and almost imperceptibly she too smiled. At first, Lu couldn't interpret the look, then it occurred to her what it might be. She had no means of knowing because, although she knew half a dozen names for 'pansies', homosexual women were only known to her through literary references. But that look was no different from those that Duke or David or any one of half a dozen of the 'Queenform' cutters gave her. Miss Lake must be a lesbian woman. Until now, she hadn't really believed they existed outside the story of the women of Lesbos. She and Bar had loved one another since they were girls, and she had been unable to imagine any other sort of love between women.

But now she saw it in Miss Lake's eyes. Miss Lake would have liked to arrange her breasts and pin on the gauze. The idea didn't offend her, neither did it excite her. What it did do though was to make Miss Lake admirable. If she was not attracted to men, then all that worrying about finding a husband was gone.

The reappearance of Mme Manet stopped her line of thought in its tracks. 'Z' gentlemen are ready Mam'selle.'

Miss Lake left, giving Lu an approving nod. 'You know that I don't approve, but you do look splendid, absolutely.'

'Please, Mam'selle, makes the body relaxed. Monsieur Lascelles has never seen the "Princess" except as the garment. Monsieur Ezzard wishes to show that here he has something which is soft and boneless, you understand? Yes, like that. Perfect. I like this very much, so that Monsieur Lascelles must like it also. It is sold, you see. Lascelles will have "Princess" on offer to special clients before the end of the summer.'

She pulled open the drapes, and at once the dressing room was transformed into a kind of small stage with mirrors on three sides. The fourth side was open to an audience of about a dozen. Lu kept Mme Manet's pose as still as a statue, and looked into a space where there were no faces. There was a little flutter of female voices voicing approval, followed by a patter of clapping. She raised her eyes and met those of Miss Lake, who nodded almost imperceptibly. As Lu had argued with Ray, there was nothing immodest in revealing no more of herself than she would on Southsea beach. True to an extent, but bathing costumes do not have six satinized suspenders topped with six little bows.

M. Lascelles rose and made a little bow to Mr Ezzard, who said, 'Well, Paul, what did I tell you?'

'Aah . . . this is the one, Jacob. This is the break with traditional styles that the modern young women do not yet know that they want, but will know that they must have it as soon as they see it.'

They walked towards Lu, followed by a group of Lascelles ladies. They all walked round her, looking at every inch, every curve, every seam and bow. She might have been a window dummy. Although the men, when discussing detail, outlined seams to within an inch of her body, she was never touched.

She must have stood there for a full fifteen minutes. Eventually Mme Manet said, 'Messieurs, may I take the model away?' Without a glance in the direction of 'the model', M. Lascelles nodded. 'Yes, yes. Then you come to my office and we will discuss with Monsieur Ezzard.'

Lu relaxed as the drapes were drawn across and the stage became a dressing room once again. 'Miss Wilmott?' Mme Manet threw a large peignoir around Lu.

'Yes, Mr Ezzard?'

He drew the curtains a little apart. 'Well done, Miss Wilmott: very well done indeed. I have come to the conclusion that in future every new style "Queenform" presents to the trade will be modelled by our own employees.'

'Even the "Empress" and the "Grand Duchess"?'

For a moment he looked blank, then he smiled. 'Perhaps Nellie Tuffnel for the "Grand Duchess". I should have to think about "The Empress".'

'I have an aunt who is exactly that figure.' You should smile more often, she thought.

'My wife suggested that you would make a good model, and she has been proved right. She often is.' You should be a little more human more often, she thought.

'Cynthia, would you mind?'

Miss Lake appeared round the curtains and took up her seat again. 'Cynthia, I should like Miss Wilmott to have something to take home, something with a Lascelles label, of course. Perhaps you wouldn't mind helping her choose?'

'Of course.'

'Don't be sparing, it won't break the bank.'

Lu noticed the sour look Miss Lake gave him, but didn't understand what it was for.

The dinner gown was so beautiful and so expensive that Lu could hardly bear the embarrassment of having chosen it. Equally, now that she had tried it on and imagined herself walking up the front steps of the Queen's Hotel and then on into the officers' mess, she could not bear the thought of letting it go.

'I think the Ezzard accounts department can stand the shoes as well, don't you? English shoes will never look right with a Lascelles gown. I'm sure Mr Ezzard won't quibble.'

The gown was so dark a blue-green as to look almost black, until the light caught the weft of the fine fabric which was somehow compressed down its length into minute concertina pleats. This was a gown only for a youthful figure; one still held together without the aid of cortiel and bone. Anything but the sheerest of undergarments would show. The bodice was two pleated cups that became wide shoulder straps which met at the back then continued on down the pleats, expanding over the hips then contracting again to become a flaring fish-tail skirt. Although it was packed in folds of tissue and placed in an enormous Lascelles gown-box, the gown itself was so fine that it could have been rolled up and slipped into a handbag. Part of the gown's appeal for Lu was its double life: on the hanger it looked nothing more than strings of crumpled cloth, but it was a chrysalis of a gown that turned into a wonderful butterfly on a woman's figure.

She had never suspected gowns this beautiful existed anywhere but in films, and when it became hers it aroused in her memory that same emotion as the amazing diamond comet hair-slide that Peggy at The Bells at Southwick had spontaneously given her. Perhaps the surprisingly generous gift of a Lascelles gown was not quite as simple a gesture as Peggy's had been. For a moment – a moment only it was true – she thought Mr Ezzard had looked at her with the same explicit interest that Miss Lake had done.

Cynthia Lake had been against this scheme to promote Lu as a model for several reasons, all of them to do with Lu's welfare. Her talents were certainly being wasted in that factory, but for her to have agreed to consider this modelling work was no improvement. That the girl's experience would be widened by the trip was all that could be said for it, but when it became obvious she was not going to be deterred, Cynthia Lake was forced to say that she would go along. Who could blame the girl; it must have seemed like a chance in a thousand, which of course it was, but not really the chance she would have wished upon a girl who had shown such promise.

On their return to Lampeter, Jacob Ezzard stopped his car outside the headmistress's house, carried her bags into the sitting room and accepted her offer of a glass of whisky. He was well pleased with himself, all affability and cigar puffing, thanks for her help, and compliments about how well the girl had performed.

'I know that you were against the idea, Cynthia, but you have to agree that the exercise was a success. I must use the girl again.'

'No, Jacob.'

He was taken aback. He hadn't even intended her to think that he was seriously asking her agreement. 'I beg your pardon?'

'I said, no, don't even consider it. Leave Louise Wilmott alone.'

'I'm sorry, Cynthia, but I don't like your tone. You might spend your days telling little girls what to do, but it doesn't wash with me. What plans I have for my own employees are no concern of yours.'

'But I make them my concern, and I shall continue to do so.'

'Now you listen to me. I've taken girls into my factory that I would not consider were it not for your friendship with Alma. She likes to think she's doing some good among the poor, and I don't mind that. She has some very confused notions for a woman who has never worked in her life, or gone short of any creature comfort, and it pleases me to help salve her conscience. When I took on the Wilmott girl, I didn't really have a vacancy – she came along weeks after the school-leaving intake – but to please you and Alma, I found one. The same with the girl who was involved in that incestuous affair. I used my influence to get training for her and found her a place in the factory. I haven't minded too much – both girls have turned out to be good workers – but I will not have you meddling in company policy. If I decide that this girl will become attached to my sales department as a part-time model, then that is what she will be. *I* decide, not you . . . not Alma.'

'Not so that you can go creeping along hotel corridors in the middle of the night.'

She had been sitting in her hotel room with the light out, smoking and watching the comings-and-goings of night-time Paris. No matter how careful, no one can move about perfectly quietly; certainly trying to creep quietly in a stiff moiré dressing-gown is hardly possible. By the time Cynthia Lake had reached the door and opened it a crack, he had already started to walk away from the room occupied by Lu, obviously having thought better of it.

'Sour grapes?'

'Ha! Why would *anyone* suppose that I would want sexual attention from you?'

No backstreet church school teacher was going to intimidate Jacob Ezzard! 'Because you don't get it from anyone else?'

The gloves were off now.

'A mile wide of the mark, Jacob.' She looked at him with a steady gaze as she lit one of her colourful cigarettes. 'Corridor creeping is unpleasant but minor. What isn't minor is Mrs Barfoot and Pansy Morgan.'

He blenched but kept his head. 'Mrs who?'

'Oh, come along, Jacob. Let's at least be straight. I know about that incident. You were on the Bench when she pleaded guilty to manslaughter. Pansy Morgan was pregnant and Mrs Barfoot tried to help her out of trouble. Five pounds Pansy paid, and all she got for it was blood poisoning.'

His expression hardened. 'Make your point, Cynthia.'

'You had no business sitting on the Barfoot case. Your brother made the girl pregnant and the five pounds came from Ezzard's. You should have declared an interest and left the court. But you couldn't, of course. Your colleagues would be most curious to know what possible connection there could be between a respected businessman and magistrate, and a backstreet abortionist.'

Jacob Ezzard burned with a sullen, silent anger. 'You're a bloody blackmailer!'

'And your brother's a bloody lecher. And you paid to clear up after him. Except that paying people off doesn't clear it up. Pansy Morgan was her father's only support. When she died, he was put in the workhouse.'

'It would be a waste of time trying to bring the case back for a new hearing.'

'Of course it would be a waste of time. But that wouldn't be the point of it. The point of it would be that people will talk, and they aren't merely going to say, Sour grapes, they're going to say, No smoke without fire.'

'You're a blackmailer.'

'You've already said that. Leave Louise Wilmott alone and do something about your brother.'

He tossed off the rest of the whisky. 'I don't know how you know, and I'm not admitting that there is anything *to* know, but this case was in the lower court months ago. If you thought that you could connect the good name of Ezzard with that business, why wait till now?'

'Because I did not know. I've been visiting old Mr Morgan – he died recently. He blamed himself for not

333

asking Pansy earlier why Ezzard's had started paying her so well, and who gave her the money to go to Mrs Barfoot.'

'Old men will say anything on their deathbeds.'

'I know that. And your fellow magistrates will certainly come to that same conclusion.'

'All this because I foolishly went along the corridor and stood outside the Wilmott girl's room?'

'All this because next time you might open the door, and there is no way I will stand by and see any more of my girls ruined at the hands of the Ezzard men.'

It wasn't easy going into work and sitting at her machine after the extraordinary experience. But she did it and, on the first evening back, she went round to collect Eileen Grigg and go down town to have an ice-cream at Palccino's.

Lu's outings with Lena were usually arranged around Lena's only two interests: films and food. They never really conversed, except in the way of questions by Lu and short, unembellished answers from Lena. The girls they worked with thought that Lu Wilmott was daft wasting her time on Lena. To them it seemed to be all one way, the benefit going to Lena. Lu couldn't have explained, she could hardly do so to herself, except that there was a particular kind of peacefulness around Lena; she made no demands, except that Lu be there. Lena didn't care whether Lu was making herself a copy of a skirt she had seen in *Vogue*, or that she had been away to Paris with Mr Ezzard. She would watch the first film and say, 'That was good, wasn't it?' Eat her ice-cream and say, 'I like choc ices, don't you, Lu?' Watch the big film and say, 'I'm glad we chose this one.' Buy her chips and scraps, and say, 'See you tomorrow then, Lu.'

The visit to Palccino's was out of their routine, but Lena wasn't put out when Lu suggested going there to meet Bar out of work and walk home with her. 'All right, then, we could have one of their ones with fresh strawberries and cream and a long spoon.' Lu would have been interested to know how Lena came to have experienced the famous 'Palccino's Pink Specials' already, but Lena was such a secretive person that to ask would be insensitive.

Bar flushed when she saw Lu and Lena waiting to be served, but she came over with her little notebook and pencil, smiling politely and asked what they would like to order. Before Lena even mentioned the 'Pink Special' she said, 'You're Lu's other friend, aren't you? So am I. We never been here together before, but we come to walk home with you. We want the strawberry one with a long spoon and I'm paying.' For Lena, a long speech.

As Bar was writing down the order she whispered, 'You're Lena, aren't you? You knew Lu a long time before I met her, so you're her oldest friend.'

Lena nodded and sat back smiling. A Lena smile was a rare thing. When Bar returned with the tall confections, Lena said, 'I shall see you every Sunday now. I got my own place. I always come in after church, sometimes I have a doughnut and cocoa if it's a cold morning,' then stopped the flow of information with a whole, red strawberry.

Lu and Lena had been going to the pictures for weeks now, but this was Lu's first insight into the rest of Lena's life. She had never liked to ask, because there was always the inhibiting memory of what Lena's life had been before she had been taken away to the Home for Wayward Girls. As they wandered home along the pebble beach, Bar told Lena that she had left home because people never forgot that her pa was a gypsy.

Lena said, 'That's why I got away from Lampeter Street.'

Bar said, 'You're not a gypsy, are you?'

'No, but everybody there knows about me having a bad baby with my brother.'

For long moments Lu didn't know what to say, or whether she should say anything.

Bar handled it better. 'That isn't your fault, no more than my pa being a gypsy is mine.'

Lu couldn't believe that she had been so deaf or blind to what had happened to Lena. 'Lena, nobody knows anything about you having a baby. I didn't know, and I lived in Lampeter Street. You went away to school, I know that, but nobody's ever said anything about you having a baby. You know Lampeter Street, if anybody had known it would have been up and down the street in ten minutes.'

'Miss Lake knows.'

'Does she? Miss Lake? But she wouldn't tell anybody, would she, not Miss Lake.'

'The doctor knows, and Mrs Steiner. Mrs Steiner wanted it to be took away, but the vicar wouldn't.'

'You mean an abortion?'

'Yes, Mrs Steiner said it would be better, but the vicar said it was criminal and a sin. Mr Ezzard knows. He got me away from the first place after they took the baby for adoption, and got me into a home where they teaches girls how to earn a living.'

'But Lena, honestly, nobody has the slightest idea about all this. That day when you came back – if anybody had known, it would have been all round the factory.'

'They must know. Didn't you know?'

'No.'

'I wondered why you never said anything. Why do they give me the cold shoulder at the fact'ry if it isn't because of the bad baby?'

'You don't speak to them.'

'Well, I wouldn't, would I?'

Bar said, 'There isn't any babies that are bad. Babies can't be.'

'Mine was. It's because of incest. Do you know what that is? It's because our Brian was always fuckin' me.' She breathed several heavy, puffing breaths down her nostrils. 'Yes. He did. Yes . . . She was a little girl. I wanted to see

336

her, but the nurse said, No, she has to go straight away to a good home. I said, Just let me see her, but she said, No, it won't do no good, she has to go to a good Christian family where she won't know she was born bad.'

Suddenly rage, like a great enveloping wave, swept over Lu, almost taking her breath away. Her emotions and her mind were in a state of agitation, yet it was in her body that she seemed to feel the greatest disorder. Her heart palpitated unevenly, her pulse raced and she felt quite terrified. She picked up pebbles and began smashing them down with all her strength, embedding them in a strand of soft sand.

When she came to her senses, she realized that the other two were standing quietly watching. Lena said, 'What's wrong, Lu?'

Lu went as close as she could, pushing her face into Lena's as Lena used to do when they were little. 'What's wrong? What they did to you! That's what's wrong! They took you away and knocked the stuffing out of you. They took your baby away.' She began to cry. 'Bar's right, there aren't bad babies. Bad people.' She clutched Lena's shoulders. 'Why didn't you punch them in the teeth like you used to punch me? Why don't you punch me now? People did that to you and when you came back all I did was take you to the pictures and buy ice-creams. Why don't you wrestle me down in the dirt, Lena Grigg? I'd let you win.'

Bar prised Lu's fingers from Lena's shoulders and Lu stood, her arms hanging loose, mucus and tears streaming down her face as though she was a beaten five-year-old. 'Here.' Bar pushed a handkerchief at Lu. 'Your nose is running.'

For a moment Lu looked at the handkerchief as though she had no idea what it was for; then she went down to the water's edge and splashed her face with water. The other two came and sat on a ridge of stones beside her.

Lena asked a bit apprehensively, 'You didn't really want me to . . . did you?'

'I don't know, Lena. Maybe I did.'

Later, when Lu and Bar talked quietly in bed about what went on down on the beach, Bar said, 'It wasn't you crying and shouting like that, it was Lena. You know, like when a message gets sent through the voice of a seer. The spirit can't talk so they make somebody else say it for them. She couldn't talk properly until you got all that off her chest for her.'

That, coming from anyone else, Lu would have said was a lot of tosh, but coming from Bar it was the most reasonable explanation of something very strange.

When Lu had calmed down, Lena stopped speaking in her usual short, lifeless sentences and spoke to them naturally, almost fluently. 'Hitting people don't do no good, Lu. First off when they shut me up in that place, I punched everybody who come near me. I was that angry that it was me shut up in there and . . . him whose fault it was didn't have nothing done to him. I could have killed him . . . not just hit him, I'd have put a knife in him if he'd a been there. Instead, I just hit *them*. Anybody. They just hit me harder. The housemother had a little cane, she used to swish it across the backs of your legs. I didn't care. They made the ones like me who caused all the trouble scrub out the lavs. That winter I had stripes on the backs of my legs and great chilblains. Some of us was sick all the time, but we didn't care, we just said all right because then we could get miscarriages. I never seemed to matter.'

Bar said, 'It must have been a strong little baby.'

'I reckon so. She used to kick the living daylights out of me. It's a queer thing, being kicked on your insides like that. You can feel the feet through your own skin. I started thinking that's a person in there, and after that I never wanted to start a miscarriage. I used to call her

Feet, and I used to say "Hello, Feet" and "Goodnight, Feet", but not so anybody else could hear. I started being good then.'

Bar said, 'It must be hard going through all that and having a baby, then it gets taken off you.'

Lu was thinking just that same thing, but couldn't say so, in case it was the wrong thing, but Bar always knew what to say to make people feel better. Lu was no good at it, so people never knew how she felt.

'They put me out to have the baby because her head got stuck. After, it's like they took everything out from inside you and left you empty. That must sound daft, but I feels like this – ' she ran her hands down her plump torso – 'is just like one of them cardboard eggs they have in the shops at Easter to put presents in. They look like they would be solid, but they're hollow. Oh well.' She gave a queer little smile. 'That ice-cream I had down at Palccino's has got lost in there already. I could do with a bag of chips and scraps. You can come in my place if you like, and I'll make us a cup of tea.'

Lu never had any difficulty in hugging or squeezing Bar, but she couldn't touch Lena; even though she would have liked to, she was too uncertain and inhibited. 'Come on then,' Bar said, and put her arm round Lena's neck, and Lu wished for the hundredth time since she had known Bar that she knew how to be calm and kind like that instead of hot-headed and distant.

For a few days, Lu felt that she could, or should, never enjoy herself again. As soon as she found herself thinking back to the excitement of Paris, or forward to dressing up in all her splendour, she forced herself to draw back and feed herself some guilt about having had the good fortune not to be Eileen Grigg.

Bar settled in easily, and took a much greater share of the chores than Kenny had ever done. Sometimes, when Bar

339

worked late on Saturday, and Lu was out with Sonia, Ray walked down town to meet her and they meandered back through the late-night markets. A couple of times he took her to a film and once to the theatre, but he never let their relationship be anything but friendly.

Ray had thought that there was no harm in them enjoying a bit of one another's company. He still felt that she was far too young for him. And after the episode last Christmas at Roman's, he decided they should have a platonic relationship.

Madrid – June 1935.

Dear Lu and Ray, In case you were wondering or worrying, it is true that there is trouble in Spain which to anyone outside must all seem very complicated, but I don't go looking for trouble. Some trade-unionists here make the NUR look like the Mother's Union, Ray.

When I started out on this 'working-man's grand tour' I had a longing to see this country, as you know, but I never thought I'd be so caught up and inspired (yes, that's the right word) by life in a republican country. I feel that I am my own man here. I love the place and the people, and would have no trouble in settling down here.

In some places there is no work to be had, in others there is plenty (labouring, of course, a lot of picking which is back-breaking) so we don't fling our little earnings about, but keep as much as we can so that we can keep ourselves fed as we walk and walk and walk.

I wish I was better with words, or that I had a camera or could paint, but come to think of it none of them would do justice to any of the sights I am seeing daily – not all good, and some are pretty terrible, but all memorable. You have to be here, smell the place, feel the hot sun and the bitter winds, taste the tomatoes and wine, burn your throat with chilli peppers. Holiday-makers come here and sit on the shores of the Med, which is nice enough of course, but they miss what's going on in the small towns.

I've learned to speak quite a mixture of languages – only words, my sentences make people laugh. But I shall get the hang of it, be sure. *Hasta luego* (see you later), Ken.

. . . Have just collected Lu's letter. What *is* going on? What on earth did the aunts say to *that*, Lu? A journey from Paris to España, not bad for a lad from Lampeter Street. Hells-bells, our little Lu giving an opinion on the Impressionists. Now it only needs you to take the plunge, Ray. You'd never regret it.

'Wouldn't you just love to do that?' she had asked Kate Roles. 'Just pack your bags and be off?'

'What? Go tramping off amongst foreigners? They eat horses. My dad was there in the Great War, he knows. You got itchy feet going off like that with the boss.'

When, in July, the day of the officers' mess dance came, Lu had still not told Ray where she was going. Bar knew, and it was she who suggested that if Lu didn't want him to ask a lot of questions, she should get ready round at Lena's and get a taxicab from there. As once or twice a year factory girls were invited into the naval base to a dance, Ray wouldn't think this any different.

After she had been to the public baths, Lu took her things to Eileen's and got ready. Eileen sat, contentedly watching as Lu fastened her stocking to a tiny suspender belt. 'An't you going to wear nothing else except French knicks?'

'It would show through. Anyway, the dress don't need anything under it.' Lu took out the Lascelles gown from its box.

'Oh, Lu, I thought you was going to wear a ball-gown. It looks like it got into a hot wash by mistake.'

341

'Just you wait and see. I've been waiting for this moment for weeks.' She stepped into the simple arrangement of straps and pleats and slid her arms into the long sleeves. As she pulled the dress up, the concertina pleats moulded themselves around every dip and curve of her figure. 'Is the back right, Lena?'

'What there is of it.' She arranged the straps correctly.

'Well? What do you think?' Lu tried to see herself in the only mirror Lena had, which was a small hanging one.

'Don't leave much to the imagination, Lu.'

Lu grinned. 'I know, lovely isn't it?'

'It shows your figure off all right, but I wish you'd got one with a big skirt. That one clings tight round your bum – you won't be able to sit down.'

'I will, look, it stretches everywhere, that's what's so clever about it.'

'Haven't you got nothing to go round your shoulders?'

'No, I don't want to spoil it with any clutter, just my little bag.'

When she was finally ready, Lena ran down the road and called a taxicab. As it drew away, Lena stood on the pavement waving, smiling. Lena had started smiling lately. Occasionally she spoke to someone at work. About this same time of year it must have been, when Lu and Bar had been dervishing by The Swallitt Pool, Eileen's grown-up brother had made her pregnant. Only a few years. It seemed hardly feasible that they could have become the people they now were in so short a time. Eileen's brother and Ray were the same age. She felt a sudden flash of regret that she had been underhand with Ray. She decided to tell him, and that she was sorry. Then, as the taxicab turned off the sea-front and in through the gates of the Queen's Hotel, she put Lampeter Street and everything connected with it out of her mind.

Several times over the past weeks she had wondered what she would do if she turned up and he didn't. But he had come. As the porter ushered her, with her heart in her mouth, into the revolving doors, David, dashing and romantic in dinner-jacket, perfect shirt and bow-tie, stood up and came towards her.

Holding her by the shoulders, he kissed her lightly on both cheeks. 'You came! I wondered whether you would, or whether you were one of those women who keep a fellow waiting half the evening.'

She smiled happily. 'Is that what they do? It never occurred to me to be late.'

The interior of the hotel was even more splendid than she had imagined. She had glimpsed a mural, and a glass dome, and longed to look round and be overawed, but she sat – as she hoped elegantly – on a comfortable, upright padded chair with her legs drawn to one side as she had learned from years of watching how the stars did it in Hollywood films. She accepted a tipped cigarette from the slim gold case David held out. A waiter placed an ice-bucket at the side of the table and deep glasses alongside. 'I took a chance on you liking dry: is that OK?'

Hoping that it was . . . It would be, whatever dry was like, she said, 'Lovely.' She had thought champagne glasses had to be flat, but these were deeper and held the fizz longer. David chinked her glass. 'Here's to it, whatever it is.' He seemed to be enjoying himself and totally at ease, which he would be, of course. He must have been here before because he had said, 'It's not a bad place.' She sipped the drink: dry must mean very fizzy or very sharp. It was certainly nice . . . most likely dry meant it dried your mouth. Tomorrow she would have to go down to the library and look up 'champagne'.

'I've quite taken a liking to this place.' He looked around, giving Lu a chance to do likewise. There were archways, beyond which were glazed doors, through which lighted chandeliers shone. She knew that that was the dining room. It faced the sea; she had seen it from a distance scores of times; sometimes when the evenings were hot, the sea-facing French doors were opened and people could be seen sitting on the veranda; strains of music could be heard as far as the promenade. Until this minute, nothing except those strains of music had connected the people who inhabited that world to the one normally inhabited by Lu and people like her. Suddenly, like Paris, like the Lascelles store, it became part of the world she *needed* to inhabit. First she needed to get away – she had told herself that before; but it was time for her to begin to think seriously about how. 'You said you knew it, have you stayed here?'

'No, I've never stayed in Southsea at all.'

He refreshed their glasses. 'Louise?' She looked over her glass at the query attached to her name. 'My name's David Hatton, and I live in Kensington. Are you going to tell me anything, or will you continue being mysterious? I can only think that you are married or something. I don't know what to make of you, except that you are extremely beautiful, tantalizingly enigmatic, and you obviously have a taste for Paris dresses. I had ordered a gardenia for you, but it would be sacrilegious to do anything to that line.' He looked for a second at the pleated cups that supported her breasts.

'I'd love a gardenia, I could pin it on my bag.'

He beckoned the bellboy, who brought the flower in a small shiny tray. It was Hollywood; real, romantic musical Hollywood. 'You still haven't answered my question. Will I go home tomorrow still not knowing who you are, or how to find you? It wouldn't hurt you to tell me your name.'

It would. She would have this one evening, and let it end there. She wouldn't be devastated, nor would her life be in ruins. She liked him, though, for similar reasons to why she liked Duke: neither of them appeared to take themselves particularly seriously. Both were totally different from all the other young men she went out with. Both inhabited worlds that were totally removed from her own. She laughed, making a joke of it: 'I would tell you my second name if it wasn't such a dull one.'

'All right, at least that.'

'Vera.'

'Louise Vera. I have an Aunt Vera . . . You see, I'm more generous with my family secrets than you.'

'David Hatton has a brother who is a tyke and an Aunt Vera. I could write a biography knowing that. I have your telephone number, I know your name. Trust me, I will keep in touch with you.'

'Promise?'

'Yes.' She smiled at him and drank some more of the champagne, not knowing what else to do or say. 'I love this.'

He leaned forward. 'Fine and simple and expensive and understated, just like that piece of crumpled stuff you're wrapped in to such effect. I can hardly wait to see how it moves when you're dancing. Shall we go? I was going to order a car and driver because my car's such a low one it doesn't usually allow for ladies' long skirts, but I'd like to drive there if it's OK with you.'

'I fold up as easily as a card-table.'

Had it really been Hollywood, then the car would probably have been white and long or black and shiny, but his wasn't. It was what she might have guessed: a new, low, sporty two-seater with the roof folded back. 'I'll leave it down, there's no wind . . . it's not far.'

That was true; within five minutes of leaving the hotel they were getting out. She had been to wave her father's ship off from the dockside, but not to this part, which was guarded by a naval patrol.

After the splendid hotel, the officers' mess was a bit of a disappointment, but it was full of men in naval officers' uniform and women wearing pretty summer dance dresses, and it was the best band Lu had heard in a long time. Almost as soon as they were in the door, David caught her round the waist and guided her on to the floor. After the dance, they stopped for drinks of fresh orange juice, soda and wine, which Lu thought a great improvement on the champagne, then danced again. When the dances were slow he held her close, his cheek against hers; when the band played jazz and ragtime they were self-satisfied at the pleasure they were getting from playing up to one another: they constantly caught one another's eyes and smiled.

When the interval was announced, they followed the line of guests drifting into the room where a buffet was laid. It really was sumptuous, with every dish a decorated exhibition of the catering art. A few men with their partners came up and said, 'David, a stranger . . . glad to see you', or, 'I say Hatton, old chap, where have you been lately? Nice to see you around. Must get together again.' They were all young, informal and on first-name terms. He introduced Lu as 'Louise Vear'.

It was easy-going and informal refreshment, and Lu loved it. People drifted in and out, to and fro; she and David took their plates and glasses to a small corner table. 'OK, Miss Vear?'

'Absolutely. The Navy does itself very well, doesn't it?'

'That's a clue. Your people are obviously not Navy or you wouldn't be surprised.'

Her people not Navy? An illegitimate daughter of an able seaman who had fallen in the drink not a hundred miles from here? Absolutely not from a naval family. Unperturbed by what she was thinking, she smiled and said jokingly, 'Keep going, Holmes, you're hot on the trail.'

There was only one incident in the entire, perfect evening that caused her a moment of panic, but she carried it off quite to her satisfaction. David had gone to the men's room and came back with a grey-haired man showing the insignia of ship's captain. 'Louise, this is Arnold Gore, a distant cousin, wouldn't you say that, Arnold? Something, something removed? Arnold, this is Louise Vear.'

'I can see a family likeness,' Lu said.

When the captain smiled it was with great charm. He took her hand and held on to it, caressing it slightly, as ladies' men did. 'We Gores are the respectable arm of the family. You'd do well to ditch David and tie up alongside me.' He had a deep-throated, pleasant chuckle. 'I watched you dancing. You do it beautifully.' As she withdrew her hand he said, 'I say, that's nasty,' and rubbed the ball of his thumb over the hard scar left by the machine needle. 'Does it hurt?'

'No. I don't even notice.'

'Accident?'

She withdrew her hand, holding the thumb in the palm of her other hand and saying lightly, 'Yes, glass. I impaled myself on a long sliver of glass. Scarred for life, I expect.' She wished he would go, but he was the type who would do his courteous duty by chatting to all the ladies. He was good at it. If he hadn't alighted on this one topic, Lu could have enjoyed herself enormously watching him operate.

'I'll tell you something interesting about just such a thing. You know we have these same shore-base evenings for ratings ashore for a short turn-round? Young women of the town are invited – sorry, no, don't mean "women of the town" – these are nice young girls from local families, they are chaperoned in, we give them a good evening, they dance with the ratings . . .'

She had been on such outings, had danced with the ratings and enjoyed the good food. Lu's mouth dried. She sipped the fizzing orange and wine, appearing, as she hoped, unperturbed, perhaps a little bored.

'I was doing my bit, saying my piece, you know . . . Anyhow, these young ladies were all from the same

347

factory. They make shirts and shrouds or some such . . . and they had scars. Almost proud of them, one might say.'

'They all had scars? What caused them?'

'They sewed their hands with sewing machines. It appears they go so fast that they occasionally can't stop, and zzzt! Pierced right through the finger. Quite often they have to take the machine apart to release them.'

'Please, Arnold,' David said, 'do you mind? I shall pass out cold if you go on.'

'Sorry, sorry, I suppose it is a bit . . . you know. I find these bits and pieces of information so very interesting . . . all these girls the same injury. It was a kind of sign that they had made it, like skiers – can't be a real skier until you've broken a leg.' He took Lu's hand again. 'Hope you're not weak-kneed, like these young Hattons. Glad to see David enjoying himself for a change. Ah well, duty calls. Hope you're enjoying it.'

'Thank you, Captain Gore. It's lovely.'

'Arnold. Please.'

'Sorry about that, Louise,' David said when he had gone. 'Nothing one can do about one's family. I should have warned you, I suppose. Actually, the invitation came from him. He likes the family to see him in his glory. He's OK, bit of a snob, terrible womanizer, too. I think I'll get you safely away before he returns.'

She laughed, relieved that the captain had been more interested in the sound of his own voice than asking how a sliver of glass could penetrate a thumb. Glass sliced, it didn't penetrate. 'No need to worry, he's really not my type. Maybe we should go, it must be late.'

'Not yet. What time must you go? Where are you going? How will you get there? May I take you? Or is it pumpkins at midnight and once again I shall be left holding the crystal cigarette lighter?'

'I like to use taxicabs when I can. If you would like to

take me back to your hotel, I will get you to order me one from there.'

'Shall we go now? Maybe we could have coffee or something.'

'Lovely.'

He drove the short way back to the promenade, but instead of turning into the hotel gateway, he pulled up on the sea-front. 'What's up with the moon, it's lurking behind that cloud, the only cloud by the look of it? I think we deserve one of those twinkling pathways across the sea. From here I should think one ought to be able to walk over to the Isle of Wight on it. Do you really want coffee now, or would you like a bit of a spin? Not far, just to get the wind in our hair.'

'Let's do that.'

'I don't know whether you know the road that goes over the Portsdown Hills from here . . .'

'I know it.'

'Have you ever seen it at night?'

'No.' That was absolutely true. Although she had been that way with Uncle Hec on more than one occasion, she had never been at night.

'It's a fantastic sight.'

He pulled the car off the road not far from the spot Uncle Hec had chosen six years before. 'There! Isn't that wonderful?'

Seen at night, the two sides of the dividing hill were perhaps as awesome as when she had first seen them on that spring morning. Far below on the seaward side, the plan of the town and its harbour was outlined by lights, on the land side there seemed to be endless dark.

'There's a rug back there if you're chilly. Or . . .' He put his arm about her and pulled her towards him, then laughed. 'Damned bucket-seats. My brother won't have sports cars, he says they're more inhibiting than knicker elastic . . . I'm sorry, I don't usually quote my brother,

349

especially on his ways with women. Arnold Gore was right, you can't take us Hattons anywhere. I only wanted to kiss you, nothing else.'

Lu held his face and did it for him. He obviously knew how to manage bucket-seats, for he enclosed her in his arms and kissed her firmly, with lips as warm as the hands that were caressing the bare skin of her back.

'We could sit on the grass, there are binoculars in the glove box . . . probably not much use until the moon comes out, but we might see something.' There were two large, soft tartan rugs which he dropped on to the grass a little way down the slope, away from the car. Then he pulled off his black tie, unfastened the neck stud and handed her the binoculars.

'I can't see a thing.'

'That wheel adjusts the eye width, and this . . . brings it into focus.' He had to sit very close to show her.

'I see something. I think it – oh yes, there's a boat moving. That's marvellous.'

'Now if I was my twin, I'd have thought to have a bottle and two glasses in the box. All I've got is chocolate and bananas.'

'I love chocolate. Look, look, the moon's coming out.'

The chocolate was like nothing Lu had ever tasted before: smooth, thin, crisp and bitter. 'Mmm, I love it.'

'Floris. My grandmother spoils me. Doesn't let me go out unless I am provided for – iron rations for if I get shipwrecked.'

'Is she a Gore or a Hatton?'

'Both. And now I shall clam up until I know something sweet about your grandmother.'

'There's nothing . . .'

He stopped her with a long kiss, during which they somehow ended up prone and closely entangled, with him looking down at her now clearly lit by the moon. 'My God you're beautiful . . . so beautiful. Seriously, now, are you engaged to be married?'

'No.'

'Or married?'

'No.'

'Or . . . ah . . . are you in the process of divorce?'

'No!'

'OK, I didn't suppose that you were, but it would answer why you won't let me into your life just a little bit.'

'I should have thought that this was being in my life.'

'Not enough. Not enough by half.' He picked up her left hand, the one with the two scars, and without looking at it took the thumb between his lips and held it there for a few seconds, perhaps apologizing for his cousin. 'My grandmother believes in kissing things better. You'd make a good criminal, you wouldn't give yourself away given the third degree.'

'I won't steal your cigarette case and cufflinks.'

'You have no intention of being serious for two minutes together. I have it! You're a nun. You lead this double life: a life of silent prayer by day, a Paris gown by night. You keep your habit and wimple in a woodsman's hut and creep back into your cell in time for matins or whatever it is.'

'What about the hair? Aren't nuns shaven?'

'Oh yes . . . the hair.' He pushed his fingers into her hairline, parted his lips and hers, and kissed her again, making a shiver rise up and spill over her whole body like a fountain of the most delectable pleasure. 'I really do want to meet you again. Please.'

She felt his weight beginning to press more heavily, the sensation of his masculine warmth raising her pores and hardening her nipples. The light scent of shaving cream, the slight suggestion of bristle when his face touched hers, the sound of his breath. She even imagined she could hear his heart, but perhaps it was her own.

She wanted to keep it like this, romantic and almost mystical, yet at the same time she longed to move on into reality where she would tell him the truth about herself. No, I'm not a nun by day, I'm a factory hand and I got this dress as a present from my boss for going to France and standing about in my underwear. Oh yes, the truth about herself.

The thought of him ever seeing her coming out of Ezzard's was appalling. It would be better if they parted tonight, leaving her with a dried gardenia as a memento, as her mother had kept her father's colourful postcards. Except that this was something entirely more glamorous than that. This was a romance, a romantic interlude. It was thrilling and wonderful.

When he slipped his hand into the pleated cup, she did not stop him, did not want to. The sensation, which started up within her pelvis, then coursed downwards and into her loins, and then back up inside her, quite taking her breath away, was overpowering. As they swallowed one another's kisses, he moved one leg over her and she was pinned by its weight. She knew what she wanted, which was to feel the bare skin of her own thighs against his own, her naked hips touching his, her breasts pressed by his chest. She had never done this before, but she knew how to do it, all the other sexual arousals, sensations and climactic dreams were feeble substitutes. She wanted nothing now except that he penetrate her until she lost her virginity. She wanted to know the extreme sensation of going all the way.

Yet, even as she made the first movement of her legs, she panicked and pushed him away. Her whole body felt moist and slick, her dress and knickers clung to her body, her hair felt in disarray. She could scarcely breathe, and a voluptuous feeling of desire hung about tempting her.

'Christ! I'm sorry.' He threw himself on to his back and lay panting beside her.

Sitting up, she inhaled quietly, deeply, and felt senses begin to return. Then he too sat up. He turned a little away from her, then he turned back and again said, 'I'm sorry . . . I . . .' With unsteady hands he lit her cigarette, and for a long minute they sat in electric silence. 'I'd say, Forgive me, except that I'm not sorry for wanting so much to fuck you.'

She drew on the cigarette, making it crackle and grow bright as she blushed. Men of her own class didn't use the word fuck in front of women they respected. Yet it was the best and only way to describe what they both wanted.

'I don't think I've ever wanted to fuck a woman so much.'

'I wanted to let you, but I . . .'

'It's all right.' He looked closely at her, his fingers twisting a bunch of her hair round and round his fingers. 'You're so desirable.'

Lu felt that anything she said would be the wrong thing.

'We'd better go.'

With mixed emotions she looked down the chalk escarpment that flattened out where houses and shops were. Where she belonged at the same time as not belonging. The houses by the sea followed the line of the shore; large, three-storey houses with names, trees, gardens, high brick walls and iron gates. The houses by the sea were owned by doctors, lawyers, high-ranking naval officers and people who appeared to do nothing except have enough money to live there. David belonged there. Lampeter Street lay further inland, in that area where the streetlights were in long, straight, close rows, unbroken by any tree.

'Say something, Louise.'

'When I was twelve years old, this was my road to Damascus.'

'God spoke to you?'

She laughed quietly, and trod her cigarette into the short grass. 'I was so full of myself, I felt like a dragonfly nymph about to burst its skin and take off into the blue.'

'And did you?'

'I think I did. This was my taking-off point. I had seen both sides of the hill.'

'I guess you must live somewhere down there?'

She liked him too much to keep on playing that coy game, yet to be honest was to change everything, and she wasn't ready to do that. 'I don't think we should meet again.'

'Please.'

'This has been the best evening of my life, but it wouldn't be a good idea to keep it going.'

'Then say you'll telephone me.'

'What is the point?'

'The point is I just can't leave it like this. Look, I'm usually at home on a Sunday, would you ring me there?'

'I don't know . . . maybe in a little while.'

'Yes, please.' He laughed gently. 'My grandmother would think that's pathetic. A mooning schoolboy, she'd call me.'

'I'll ring on the first Sunday in September, in the morning. Don't say "Promise?" because I will do it.'

'First Sunday, right! I will be there come hell or high water.' He held open the car door.

'Would you . . .?'

'What? Ask.'

'I'd love to drive your car.'

He didn't hesitate, but picked her up and deposited her in the driving seat, then threw the rugs in the back. 'She's a roaring monster, and I shall absolutely love to see you controlling her.'

The controls were as simple as Ted's pick-up, the great difference was in the engine capacity. Even so, she discovered that she could feel her way easily into the gears. She had never imagined an engine could be engaged so smoothly. She never doubted that she could drive it. She could and she did – not fast, but competently and enjoyably. She was aware of him sitting sideways on, watching her; she did not feel intimidated either by him or by the roaring car.

When she stepped out she said, 'I'd love a car like this. I would fill it up to capacity and drive away and see where it took me.' He looked puzzled; she knew that he must be. Then he would have to be puzzled.

Their goodnight kiss as he handed her into the taxicab was as gentle as the one with which he had greeted her earlier that evening. She let the driver draw away before she told him where to take her.

From the Queen's Hotel to Lampeter Street. He probably thought she was an expensive street-walker.

In spite of Ray's insistence that he was too old to think of Bar romantically, their relationship slowly evolved into that of a couple – not lovers, but people happy in each other's company. When they took to occasional outings to the cinema, which Bar adored, the usherette would show them to back-row seats but Ray would press on to find seats in a safer position, cross his legs away from her, and keep his eyes firmly on the screen during love scenes.

Lu went to May and Ted's only once during that summer. She had a good many things on her mind and, at the moment, Lampeter Street was not the place where she could think clearly. Certainly she felt very confused by Ray and Bar.

Bar not only loved Ray, she admired him, and Ray knew it and would not want to lose that admiration. But Ray was cautious, he had grown up having too many responsibilities. If he wasn't careful, Bar would think he wasn't interested in her. One thing Lu did know, he'd got it fixed in his mind that Bar was too young for him. He imagined people saying he was a cradle-snatcher. Against the concern that Ray and Bar would not get together was an equal concern that they would; they had more in common with each other than with her. She was changing, growing away, she could see it with every month that passed, not only from them, but it seemed from everyone who had been part of her life till now, except perhaps Gabriel Strawbridge, who had always treated her as an equal.

In the peaceful atmosphere at Roman's Fields, Lu was able to tease at these tangled threads of her confusion and make some sense of herself. To make sense of her feelings towards David and the tangle of deception she had woven for herself, she told May about him. May, as always, was direct.

'Do you want to see him again?'

'I don't know, sort of yes and no. If I was his sort, then yes, I would, but he's a toff, Aunty May.'

'When you call me Aunty, you're usually trying to hide your real feelings.'

'My real feelings are that he's a toff and I'm a factory hand, and if he ever found out I'd be mortified.'

'Well, he isn't worth spending time on then, is he, Lu?'

'I know what you're getting at, but it's not him, it's me. He quite likely couldn't be bothered if I'm Lu Wilmott or Princess Elizabeth, but because I'm not Princess Elizabeth I don't want him to know who I am. Perhaps it is childish and shallow, but that's how I feel.'

'What are we wasting time talking about it for, then?'

For a while Lu went on sorting reusable bean-sticks from firewood. 'Because I said I would telephone him.'

'What for?'

'Because I wouldn't give him my address, and he wanted to keep in touch.'

'That sounds like you're keeping him on a piece of string to me. I must say I feel sorry for the poor chap. He must think something of you or he wouldn't put up with all this secrecy.'

'Aunty May! It isn't like that.'

'If it isn't, then stop messing him about. When you do ring him you should say to him, That's it, and finish, or be straight and tell him, and then see what he's made of. There's nothing to be ashamed of working for your living.'

'He works for his living, too.'

'What at?'

After a pause, Lu said, 'I don't know, but he has to travel. He's got this lovely sports car.'

May's 'outspoken' expression melted. 'Cat burglar, d'you reckon?'

Lu beamed, as though May had stumbled on a truer perception of the situation. 'And not a toff at all?'

'Perhaps he thought you were, and played up to you?'

'But he's got a cousin who's a naval captain.'

'We've all got something other people are impressed by.'

Lu's face fell again. 'Oh? And what have I got that would impress anybody?'

May twisted binder-twine around a bundle of sticks, threw it on to the trailer, then stood looking at Lu. 'You've got yourself, Lu Wilmott, a beautiful, well-read and intelligent woman. Anybody who isn't impressed by that, isn't worth knowing.'

'Aunty May, you always knew how to make me feel good. I think I'll telephone him at that number. I don't really want to get serious about a man yet, do I? I still haven't got my ticket for Xanadu.'

May's love showed. She smiled. 'Of course, if you really wanted to impress somebody, there's always the Louise Wilmott loom-weight over there at the Alton museum.'

When Lu went back to Portsmouth, she was set in her mind about what she would say. Light-hearted, but firm. She was young; the way out of Pompey wasn't by means of a man, no matter how exciting and intriguing. She regretted that they had not satisfied the sexual craving they had experienced that night, but in one way it was good, because now she knew how easy it was just to keep going, she would go back and see Mrs Steiner. When she thought seriously about it, she had really had a narrow escape; a second time she might not.

The next morning, when Lu arrived at work, the road outside the factory was thronging with women and girls, the gates locked. George Ezzard was trying to make himself heard as he nailed a notice to the gate. 'Fire in boiler room. Closed until further notice.'

Kate Roles said, 'They shut us out, Lu! We're stood off.'

Lu said, 'They treat us like bloody dirt!'

'Language, language,' Nellie said.

Lena Grigg, standing close to Lu, said, 'Two girls dropped their scissors on Friday.'

Lu said, 'Don't be daft, Lena, dropping scissors don't start a boiler-room fire.'

'Don't you be daft either, Lu Wilmott, bad luck's bad luck and it comes in threes, anybody knows that. People don't make these things up.'

George came out and, standing on a box, announced that the damage would take three days to put right. Until then everybody was laid off.

As Lu pushed her way towards him, she was suddenly struck by the notion that George Ezzard could not stand her. 'That's not fair. It's not our fault your blinking boiler caught fire. We can't afford to be stood off for three days. Who's going to pay people's rent and groceries?'

'You, Wilmott, are a damned trouble-maker.'

'That's not fair either. I'm only saying I don't see why we should be the losers if the machines stop.'

'You think we should pay you lot to stop home enjoying yourselves?'

Somebody shouted, 'I could be home enjoying myself at the wash-tub.'

George went on. 'Money for not working, that's a good one.'

Lu raised her voice. 'But we will work. That's what we've got out of bed and come here to do, only you've locked us out.'

'You can't work without machines.'

'And you shouldn't let the boiler break down.'

'That's all I've got to say. Factory's closed until further notice!'

'No!' she shouted as he went to get down. 'We kept our end of the bargain.'

Flicking her comment aside contemptuously and addressing the crowd, he said, 'Well, Madam Wilmott, if you can find a clause in your contract says we got to pay you, then you'd best consult your solicitor and sue us.' He jumped down and dived through the small door in the chained and bolted factory gate.

In the midst of all the noise, and an atmosphere tense with frustration and anger, Lu saw quite clearly that his contempt for their arguments had been directed at her. That riled her. Oh, this place! Why did she even care what happened? She turned on her mates. 'You lot might be scared to speak up for yourselves, but you don't have to let him insult you . . . It wasn't just me he was jeering at – it was all of us. He knows they've got us where they want us . . . If they've got the upper hand, you don't have to kiss it!' Nobody wanted to go home, that seemed too final. No work, no money.

Once George had disappeared, there was really little point in hanging around the factory gates, but this they felt compelled to do.

Women waiting for no reason other than they were with others in the same boat. Three days. They calculated what debts they could 'leave' this week, and who must be paid, what would husbands and mothers say about a two-and-a-half-day pay-packet. It wasn't that they were unused to being laid off. Regularly each summer they were sent on 'holiday' for a week or two when orders were short or the walls whitewashed or the engine dismantled and serviced. If there was a week off, they could draw six shillings from the dole office, but there was nothing for this sort of casual shut-down.

Kate and Lu, with a number of other girls from their floor, stood leaning, backs to the factory wall, face to the sun, smoking cigarettes and grumbling. Nellie joined them. 'Any of you girls going to be in real trouble over this?' Nellie would do her best to try to bail anyone out if things got really bad. She was as good as they came, and none of the girls would ever try to put one over on her. Nellie was their harsh task-master and their good fairy. She put them through the hoop for their own good, they knew that; slap-dash work was only thrown out, so they might as well do it right first go. The girls looked at one another and shook their heads.

Nellie said, 'I was thinking to myself, only an idea, like. Maybe if we had a kind of "Sinking Fund". Say we all put in a few pence a week. It'd be like the Doctor's Club: you could get help from it when things got bad. It wouldn't be a lot, and we'd have to work out how to do it. What do you think?'

What Lu thought was, why haven't I suggested something like that? In her heart of hearts she knew why. She preferred Mr Matthews' classroom theory of politics to its practice in the factory. She had grown up seeing what commitment to other people had meant to Ray. She went dancing and he went to union meetings. He didn't know how to be frivolous.

Kate said, 'I reckon it's a good idea. I'd be in!'

Others said that they would too. A new machinist, a married woman, said, 'If they was anything of employers, *they'd* set it up. You need somebody who knows what they're doing handling other people's money.'

Nellie said, 'I was wondering about Lu.'

It was a good idea, but what they really needed was proper insurance. What she needed was not to be drawn into it, not to be asked to run the thing. All summer she had had the feeling that her time at Ezzard's must soon come to an end. Something would happen, would present itself, as the Palccino's job had to Bar. She'd already decided to use the three days off work in making up some winter remnants she had bought in the spring sales on Vera's old sewing machine.

But first Nellie called to her. 'We thought of getting up a delegation and going to ask Mr Ezzard if he didn't ought to pay us something for being laid off. It has to be women who won't suffer too much if he gives notice. There's Rita Bell from the box-making room says she'd do it with me; she's got her two sons working, and there's only me and my Fred. Me and Rita are getting on, anyway. We thought we should ask one of you young ones. Katie would probably do it, her dad's in a good job and Katie's going to leave anyway when she gets married, but you know Katie, you never know what she'll say next and she's got quite cocky since she got that engagement ring. We don't hardly like to ask you, but you've got the gift of the gab, Lu. I mean, the rest of us'd be struck dumb and peeing our pants at having to go off abroad like you did.'

Jacob Ezzard may well have been surprised by Lu's telephone call to his office – surprised enough to agree to see them. Word had got about, so that when the three of them arrived at the office entrance, quite a crowd had gathered.

Because of her gift of the gab, Lu was elected spokes-woman. Mr Ezzard's face was expressionless; it was difficult to believe that this was the same person who had been so affable and generous a few weeks ago. 'Well, Wilmott, if you have something to say, get on with it. My time's money.'

361

'Well, Mr Ezzard, so's ours, and that's why we're here. We can't afford to be stood off. Three days is nearly half our money.'

'You don't think I want the factory closed, do you? Three days is half a week's output.'

'But we haven't got insurance, Mr Ezzard.'

His face darkened at the accurate point of her argument. 'What do you expect me to do? Give you three days' holiday and pay you all for hanging around in the streets?' He indicated that he was aware that there was a crowd below.

'No, Mr Ezzard, but we think it might be fair if you did pay something. After all, we all turned up for work. Nobody wants to hang around in the streets.'

His eyes slid to Nellie and Rita. 'You've been working at Ezzard's for a long time.'

'Since we were girls, Mr Ezzard.'

'Would you say that conditions are better now?'

Nellie and Rita looked at one another.

'It was treadles when you started, and now the entire work is mechanized. These days girls can turn out the kind of piecework you could only have dreamed of. Right?'

Rita nodded. 'And you got us that new glue that didn't get on our chests. That made a difference.'

He changed tack, became patronizing. 'I've made huge investments in bringing "Queenform" up to date. Where do you think the money came from? Come on, Nellie, where?'

'The bank?'

'But how did it get into the bank?'

Lu jumped in. 'Capital investment. Profits set aside for the purpose.'

He engaged her eyes dominantly, but she would not back off her own gaze. 'Which have to be earned.'

'And which *we* all have a hand in earning, Mr Ezzard.' She was impeccably polite.

'And which with a three-day shut-down for repairs are not likely to increase, and will certainly not allow for a pay-out for non-productive factory hands. No. The answer is no. The gates will be unlocked on Thursday morning and there'll be overtime working until Saturday evening ten o'clock. Plenty of opportunity for making up for lost time.'

Before Lu could add anything, Nellie took over. 'Thank you for seeing us, Mr Ezzard. Will you put a notice up to that effect?'

'All right, why not? I'll get George to see to it.'

As the three were leaving, he did his usual trick of making a parting shot. 'I would have said that you were perhaps three of "Queenform's" most reliable employees, not at all the hot-heads who want to upset the status quo with unions and conditions of work. I shouldn't like to lose you.'

Lu could have spoken for herself, but not for the two older women.

Outside there was a great deal of jeering up at the office windows. Some stones were thrown, only one of which reached the offices; the others went through the barred windows of the ground-floor machine room where Nellie and Lu worked.

As she had promised, on the first Sunday in September, Lu rang the number David had given her. A woman with a London accent answered, Lu asked if David Hatton was there.

'I'm sorry, no.'

'He was expecting me to call.'

'Was he? May I ask who is calling?'

There was a beat of pause before she answered. 'He won't know me except as Louise . . . he *was* expecting me to call.'

'I see. Could you hold on for a moment, please?'

Lu heard her saying something with her hand held over the mouthpiece, then it cleared. 'Lady Margaret will speak with you.'

'Who?'

'Lady Gore-Hatton, Mr Hatton's grandmother.'

'Hello.' The voice was loud, the manner imperious and tetchy. 'Who is that?' In Lu's terms the voice was top-drawer, cut-glass, posh, and associated with arrogant authority. Her instinct was to put down the receiver but she managed to stammer out, 'Can I speak to David, please?'

'No, I am afraid that you may not.'

'Well . . . ah . . .' She slammed the earpiece into its clip and left the call-box blushing and confused, then went into one of the many little cafés in the Lampeter area that opened despite it being Sunday. There she sat and drank tea until she had got over the shock of that voice, that title. He had said, hadn't he? 'My grandmother is called Vera.' Not with an accent like that, she wasn't. Lu felt extremely foolish and naïve. Lascelles gown or not, he had probably seen right through her. Embarrassment at her silly deception was replaced by indignation at his more serious one of not being there on the day she had arranged to telephone him. She left the café feeling quite justified at having crashed the earpiece into the holder.

Miss Lake wanted to hear from Lu about the delegation. 'Mr Ezzard's a hard and proud man, Lu; he's not going to forgive three women trying to tell him what he should do.'

'He can do what he likes. It's time I left there. If I just knew what to do, I would be gone in a flash.'

'Well, I'd appreciate it if you didn't fly off for the moment. Did you know that Eileen Grigg's brother is home on leave?'

Lu's heart sank. Not now! She had quite enough on her plate just now, thank you very much. She felt irritable and put upon. She wanted to say, What's it got to do with me?

She would stay, of course. If Lena wasn't exactly a friend in the same way that Bar and Katie were, she and Lu were part of one another's lives, and if Lena had taken some things for granted, it had been Lu herself who had been the intruder into Lena's world which, until Lu had persuaded her to go to the pictures, had been self-contained.

'OK, I will. Is he much of a threat to her these days?'

'Lena still thinks so.'

'Yeah, well, it'd be a pity if she went back into her shell again.' It was a habit of Lu's when she was irritated with Miss Lake to revert to her old street-talk.

'Don't expect too much of her, Lu.'

'I don't expect nothing of her.' Which wasn't true, and Lu knew it; she still thought that somewhere inside the phlegmatic woman was the old Lena.

When Lu went round to Lena's room the door was bolted and the key turned in the lock. It wasn't opened until Lena was assured that Lu was alone. The normally spartan and tidy place was in a mess; Lena was sitting in bed, dressed, flicking through a pile of old magazines and drinking from a large bottle of cherry-red fizz. Her dull, toneless voice had returned. 'He's come back, Lu.'

'I know. He's not likely to come here, is he? He'll be off round the pubs with his friends.'

'He's worst when he's had a skinful. He'd think it was funny to bring them all round here.'

'Do you want to come round with us until he goes back?'

'No. I'm safer here. This is the top floor. He'd have to take a chopper to get through that door. If he did . . .' From within the pile of assorted blankets she produced the type of thin, pointed knife used to bone out ham.

'Eileen! That won't do any good. Come and stop with us.'

'My ways are queer, Lu. I wouldn't fit in. It's why I like my own place.' Her own place was pathetic, but Lu supposed that after life with the Griggs and then time spent in various hostels, a little attic room with a key to its door was better. 'When the factory starts again, you could walk home with me. Specially if we got to work extra shifts.'

The last of the summer visitors to the seaside had gone home. Palccino's Ice Parlour turned to its winter role providing 'Bacon Breakfasts and Hot Snacks All Day' to workers and shoppers in the centre of town. Bar's tips became less, but during the summer she had accumulated a tidy sum of money in a tin box.

Ken and his friends continued walking and working, sometimes stopping for weeks at a time in the same area, helping with the harvesting of olives, oranges, tomatoes and garlic bulbs. Sometimes, where a small bit of land was cropped by a family and could not stand the cost of extra labour, they would work for their food and a place to sleep. 'You'd not recognize me now, Lu. I've got big and broad and brawny and brown (which goes down a treat with the girls).' It was the day he mentioned Guadalajara in one of his letters that Lu truly began to feel resentful. It was one of the places she had claimed for herself, for her future away from Pompey. Guadalajara was one of the places that had hummed a siren song which had reached her ears in a classroom in the slum streets of Portsmouth. She grew even more envious of Ken's carefree existence.

Ray too began to have moody silences. He seemed happy enough at times, especially when the three of them had been to a show in town, or when Lu had gone dancing in Southampton, and he and Bar had gone to the cinema, but many times he would sit after his meal staring at the newspaper but not reading it. Whatever it was that was going on in his mind clearly troubled him.

On the machine floor at the 'Queenform' factory, the

windowpanes broken during the lock-out demonstration stayed broken. George said that they had a choice: give him the name of who did it, or have money docked to pay for the repairs. Nobody wanted to or could say, and nobody could afford to have money docked, so that those girls who were affected most by the draught wrapped themselves up in something extra where the cold hit most.

One evening after she had seen Lena safely locked up for the night, Lu returned home to be shocked at the sight of a gleaming car parked outside Number 110. David! Her stomach turned over. It was a new car, but a similar model. How could he possibly have tracked her down? It was Bar's half day, so the light was on in the house and the curtains drawn; she must have invited him into the house. Lu didn't know what to do, except to go back to Lena's and wait there till he had gone. Wrapping her scarf round her head so that it partly covered her face, she turned and, head down, walked quickly in the direction from which she had just come.

When she reached the bread shop she caught a glimpse of Bar's black hair with its red ribbons, so she stepped out into the road away from the light. As she did so, someone she hadn't noticed waiting on the corner grabbed her elbow and pulled her back on to the pavement, holding her tightly and pinioning her arms. Duke Barney!

'You'll get yourself killed bucking away like that.' She had not heard that half-mocking, half-insolent tone for months. He was smartly but unconventionally dressed in a roll-necked jumper and narrow trousers; she had seen such costume at the pictures on wealthy Brazilian cattle-ranchers. He still wore his hair tied in a club; pulled back from his face it emphasized his racial features. 'I said I'd call round, didn't I? Come on, I've come to take you up to see the Fire Boys Fair.'

Later, when she tried to recall that evening, she couldn't remember much about what they had said to one another on that drive. Perhaps they had said nothing.

She got into his car, just as she was, wearing her work clothes, and they drove off to Heathfield, a small village twenty miles away. Surprisingly, he was a steady, slow driver, perhaps from years of travelling by the one horse-power of little mares like Pixie. The car smelt of new leather, and its engine performed perfectly. For Duke it would have to be a car to impress. Even when he had been a youth, he had never galloped any horse as Bar would do, but preferred to sit erect, composing himself into a noble image. She had seen him do it. It was the same with his driving; straight-backed, head erect, looking at the road ahead down his long nose. He didn't mention the car, or how he came to be so prosperous. He didn't need to, it would be sufficient for Duke to be seen as such. Lu did not want to know.

Although he behaved with authority, Lu sensed that he was not entirely at ease. She wondered whether what he required was for her to see that he had succeeded, that it should be herself in particular – having known him as a half-breed village boy gypsy – who should see that he had made Duke Barney into a man of substance. He had come to show off to her, much as he had that day in Swallitt Wood when he had dived into the pool.

He was certainly a very attractive man, but with some-thing about him that was unknowable; he had that same mystical spirit that was part of Bar's enigma. There was part of them that was difficult to understand. Perhaps they had been born with extra senses. Lu had felt that about Bar, and about her mother, Ann Carter, which was strange because you would have thought it would have come to them from their gypsy side. Duke's unknow-ability was quite different from not knowing David Hatton. Her ignorance of David was because she had made the choice not to continue to see him. It wouldn't be difficult to discover David if she chose. It would be a challenge to know what made Duke Barney tick.

She would never take up that challenge, for she felt that the more one knew about a person, the more one became bound to them. To love was worse, love dragged like an anchor on people's lives. She had seen it everywhere. If Ray had not loved her and Ken and their mother he could have done as he pleased, as Ken had. Girls at work who had always been one of the bunch, free to do what they liked in their own time and with their own pocket money, free to dress as they pleased, wear their hair as they pleased, fell in love with the idea of falling in love and changed. They gave up everything that had made them who they were to become attached to their young man. Not only attached, they became part of him, his life became theirs and in a matter of months the carefree girl became weighted down by all the rules and traditions that went with falling in love.

But that did not mean that she wasn't enjoying being here with Duke. Indeed not, she was elated.

After he had parked, they went along with the thronging crowds making their way through the narrow streets. As they passed street-hawkers, he bought bunches of balloons and flags on sticks and insisted that she carry them. He put coins into every collecting box. Taking her by the hand, he pushed a way through the crowds. He said hardly anything, but from time to time looked back at her with an amused expression. She felt that he might be daring her to protest, or pushing her to see whether she would show some curiosity. But she did not; she felt elated by the surprise and excitement at the dramatic change of scene. One minute she had been in dimly lit Lampeter Street, and almost the next she was part of a thronging crowd, marching bands, fife and drum troupes, tableaux, floats, decorated wagons and lorries, little girls dressed as fairies and princesses and little boys as Zulus and fire chiefs, all lit by flaring torches.

'You ever been to the Fire Boys before?'

'No, I thought it was just a carnival with fireworks.'

He nodded. 'Come on, the bonfire's down yonder meadow. I never miss the Fire Boys.' She followed where he led, wondering as she went how had he travelled to this place on other occasions. Riding one of his horses bareback to sell or exchange with other horse traders perhaps? In a van like some of the travellers? She guessed that he wouldn't have been so keen for her to have seen him then.

He had said earlier on, 'I was waiting for Bar when she came out of work.' How had he known where to find her? Perhaps he had been back to Wickham first to display his prosperity there. Bar wouldn't have withheld her praise or curiosity as Lu had done. Then he'd said, 'She's found her right place. She belongs where she is. She's happy all right, and she wants that brother of yours, don't she? She wants to be married like house-living people.'

She wondered whether he would offer an opinion to Bar about herself. How *did* he see her? There were ways in which she and Duke were two of a kind. He would be wary of any display of emotion that would give another person a hold upon him, he too must think that he was separate, different and, she guessed, he recognized that in herself. What an admission. Wasn't it Tess Durbeyfield who, although she thought herself less worthy of Angel Clare, knew herself to be more impassioned, cleverer and more beautiful than the worthier women? Not that Lu had any such humble thoughts of her own worth. Had she been here with David Hatton, his amiable conversation would have cut into her thoughts, but uncommunicative Duke left her thoughts to ramble on. Quite risky thoughts too.

In the field a bonfire was alight at one end of a roped-off lane, lined several rows deep with people whose faces were lit sporadically by coloured flares and silvery showers of fireworks' sparkles. Standing at the end furthest from the bonfire, he confidently put an arm about her. How natural and friendly that seemed.

From the moment when they had set eyes on one another in Lampeter Street, mutual physical desire had flickered about them like an unseen St Elmo's Fire. Her own eager libido was distracting. He did not make any other movement, yet she had a strong sensation that her whole body was enveloped by him. Taking his free hand she drew it into her coat and held it against her midriff, where there was bare flesh at a gap between skirt and top. He flexed his fingers upwards and found her breast. That contact effected a circuit.

They did not look at one another, but stood in total awareness of each other's presence within the dense, noisy crowd which was illuminated redly by the raging bonfire. The stillest and most silent stimulation.

Suddenly he drew away, ranted off his hacking jacket, thrust it at her and dived into the crowd. When he re-appeared, he was inside the roped-off lane with a group of men who were preparing to be Fire Boys by wrapping themselves in sacking aprons.

The climax of the Fire Boys Fair was a much-tempered twentieth-century version of what in the far distant past was possibly a rite of passage. Lu had, during one of her visits to Roman's Fields, found a book about such rituals in Gabriel Strawbridge's shelves. A man must prove himself fit for coupling – wasn't that how it had been put? Bundles of straw, resin-smeared and bound into rolls, were set alight; young men carried these bare-handed, tossing them into a fire as an offering to a winter god. Lu felt almost breathless with anticipation. It was not difficult to make the connection between the crackling, burning symbols and male potency. Had Duke intended her to make another connection between this ritual and the one she and Bar had performed at Swallitt Pool? Water and Fire. This time it was she who was hidden but looking on. He must be aware of it, she was certain.

He ran, knowing how to control the dangerous burden. He was not intent on out-running other men, many of whom were pie-eyed from day-long drinking. Lu supposed that it was enough for him that he was part of the ancient masculine rite, and that she was there to see it. Having tossed his fiery offering into the heart of the fire, he returned to her, put on his jacket, and guided her out of the field.

By the feel of its bark she knew that this was an oak tree against which her back was pressed. Its solid trunk buttressed her against the pressure of Duke's strong, lean body, making a trio of them. This was no suddenly awakened desire as it had been with David Hatton; this mysterious lust had been burning underground since the day when he had walked out on to the bent willow and dived into Swallitt Pool.

No preliminaries, except the swift, practised rolling of rubber. Body to body standing in the chilly woodland. 'It's what you wanted, and now you've got it.'

'And I wanted this. Red hair, main thick. I watched you spinning round with Bar. Red hair, red hair, red hair everywhere. I was cross-threaded to see that.'

That day, ages ago . . . years ago. She hadn't seen him watching, but she'd known that he was. She'd felt his presence, hadn't wanted to cover herself – that would have been too childish.

'You watched me, too. This is what you saw and you wanted it ever since.'

Not in the way he thought she had; her desire for him had been buried under newer desires, of which many were nothing to do with wanting Duke Barney to be her lover.

'That Christmas, when I had supper at Roman's, you'd a come with me if I'd a said half a word. We was both cross-threaded that time. You thought to see Eli Barney's rag-ass youth, but I had grown to a man, and I didn't look like no man you had ever seen. I know that . . . I know what I look like. Nobody ever forgets meeting Duke Barney, do they, Lu?' He was mocking her with his voice, 'Nor will you forget tonight, I'll see to it you don't,' teasing her with his hands. 'That Christmas, I thought you would have got yourself into a snooty college girl, but you was a woman working for her own keep. I could have had you then; you couldn't take your eyes off me. I licked my lips a purpose to see what you'd do and you damned near come there and then. If I'd have sucked your finger when you touched my mouth you would have, you was that hot for me. Like now.'

'I never knew a man as cock-sure as you, Duke Barney.'

He had pulled away, just his head and shoulders, as he tried to see her by the light of the moon and stars, his hips still pressed against hers, the smell of tar strongly about him. He laughed as he leaned back. 'Buggered if you ever will again, Lu Wilmott.'

She was no more gentle than he, but her body was soft and rounded, so that the thrusting of her hips did not bruise; so she used her teeth and fingers.

For both of them standing against the oak tree, they tempted and teased, holding out against the moment when they must give in to – not a long-awaited love-making – but to fierce, vibrant, earthy lust. 'This is what you wanted since you saw it showing itself off to you over at Swallitt Pool.' He was manly, insecure, and needed to know that women wanted him . . . wanted it.

Often over the last year she had experienced panting, perspiring, erotic dreams. Duke, from an earlier existence in his faun guise. David, with his weight impressing the pleats of the Lascelles gown into her skin. Casual boyfriends who had kissed her. Miss Lake and other people who disappeared at the moment of waking up. Her need to be satisfied by real sex with a real man had been spreading in the way that a forest fire can burn below the surface of the soil, insidiously, until it can no longer be contained.

It seemed inevitable that it would be Duke who would turn up. When he did, it seemed inevitable that he would supply the oxygen that would set her afire.

'I reckon you didn't want to stand up for a man till I came and broke you.'

'Think what you like, Duke Barney, but just stop talking like a horse-dealer trying to talk up your stock to the crowd.'

He laughed, pleased with himself, pleased with her. 'There wasn't never no doubt that we'd got a deal.'

When their moist skin came into contact Lu remembered vividly how white his youthful skin had been. Now as it touched her own it felt hot, and soft. He clutched her hips, lifted her, drew her hard against him whilst she held him tightly about his slim waist, responding instinctively. Easily, expertly perhaps, he moved into her. There was no virginal resistance, no momentary recoil. No hesitation. Mrs Steiner's little device was in the box with her Saturday-night dance shoes, where it was least needed. But at least Duke Barney had come prepared.

What she and Duke were, each to the other, was the missing half of their sexual whole. No matter who or what she might pretend to be at other times, with her body in contact with Duke Barney's, she was a sexual and lustful woman, and he would have found her no more desirable had she been dressed in the Lascelles gown.

Separately, using each other selfishly, they each strove to satisfy their own lust, but all the while aware that if they were going to experience the profound and supreme climax they expected, they must reach it simultaneously.

To extend the last moments they held one another still. Kissing, hardly breathing. Their bodies alive to every last spark of erotic anticipation before they let themselves go. Their senses were raw as they climbed to the peak of this most physical kind of dervishing. When they reached it, the extreme sensation was almost violent in its power. Not an encounter in any way spiritual, just elemental; lusty hunger being fed the sensation it craved; bodies of positive and negative force drawn by a primitive instinct neither of them questioned.

Their parting was as unceremonious as their meeting a few hours earlier. She let herself out of his car outside the corner shop. David Hatton would have been there holding it open, offering a hand to help her step out. Duke did at least casually walk round to her side, hands thrust into his trousers pockets.

'Here, I got this for you.'

It felt like a small pebble wrapped in crumpled tissue paper.

'What is it?'

'Near as I could get to your birthstone. It's not polished or set or anything, just its natural self as it was when it came out of the rock.' His voice had a much gentler edge than earlier. 'Just put it in your pocket. If it falls in the gutter you won't find it again.'

'My birthstone?'

'Should be a moonstone, seeing as you was born to the summer solstice, but this is better.'

Lu, unable to contain her curiosity, carefully unrolled the ball of tissue paper in the light of the car's big head-lamps to reveal a piece of stone in which another stone swelled like a bubble. 'I can see it's not a moonstone. What is it?'

He came round to where she stood and leaned nonchalantly against the radiator grille. 'It's an opal – a black one, pretty rare.'

'I know.'

'It don't signify nothing. It's just that I had the chance to get it, so I did. I always knew I'd be down this way some time, so I kept it about me.'

'But I can't – '

'You can. What would I do with it? It an't any use to anybody else. In any case, it's yours now. If you don't want it, give it away . . . chuck it away if you like. It an't mine now.'

'It must be valuable.'

'It is. Duke Barney don't give away trash. Only remember, I said it don't signify nothing.'

He was lying. It signified that he must have been thinking of her a lot more than she had been thinking of him, knew a lot more, remembered a lot more.

'When I left home my pa give me his earring. He said, "Don't be afraid to sell it, but sell it for something worth having. Don't get sentimental over it: it's only gold and there's plenty more where that came from."'

'And did you sell it?'

''Course I did. When I bought my first stud, I had to put up a year's rent for the stabling. I didn't have enough, so I sold the earring. It fetched a good price too. Pa said I got a good deal on it.'

He went back to the driver's side of his car, and started the engine. For a moment Lu wished that she loved him, or could fall in love with him. For a moment too she wished that she was going wherever he was going and not back home. She hurried along the pavement. The car drew away. The lights in the house were out. Ray and Bar had not waited up. A little way on he stopped the car and began to reverse. He stopped it beside her and, keeping the engine running, leaned over and wound down the window.

'You don't belong here. You should get out.'

He revved up the engine and was gone.

She sat for a short while on the front doorstep. Front doorsteps in Lampeter Street were as near as the people there would ever get to the seats on the balconies of the Southsea villas, a place to watch the world go by. She held the stone up to the gas-lamp outside Number 110. In the overnight case she had bought for the Bournemouth trip, she kept certain possessions that would go with her when she left home. Her journal – pages and pages of which were now filled with her clear, round handwriting – the sparkling diamond hair-slide which never failed to bring a great longing to her mood. She never knew what it was she longed for; perhaps that experience when, in the course of a few weeks, the whole world seemed to open up and spread and grow like a Chinese paper flower in water. Ann Carter's pocket-piece: a strange item, containing a kind of power she did not believe in; yet she often sat holding it, rubbing her fingers over the smooth surface. The photo Ted had given her, the cross and chain that had been her mum's. Not much else really.

Now she had this. This large and valuable piece of precious stone that Duke Barney said he had 'kept about him'. She fingered its unusual surface. What made it precious? Rarity. No rarer than the ash pocket-piece which was unique. Her virginity was even more so. What did Duke Barney think of that? Only two men had aroused her to such heights of desire, the kind of passion where, for its duration, only that matters and nothing else. She could have given her virginity to either of them, it wouldn't have mattered which, really. It just happened to be Duke. Another of those coincidences that had often exercised her mind: the what-ifs. What if she hadn't hung up on Lady Margaret? Would David have thrust upon her a rare opal still embedded in its rock? A dark stone that had the power to flash out red fire? No, it was not David's style, he would be more likely to give polished and set moonstones. How different they were, the two men who captured her imagination. Or were they? What did it matter, she had at last experienced real sex as she had always imagined it would be. It happened with Duke, and it had been a marvel.

* * *

Ray had taken Bar to the pictures, a romantic film full of laughter and tears, the kind of story Bar loved and wept at unashamedly. At a point where a baby had hovered between life and death, with tears streaming down her face, she had said, 'Oh, that poor little mite.' Ray had been quite unable to do anything but put his arm about her and let her cry on his shoulder until the baby recovered.

All the way back from town to Lampeter Street, he had kept his arm round her as she chattered away giving her own idiosyncratic view of the story. 'I wouldn't a let it get that far without doing something about it. Anybody could see that baby was bad. Keep trying to feed it milk like that was bound to make things worse . . . cool boiled water, that's all it needed. People in films are so daft at times.'

Ray had let himself go as far as to press her to him and say, 'I never knew anybody like you in my whole life, Barbara.'

Then, as she had done once before, Bar took the initiative and kissed him. A group of youths lounging outside the billiard hall whistled. Ray said, 'They're probably wondering what a pretty young girl is doing kissing an old bloke.'

She waved at the youths and called out, 'It's because I love him.'

'You might think you do, but – '

She cut him short. 'Ray, I can't help it if you don't love me, nor can you help it if you're set on somebody older.'

'It's not – '

'Let me finish. I know what the matter is. But I think if you just stopped for half a minute and tried to see things like they really are . . . Lu isn't your baby sister no longer, she's a grown woman. Duke knows that, he'll treat her like a proper woman.'

'I know she is, but it's hard to accept, and I have to be

honest, when you said she'd gone off with Duke. In her working clothes, too. It's not like Lu to go off like that. I didn't like it.'

'You don't have to tell me that. Anybody'd have thought he was the goat-king himself had carried her off.' She was not far wrong. He didn't reply. 'The thing is, Ray, even if they was going off to do that sort of thing to each another, it's their business.'

'I'm still responsible for her.'

'You're not! You still wait up for her when she's been to a dance – that's treating her like a child. It's time you let her go her own way.'

When they were back inside Number 110, she took his face between her hands and gave him a nice, comforting kiss. 'I don't know about me being too young for you, there's times when I feel I'm your wise old grandmother.'

He put his arms round her, linked his hands in the small of her back and looked closely at her. 'Are you sure about it? I couldn't bear it if you went off me when my hair starts getting grey and you're still young.'

'There's about the same difference between you and me as between your aunty at Roman's and Mr Wilmott. She haven't gone off of him.'

'I do love you, Barbara. Really love you, and I know I shan't ever love anybody else.'

'Well, then . . . are you ready to go to bed with me?'

He really had no more strength to resist her. He no longer wanted to. It would be a long time before he could face up to what Lu might get up to with a man like Duke Barney but, in admitting to himself that she might get up to something, he was admitting to himself that she was now a woman. 'Not in your bed.'

'Of course not. It's Lu's bed, anyway.'

'I wouldn't want Lu to find us . . .'

'Making love like grown-up people?' She grinned and began unknotting his tie. 'Best hurry up then.'

Ray's bed was narrow, but they found as much delight in it as in a four-poster with a feather mattress strewn with rose petals. It would never have occurred to Ray that they might be better on the floor. So, predictably conventional, behind closed doors, curtains drawn, Ray made love to Bar. Man to woman. Lover to beloved. Gentle kisses. Happily satisfying. A real act of love. Not to be likened to the transaction between the other couple, hungrily taking of one another in the open air, instinctive, lustful, hedonistic, standing with the oak tree, joined at the hips.

As usual that winter, a general invitation was sent to the 'Queenform' girls to attend one of the buffet-suppers given to entertain the crew of a visiting ship. It came just at the right time to cheer them up a bit during the dark days. It was a star event for the Ezzard's girls.

Kate Roles was full of it, all the girls were. Except Lu.

'It's only one step up from taking girls out on the bumboats to entertain sailors like they do in the South Seas.'

'Oh, shut up being such a Jonah. You've always wanted to come, I don't know why you're being like this.'

Now that she knew what she knew about David's background, nothing would induce Lu to put herself in the way of an accidental meeting with Captain Gore.

'Lu! You haven't heard a word I said, have you? You've been in a right queer mood lately. You need taking out of yourself, you should come.'

'No, I said I'll go somewhere with Lena.'

'I don't know why she don't come too. Always shut up on her own.'

'Not everybody wants to be always gadding about like you and me.'

'Yes, but it isn't natural, the way she won't go nowhere.'

Lu knew that Kate was right, but Kate didn't know how afraid Lena was of her brother. Lu wished he would hurry up and sign on again. He had been home for weeks now.

Lena found some comfort in repeating that his money couldn't last for ever, and then he'd have to sign on. But until he did, Lu and Bar did what they could to stop Lena becoming a total hermit when she wasn't at work. Lena had said that she would go to a show with them, but she probably wouldn't when it came to it.

Although he would have denied it as too daft for words, Ray was a bit resentful of Lu and Bar's attention to Lena. 'I can't understand why you want to sit in a garret when you've got a nice comfortable place here.' Bar had said, 'She's just a poor thing, Ray, how would you like it being shut up on your own?' and Ray had said, 'You're too soft-hearted.' Bar had answered back sharply, 'What would you do then, let her get on with it?'

All around Lu, on the afternoon of the day of the dance at the base, were girls with their hair in pins and covered with scarves tied into turbans. Early in the evening, a coach from the naval base would arrive at the works gate to collect them, dressed, lipsticked and earringed, and looking vastly different from their daytime selves. What they loved most of all was the elaborate buffet, the politeness with which they were greeted by the sailors under the watchful eye of their officers, and the general air of being special for the one night.

'I shan't be able to eat a thing,' Kate wailed. 'I never can. I starve myself all day, and get that worked up that when I see all that lovely food, I can't swallow it for excitement. And it's a Yankee ship, too; they always have the best food.'

'Rubbish,' Lu said. 'One dance with a jivey American sailor and you'll love it.'

'I know, it's just the anticipation. Perhaps nobody will dance with me.'

'Oh Kate! In your red dress and your hair all in ringlets, they won't be able to resist you.' On these occasions, Kate took infinite pains over her thick, blonde hair, keeping it rolled around sausages of cotton wool all day and then teasing it out into a thousand curls.

'Would it look bad if I didn't wear my engagement ring?'

Knowing what was expected of her friendship, Lu said, 'Of course it wouldn't. If I were you, I'd leave it at home. Then you'll be sure you won't lose it.'

'You're right, it is a bit loose. Only I wouldn't want anybody to get the wrong idea.'

They were talking quietly without looking up from their machines. Kate had taken out her cotton wool and had wrapped an artificial silk scarf loosely about her head. 'Damn! The belt's come off.' As the belts deteriorated, they slackened: it was a common enough occurrence that Lu didn't even look up. All machinists were adept at slipping the belt back on to the drive-wheel without the need to call the mechanic.

Suddenly, Kate let out a shriek of pain and horror. Lu was off her stool in a flash. Other girls fell over one another to get to Kate's station as they realized that her scarf and hair were being twisted around the belt. Kate was screaming and holding on to her hair like grim death. Lu jumped over her own table to get to the belt and help Kate hold on to her hair.

George rushed out. 'Turn it off . . . turn off the power,' Lu yelled.

But there was no power-switch on the factory floor. The belts were power-driven from the basement, and it was only there that the power could be cut.

Nellie thrust scissors into Lu's hand. Without knowing how she managed it without the scissors being flicked out of her hands by the belt, Lu sliced through the mass of Kate's yellow-blonde hair which was fast becoming saturated with blood. The belt slapped on and on, free now to take a great bundle of Kate's hair with it. The security man had run downstairs to get the power turned off there, but it was a bit late now.

Kate fainted, blood running down her face and dripping on to her apron. Lu caught her as she fell and they lowered her to the floor. Lu became almost as bloodied as Kate herself.

Nellie shouted for someone to fetch a bowl of water. There was a general unhelpful move by some of the girls. Others stood around helplessly. There was nothing to fetch it in. 'Isn't there a bowl in this whole shop, George?' George watched the growing pool of blood as Lu made an effort to bind the wound with her apron. Nellie shouted at George, 'Move, you useless article! Get that fruit-bowl thing from your office. Bring your brandy bottle, and tie up that dog!' Nobody had ever heard Nellie speak so harshly, or seen George move so fast.

George sloshed brandy into a teacup and held it to Kate's white lips. 'Come on, sweetheart, come on,' he said, shocked into gentleness. 'Take a sip of this. Go on, just a sip, Katy love, that's my girl. Good girl, good girl.' When she pushed the cup away, George drank it himself. He looked as though he needed it.

'We'll have to get her to the hospital,' Lu said.

'No, I'll be all right.' She trembled violently, then grew cold and clammy, beads of sweat formed on her brow and upper lip. She became deathly pale. 'I couldn't help it, the hair-slide broke and it all fell down.' She began to cry, then, when she caught sight of Lu, who seemed to have blood everywhere, she collapsed again into a dead faint.

Lu said, 'Get her to your office, George. Phone for an ambulance.'

'I can't, there's no outside line down here.'

Lu flew out of the factory. Taking no notice of the protests of Mr Ezzard's secretary, she ran through the outer office and, without hesitation, opened Mr Ezzard's door. 'There's been a terrible accident. Kate Roles's hair caught in the driving belt and her scalp's torn away from her head. She's lost a lot of blood. You've got to get her to hospital.'

His secretary appeared at Lu's side, waiting for instructions to throw her out, but Lu was a daunting and bloody sight.

He too seemed intimidated and, waving his secretary away, reached for a telephone and ordered his driver to take the car over to the ground-floor machine shop. 'Go with her.'

Lu turned on her heel. 'Thank you.'

It was only when she was pushing her way past the clerks and typists gaping at the astonishing scene that she realized how bloodstained she was.

The surgeon ordered Kate to be kept in hospital, and when Lu went to visit her that evening, Kate's father and mother were already there. The ward sister said testily, 'You can't go in there – only two visitors at a time!'

Lu bore into her the same self-confident gaze that had made Mr Ezzard move. 'I'm probably more concerned about my friend than you are, so you can be sure I won't do anything to make her worse. I'll be five minutes, that's all.'

Before the sister could cite matron and hospital rules as higher authorities, Lu had walked on into the ward. Mrs Roles started back when Lu appeared round the curtain. 'Only two visitors,' she whispered. 'I'll go.' Lu pressed her back down into the only visitor's chair. 'I shall only be a minute. I just wanted to see what they said.'

Tears welled in Kate's eyes. Mrs Roles said, 'Katie love, they never said it was definite.' To Lu she said, 'One of them said that her hair might not grow again . . . it wasn't very tactful.'

'I might as well be bald all over as just in a patch. And it hurts, Lu, you've got no idea how much your scalp can hurt.'

Mrs Roles said, 'Don't get worked up, Katie, it never does no good to work yourself up when you're bad. It could a been worse.'

Mr Roles said angrily, but keeping his voice low, 'Aye! If the scarf had a got round her neck she could a been throttled. They should a let that bloody sweatshop burn when it was going. If you had a union, the lawyers'd fight for compensation for an accident like this. I'd like to see him in court, but folk like us haven't got that sort o' brass.' Mr Roles, like Ray, was a railwayman, and so could safely talk glibly about unions. He also came from the north, where people did not seem so prone to tugging their forelocks.

Surprising herself, Lu said, 'I'm going to start one.'

Yes! It was as though the last digit in a coded sequence had been entered, tumblers fell into place, and the door to her subconscious swung open to reveal an idea almost ready-formed.

'You'll not work as a staymaker any more if you do.'

'I know.'

'You'll be needing help.'

'I know that too.'

'You can count on me.'

After she left the hospital, Lu went round to Lena's to see if she was all right. In the confusion she had forgotten her. Although her brother had not yet bothered her, she still waited for Lu to walk her back to her room after work. It was disappointing that she had returned to her old uncommunicative self just as she seemed to have begun to come out of her shell. Occasionally Bar would bring home a magazine left discarded by a Palccino's customer, or the last of a box of biscuits which Mama had told her to take, and drop in with them to Lena's room, staying there for a couple of hours. When Lu asked what they talked about when she wasn't there, Bar said, 'I don't know. Nothing much. She likes me to tell her hand. It isn't a good hand, so I read the good bits, which is that she's good with her fingers and she's got a strong lifeline. Actually, you don't have to talk to Lena if you don't want to, so it's quite a nice change after being nice to customers all day long.'

What were they going to do about Lena, though? When Kenny had gone away to live his dream, he hadn't had any Eileen Griggs or Bar Barneys or Kate Roleses to think about.

The spur-of-the-moment decision to try to start up a union caught fire. She felt certain she could do it. So, on the following evening, she went to call on Nellie, whose co-operation would be vital. Nellie, without her cap and large white apron, was quite transformed. Her hair was white and fluffy, and she was wearing a soft dress with a bar-brooch on the bosom, and a locket on a chain round her plump throat.

'I called round at the hospital. Oh, poor Katie, she's always been that proud of her hair. They used to call her Buttercup when she was little, but then you'd know going to the same school. Fred, this is Lu, one of my girls.'

'Sit yourself down. You just caught us right, we've been to a meeting.'

'That's just what I've come about.'

Nellie smiled, 'Not a Baptist meeting, though.'

'No, a meeting to start a union.'

'Do you know what you'd be taking on? I don't know that it's a job for an eighteen-year-old.'

'I can do it.'

Nellie nodded thoughtfully. 'I believe you can, Lu.'

Fred Tuffnel said, 'Why not? It don't take anything except a bit of guts and an ex-marine on the door to keep out any riff-raff.'

'All right,' Nellie said, 'we'll help. It's time we got on an' did something instead of hoping and praying.'

* * *

Seeing Nellie and her husband like that gave Lu heart.

A meeting was arranged in the greatest secrecy, and in secrecy too they were visited by a Mr Gus Greenfield, who already had experience of establishing a branch of the Garment Workers' Union in the West Country. It was all a bit fraught having to organize it under the very noses of the Ezzards, and they were forced to distribute leaflets only on the day of the meeting. But Gus Greenfield seemed confident that, if it had worked in his part of the country, it would work anywhere.

It was March now, and although the evenings were getting lighter, it would be cold in the hall. Lu became ever more anxious and edgy. She knew their opponents well enough to understand that this was the only real chance they had of a shot; if it misfired there wouldn't be a second. But if it worked . . . If it worked then tonight they would form a branch and sign up members, but from then on they would be forced to function under cover, because it was a dead certainty that anyone found having a paid-up card would be O-U-T, fast. They had no idea how many would turn up; all they could do was hope. It was an upstairs hall, so that with Fred Tuffnel and Mr Roles, who knew just about everyone in the area, they felt fairly certain that they could keep an eye out for anybody who might be there to make trouble. They knew that it was bound to get back to the Ezzards after tonight, but hoped that enough people would turn up to feel that there was safety in numbers.

When Lu was still bothered about whether it was fair asking people to risk their jobs, Fred Tuffnel said, 'It's always been a fight between Them and Us. We have to fight.'

Nellie said, 'When I was a girl, women didn't have a vote – it all had to be fought for. In the end all the factories are going to have to let in the unions.'

Before Lu left for work that morning, Bar said that she

would see if Lena was all right and then come on to the meeting. 'You look as white as a sheet,' she said to Lu. 'You eat something before you go or you won't be any good to anybody this evening.'

'I already feel sick with fright, and that's the truth. I told Ray not to come, I should feel worse knowing he was there.'

'You'll be all right. You're good with words.'

'I shan't remember any of them if there's a room full of people.'

'Just fix your eyes on me and you'll be all right. I shall be proud of you.'

'What would I do without you, Bar?'

'You'd stop eating altogether and drop down through a crack in the floor.' There were times when she reminded Lu of little Bar as she had first seen her, carrying the tray of milk and Sunny Jim's.

'I don't think I ever met anybody so contented with what they've got.'

'That's because I've got everything. I used to wish I could be like you and live in Portsmouth, and then my dream came true and I do.'

How could anyone have a dream to live out in this place? For Lu to live her dream there would need to be ancient olive groves and sunshine, or mountains with winding tracks leading to ancient walled cities, or a place like Paris or New York where the people were elegant and interesting. Her dream could be lived in any number of places – but not here. Not here in Pompey.

She'd have to leave to do that. This morning they had received a letter from Kenny. Although he didn't write a lot about the threat to the new republic, it was worrying what was happening in Spain: the uprisings, the threat from the Fascist powers on its borders. Lu went almost daily into the public reading room of the library to see what she could find in the newspapers about the area in which Kenny was working. Worrying and inspirational. In Spain, long before the people took over, there must have been any number of small groups doing the sort of thing the Ezzard's workers were doing. In one of Kenny's letters he had said the most powerful nation in the world was the nation of workers. Lu had liked that. It was the kind of inspiring statement she had heard that time at Bournemouth, the kind of thing that cheered people up.

She knew, though, without it having to be spelt out, that she was about to reach some kind of peak, some crossroads; that the various threads of her life over the last seven or eight years were coming together and making some kind of significant pattern. But, for the time being she was too involved in what was going on day to day, minute to minute, to think about it.

One thing was for sure, though: she would be called to Mr Ezzard's office and made to account for herself before she was sacked. Maybe she wouldn't even be given that satisfaction, and would find herself being given her marching orders by George, or even shut out by the gateman.

Mr Tuffnel was already guarding the outer door and Mr Roles waiting with a collecting bag upstairs when Lu arrived. Mr Roles patted Lu's back. 'Good lass. We brought our Katie home today. She reckons she's coming to the meeting, but it depends who gets top-side in the argument wi' the missis.' He smiled, proud of his two strong-minded women. 'I'd back ower Kate. If she comes, she'll have summat to say.'

By seven-fifteen, only about thirty of the seats were taken. Spread around the hall, this audience looked very sparse. Gus Greenfield arrived, his West Country voice assuring them that people would come. 'Last minute. The fellers'll be having a pint, and the maids putting on their faces. You won't get none of the women who've had little childer.'

He handed her a cigarette straight from the packet, lit it with the match cupped as he would for a mate.

Soon the room was two-thirds full, then more and more people began streaming in. 'You see, my gel, I told you it a be standing room only. When the time's right for summat like this, it will go.'

And then they were on the platform. Gus Greenfield and Lu. She felt pale and sick, her throat was dry and her hands cold and clammy, and she knew if she should unclasp them they would tremble uncontrollably. Her stomach was rumbling horribly; she hoped the sound wouldn't carry beyond the table.

Gus Greenfield said something formal. Lu tried to attend but she was thinking of what she had in her notes, at the same time scanning the audience for Nellie or Bar or anybody she knew; but without aprons and scarves tied round their hair, all the women seemed to be strangers. By the time she returned her attention to Mr Greenfield, he was getting towards the end of his remarks about the need for unity, about recognizing that labour and capital had equal value, and about the benefits of a unionized workforce to workers and management alike.

'But this is not my show tonight. This is an inaugural meeting, the start of a new branch of the Garment Makers' and Tailors' Union . . .'

As Lu looked, more and more unknown faces became people she recognized. Workers from other factories, but who lived in the Lampeter area had come. They'd be saying, She's only one of the Wilmotts. You know, her dad was that sailor who drowned, brother of him that drives the beer-lorry. Who the 'ell do she think she is? She wished she could run away, but she was trapped by her own cockiness now.

Then, at the side of the hall, she saw Bar's familiar topknot of black hair tied with a red ribbon, and standing close beside her was Ray. She should have known he wouldn't be able to stay away, was glad that he hadn't. She spotted Nellie, standing as she did in the factory, arms folded across her large bosom. Then Miss Lake! Miss Lake winked . . . surely she had winked?

'. . . and she is a local young woman, who knows the staymaking industry, having worked in it as a skilled machinist for several years. Miss Louise Wilmott.' He turned to Lu and suddenly she was on her feet.

The voice she heard coming from her own mouth was amazingly clear, unbelievably confident as she said how glad she was that so many people had been willing to come and sit in a cold room on a Friday evening. 'But we shouldn't look upon it as giving up the picture-house or the pub, because we're doing something for ourselves. We're not here by permission of our bosses, we are here because we want to be, we need to be. We are here because many of us believe that it is high time the health-hazards, the long hours, the unpaid work, the shut-outs, the stand-offs and poor pay need to be talked about openly. There's nothing shameful in expecting good, safe working conditions and honest payment.'

A burst of applause surprised her, and when she looked up from her notes, Kate Roles was taking a seat on the end of a row, bits of her buttercup hair ringleting from a silk scarf fastened by a diamanté brooch covering her bandages.

Abandoning her prepared speech she said, 'I was going to say all these things about wages and conditions, but I won't, I'll just tell you this story about a girl I went to school with, who works the machine next to mine. Let that say it for me.

'In my time as a machinist I've seen the usual accidents, I've had a burnt arm and twice been run through by the needle. In the staymaking factories we say a needle through your finger shows you've served your apprentice-ship, don't we? But recently I saw an accident, one I shall never forget, and it's that which has made me determined to get this union started.

'If there'd been a safety-guard on the machine, this accident couldn't have happened. If there had been an emergency switch, it wouldn't have been so bad. But it *did* happen and it was bad and it happened because the bosses don't bother about us. We're not people, we are "hands", just so many hands pushing hundreds of miles of elastic and cortiel through the machines.

'The girl who had the accident is the same age as me. She is very pretty. She likes dancing, going to the pictures, and pretty clothes. She's engaged to be married. She was just like all the rest of us. But not any longer, she isn't.'

She looked at Kate and held her eyes, momentarily reliving that terrifying moment, the horror of it flowing into her voice and expression as she told the audience about the accident.

As they listened to the horrific tale, women and men shuddered, and men turned down the corners of their mouths squeamishly.

'I'm proud of her, so should you be, because although she still wants her old job back, she's here to support the start of our union branch.' Lu indicated Kate, who stood up. Dressed to kill as she always was, thinner than when she went into hospital, but looking pretty and defiant, Kate walked forward, unfastening her scarf as she went dramatically to uncover her swathed bandages. Gus Greenfield gallantly helped her on to the raised platform, where she stood between him and Lu, facing the audience.

'I haven't got much to say, but I'm going to say what I've been thinking about laying there in hospital. This sort of thing happens because we are women, and because there's a lot of unemployment. We get treated like dirt, and nobody cares if we lives or dies, just so long as there's two women for every job. If I was a railway labourer got injured, I would have had a union solicitor to fight a case

392

for me. Like Lu says, we women and girls are skilled workers, we deserve better treatment, but we won't get it till we respect ourselves and make our bosses respect us. So join the union!'

Fifty members signed up that night. Fifty in an industry of twelve thousand. An industry that outdid the naval dockyards in contributing to the economy of the town. But fifty was good. Fifty was a start.

Wealthy industrialist and factory hand. The encounter between them was as inevitable as between Lu and Duke. There had been no ignominious shut-out by the gateman, no instant dismissal by George; Lu was, as she knew was fitting, to be dismissed by the managing director. A small triumph, an acknowledgement that what she – they – had done was significant.

The machines had stopped and all eyes were on her. Her mates knew she was for the high jump, and that this was no ordinary sacking. Nobody was fanciful enough to say that she was a contender in an unfair fight who had been forced to surrender, but as she shut down her machine and made her way slowly between the rows, touching girls on their shoulders as she passed by, that was not far from the general idea. As she walked through the factory knowing that this must be the last time, she was more filled with emotion than she would have believed, and she found it hard to hold back some tears. As she went through the big bay doors she did not look back. Her life as a factory girl was over. Every name, every voice, every position of every girl would be in her mind for ever. Set in aspic, domed in glass, they all would be a set-piece shelved in her memory, much as the loom-weight in the Alton museum. An appropriate label would be affixed: *Machine room – Ezzard's 'Queenform' Factory, Lampeter, Portsmouth, circa 1936.*

In his office, Jacob Ezzard made no pretence at being

occupied. He knew that she must be on her way to see him now; all he could do was sit and wait and try to ignore the effect this business was having on his self-possession. He had never been able to understand how it came about that of all the hundreds of 'Queenform' factory girls, this one had made such an impression upon him.

Even now he could remember perfectly clearly how she had stood there on the day when she came to be set on. He hadn't looked up at her, but had come to be aware that a contest was going on between them. She had stood it out, though, and when he had at last paid her some heed, he had thought that she meant to give him a reason for turning her down, yet there had been nothing . . . nothing at all to take exception to – the opposite, in fact.

Until now, she had never behaved less than well. Her best piecework figures had never been topped before or since. She came from the Wilmotts, one of the true stay-making families who had been in the business as long as the Ezzards. Had she been a man, then he would have had no hesitation in promoting her to foreman and most likely to a sector manager.

One thing he did have to thank God for: that he had not given in to the temptation on that visit to Lascelles in Paris. Perhaps it was best that she herself had given him this unquestionable reason for banishing her. There was not an employer in the whole city who would not do the same with such a trouble-maker. Even so, the reported success of her action had sent a cold chill through him. He was realist and intelligent enough to know that this could be the beginning of the end. Ideas had their time, and the idea that there should be some sort of accord between worker and employer was taking hold. Such ideas had struck at the foundations of the old order in Spain, then in France, and it was happening in a different way in Germany.

The details of the meeting had been given him by, of all people, his own wife. Cynthia Lake had attended the meeting, that was obvious. Alma had thought that she would have loved to have been there to listen to the thrilling speech Cynthia's girl had made, and to see that other pretty girl mount the stage so dramatically. 'Like some heroine, Jacob, all swathed in bandages.' He sometimes wondered whether Alma's apparent prattle was as ingenuous as she made out: she'd sprinkled that information cleverly into a whole serving of inconsequential gossip.

He had no choice but to get rid of her, and get her blacklisted in the city. Nellie Tuffnel and the Roles girl must go too, because they had presented themselves as obvious organizers. More than that was not necessary. He knew his workers, and this morning when he looked down upon them as they arrived, he had sensed their tension. He wanted no more trouble to upset production figures, especially now that they were getting enormous orders for the 'Princess' model. The dismissal of the three ring-leaders could stand for all the others he knew about. The Roles girl's father had apparently threatened taking legal action, but he hadn't a leg to stand on, or the money to go to law. The girl should have had her hair securely pinned.

Jacob had read an article that purported to prove in terms of production figures that a happy workforce produced higher profits. Well, he wouldn't go that far. In his own experience workers jumped when you said jump, because if they did not, then they knew that there was always somebody prepared to jump in their stead. Still, he could institute a few improvements that would show he was prepared to move with the times, but not prepared to set a trend that would upset his fellow factory owners. The whole of history proved that no one kept the upper hand by showing weakness. But, he saw sense in providing a few chairs in the women's lavatories, and an experienced rodent exterminator would do a lot better than George's dog. Simple medical kits on the premises made sense. He had already decided that George must investigate some form of safety guard around the belt drives. If the scarf had been around that Roles girl's neck, she could have been strangled by it.

They faced one another across his desk.

'You are a very foolish and hot-headed young woman,' Jacob Ezzard began. 'You might have done very well for yourself at "Queenform", instead of which you set yourself up as a spokesman for the rabble. You're a trouble-maker, and now there's not an employer in the area who would let you through his factory gates. There is a black-list, and you will find yourself at the top of it.'

She was not wearing her working clothes, but a street coat with side pockets into which she thrust her hands nonchalantly – he couldn't help finding the gesture seductive. 'I know that,' she said. 'And of course, by the same token, there is a blacklist of bad employers, and you'll be at the top of that. Do you really think you can stop us? You can't.'

'I'm sacking you.'

'You can sack me, sack Nellie, and Kate Roles, but we're like the Hydra: try to kill us off and twice as many others will come in and take our place. But you won't know who they are. How will you know who holds a union card and who doesn't? They'll all be there, gathering in numbers. Then one day you will discover that "Queen-form's" got a hundred per cent union membership. Then the machines will go off and everybody will walk out and you will have to meet your employees and talk to them like human beings.'

She turned her back on him and walked out. He noticed that she wore high-heeled shoes and silk stockings. That was like cocking a snook.

When Lu and Kate and Nellie came to collect their wages the following Friday, there was what seemed to be a spontaneous large gathering of girls and women waiting outside the factory gates. Among them, Eileen Grigg took her place beside her best friend, knowing that she was no longer going to be able to rely on Lu now that she had been given the sack. They said how sparkling Lu seemed to be, more like she was off on another trip like the one she'd had to Lascelles. Lu was delighted at the unexpected show of solidarity. Kate shook her wage-packet. 'Come on, I don't know how much there's here, but let's blow it down the Pier Café.'

Lu said, 'Yes, I'll put mine to it. You coming, Nellie?'

Nellie, who knew that the gathering was not entirely spontaneous, said, 'No, these dos are for girls, but I'll put in my packet.' The Pier Café was a favourite rendezvous for factory girls; they could sit for ages over pots of tea and plates of buns and doughnuts, gathering tables together to accommodate whatever number of girls assembled. So, in dozens, they crammed on to the passing trams and tumbled off laughing at the pier.

After half an hour, the initial hubbub quietened, and Kate Roles stood on a chair and told everyone to shut up. 'I got something important to say, and now I've got the taste of spouting at meetings, it's going to be hard to give it up. And I don't intend to. I might be on the dole, but that won't stop me going to all sorts of meetings and standing up and asking awkward questions. But that's not why I'm perched up here where half of you can see my stocking tops. I'm up here because of you, Lu Wilmott.'

Lu, feeling intoxicated from the essential gaiety that groups of women exude when they are enjoying themselves and there are no men around, said, 'Well, don't blame me if you drop off your perch.'

'Oh, dear, I said I wouldn't cry. Here, Lu. We put together and got you this. It's the dearest one we could find. There isn't one of us here could make much use of one ourselves, but we know you will.' Unceremoniously she thrust the highly decorated package at a surprised Lu.

Although they all knew what the package contained, they still crushed around to see Lu's reaction when she opened the leaving present. In a world where electric irons, sets of picture table-mats and embroidered tablecloths were luxuries, this was the first of its kind. Lu let out a 'Waah!', Portsmouth's own particular expression of shock and surprise. 'A proper fountain pen!'

Lena said, 'With a real gold nib.'

'And my initial on it. I don't know what to say.'

'Go on,' Kate said, 'say it just the same. Come on, get up and show us your stocking tops too.'

Lu went one better than Kate and climbed on to a table. 'This . . . is the nicest thing anybody could ever ask for. Not just the pen, but that's just wonderful too, but all of you coming here like this. I said to Nellie that we had got to find a way of getting together and making sure what happened a week ago don't get lost, and this is the perfect chance for me to start getting on to you.

'Keeping the union going isn't going to be easy. You can be sure every time somebody puts their head above the parapet, the bosses are going to try to shoot it off. This time it was Nellie, Kate and me got our heads shot off, but we knew it was sure to happen when we organized the meeting, and none of us regrets it. But what you have got to make sure is that nobody else loses their job because they joined the union.

'The bosses have got their secret ways: you might not have heard of what goes on, but there's a club called the Freemasons that practically runs the city, there's business-men's clubs, there's associations, they meet at golf clubs, sailing clubs, they have dinners, visit each other in their homes . . . They settle things amongst themselves, to suit themselves, and none of them thinks that's wrong.

'The only weapon girls and women like us have against all these societies the bosses have set up to look after their interests is ourselves. They need us, they can't do without us. Even if they tell you: There's plenty more where you came from, don't go into a panic and start kissing their feet. Sticking together is what counts, and sticking together is what being in a union means. In our factory, we've done the worst bit, we've had a meeting and got it going.' The young women looked at one another and nodded: they knew that they had done something important last Friday.

'When Mr Ezzard called me into his office to tell me what he thought of me, I told him that there would come a day when every woman and girl in "Queenform" would hold a union card. Then one day, when there's a shutdown, or somebody asks for a washbasin to be installed and you refuse, you're going to see every woman in the factory get up from their machines and walk out through those gates.

'He knew I was right. You could almost hear the cash register in his brain working out how much profit would go down the drain. They've done it in other places, in other trades – the mines, steelworkers, ship builders. Not because there was more jobs than men, they got their unions working because they saw the sense in sticking together and standing up to the bosses. Now, a lot of the men's trades have got proper arrangements with union leaders to speak up for them – '

A young girl called out, 'But you're our leader aren't you? If you go, who's going to keep us together? Who's going to take our subs and go to meetings and that?'

The room was now totally quiet. Others were nodding in agreement with the girl, as Lu looked around at a sea of wide eyes. 'Listen,' Lu said firmly. 'I'm not your leader, I never was. I was just the one who got mad enough to start the ball rolling. You don't need me. You've got each other, you've got all this strength and spirit. It's what keeps us slogging away day after day in a place that's hardly fit to be called a dungeon, and still able to keep tabs on where George's hands are, and still able to see the funny side of things.

'And the other thing none of us must ever forget – and it's easy to forget it because nobody ever gives us credit for what we do, and we never get a certificate saying we passed anything – but we are *skilled* workers. It takes ages to learn how to do what we do at such speed. That's part of the skill, the speed; we work so fast that you can hardly see the needle.' She held up her damaged finger and thumb. 'Too damned fast sometimes.' They laughed, they reviewed their own scars, the tension dropped, Lu Wilmott was one of them.

'We aren't female "hands", we aren't "factory girls", we are women workers employed in the staymaking industry for our skill and knowledge. And now we are Members of the respected Garment Makers' and Tailors' Union. We count for something.'

Somebody asked, 'What you going to do, Lu?'

'I don't know. I'm blacklisted in the Portsmouth factories – not that that means much. Kate and I have had offers to go into the Co-op bespoke tailoring department. Kate might go, but I don't know yet. And as far as Ezzard's is concerned, it doesn't matter, I'm finished there. All you need for now is to decide who is going to take on collecting the weekly subscriptions and keeping tabs on things. You'll get help from people like Gus and my brother if you need it. But why should you: you're as good as any of the men.'

'Please, Lu.' Lena held up her hand as though in school. 'I'll do it if you like.'

Lena. Lena Grigg, of all people, coming forward, offering herself in front of a room full of girls. Lena would be perfect. Conscientious and unlikely to allow defaulters to backslide.

'I was always good at figures, wasn't I, Lu?'

'You were, Lena . . . She was. She was always near the top of the class.' Lu grinned at Lena. 'The times I could have thumped you for coming out top over me. I tell you what, I propose we make Eileen Grigg our . . . what? I don't know. It's going to be a Jack-of-all-trades job.'

'*Jill*-of-all-trades,' Kate said.

'What shall I propose Lena as?'

'I'll be the "Queenform Union Representative".'

'Good!' Lu said. 'Then I propose Lena as Representative of the "Queenform" branch of the Garment Workers' Union.'

Back home, Lu related what had taken place in the Pier Café. 'Lena got up on a chair and made a little speech . . . can you imagine? She was wonderful. She said, "Anybody who don't know me, I'm Lena Grigg, I'm Lu's friend, and like she said, I'm a skilled machinist and I'm proud of that. I never owed nobody a penny piece, and I'm proud of that. If you don't know me now, you soon will. I shan't never try to collect money from you at Ezzard's – I might look green, but I'm not a cabbage." She was good, she made them laugh.'

Ray said, 'It's amazing what people can do.'

Bar said, 'Not when it's women, Ray, you shouldn't never be amazed at anything women do. We can do anything when we puts our minds to it.' She touched Ray on the back of the hand with one finger. Lu was astonished at how intimate the gesture was, and suddenly saw what she had been blind to: that Ray and Bar were openly in love. Bar continued, 'Some of us can even get stiff-necked old railwaymen to propose to us.'

'You and Ray?'

Ray flushed, actually flushed like a youth when he said, 'That's right, Lu, we're going to get married.'

'We're going to have a baby.'

Bar and Ray were married quietly at the Register Office. May and Ann Carter had come down by train, and Chick Manners and Lu stood as witnesses. When the small celebration in Palccino's was over, Lu collected her bag from Number 110, boarded the train with Ann and May, and went to Roman's Fields where, as May put it, she would have time to sort herself out. It was one of the busiest times of year, so her labour was welcome there.

They were strange days, for although Lu was as fit as a fiddle and as strong as a horse, she sometimes had the feeling that she was once again recuperating after an illness. She reasoned that she must be gathering strength for whatever came next. Something was coming: she knew it, sensed it.

Sometimes in the late evening she would walk alone through the wood down to The Swallitt Pool, where she would sit on the bent willow and swish her toes in the still water. Inevitably she thought of Duke. She would hear a horse pass by in the lane and wonder what would happen if Duke were to show up there. Not that it was likely, for Duke now preferred to ride his thoroughbred motor car. Paid for, as Lu had learned from Ann Carter, by people who paid him very silly amounts of money to have their mares serviced by one of Duke's two thoroughbred stud horses.

She felt a strange detachment about him. It was as if he was somebody interesting she had read about, a character in fiction or mythology. She had no particular wish to see him again. She had erotic dreams in which Duke and David became one lover, being at the same time both dark and fair, slim and broad, courteous and negligent. The one thing they had in common was a long, fast racing car which only she was allowed to drive.

During those weeks at Roman's Fields, Lu was in limbo, gathering her wits and strength about her as well as building up her Post Office account. The outside world came in the form of Ken's letters, which Ray sent on. These were to a great extent about the political situation in Spain and France.

Imagine, the Left has come to power here and there's a Socialist coalition in France. I almost persuaded myself to go see how it is working there, except that I've begun to feel a great loyalty to this country and the people. For the first time in history the Spanish people have not got the Church and the monarchy on their back. But nobody is hiding their heads under the sand; the Fascists are at the gates and they have Hitler and Mussolini itching to try out their new armies and air forces in somebody else's war.

But if only the working class back home could sniff the air of the true kind of democracy. Here is where Spaniards are citizens, *not subjects*, as we British are. In France, the new prime minister has ended the strikes – pay rises of twelve per cent! A forty-hour week! Two weeks' paid holiday a year and free collective bargaining. Socialism and unions, Lu. I expect the Ezzards and their like are sweating bricks.

Ray and Bar's baby was due in August. Not only was Ray behaving as though nothing like it had ever happened in the world before, but Mama Palccino and Lena were knitting and sewing enough small garments to set up a shop.

Lu, who loved driving Ted's truck, took over the daily delivery of strawberries to the Portsmouth and Southampton depots. She started calling in at The Bells, where she was always greeted with great enthusiasm by Peg and Dick Briardale. They now had four children, of which they were both very proud, and another was on the way. Peg, who was now as plump as Dick, always joked that, 'He's trying to grow his own cricket team.' Lu would sit with Peg and the children in the garden which, although it was quite as charming as it had been when she first saw it, seemed to have shrunk. But then so had the village, and the strawberry fields and the journey between Wickham and Portsmouth.

Two things had not changed, perhaps never could be changed. One was the panoramic view of Spithead and the Solent from the top of the Portsdown Hills. The other, Swallitt Woods and Pool, where serene nature and pagan mystery were still undisturbed.

When her deliveries coincided with the 'Queenform' dinner-break, Lu would drive round to the factory, taking a basket of fruit for her old workmates. There she would park, blocking the gates, and make several blasts on the horn, always hoping that one day Jacob Ezzard would want to drive through and would have to ask her to move. He never did, of course, it was a petty game, but she enjoyed it. He would know that she was there. Her skin was tanned and her hair lightened by the sun to a pale gold on top. She knew that she looked well and she took trouble to appear carefree and happy, even though, as the weeks went by, she became increasingly tense at not having resolved her future.

She still believed that her dream to go somewhere and be somebody was attainable, but could not see what move to make next. Life at Roman's was mesmeric. She half-heartedly did a bit of French language with May, having some vague notion that she might ask M. Lascelles if he would take her. It wasn't likely, given the Ezzard connection, but the idea fired her imagination. She imagined herself as a chic and stunning sales assistant, but she knew only too well that she would not last five minutes being ordered about by the kind of Parisian who patronized Lascelles'. French versions of a Lady Margaret Gore-Hatton.

She still thought of David Hatton quite often, and one day, when she and May were eating their midday sandwiches, she mentioned how much she'd liked him.

'You should have persevered, Lu, told him the truth. You don't want to take much notice of class . . . posh voices and cockroaches in the kitchen. You don't need to apologize to anybody for being who you are.'

'I know that. But how do you think the Gore-Hattons would treat me if they suddenly found out it was a factory girl David took to the dance in the officers' mess? I'd die of shame. I made out I was one of them. I can "put it on" all right . . . I know a fish fork when I see one, I don't look "common", but I wouldn't want to be questioned about the Wilmotts by that cousin of his, Captain Gore, or Lady Margaret – she sounded like the old queen looks.'

There is a low time at the end of the strawberry season, during which Lu spends whole afternoons alone in Swallitt Wood. Bar's old cairn is still there, a bit toppled where a branch has fallen on to it, so Lu sets about rebuilding it. Sometimes she slips into the cool green water and floats lazily, watching the sun through the filtering willow and birch leaves. In the quiet solitude in and around the pool, she finds herself more and more thinking about her father. What *was* he like? It starts with thinking about herself and Duke, and then more generally about her tendency to act impetuously, her capacity for anger, her strong sexual desires. How is it that she has turned out to have such traits? Has she inherited them from him?

Stiff from having floated too long in the pool, she climbs out, stands on the flat dervishing stone where Bar showed her how to spin into a trance. Smiling at the sweet memories she has of those two young girls spinning their way to ecstasy, she spreads her arms and begins to revolve. She remembers how wonderful it felt then. At first the leaves quivering against the twinkling sun, the smooth green surface of the pool appearing and disappearing. She remembers Bar, a short girl with womanly hips and breasts. Don't start raising your arms till the pool is all round you.

It was like that, when you were spinning fast enough: the pool became a shining blur.

Still smiling, she raises her arms, stretches them until she can temple her fingers. Trees, sun and pool become a cylinder of twinkling green, with herself whirling at the centre, twisting on the ball of her left foot, giving herself spinning impetus with the right.

Now she can see nothing except light, feel nothing except the air moving across her bare skin, hear nothing except her own shallow breathing.

But all that happens is that she gets giddy. Warm now, she slips on her clothes and makes her way back to Roman's. The sky spirit has not sent a nice dream down the invisible thread. Perhaps it dealt only with girls, women have to find their own dreams.

She has at least decided where she should look for them.

Leaving

Lu, determined now to become Louise Wilmott – she might well change her surname too – is leaving on the London train. Travelling third class, she watches the beautiful, undulating landscape of rural Hampshire rolling past, a diorama of crops and grazing animals.

Since she left the factory, she has used some of the time at Roman's Fields in solitude, trying to take an unbiased look at herself. She amended the thought that had passed through her mind that evening at the Fire Boys Fair. She was cleverer than many of her peers, but whereas she had thought herself less worthy because of her desire for something better, she has begun to allow that a desire to get out and get on in the world is not shabby. She now acknowledges what her subconscious has been telling her since Kenny left home. Do what you want. Be who you want.

She had turned her back on what mattered for too long. It took the sight of Kate Roles' bloody accident before Lu realized that what she had learned at the evening classes was just theory, just the ideal. Jacob Ezzard might live in a democratic society, but the girls who worked for him did not.

It was this thought that gave her a fierce determination to do something about the poor hand she had been dealt. She might have been born the daughter of a beached woman, and brought up in the slums, but now she is resolved to play and win.

She has got a passport, has paid off her clubs and debts, withdrawn her savings, sold most of her clothes except her gold satin dance dress and the Lascelles model, packed her few possessions in the overnight case that has served her on two previous important journeys. Sonia has cut her hair short.

She left Number 110 quickly and early in the morning.

The Waterloo express thunders through small stations. Rowlands Castle, Liss, Liphook; all that part of the rural south she first glimpsed from Uncle Hec's lorry when she was twelve. This time she sees a landscape that is familiar and loved. For a second the thought occurs to her: this could be the last time I shall ever see the downs.

This is a big step. As big a leap into unknown territory as when she left Lampeter in Uncle Hec's lorry. A clean break. The only way, or she would have stayed there for ever. This time, though, it is a more permanent leaving. It is the start of the rest of her life.

These days in the newsreels, there is always something about Spain.

Basque refugees. The bombing of Madrid. Fascist troops, Fascist war planes, Fascist wounded.

Republican wounded.

Neutral corpses.

The first news item shows a small group standing outside Victoria Railway Station in London. They are surrounded by a large crowd and a parade is passing. The commentator explains that ten thousand people have come from Hyde Park to march past and honour these brave youngsters.

The group is swamped, flowers are pressed into their hands. Mayors and mayoresses from six London boroughs, representatives from the London County Council, the Labour Party and the Trades Union Congress, have all come to wish them Godspeed.

'The brave adventure of these doctors and ambulancemen has started, and we too wish them the best of luck.'

The camera plays on the faces of the doctors and the ambulancemen.

One of the doctors is a woman.

Seven of the ambulancemen are women.

'Look, look!' says Lena. 'There she is!'

The red 'Exit' light flickers on.

Bar absorbs every detail of the scene she and Lena have already watched at the matinee. 'She looks happy.'

Lena says, 'See that bloke: he had his arm round her.'

'They all had their arms round each other.'

'I just wondered if it was that one you said she was keen on.'

'She don't want any blokes now.'

The house lights go up. Bar and Lena stay put as the familiar pretentious voice booms, 'The Eyes and Ears of the World!' and the 'Gaumont British News' symbols fade away.

'Yeah,' Lena says, looking admiringly at the happy face of Lu, whom she can still see in spite of the velvet curtains that come swishing down. 'Yeah, Lu don't want no blokes now.'